CW00665374

THE
Ro Bro
JA
Huss
Johnathan
McClain

CHAPTER ONE — CORDELIA

THREE WEEKS BEFORE THE CONVENTION

I know I shouldn't bite my nails.

But I can't help it.

It's the whole reason I've never gotten a manicure.

I can hear my mother's voice in my head even as I'm doing it: "*Cordelia. Don't chew at your fingers like you're some kind of rabid wildebeest. It's a filthy habit.*"

Never mind that wildebeests can't chew their nails because they're basically antelopes and antelopes don't have fingers and even if they did are unlikely to be able to get one of their hooves up to their mouths to chew on it in the first place, so it's a bad simile and she could have just said 'wild animal' and also left out the part about it being rabid because what does that have to do with anything, but my mother has never been one to go for simplicity, much less use only two words when fifty will do…

Which, as I play back my run-on sentence to myself, occurs to me, not for not the first time, might be a heritable quality.

But putting all that aside, it's not the most constructive way to get a kid to stop doing something. By lecturing them.

Or, at least, it wasn't for me. The more I'd get lectures to stop, like, biting my nails, or touching the door handle five times on each side before turning it, or rearranging the silverware by my dinner plate in three very distinct formations before I could begin eating, the more it made me anxious and drove me to do the thing she was telling me not to do even more.

Like when she said, "*You don't want to be a writer, Cordelia. You really don't. It will break your heart. Then, when it's finally beaten you all the way down, it will cause you to become filled with hope just when you least expect it only to break your heart once more,*" it made me decide: *Okay. Well, guess I'm gonna be a writer then.*

At least that particular lecture was founded in something more substantial than just her not wanting me to look like a wildebeest. Mom and Dad are both writers, and neither of them ever really achieved what I think they thought they would when they started out. I mean, all things considered, they've had pretty good lives. They wrote as a team for some of the most successful TV shows ever to be on TV, back when TV was just on, like, TV.

Changing tides and all that caused them to realize that the world of entertainment was moving in a direction they really didn't want to try to keep up with, so they took all the TV money they made over the years and moved to Mykonos, where Dad's side of the family is originally from, and now they wake up every morning, drink their coffee, look out at the ocean, and then spend a few hours each working on their own 'great literary novel.' Which, I mean… if the cost of a repeatedly broken heart is having enough money to retire in your early fifties to an island off the coast of Greece? I'd be willing to take that trade.

But the point is I sometimes wonder if maybe I should've just listened to her.

Instead of pushing back like I tend to do when given advice I don't want to hear, maybe I should've considered that what she was saying was a genuine attempt to look out for my best interests. I was a pretty high-strung kid. I think I'm less of a high-strung adult, but I can't deny that one of the things my mom encouraged me not to do—bite my nails—is happening at the moment because of another thing my mom encouraged me not to do—become a writer.

Sitting in my favorite sling chair—that really needs to have a section of the canvas back reupholstered so I stop playing obsessively with the bits of loose thread that hang from it—by the side of the pool, waiting for Britney to finish reading the last two chapters of my latest manuscript, I find myself unable to avoid biting at my nails and letting my brain wander all over the place.

I actually first tried my hand at being a TV writer like Mom and Dad, but I wasn't cut out for it. You have to write in teams with a whole writers' room filled with other maybe-up-and-coming writers and *collaborate*, and be willing to have all your writing rewritten by someone else and just a whole lot of other stuff that made it feel less like writing and more like going to work on some kind of assembly line. Just, instead of assembling widgets or car parts or something, you're supposed to be assembling art.

Or, no, that's not quite right. It isn't art. It's *entertainment.*

And there's nothing wrong with that. Entertainment is great. I love being entertained. I find many things very entertaining. Circuses, for example. I think circuses can be super fun. But I don't wanna be a clown.

I wanna do something that I feel *matters*. That touches people. That makes them think and has a real impact on their lives. I want to write the kind of thing that stays with someone long after they've finished the story. That's my goal, anyway.

And that's why I became a romance writer.

Well, that and the fact that I've been addicted to romance novels since I read my first one when I was, like, nine.

I was in the library down the street from our house in Santa Monica, by myself (partially because I didn't really have a ton of friends and partially because the friends I did have didn't want to spend their afternoons hanging out in a dusty old library when they could be at the beach), and I just happened to wander out of the kids' section and into the grown-ups' section.

And there I found an old, weathered, beaten copy of *Pride and Prejudice* by Jane Austen. I don't know what drew me to it. Something about seeing the words on the spine, maybe. The P and the P so elegantly alliterative and simple all at once. Or maybe it's just because when I pulled it out and saw an artist's rendering of a busty Elizabeth Bennet on the cover, looking like a porcelain doll, it made my mind wander to far-flung places that my nine-year-old brain didn't even know existed yet. But, whatever the reason… I started reading.

And I was done. Cliché though it may be to say, I was… *transported.*

And that's been my dream ever since. To transport someone the same way. To ferry them away to magical places where love conquers all and happily ever afters aren't some unachievable fantasy, but real, honest, sincere aspirations that we shouldn't feel embarrassed to want.

My dream—candidly and with a little embarrassment of my own—is to be one of the greats.

I'm not there yet. But I'm getting there. I really believe I am. And that's why I'm particularly nervous just now.

Because I think this book is the best thing I've ever written.

I spit away another bit of nail shaving from my index finger, noticing that if I chew anymore I'll surely draw blood, and attempt to still my thoughts by taking a deep, deep breath. I close my eyes and just try to feel the sun streaming down onto my face. It's nice out today. There's a tiny bit of a breeze that's causing the palm trees to sway gently, the rustle of the fronds creating a pacifying white noise.

It's been hot this summer, even for LA. Or so I hear. I haven't really gone outside much. Just been working on getting this book finished.

I really feel like I turned a corner. Unlocked some kind of code. I think maybe before I was too hung up on 'rules' and 'expectations.' And this time, I just let my imagination run wild and allowed the story to take me wherever it wanted. It was almost like I wasn't in control anymore. There was some kind of muse who entered my body and came pouring out through my fingertips, conducting the orchestra of my imagination and allowing me unfettered access to my own creative freedom.

Which, I suppose, sounds awfully grand, but it's how it felt while I was writing it.

But now I'm a little freaked out, waiting for Brit's notes. She's taking an awfully long time to finish and give me her thoughts.

I trust Britney. She's one of the only people I can say that about. It's why I asked her if she'd be my assistant. My first read on everything. Because I'm writing exactly the kinds of books she reads too.

We met online, in a reader group for one of our favorite authors, SS.

That's it. Just 'SS.' Her real name is Essie Smith-Scott, but SS is her pen name. I like it. It's simple. The S next to the S. For some reason, something about it reminds me of the P and P in *Pride and Prejudice.* To be clear: SS writes very different kinds of books than Jane Austen and Charlotte Brontë. Jane and Charlotte had far less, um, choking, and, y'know, fellatio in their books (at least on paper; you can't tell me that Elizabeth and Mr. Darcy weren't getting all kinds of freaky off the page), but there's just something about the way she writes. It's… I don't know. There's a real beauty to it that makes me swoon. Even with all the choking and handcuffs and stuff.

But that's where Britney and I first became friends. And then we discovered that we both live in LA and decided to meet up IRL. It was Britney who encouraged me to try writing romance.

"Oh, no, no," I said. *"I don't think I could."*

"Why not?" she asked.

And I enumerated for her the number of reasons I thought I was not cut out for it.

—I haven't had the greatest personal track record with 'romance.' My last boyfriend lied to me about… well, everything. And then he stole from me. Money. A pair of earrings my grandmother gave me. My remaining trust in humanity.

—I don't really, um, go places. Or do things. (What I have heard some refer to as 'peopling.') When I'm overstimulated, I get kind of… manic, I suppose. So, I try to avoid it whenever possible.

—I'm what some might call 'cynical.' (They'd be right. I am. But at least I'm self-aware.)

—I'm a snob. I really am. I'm not proud of the fact, but I grew up in a house that was so filled with snobbery and self-judgment, and, frankly, fear of failure and of what others think, that I actually feel like I should pat myself on the back for turning out as well as I have so far. (I won't though. Pat myself on the back. Because of the aforementioned self-judgment.)

Britney countered all of my arguments one by one.

—So? You think crime writers go out and commit murders? I mean, unless they're really, *really* good at hiding it, probably not. (Probably.)

—You don't have to have gone places or done things to know they exist. Have you ever been to Saturn? No. Do you believe it's there? Of course. So, just make up what happens there. It'll be fresh and original!

—Cynicism is amazing! What better to write about than someone whose cynical, hardened heart is made all gushy and soft by the magic of love? (Note: Britney is *not* a cynic. Clearly.)

—You think *all* writers aren't snobs, no matter what they're writing? That's what makes you a writer. The kind of introversion that requires you to stay locked inside your house, scribbling away, but, at the same time, the kind of ego necessary to believe that anyone wants to read a hundred thousand words that just happened to fall out of your brain? If you're going put that kind of energy to use, may as well put it to use writing the kind of thing you like.

She is incredibly persuasive.

And so… I decided to go for it. I followed my dream. I became a romance writer.

I haven't told my parents yet.

They know I'm writing, but I've just been cagey about *what* I'm writing. Because if I can get judge-y about stuff, they can get *Supreme Court* judge-y about stuff.

(Which is also ironic, given that they spent almost half their lives writing jokes for sitcoms, but I know if I told them I was making a go of it self-publishing my own romance novels they'd give me grief about it.)

Ugh. I need to cut them some slack. I have this tendency when I'm feeling anxiety about anything to pivot it back onto them, and that's not fair. They're not bad parents, they're really not, they're just very… specific in their opinions.

I mean, look, it's not like I don't still have an aspiration, just like the ones my parents still have, of writing a great literary novel someday, but I have to tell the truth: I'm *happy* writing what I write. I really, really am. It gives me joy in a way that not a whole lot of other things do. And I have to believe that makes it right. They say if you eat a meal prepared by a chef who's happy and loves the food they're making, you can taste it. And if you're eating something made by someone who's just going through the motions—cooking by the numbers—you can taste that too.

I have to believe it's the same with writing books. I want the people who read what I write to *feel* that I put everything I have into it and to get something out of it that moves them in a real, meaningful way.

And I think it might be working? Maybe? Because the first two books I've written—the start to a series I call The Purity Principle (a blatant homage to my girl Jane and *P&P*)—have sold okay(ish) and I've begun growing a little bit of a fanbase.

But, even more exciting…

I've now been invited to attend the Sin With Us Romance Convention in a few weeks! *SS's convention!* She runs it and only invites all the hottest authors. It's, like, the biggest romance novel convention in the world and they want *me* there!

(Okay, so I realize I probably got invited last minute because someone dropped out and I just happened to be the first one to respond when they sent out the mass email asking if anyone wanted to take their place, but still…)

I'm going! And this book I just finished is going to be the thing I lead with at my big romance con coming-out party.

I've taken a little break from writing book three of The Purity Principle because I had a new idea come to me in the middle of the night and I *had* to get it out there. It shook me to my core and I knew that if I didn't write it down, I'd never forgive myself. So I put my scheduled release of the next *PP* book to the side to focus on this one.

I'm calling it (coincidentally) *Filling the Gap*.

It's taken a while to finish. Normally, when I'm in my flow, I can write pretty fast, but as I started writing *FTG*… I dunno. I just *felt* it in a different way and wanted it to be perfect, so I've taken a little longer than I normally would to revise it and rethink it and really hone it to the best, most pristine, gleaming version of itself that it can be.

My plan is this: Show up at Sin With Us with bunches and bunches of free copies of the new book, hand them out to whoever I can hand them out to, make friends with the biggest writers there, get them to co-sign how swell my new book is, get one of them to introduce me to their agent, get a big, traditional publishing deal, and *then* blow everybody's mind with my grand literary opus that tops the *NY Times* bestseller list and gets turned into a movie that I have complete creative control over and that changes people's lives and leaves a mark on history.

Doesn't feel like too much to shoot for.

So, I *really* need Britney to tell me that she likes it. That it's good. That it's special.

Because I'm ready to explode out of the middle-tier writer purgatory place I'm in. And I know. I know I sound like kind of an asshole. I know I should just be happy that anyone reads anything I write at all and grateful that I'm making a go of it, but if I'm being honest with myself… I really, *really* want to graduate to the big leagues. Like I say, not *just* because of attention or money—

"Cordelia, can you rub some more lotion on my back?"

—although I wouldn't mind moving out of this pool house and buying a house of my own with its own pool and its own pool house that I could rent to someone else, rather than being the one doing the renting and serving occasionally as the impromptu pool girl.

"Uh, sure, Sheila." I pull myself out of my stream-of-consciousness reverie and push myself out of my seat, padding barefoot around the deck to the other side of the pool where Sheila lies face down on the fully supine lounge chair, wearing only the thong portion of her micro-bikini, tanned butt cheeks glistening in the sun, the top half of her barely-there-in-the-first-place bathing suit discarded off to the side to avoid any unsightly tan lines.

It's quite a sight. Especially given that Sheila is at least twenty years older than my mom and dad.

I've never asked her outright how old she is exactly, but if the internet is to be believed she's somewhere between seventy-five and maybe, like, ninety?

Her first movie credit is listed as 'Girl In Candy Store,' and that was seventy years ago. She could've been five at the time or she could've been twenty-five. Hard to know. I've looked for the movie but can't find it. It is, like so many things about Sheila, a mystery.

In any case, however old she is, it's safe to say that it's a fair bit older than most women you might see hanging out by a pool wearing almost nothing but a smile.

I appreciate that she's wearing anything at all. It took about six months after I moved in here to work up the nerve to ask her, politely, if she wouldn't mind wearing some kind of a bathing suit when she came out to tan rather than just being totally naked all the time. I mean, it is her house. She can do whatever she wants. But it could be kind of distracting sometimes when I would look out the window as I was trying to work.

Not that Sheila isn't beautiful. She absolutely is. I mean, either she looks *really* good for her age or she looks *impossibly* good for her age, so I'm not saying she shouldn't do what she wants and wear what she wants or not wear what she doesn't want. I'm just saying that when I'm sitting inside my little cottage tucked away behind the main house, trying to drill down and write a hundred-thousand-word novel, a naked septua-, octo-, or possibly nonagenarian parading around outside makes it tricky to focus.

"Just the middle area, dear," Sheila says as I arrive beside her and pick up the bottle of sunscreen, squeezing the creamy, warm solution onto my hands and rubbing my palms together to distribute it evenly.

I have to have an even distribution or everything will feel off and I'll have to start over and do it all again. I'm aware that everything won't actually *be* off. It'll just *feel* that way. But, ultimately, I'm the one who has to live with the feeling, so I'm not sure it makes a lot of difference.

"Mmmm, that feels good," she says as I massage the SPF into her already dappled, suntanned skin. It makes me a *little* nervous when she says it like that? I'm never quite sure if she's just expressing herself honestly or hitting on me. Not that I'd be offended. I've seen pictures of Sheila when she was around my age. She could probably have had her pick of anybody she wanted. Honestly, the idea that she might be flirting with me is pretty flattering. But it would also still be a little awkward. I have to live here and everything.

"That's good, dear, thank you."

I stop rubbing, pick up a hand towel, wipe the excess sunscreen from my fingertips, fold the towel neatly, and place it back down on the side table next to Sheila's piña colada.

"Is everything okay?" she asks after a moment.

"Yeah, sure, why?"

"Your leg."

I look down at my leg and notice for the first time that it's bouncing. To be clear: *It's* bouncing. I'm not bouncing *it*. It's like it has a mind of its own. "Oh, sorry." I work to still the movement and start biting my nails again.

"I thought we might be having an earthquake," Sheila says, voice muffled in the beach towel she has rolled under her face. "What's got you anxious?"

"Oh, nothing. Just, y'know, my book. Vegas coming up. All that."

"I understand."

"You do?" That's surprising. I mean, I haven't known Sheila that long, but she doesn't seem like the type to get anxious about anything. Maybe when she was younger. Whenever that was.

"Of course I do. I remember when I first went to Vegas and how intimidated I felt."

"I don't think it's really the Vegas part itself, that—"

"So many hopes and dreams. Glitz and glamour. It'll wrap you up and spin you around like you're on a rollercoaster. Crazy, crazy times."

I would ask her to say more, but she does this sometimes. Says some partial thought about some long-ago memory out loud and when I ask her to expand upon it, she just moves on or acts like she didn't hear. Like the time she fell asleep out here and I heard her mumble in her slumber, "*If we don't bury it deeper, someone will find it.*" Then she startled herself awake and, when I asked her what she was dreaming about, she said, "*An old boyfriend.*"

I told her she was talking in her sleep and what she said, and she just smiled, stood up, went inside the house and asked if I wanted lemonade.

So I've stopped asking. But it seems like Sheila has *lived*, from what I can tell.

"Why don't you jump in the pool, dear?" she offers. "Swim a lap or two. Work out some of that excess energy."

"I'm okay. Maybe later."

I actually hate going in the pool. I don't like getting recreationally wet. Not sure why that is, apart from the fact that getting in water means eventually you have to get out of the water, get in other water to clean off the water you were just in, and then get yourself cleaned up and ready to face the world looking like you were never in water in the first place. Seems like a lot of work just to do something where you could drown.

I stand and start pacing instead. Pacing, chewing at my nails, pushing back behind my ear the one errant strand of hair that keeps falling in my face.

Owing to the fact that I haven't gone outside much this summer, I also haven't had my hair cut in months. It's down almost to just below my shoulder blades, which is the longest I've had it since I was a kid and this boy who sat behind me in homeroom used to pull on it and make fun of my name. Cordelia Sarantopoulos. He'd say things like, "I thought Greek girls were supposed to be pretty. What happened to you?" And stuff like that.

I wrote him as a character into *The Clock Chimes for Love*, the first book of The Purity Principle. He got hit by a train.

Suddenly, the door to my little pied-à-terre opens and Britney steps out. My breathing speeds up. I stop biting my nails, but I'm now wringing my hands together feverishly, twisting and turning at my fingers like I'm trying to wash them clean of something that won't come off. Straight-up Lady Macbeth.

I can't read Britney's expression. She's got a neutral face on like the one she puts on when guys start hitting on her at the bar or the club. It happens a lot—that she gets hit on—so it's a very practiced look. And I know what it means when some Chad is trying to get her Insta or whatever, but I have no idea what it means here, now, in this context.

My hope is that it's a preamble to her bursting into a wide smile, throwing her arms open wide, and saying, "It's a-MAY-zing!" in that way she does. But I just don't know.

I step forward a few paces around the side of the water as she crosses over to meet me. She looks at me with an admixture of… something and… something else. I've never seen her look like this before and I have no idea what this look portends.

I think I'm gonna have a heart attack.

"What—?" I start. But before I can get any more of the sentence out, Britney just grabs me, pulls me close and wraps me up, enveloping me in a hug. She whispers in my ear…

"You are so goddamn talented, I can barely stand it."

I'm glad she's hugging me because I feel like I'm going to collapse. The relief I'm experiencing is like… I dunno. Like someone who just found out they had their death sentence commuted. Which is a terrible metaphor because it trivializes death and almost sends me off into a brain spiral about the complicated ethics of the judicial system, but I rodeo my mind back into the moment and just let the feeling of release and gratitude roll through me.

Britney pulls back and I can now see she is, indeed, smiling. Which, in turn, causes me to smile through the tears of joy I can feel forming around the corners of my eyes.

"Really? You think it's good?"

"It's beyond good. It's a masterwork."

My heart leaps. I have so many things I want to say. So many questions I want to ask. So much I want to talk about. I want to throw my head back and laugh to the heavens. I want to pop champagne and go shopping. Which are not things I typically enjoy or think about doing, but right now it's what I want.

Still smiling, Britney takes me by the shoulders, looks me in the eyes, and with a tilt of her head and an apology creeping into her expression that is at odds with the mood I feel like we should be sharing, she says something that you don't expect to hear from someone who's basically just told you you're a genius.

She takes a deep breath and says…

"You can't publish it."

CHAPTER TWO – STEVE

THE DAY BEFORE THE CONVENTION

I'm just about to throw a dart when my phone starts buzzing on the kitchen counter behind me. I pause. Close my eyes. Count to five.

"You gonna get that?" That question comes from my friend, Terry.

"Want me to grab it?" That's our friend, Luke.

"Yello." That's Shawn, who doesn't ask questions. "This is Steve." He's also a big believer in the idea that every moment is an opportunity to be someone else. I guess that's why he's such a great fiction writer. He pauses for a moment, listening, and the rest of us look at him expectantly, waiting to see what will happen next.

"Mmm. Wow." Shawn looks at me and winks. "Glad you're all OK." He nods, listening again. "Yep. OK, Mom. See ya when ya get here." He ends the call, trying not to laugh. Then he tosses me the phone.

I catch it. "Well?"

"Your mom and dad are about twenty minutes away—there was a fire on both sides of the 10, just east of Palm Desert, they had to drive right through it and she thought she was gonna die. Oh, and she says you need to get a real job and stop mooching off your sister."

This is why I don't answer the phone when my parents are coming into town. I throw my dart, stick it in the bullseye, and then grab a beer from the fridge.

When I turn, I see nothing but ocean and sand though the completely open wall of the lower level of my Malibu home. I hear waves and distant laughter of people outside enjoying a day on the beach.

I count to ten, looking for my Zen. But my parents, man. They're not easy to be Zen around. And I have to spend the next six days with them.

A hand slaps my back and I turn to find Terry standing next to me holding his own beer. "You'll get through it, dude. Just… just…"

"Just think about the money." Luke is the one who finishes that sentence. He throws his dart, hits my *wall*, and says, "Oops. That'll buff right out," as he snags the dart and grins at me.

Shawn has started a game of Pac-Man over in the corner so that stupid waka-waka-waka noise drifts through the room. As far as man caves go, mine is pretty spectacular. Ocean front view, sand just ten feet down, air hockey, darts—obviously—pool table, fridge stocked with beer, and a variety of arcade and pinball machines lining one whole wall.

It's also my living room. I don't even use the other two floors of the house.

I am living the dream. Every man wants what I have. Hell, it's an empire at this point.

Pac-Man dies and the death sound that comes with it is the perfect background noise for how I feel about what will happen tomorrow.

Shawn abandons the game and walks over to stand next to Terry. Then Luke is on my left. The four of us stand there, inside the pinnacle of my success, gazing out at the dream, and sigh.

The money isn't enough to get me through the eighth annual Sin With Us in Vegas Romance Convention where I am the headliner.

Correction, my alter ego, SS—otherwise known as my twin sister, Essie—is the headliner.

I am the number one romance writer in the world and everyone thinks I am my sister because when I first started writing romance ten years ago, it was… it was… I mean, I hate to say it was a joke, but it was a joke.

Terry, Shawn, and I all did it. We were newbie writers, struggling to get that one breakthrough novel, marketing our asses off trying to sell science fiction. Cyberpunk was big back then. But it was fading, so nothing we were doing was hitting. And after a dozen books with no luck, we were getting desperate.

At the same time, erotica was huge. And then, like overnight, every kind of romance was in the top one hundred on Nile. You couldn't find a sci-fi book to save your life. It was nothing but man-chest covers and titles like *Own Me, Master.*

All four of us met at a fiction writers' retreat at the Holiday Inn and Suites in Thousand Oaks, California, that summer. We got drunk that first night of the retreat in what passed for a motel bar—fuckin' Luke was only seventeen. He was using a fake ID. Then Shawn made a joke. All we needed to do to find success was write our version of *Own Me, Master*, slap a man-chest on the cover, and wait for the money to roll in.

That's literally what happened to me. Only my book was called *Master Choke*.

One minute I was snickering in the corner of my shitty Encino apartment, writing salacious sex scenes, and the next thing I know, I'm number thirteen in the whole Nile store. I made over a hundred thousand dollars in one month. My SS Facebook page, which had twenty-seven followers before I published that first book, suddenly had fifty thousand.

I banked the money, still snickering like an asshole, and then thought… *Hell, maybe I'll write another one?* Maybe Sugar and Master Choke had more story in them? I can't believe I named that girl Sugar. What was I thinking? How can anyone take me seriously?

Book two, *Sugar Push*, made it to number seven in the store. *Sev-en.* They loved it. Artists were sending me fan art—like hand-painted renditions of my characters. I was getting invited to indie book signings all over the country, as SS, of course, and my bank account was overflowing.

This is when it kinda became an addiction. I started publishing one story a month. They were mostly long novellas and every single one of them made it into the top twenty in the Nile store.

Shawn, Terry, and Luke were all cheering me on. We kept in touch after that writers' retreat. Terry and Shawn tried their hand at the romance, but they never could get the sex scenes as dirty as mine. I tried to get my readers to buy their books too, but it didn't work.

Eventually they gave up and went back to science fiction and now, ten years later, they're all icons in the industry. Hell, Luke is the top humorous military sci-fi author in the world.

Shawn has a twenty-seven-volume series about time travel and a huge comic company bought the rights to his shit and they're making it into a whole graphic novel series.

Terry's got a deal with the number one online streaming network in the world to bring his fifteen-tome shit-hits-the-fan apocalypse series to the small screen with a three-season guarantee. *Three* seasons.

Meanwhile, I'm still writing the salacious sex scenes. Only now I run online webinars, and retreats, and this fucking Sin With Us in Vegas Romance Writer Convention. *Master Choke* was made into a movie several years back. It did OK. But I did very well off that thing.

Thankfully, Sugar and Choke's story ended a while ago now, but I've got nine other series just like it.

I have written other stuff under my real name—Steve Smith. It's good, intelligent sci-fi. Lots of virtual reality and Matrixy-type shit mixed in with the technical details. But no one liked it. The readers were… murderous. The reviews were terrible. They called me the 'worst writer in the history of science fiction.'

I just don't get it. How can I be the number one writer in romance and the worst writer in history in sci-fi?

Needless to say, I haven't really been in the mood to write since that happened.

"Maybe you should just come clean, man?" I look to my left at Luke. He's like a little cherub of innocence. No clue how the real world works because he found success at the age of eighteen and he's been living the dream life of a number-one science fiction author for a decade now and he's not even thirty yet. "Just… tell people it's you. They'll still like your books."

"Do you think he hasn't considered this?" Terry is the one who comes to my defense.

"You remember what happened with the sci-fi stuff." That's Shawn. "They hated it."

I feel like defending myself here, but he's not wrong. They did hate it. I wrote a trilogy and the first book has over ten thousand reviews with a two-point-five-star rating average. It won online blog awards for worst book ever two years in a row. They turned me into a meme, for fuck's sake.

And two years in a row? How does that even happen? Give it a fuckin' rest already.

"Steve!"

All four of us look at the pretentious set of open stairs that lead down to the lower level of the house from the middle-level front door. My home is grotesquely opulent. Not like… French opulent with ornate shit everywhere. But the windows, and the blond-wood floors, and the Swedish-style furniture, and the pristine white walls—it's so fuckin' Malibu, ya just wanna throw up. It's three stories tall, has a pool on the roof, and has a view people would die for.

I do love it, though. Living on the beach is awesome. Hell, my whole life is awesome.

So why do I feel like such a failure?

Essie appears, bouncing down the stairs in her white bikini. I nudge Luke to remind him not to drool—she's married, for one. And for two, she's my fuckin' sister.

As far as twin sisters go, Essie is top-notch. When you think of a 'romance writer,' my sister's face is what you picture. She's cute, she's curvy, she's bubbly, she's smart, and she's friendly. She's a walking rom-com.

Which is why I asked her to be the face of my alter-ego, SS.

She was in the middle of a huge reno project inside the Paradise Cove Mobile Home Park—famous for being the most high-priced trailer park ever because it overlooks the beach. She bought this old, run-down mobile home before all the property values went through the roof. It was a steal and it came with the most private location on the hillside. She blew all her savings on this risk and then, little by little, she tore it apart and put it back together. That's how she met her husband, Mike. He was renovating one next door. They had the same idea—the same dream—at the very same time. It was fate. Love at first sight. The happily ever after, if I may be so cliché.

Now they own seven mobile homes and rent them all out by the night. I let them use my top-floor master suite here at the house because sometimes all the mobile homes are full at the same time and they need a place to crash until the rush dies down.

Everyone but my sci-fi writer friends in this room and Mike thinks that Essie Smith is SS, the world-famous romance writer.

Even our parents think this, which is why they constantly tell me to get a job and stop mooching off my sister. They think this is her house and I'm her assistant. They think she's throwing me a bone because I have no ambition.

I would tell them the truth, but my parents couldn't keep a secret if their lives depended on it. Thanks to me, they are living the dream too. When they wanted to retire to Lakeside, Arizona, several years back and buy in to a multimillion-dollar luxury senior co-op (aka commune) where bragging about your overachiever kids is more popular than bingo, I had Essie offer to pay for it.

I love them. Like them too, most of the time. But living a lie this big with my parents twenty minutes away was more than I could handle. And I know, *I know* I could've just told them the truth. Then I wouldn't have to live that lie. But my parents cannot be trusted with a secret this big. They would blab it to anyone who would listen.

So it's Essie's face on the inside back cover of the dustjacket. It's Essie's face on the website, and on Nile, and the socials, and in front of the webcam for the webinars.

She is the one who signs the books at the conventions, not me. She does all the marketing too. I'm just the chump who writes the books. I even narrate the books—I've got something of a cult following there—and Essie is the glamorous persona.

It feels a little silly these days. There are… well, not a *lot* of men writing romance, but it's a thing. Back in the day though, I dunno. I was… embarrassed, I guess. I didn't want anyone to know what I was doing.

Even if I wanted to come clean, it's too late. We've been living this lie for way too long to start telling the truth now.

"Mom and Dad are here." Essie directs her gaze to Luke, Shawn, and Terry. "Can you help them with their luggage?" She says this in her sweetest voice. They rush to put down their beers and start for the stairs.

I roll my eyes.

Essie just smiles, watching them disappear up the stairs. Then she turns to me with a serious face. "You're gonna get through this. It's gonna be OK."

I have the best sister on the planet. I upended her entire life and now she's gotta live a lie because of it. Not only that, she knows she's the favorite and she never lets our parents get away with treating her better than me. She's always sticking up for me.

"I know," I tell Essie. "I'll just… stay down here and keep out of the way."

It's not like my parents are bad people. They're not. My father was a hardworking plumber the whole time we were growing up in Encino. My mother was a housewife. She stayed home and raised us kids. She made dinner every night, and took us to after-school sports and activities, and she was always our number-one fan.

But now I'm thirty-five and they think I'm a mooch. They think I do nothing, even though my fake job description for the SS Corporation is head of marketing, which is literally the same title Essie has working for me. They think Essie feels sorry for me because I am a failed science fiction writer and is throwing me a bone.

And whatever, right? I'm not that guy. I'm super-rich, I'm super-ambitious, and I'm super-successful. It didn't really bother me until… until I really did become a real-life science-fiction writer failure.

And now… I dunno. I feel like something's gotta give. Because despite the fact that I live in a ten-million-dollar house with the ocean as my backyard and have literally lost count of how many times I've had a book on the bestseller lists, it's this one failure that dominates all my thoughts and every day feels like a pointless challenge.

Essie is making a pouty face.

"I'm fine."

"We should stop doing this convention, Steve. It's not good for you."

"I don't even do anything. You do all the work."

"That's not true. You're the one who writes the books. You're the reason they come. And by the way, I got seventy-five requests for the name of my narrator last week."

Despite my current mood, this makes me smile. "Really?"

"Do you want me to give them your name? It's so stupid that you don't want people to know you narrate sexy audiobooks. You should run with it. Turn it into something real. Something big. You could make so much—"

"Money?" I snicker. "Essie, do you really think money is the problem here?"

"No. But I'm desperate to fix whatever is wrong with you right now."

"Come on. Like I have time to narrate other people's books."

Essie shrugs up one shoulder. "Well, it's not like you're writing much these days."

She's right. I'm not.

"You could do the narration on the side. Until you get your mojo back."

"Have I lost my mojo?"

She makes one of those all-teeth smiles. Yes, I have. But she's not going to say it out loud.

I sigh, then kind of give in. "Maybe."

This makes Essie clap her hands and put them up to her chin like she's praying.

"But don't say anything yet, Essie. I have to think it through."

"OK. I won't. But you're great at it. Hell, Steve, you're great at everything. If we could just tell Mom and Dad the truth—"

"No! They can't know. The whole thing will come tumbling down. And I'm not ready for that kind of attention, OK? I'm just not. You don't read the reviews—"

"And you shouldn't either."

"I know, but my point is, they will crucify me, Essie. It's not the money, either. I'm not worried about the fuckin' money. But they will write terrible things about me, and give me the worst online blog awards, and turn me into a meme, and have Twitter wars, and—"

She puts up a hand to make me stop. "I get it. I won't say anything." Then she hugs me. "But you know, I'm your number one fan. Never forget that. I know exactly how spectacular you are."

And, with the pep talk over, she turns away and goes up the stairs to welcome our parents into my home like she owns the place.

♥♡♥♡♥♡♥♡♥♡♥

Later that evening, after Terry, and Shawn, and Luke have all wished me the best and gone home to their wonderful iconic-science-fiction-writer lives, I'm counting down until dinner is over and I can go back downstairs and forget I even have parents.

I've managed to make it twenty-three minutes, my pasta has been demolished, I've declined dessert and coffee, and I'm just about to push back from the table and make my retreat when I make the mistake of meeting my father's gaze.

"Have you at least *tried* to get a job?"

"Dad!" Essie throws her napkin down. "We've talked about this. Steve has a job. He works for me."

"He shouldn't have to work for you. He should've finished school."

"School?" I deadpan. "Dad, you wanted me to be a plumber."

"What's wrong with being a plumber? It paid for this family, didn't it? And Essie's college. At least she took her education seriously."

Essie has an associate's degree in interior design. I mean, it's more than I have, but still. He acts like she went to MIT or something.

I don't want to have this argument. Essie's smart, and talented, and she's one of the hardest-working people I know. I hate that he pits us against each other because that's not how it's supposed to be. And I hate that she feels obligated to stick up for me because of the lie I've made her tell.

"And look at you! You're living in her basement!"

Oh. This again? I point at my father. "First of all, it's not the fuckin' basement."

"Steve! Your language!"

Every time I say the word 'fuck' in front of my mother, she acts like she's never heard the 'F' word before. So I direct the rest of my response to her. "It's not the basement. It's the main level. I mean, what the actual fuck? How is that not obvious? That's where the two-hundred-thousand-dollar kitchen lives."

Granted, I have two kitchens. The second is an outdoor one on the rooftop adjacent to Essie and Mike's guest suite, so that's the one they use. But come on. I don't live in the fuckin' basement. This is a Malibu beach house. The lower level is prime real estate.

My father is not done. "That's where the Pac-Man lives, too, Steve. That's where the air hockey lives, and the pool table lives, and the dartboard lives. It's like you never grew up. You're going to be fourteen forever. And if you're gay—"

"Dad!" Essie is standing now.

He thinks I'm gay because I don't date. "I'm not gay, Dad. How many times do I have to tell you this?"

"Then why don't you have a girlfriend? Did you ever consider that your mother might want grandbabies?"

I would like to point out that Essie is married—why don't they bother her about babies? But I don't point that out because Essie and Mike have a baby plan and it's still three years out. We all know this.

Still, how do my parents even think it's possible that I could meet a woman, marry her, knock her up, and give them grandbabies in less than three years?

It doesn't even make sense. Mike and Essie's babies are a sure thing. All Mom and Dad have to do is wait it out.

But they won't. They just keep bringing it up. They're just… they just… it's just *nagging*. They want to nag me to death.

And of course, I *would* like to marry one day. I love women. I love everything that comes with loving a woman. I would like a family. The kids, the dog—all that shit. But I'm walking the edge of a knife and living a lie.

How do you date a woman while you're living a lie? When do you admit you've been deceiving the entire world?

Third date?

Engagement party?

Wedding night?

Dating is pointless. And this is yet another irony. I'm rich and successful but have to pretend I'm mooching off my sister to get by. I write the hottest fucking romance books on the planet and I haven't even been on a date in almost two years.

This is my life.

"I'm just saying…" Oh, my God, my dad is still talking. "If he's gay, he can tell us. It's fine, Steve."

My mother shoots me a look of love and compassion. Which is funny. That me being gay would delight them and make everything OK. Because me *not* being gay seems to indicate that I'm some kind of layabout sociopath. "It really is OK, Steve, honey. I'm opening the closet door for you, sweetie."

For fuck's sake.

Mike stands up and smiles at everyone. "Why don't we put on a movie?"

Everyone, including Essie, shoots him a WTF look. But he's anti-confrontational. Changing the subject is a life goal for Mike.

So I decide to be the adult in the room and shoot my dad with my finger. "Good talk, Dad." And then I just leave them there, mumbling and whispering—my mother telling my father to be quiet, Essie interjecting, Mike trying to change the subject.

"Six days. *Six days.*" I whisper this under my breath all the way down the stairs. "I can do this. I can make it six days."

But I'm not sure I can. We're leaving for Vegas tomorrow morning so we can get there a day early and make sure the whole thing is on track. Of course, we have hundreds of people doing most of the work for us, but when something goes wrong, they take it to Essie. Which means I have to handle it because she's too busy playing the part of SS to manage things like seating chart complaints from all the authors.

"It's only four and a half hours." This is my new mantra as I stand in front of my open wall of beach. Four and a half hours in the truck with my father sitting next to me and my mother in the back seat.

I would make them go with Essie and Mike, but Essie's SS car is a little vintage Mercedes. When we show up at a signing, she drives that thing up so she can make an entrance. And Dad doesn't quite fit in that backseat.

It's only four and a half hours.

CHAPTER THREE — CORDELIA

DAY ONE — THE ARRIVAL

"Welcome to the Aria, ladies."

Stepping out of the passenger's side of Britney's car, I look around and take in the enormity of the place. I've never been to Vegas before. You'd think, growing up in LA, I would've been, but somehow the whole 'Vegas, baby!' thing just never grabbed me, so this is my first time and I don't think I had a clear picture of what it would be like.

The hotel is massive. The parking lanes are massive. The billboards are massive. The whole shebang, from what I've observed so far, is over the top. Which is something I understood it to be, intellectually, but seeing it in person is a bit overwhelming. Which is maybe why I've never been here before. I can 'people' okay if I have to, but concentrated throngs of people all 'peopling' at once in thirsty and desperate ways isn't my jam.

With me being half-Greek, you might think Dionysian debauchery would be in my natural wheelhouse. Not so much. The more puritanically repressed British vibe I inherited from my mom seems to have won out as the dominant one.

Probably why I respond to the Austens and Brontës of the world so much.

And speaking of classic, romance-novel sex bombs…

Britney slides out of the driver's side and I see the eyes of the young valet who's holding her door open go wide.

Britney's six feet tall, blonde, and exudes an effortless sexuality that may predate all the attention she receives from men, but at this point is most certainly reinforced by it. She can't help it. I think, if given the choice, she'd probably opt to turn it off because of how exhausting it can be for her, but since that option doesn't exist, she's learned to harness it and use it like a superpower.

"Thanks," she says, handing him the keys to her Mercedes SUV and smiling politely.

"Are you here for the convention?"

"We are."

"Amazing." He smiles and nods his head like it's the coolest thing ever. "Are you one of the authors?"

"No. No, she is." She points at me and I give a small wave to the cute boy wearing the white polo shirt tucked into dark blue club shorts.

"Oh," he says, looking at me across the roof of the car, still smiling, but now with something more like practiced courtesy than eager enthusiasm. "Cool."

Another couple of white-shirted, blue-shorted parking attendants pop the liftgate and proceed to pull out the many cardboard boxes of paperbacks stacked in the rear.

"Can I get the name on the reservation?"

"Cynthia Lear," Britney tells the kid.

It took me a long time to come up with that. I workshopped a variety of nom de plumes before I settled on one that felt right. When I started writing romance just about twenty-four months ago, I had to make a decision—do it under my own name or pick a pseudonym.

Ultimately, I decided to go with a pen name.

Not because I don't want people to know what I'm writing or because I want to protect my identity or anything.

If anything, it's the opposite. I definitely want to be recognized for my work and I'd love to see my actual name on the covers of my books, but unfortunately 'Cordelia Sarantopoulos':

A) doesn't really fit that well on the covers. I tried fifty ways of placing it, with a bunch of different fonts, and it always seemed to crowd out the title somehow, and…

B) is not terribly sexy.

Cordelia's not bad, I suppose, but Sarantopoulos doesn't really get the job done.

So, after much consideration, I settled on 'Cynthia Lear.'

'Cynthia' just because it has 'sin' built into the pronunciation and I thought that was kinda cool, and 'Lear' as an homage to my actual name. King Lear's youngest. His favorite daughter whom he banishes, but who returns home to care for him after he goes mad.

Dad once told me that when they found out I was going to be born a girl, he and Mom went back and forth between Cordelia and Ophelia, but ultimately decided that if I was going to be named after someone from a Shakespearean tragedy they'd rather not have it be the one who goes nuts and drowns.

(Coincidentally, I still do have a pretty well-articulated fear of drowning and I suppose it's debatable whether or not tapping out the 'one, two, three, four… one, two' pattern on the roof of the car—like I'm doing right now—before I can walk away technically qualifies as 'nuts.' Ah, well. Best-laid plans…)

The valet writes the name on the parking ticket and hands the stub to Britney, who winks and gives the kid a five. "Thanks," she says, sashaying around the car and heading with me inside as he and the other two set about unloading the boxes.

I grind my teeth thinking about it as we enter the hotel. Because what's in those boxes is not what I thought would be in these boxes.

It mostly is. About eighty percent of what I thought I'd be bringing with me is there, but it's not the exact thing I intended to have with me. I still haven't gotten fully over the shock of Brit walking out of my little pool house, filling me up with hope and happiness, and then saying…

"You can't publish it."

There's a slow, gut-punched beat during which I can feel the smile sinking from my lips and the light in my eyes going dim.

"What? What are you talking about?"

"Or you can, but you can't try to sell it to the readers you've already built up."

"Why not?"

"Because it's not a romance novel."

I blink. Once. Twice. Thrice. Then three more times quickly, counting as I do. "It's absolutely a romance novel. There's romance all over that novel. It's practically oozing off the pages. I don't—"

"It doesn't have an HEA."

An HEA. A happily ever after. A promise to the reader that no matter what the lovers in the book have had to endure to get to where they are at the end, they are rewarded with a bright, hopeful future, free from distress and trauma, and filled with the possibility of an ever-better tomorrow. It is the hallmark of romance. Certainly of contemporary romance.

I know this.

And Britney's telling me it's not there.

"What are you saying, it doesn't have an HEA? Elpida quite literally goes walking off into the sunset."

"Alone."

"Yeah, but—"

"Because Apollo is dead!"

"Yeah! He died for her! What's more romantic than that?"

"He gets crushed to death by a rockslide and she watches it happen!"

"Exactly! And even after all that, she finds the inner strength to make her way to the ocean and back to civilization so that she can begin her life over again! It's about renewal and self-reliance. About discovering that you are enough and you don't need anyone else to hold you up. About filling in all the empty places inside of ourselves and making ourselves whole. That's why it's called Filling the Gap!*"*

"Cord, that's nice and all, but if I pick up something called Filling the Gap, *my expectation isn't gonna be that the title is a metaphor for some chick seeking to 'make herself whole.' It's gonna be to read about somebody getting poked in a lot of holes."*

"But I—"

"I'm sorry, Cord. If you put this out there, you're going to get crucified."

"Listen to your friend, dear," I hear Sheila mutter. "You gotta give the people what they want. Until you've given 'em what they want for long enough that you either retire or outlive everybody else, then you can do whatever you like."

"Also…" Britney starts hesitantly. "It takes a long time to get them together."

"What?"

"It just takes a long time for them to meet and, y'know, actually get to the sexy stuff."

"It's called character-building. We need to grow to care about them as individuals before we put them together."

"I understand that, but—"

"Unless we understand them, how can they understand each other?"

"Okay. Great. Fine. I get it." She takes a long pause and I can tell there's more she's not saying.

"What?" I prompt, against my better judgment.

"Nothing, no, it's not… Just…"

"What?"

"I think you should maybe take a look at her name."

*"*WHAT'S WRONG WITH HER NAME?*" Now that the floodgates are open, a whole lot of unexpected shit is likely to come pouring out.*

"Elpida? It's not terribly sexy."

"It's Greek! It means 'hope!'"

"You know what other name means 'hope' and is *sexy? Hope! Why don't you go with that?"*

My head is spinning. I feel like I'm going to fall into the pool. And I don't want to fall into the pool. I'm wearing shorts and a t-shirt. The only thing I dislike more than getting recreationally wet is getting inadvertently wet while fully clothed.

"I—you—are you—?" I semi-successfully stammer out before Brit puts her hands on my shoulders in what I know is a loving attempt to keep me calm, but at the moment feels more like an assault.

"Cord, there's so, so much good stuff in there. It really is great. But..." She pauses, I assume to calculate how likely it is that whatever she has left to say might send me into a full-blown breakdown. She chooses her words carefully. "It's like... okay, it's like you made a steak, right? A beautiful, tender, juicy, perfectly cooked steak that is so mouthwateringly delicious that it rivals the best steak ever made by the finest chef at the best restaurant in Paris."

"How is that a bad thing?" I can't believe she's using my own food metaphors against me.

"It's not! It's a great thing! The problem is you don't run a steakhouse. You run a candy shop. And when people come to the candy shop to buy their gumdrops and chocolate balls and stuff and you instead hand them this other thing that they aren't expecting and didn't ask for, they're going to be disappointed. That doesn't mean that they wouldn't enjoy your steak in a different context, but you're not selling them the thing your store claims to sell and what they came in to get."

I stared at her for a long time after she said that last bit, trying to come up with counterarguments and defenses of the thing she had just read.

But, ultimately, she was right.

I cooked a filet mignon instead of making bonbons. And so, as much as I fought and railed against the notion internally, I changed it.

I changed her name to Hope and I rewrote the end so that instead of Apollo getting killed in a rockslide, they just fuck on the side of the mountain instead and are rescued by the National Park Service.

And that's what's in the boxes being unloaded from the car. A thing that's mine and also not mine all at once. And, I mean, look… I'm okay with that. I really am. I don't want to turn into one of those arrogant asshole writers who wears tweed jackets with elbow patches and thinks they're better than everyone else. But it's tough to feel really, really good about a thing you've written and have nobody else see it.

I kept one copy of the original manuscript. I have it right on top in one of the boxes. As I'm standing at my table the day after tomorrow, handing out free copies of *Filling the Gap* 2.0, I want to keep the original source material close. I don't know why. But I gave up trying to figure out some of my odder habits a long time ago.

Right now, I'm putting all that aside. Because as we enter the lobby and I see all the 'WELCOME, SIN WITH US AUTHORS!' banners and signs everywhere, I get kind of giddy. I'm here. I got invited to a real book convention with real, big-time, bestselling authors, and I'm here with them. I'm included. I'm part of the club.

I've wanted to be a writer since I was a little kid, and I am one. And this is evidentiary proof of that. And that's the only thing I'm going to focus on. I'm going to quiet my mind and my anxiety and just be glad to be here.

Where I'm supposed to be.

Where I belong.

"What do you mean I don't have a room?"

The woman behind the check-in desk keeps looking down at her computer monitor, shaking her head. Her name tag says 'Rhonda.' "Yeah, I'm sorry, I only have one room on the reservation."

"Well, that's a mistake," Britney says, tapping on the counter with her claw-like nails. "I made the reservation and I very definitely reserved two rooms."

"I believe you," Rhonda, who wears a blazer and ruffled neck shirt that seems anachronistic and out of place on a young woman in Vegas, says half to herself as she keeps typing and looking at the screen, "but I only have one room here for Cynthia Lear. Strip view, king bed, that's what I've got."

"Well… Can you check under the name Cordelia Sarantopoulos and see if you have a second room under that name?" I ask.

"I didn't give them your name." Britney.

"How do you spell that?" Rhonda.

"S-A-R," I start.

"There's no way it's under your name." Britney.

"S-A-R…" Rhonda.

"Did you maybe reserve another one under *your* name?" Me.

"No." Britney. "Why would I reserve one under my name?"

"S-A-R…" Rhonda.

"Okay, fine," Britney says, spinning back to the ruffle-necked young lady. "Whatever. Can you just give us another room now?"

"I'm afraid not," Rhonda says. "We are *completely* sold out because of the convention." She really leans into 'completely,' making a special point of emphasis on the word to let us know that completely means *completely*.

"No sky suites? Nothing?" Britney asks.

"I'm afraid not."

"Okay, listen," Brit says, tilting her head at Rhonda confidentially, "I know that you always hold out one or two rooms for VIPs. Do you know who this is?"

"Brit," I start, "don't—"

"This," she kind of stage-whispers, "is Cynthia Lear. *The* Cynthia Lear."

Rhonda looks at me and I try to smile. I hold up my hand in a tiny wave.

"I know," Rhonda responds with a nod. "I have the name on the reservation for the room. The one room. The one room booked under the name Cynthia Lear."

"Rhonda, you gotta be able to—"

"I'm sorry," Rhonda interrupts. She makes an apologetic face and shrugs. "There's really nothing I can do. There are several other hotels you can try…"

♥♡♥♡♥♡♥♡♥♡♥

There are several other hotels we can try. It's Vegas.

And we try them all.

And after seeking a room at what feels like every other hotel on the Strip for the last three hours and coming up bafflingly empty, we find ourselves standing in the bedroom of a *kind* of apartment in a place I've never heard of before called 'The Siegel Suites.'

It's not on the Strip.

It's not exactly a hotel.

There are used syringes in the hall.

As far as I can tell, no one else is staying here. At all.

And I'm pretty sure I saw the remnants of police tape across one of the doors.

"It says it's part of the Tropicana," Britney reports, reading from her phone.

We look around at the space. I see a roach trap in the corner. It's empty, which I'm not sure makes me feel better or worse. After a second she says, "This is silly. Why don't we just share the room?"

"What? At the Aria?" I ask. She nods. "It's only got the one bed."

"So?"

"I have a hard time sleeping next to someone unless I'm having sex with them."

"… What? Really? Why?"

"If we've already had sex, I'm not worried about germs."

"But… if you haven't had sex, you are? That's—"

"Don't try to make it make sense. It's just how it is."

I gave up working to justify things that aren't rationally justifiable a long time ago. Like most things about me, I can't worry if other people get it or not. I have to just go with what my various, frequently annoying impulses tell me are right.

After a long beat, Britney finally says, "Well, should we—?"

"Have sex? No! I mean, I'm sure it would be awesome, but—"

"I was going to say, 'switch places.'"

"... Oh."

"Like, why don't you just stay at the Aria and I'll stay here?"

"No, no, it's fine. You have to set up the booth in the morning while I do all the author-y stuff and… it'll just be easier if you're already there where the convention is. All the books are upstairs and… it'll just be easier."

It's kind of bullshit. It would be just as easy for me to stay there as it is for her. I don't know why I demur. Or, no, that's not true. I do.

It's because I feel guilty. I don't pay Britney anything. She's not really my assistant. She's just my really good friend who's always there for me and keeps me from freaking out about things that don't deserve my freak or making decisions that are based in emotion rather than logic.

She doesn't have to do any of it. Her mom started the second-best-selling 'slimming undergarment' company in the world. Britney could just be one of those stereotypical LA wealthy scion kids who does nothing but show up on *TMZ* for all the wrong reasons, but she isn't like that. She gives all of her free time to me and helping me build this career I'm trying to establish.

And because of all that… I just can't let her stay here. I can't. I wouldn't be able to sleep and I need to be able to sleep. If I don't sleep, I get foggy. And if I get foggy, I get weird. Er. Weirder.

I suppose.

"Are you sure?" she asks.

"Yes."

"Are you *sure* you're sure?"

"Absolutely," I say. She gives me a long, skeptical look. "Brit, I'm fine. It's okay. Look, I'm here. I'm going to be signing a book I almost-like at the biggest book convention in the world."

"Cord—"

"I'm kidding. It's a joke. I'm good. Really. I just want to take a shower and get some rest. I'll meet you over in the ballroom in the morning. Seriously."

She sighs, heavily. "Okay. But if it feels off here at all, like in any way, or you just decide you want to get out of this place, you call me."

"I will."

"I'm serious."

"I know."

She stares at me for another moment, nods, then gives me a hug and says, "This is gonna be awesome. I'm proud of you."

"Thank you." I smile. She smiles back. And then she leaves, reluctantly, trying to close the door behind her, but it sticks. I go over to help her slam it shut. She rolls her eyes in that way she does when she's not happy but decides to give up and not fight me anymore, and exits.

And then…

I'm here. On the eve of what I had planned as my big coming-out party into the world of big-time authorship. It isn't like I had imagined it, that's for sure, but it's still happening. I'm still here. And she's right. It's going to be awesome. It's going to be—

"Yes, Daddy! Yeah! Fuck me, Daddy! Fuck meeeeeeeeee!"

Oh.

There *is* someone else staying here.

That's comforting.

CHAPTER FOUR – STEVE

DAY TWO — THE SETUP

In the early days the parents didn't come to all the signings. The first two years were pretty nice. It was just me, and Essie, and Mike, once they were married and we let him in on the secret.

It was fun. Meeting the fans was so cool—still is the best part, even though I have to hear about it second-hand because I make a point of not hanging around Essie's signing table during the event.

And the authors were closer back then. We were a smaller group, I guess. We all came up together. I actually wasn't the first to break out so big. That was Leslie Munch, pen name Raylen Star.

For more than a year, Raylen Star was my idol. I looked up to her in my early days. I stalked her socials, entered all her giveaways, and read her books. I *read* them. They were… well, not good. Let's just say they were better than most at the time. Indie authors have upped their game in an incredible way. But back then, we were making it up as we went.

I used her as a role model. I paid close attention to her publishing strategy. How long she went between releases, how many ads she ran, how many signings she went to. And I just tried to do everything better.

Oh, man, did she ever notice. She has accused Essie—i.e. me—of stealing her ideas at least a dozen times. And when my seventh book—*Choke the Sugar Outta Me*—made it all the way to number one in the Nile store, she accused me of plagiarizing. Lawyers and everything.

She lost in court—because let's be real here, OK? You don't get to be the number one romance writer in the entire *world* by copying the words of Leslie fucking Munch. She had to pay my attorney's fees and issue a public apology—that was Essie's idea. Essie made a Facebook Live asking for it in lieu of us suing her back for defamation, and this whole thing split the romance world in half. One group on Leslie's side, one on Essie's.

So yeah. Leslie Munch had to eat crow. And she kinda faded away after that. Not entirely—every once in a while, she manages to pull together enough words to make a book. OK, I'm just getting snooty now, but she was a bitch to me and I seriously idolized her. But more importantly, she was a bitch to Essie. Sweet, fair, honest (mostly—it's me who makes her a liar) hardworking Essie.

You can call me out all you want, but do not fuck with my sister. I will go all alpha big-brother on you. Even though technically she was born three minutes before I was, so I'm the little brother in real life.

The point is—Leslie Munch burned this bridge to the fucking water. There's not a splinter of that bridge left.

She became our mortal enemy.

But losing that lawsuit did shut her up. At least in public. I've heard rumors that she's got some private fan forum where she talks all kinds of shit about other authors, but those fans of hers must sign NDAs in blood, because no one will admit to it. Maybe it doesn't even exist. It takes a special kind of psycho superfan to not screenshot that shit and blast it all over socials.

Anyway…

The Sin With Us Romance Con started that same year. It was kind of a shit show. Let's just put it this way—we didn't have it at the Aria. It was at Circus Island. There were cockroaches in the ice cream machines at the buffet.

But no one really cared back then. It was all so different. We felt lucky to be there. It was like a dream come true. I mean, yeah, cockroaches in ice cream is gross, but pretty much every author there—and there were only about fifty back then, this year we have three hundred coming—pretty much all of us just walked around like we were living a fever dream. Like it wasn't real. None of what was happening to us as a group had sunk in yet. I mean, people were cheering for us. They would line up at our tables and wait there for hours just to get a signed book. Our bank accounts were filling up, our socials were growing, and there were deals being made.

Movie deals, publishing deals. Not just me, either. Lots of us got deals like that back then.

Even Essie was enthralled with it all, and she didn't even write the books. This was before Mike, so I had to participate more, and that first year I sat at the signing table with her as her twin-brother assistant.

We only did that once. The ladies were kind of obsessed with me. Started asking for my picture. A few of them even asked if I was her boyfriend.

That's when I bowed out and never sat at that table again. It's bad enough that I have to write sex scenes for a living, but my sister has to read them all so she knows what the hell the fans are talking about when she interacts with them.

It's… not ideal. Embarrassing is a better word. Especially since she's pretty much my beta reader too, so sometimes she wants to give me pointers.

I can't, man. I just can't. These days she tells Mike if she has an issue with a scene in the book and he tells me.

Needless to say, I never sat down at the signing table again after that first year. Mike sits with her now. The fans love him too. He looks like a soap opera star. They flirt with Mike non-stop.

I'm the guy behind the curtain. Kind of literally. Every author gets a table and they bring banners with them. Some banners are big, some small, but ours is huge. I mean, like fifteen feet long and eight feet tall. We take up double the normal space because—well, it's my convention.

All the authors keep boxes of books behind the banners, so when you're back there, it's a like an alleyway. Like a little secret passage in the middle of the convention room. And that's where all the second-string assistants hang out, waiting for the first-string assistant to peek her head around the banner and bark out book titles. Then we dutifully hand them over and go back to organizing swag.

When Essie, Mike, the parents, and I enter the Aria signing hall on Wednesday just before noon, this is where I'm headed. I already know where our table is, so I'm aimed in that direction, focused and intent on getting there so I can start organizing my books and get back to pretending Mom and Dad aren't here. It was a rough four and a half hours from Malibu.

But on my way to the table, everyone starts saying hi to me.

"Hey, Steve! We need to catch up at the mixer tonight!"

I raise a hand to Winter Page, but keep walking.

"Steve!"

"Fuck." I mutter this under my breath. "James. How's it going?" This is Audrey Saint's husband. For some reason, he thinks we're friends. Every year he's trying to fist bump me. I point at him, evading the bump. "I'll catch ya tonight at the mixer."

He raises his hand. "See ya then, bro!"

I'm tracking our huge banner in the middle aisle of the signing hall when, all of a sudden, a familiar voice calls out.

"Excuse me."

I keep going. Because I'm clearly delusional. I've been in the truck with my parents too long. I didn't get enough sleep last night.

"*Excuse* me!"

I'm on drugs. Maybe. It could happen. Because that's the only way *this* voice is invading *my* privacy inside *my* signing hall.

"*Steeeeeeve*! I know you hear me!"

I stop. Take a deep breath. Close my eyes and ask for patience. Then I turn. "Hello, Leslie. Why are you here?"

She hisses at me. "It's *Raylen*, Steve. Not Leslie."

"Right." I force that smile. People are watching us. There's a BookToker with a phone at three o'clock and a Bookstagrammer right behind her. And even though I'm Steve, not Essie, they will virtually crucify SS on the socials if I make a scene. "Sorry, Raylen. What can I do for you?"

She starts talking and I just stare at her mouth. It's bright red. Like… candy-apple Corvette red. It's not even noon yet. Even I know you don't wear bright red lipstick for brunch. And all I keep thinking is… *Why is she here? We banned her eight years back.*

"OK?"

I blink. "Sure. You bet." Then I turn and keep walking. I don't acknowledge anyone else. I just hit the booth and slip behind the banner.

I stop short because there's a woman back there. She's got her head buried in a box of books and she's simultaneously scratching her arm and muttering to herself. Grumble, rumble… "Where the fuck is it?" More grumble rumbles. "I know I packed it."

"Hello. Did you lose something?" I say this in my booming narrator voice. I'm not sure why, but it's deep and commanding. I made this voice up when I narrated all my Master Choke books years ago.

She looks up, wide-eyed and startled. "Oh." Then her eyes go even wider. "Oh!" She stands up, wipes her hands on her jeans. "Sorry. I did. Or no, I didn't. It's here. You're…" She squints her eyes at me, confused, I think.

I smile. Kinda big. Because maybe she doesn't know me, but I know her. I'm the one who got her invited this year. Someone canceled last-minute and Essie asked me if I had a preference, and as a matter of fact, I did. After I gave up on Leslie Munch as an idol, I gave up on professional idols altogether. Until Luke, of all people, sent me a free book saying it was 'right up my alley.'

It was a romance by an author calling herself Cynthia Lear, aka Cordelia Serendipitous. But it wasn't like any other romance I've ever read. It was… *literary*.

And even though I'm not a book snob—like at all. I mean, my major talent in life is writing sex scenes—I do love a good sentence and this woman right here knows how to write one. I point at her. "You're Cynthia Lear, aka Cordelia Serendipitous."

"Um." She looks uncomfortable for a moment. "You got the first part right, but it's Sarantopoulos, actually."

"Right. Right. I knew that." I even point to my brain to prove it. "I just never knew how to pronounce Sarantopoulos, so I made up a new word. Am I the only one who does that?"

"Yes."

"No. I'm not. Everyone does that, right? Especially readers. Right? I mean, if you had to stop reading every time you got to a word you couldn't pronounce, you'd never get through the damn book. I'm right, right? Seriously, who the hell stops mid-sentence to figure out how to pronounce Hercule Poirot? Just call him Hercules Parrot in your head and keep going."

She blinks at me. Twice. Then bows her head and resumes searching for whatever it is she didn't lose.

"Sorry." I take a deep breath and dial down my enthusiasm. "I didn't mean anything by that. And by that I mean I hope I didn't insult you. I'm a lazy reader, I guess."

She looks up at me again. "Hercules Parrot is kind of genius."

"Thanks."

"Um… what are you doing back here?" She looks around, like maybe I was meeting up with someone else and she's just the one I ran into first.

Which isn't the case. I mean, it could've been the case. I didn't know she'd be back here. But now that she is, and so am I, she's exactly the woman I was looking for.

"I'm Steve. SS's sister. Brother, I mean."

She laughs. And damn, she's pretty when she's wearing her trademark scowl, but that smile is a whole other level of beautiful. Her whole face changes. "Yeah. I know who you are. I'm a bona fide SS disciple. I'm even in her reader fan group. Everyone knows who you are."

Hmm. I frown a little. Because… *do they*? Do they really? "You know me because I'm everywhere Essie is? Her unassuming doppelganger? Hovering like an asshole fishing for compliments to boost his ego so he doesn't dwell on what a mess he's made of his life?"

"Umm… OK. But you narrate her books, right? Under the name Tank Watson?"

"What? How do you know that? I mean, it's not public."

"I'm not a stalker or anything, I'm just saying… it's just… your voice." She sighs a little. "I've heard you behind the scenes at Essie's writing webinars. And…

well, it's really not a secret. We've all listened to the audiobooks. Jesus. That scene you narrate with Choke and Sugar?"

"Which one? There are hundreds of them at this point."

She blushes. Bright pink.

"Ohhhhhhhhhh. *That* one."

"That one." She looks down, a little bit embarrassed. "I could never write stuff that dirty. I'm mostly a fade-to-black kinda girl. I like classic romance the best. Not that I don't love your sister's stuff. I do. I absolutely do. It's just…" She lets out a long breath. "*Pride and Prejudice* is my all-time favorite. So. Yeah. I still find the sex scenes to be difficult. But I'm learning."

"Well, it's not as hard as you think because—" *For fuck's sake, Steve. Shut. Up. You were about to give yourself away.*

"Because what?" Cordelia is squinting her eyes at me. "What were you gonna say?"

"Well, Essie and Mike are…" Oh, my God, what am I doing?

"They're…?"

"Experimental. In private."

"Oh." She squints again. Probably because as her brother, should I know this about them?

No. No, I shouldn't. It's weird. And she's just about to say this, I'm sure of it, so I quickly change the subject. "By the way, I read that first book of yours—*The Clock Chimes for Love*—and it was… pret-*teee* amazing."

Her eyes go wide with shock. Then they narrow down. "You're making fun of me."

"What? No! I loved it. Oh, my God. When you made Marcus sell his soul to that corporate asshole to save the corporate asshole's daughter from a life of implied financial slavery—"

"Oh, my God! You *got* that?"

"Got it? Woman, it inspired me to—"

But I stop. Abruptly. So abruptly she rolls her hand in a keep-going gesture. "To what? Inspired you to what?"

I am so off my game today. I feel like I'm bursting with secrets, so full of secrets that I might explode and spill them everywhere.

Alternatively, perhaps it's just lovely Cordelia casting a spell on me, making me feel like we've known each other forever. Because, for the second time in thirty seconds, I was about to admit that I am the one who writes the books and tell her all about how that final scene made me change my whole ending in *Slay Me Wild.* Her ending was so courageous, and wordy, and perfect, I stalked her relentlessly online for like four days solid, looking for all her other books.

But she only had the one back then. And, unfortunately, I kinda forgot about her until I saw her name on the cancellation waitlist and decided to send her the invite.

I wonder if Essie put her behind us in the signing hall so Cordelia and I would have ourselves a little meet-cute?

I wouldn't put it past her. Essie hasn't said anything about me not dating—not the way the parents have—but she's concerned about me. Everything about me seems to be concerning these days.

"Steve?"

"Hmm?"

"You were saying? Inspired you to…"

"It inspired me to tell my sister to rewrite the ending of *Slay Me Wild*."

"Stop it."

"I swear."

Cordelia's mouth drops open. "Wow. Ya know, I thought the ending rang out with familiarity. I mean, not that her book is anything like my book—"

"No, of course not." I don't mean to chuckle here, but come on. Cynthia Lear, aka Cordy Serendipitous, writes some highbrow shit.

I write… well, sex scenes.

Really, really good sex scenes, and of course, I nail that happily ever after each and every time. But you can't even compare the two of us as far as style goes. She's… literary. And her romances are mostly sweet, which I find refreshing. There's nothing I want to read less than a fucking sex scene after I've been writing them all day.

Not that I write all day. Not that I write at all, these days.

While I've been musing on our complementary differences, Cordelia's face has morphed into an expression of… confusion. Then quickly turns to… disappointment?

Did I insult her with my chuckle? Should I explain further? Tell her how artistic her voice is and how her natural ability as a writer would make the hacks cry?

But I've missed my chance. Because Cordelia huffs, bends down again, and resumes looking for whatever it was that she didn't lose. Then her face pops back up, eyebrows knitted together. "Hey. How did you know my real name?"

"You did an interview on a blog called Hot, Sweaty Reads once and spilled all the beans."

"Oh, wow. I had forgotten about that." She pauses to look at me again, her eyes dark, and mysterious, and unexpectedly sexy. Her full lips tremble a little as her tongue peeks out. She's taking me in, sliding her gaze down my body, then back up again. She locks eyes with me.

Holy shit, am I writing a salacious scene in real time in front of a classy woman? What the hell is wrong with me?

"Hey," she says. "I've got a question for you."

"Shoot."

"What do your parents think of Essie's books? I only ask because my parents don't know I write romance."

"Well, our parents love Essie, so of course, they also love Essie's books."

"Oh." Again, I have confused her.

I seem to be good at that. Of course, it's pretty easy to confuse people when you're lying to their faces and leaving out all the important details. So I elaborate. "She's the favorite. She can do no wrong."

"Hmm. I'm sure that's not true. You're… *you*. But do they read them? Wait. Do *you* read them? You don't. Tell me you don't."

"Because that would be… awkward?"

"Gross?"

"Right. Well, I'm a sci-fi guy."

"Yeah, what's your favorite book?"

"Well, actually…" Should I tell her about the books I wrote under my own name? They are damn good books. I don't care what the critics say. I'm a sci-fi book expert and I loved them.

I'm just about to open my mouth and spit out the title of book one when my sane inner voice intervenes. *Steve, that's a big fat no. Two-point-five-star rating. Any chance you have with this lovely creature would be gone the moment she looked that book up on Nile and figured out you're a meme.*

"*Starship Troopers.*"

Her face lights up. "Oh, my God. Heinlein? I love him."

"Really?"

"He's a classic."

"He is indeed."

We smile at each other for a few awkward moments. And I'm pretty sure she's about to get up and be on her way, so I say, "What are you looking for?" to stop that from happening. "Maybe I can help you find it?"

"A book. Well, an ARC."

My eyebrow shoots up. "Advance copy?"

"Not even. It was a beta copy of my latest book. I mean, before I changed it to… whatever it is now."

I'm confused. So I say that out loud. "I'm confused." I make a face to emphasize this.

She sighs. It's long too. Very dramatic. "I wrote a book. Like… the *best* book ever. Even my assistant loved it."

"OK. So what's the problem?"

"The problem? I can't publish it."

"Why not?"

"Apparently, killing the hero of your story and letting your strong, female main protag walk off into the sunset by herself doesn't qualify as a HEA."

"Ooooooh. Yeah. That's a big fat no, Cordy."

"Cord. I really hate Cordy."

"Can I give you some advice?"

"I know, I know. I changed the book. Instead of my dramatic ending filled with personal growth and self-acceptance, they fuck on a mountain and get rescued by the National Park Service."

I laugh. It's very loud too.

She points to the box of books she's been searching through. "That's what all these are. The real ARCs. For my ARC team. Which sounds more important than it is, because there are only nine people on it. My team, that is." She ends this with a powerful exhale that sends the hair around her eyes billowing up. "But I had one copy of the real book and now I can't find it."

"What does it look like?"

"It's a plain white cover with the title on it."

"*Filling the Gap*?"

"Yeah, but not these." She points to her box of books.

"Right. But what about that one?" I point to another book, sitting on the floor right behind her.

She turns, grabs the book, and squeals, holding it to her chest. I don't think she meant to do this. I think it was a genuine display of relief because she immediately looks embarrassed. "Sorry. It's just…"

"Your perfect book."

"Yeah. It's my perfect book. And even though I had to change it to satisfy the commercial nature of the business and meet my readers' expectations, I will forever know in my heart that this is the real story."

I smile. "Nice. Hey, can I read it?"

"What?"

"I'd love to read it. I'm a fan, remember? And if it's your best book ever I'm very interested."

"I don't know. You might hate it."

"So? I mean, I'm sure I won't. I love that first one. Come on. You wrote the best book of your life and now you're just gonna… what? Put it in a trunk and pack it away? Never to see the light of day again? Let me read it. Please."

"What if you lose it?"

"*Cynthia.*" I shoot her a look that conveys a moment of shocked incredulity and trust-me-I'm-a-grown-up at the same time.

She giggles a little.

"Hand it over. I'm gonna read it cover to cover and report back to you at the mixer tonight."

"Oh…"

"Stop." I know what she's gonna say. I can see it coming. She's not going to the mixer.

Lots of first-time authors get too nervous to attend. It's common. Hell, lots of old-hats get too nervous to attend as well. We *are* writers, after all. Well, I don't quite fit the whole writer stereotype, actually—I'm sort of a social butterfly. Which is super ironic since I haven't had a date in two years.

Regardless of my relationship issues, I decide to intervene so I can save Cordelia from an internal debate whereby she talks herself into room service and pay-per-view tonight instead of the fabulous mixer where she can bump elbows with romance giants. "You're going, woman. You're signing books at the biggest romance convention on the planet. You're back to back with SS. She's gonna be right there." I point at the back of our banner. "You're in the big leagues now and you're not allowed to miss a single moment of it, understand me?"

She presses her lips together, then gives me a little nod.

"And I would be honored to read your book. *Please*." A moment later, she hands it over.

CHAPTER FIVE — CORDELIA

I have a hard time letting go of the unadorned, white paperback with the black lettering that contains within its pages what Britney called 'a masterwork.' As he grips it, I suddenly get a little… if not panicky, then breathless. It's unexpected.

And while I'm used to little things triggering an unexpected reaction in me, I can't possibly be prepared for when or what those things might be. That's why they're called 'unexpected.' Being prepared for them to happen would defeat the whole purpose of their stupid, annoying existence.

"You all right?" Steve asks. I nod. "May I… have it?" he follows up, raising his eyebrows and giving a tight-lipped smile that's about fifty-seven percent more charming than I was anticipating it to be. I mean, he's a handsome guy and seems nice, but the sort of aw-shucks, super-handsome but self-deprecating thing he just slipped into so insouciantly is disarming on a different level.

But still… I just met this guy. He rolled up on me all casual-like, knowing who I am, and just started talking to me. Which makes me reflexively wary. Not owing to anything about him specifically, but because of my well-documented lack of trust. And because I think I'm a little bit jealous of people who have that quality about them.

I don't know if my natural tendency toward solitude is what actually drew me to the solitary art of being a writer, or if being a writer has fostered in me a tendency toward avoiding interaction with other humans. Probably a little from column A, a little from column B.

I try not to make a big thing out of it, just like I try not to make a big thing out of my anxiety or habits or any other part of my behaviors. Because I have decided that those things aren't actually *me*. My idiosyncrasies are not the sum and substance of who I am. I'm wary of anyone who defines themselves as one thing or tries to turn the fact that they… don't care how much charge they have left on their phone, or whatever… into a personality trait.

We are not a collection of our behaviors and tendencies and actions. Hell, I'm not even sure we're a collection of thoughts, feelings, and ideas. I'm determined to believe that we are more than that, some unknowable, ineffable thing that is beyond description or definition, and that all of us have the ability to become more than we are.

And I don't think that's just something I tell myself on the days I can't get out of bed because the world outside seems too big to deal with.

I really don't.

"The book. May I read it?" Steve, the brother of SS, the biggest, most bestselling, independently published romance novelist in the world, asks me again as he continues to tug at the manuscript in both of our hands.

And that's when I realize it's not because I don't know this distractingly handsome and charming guy who I just met and have no reason to trust that I don't let go. It's not him that I'm anxious about. It's his sister. SS.

This is sort of what I wanted. Sort of. My plan had been to come here, meet some big authors, get something like a co-sign or a validation from them, and start fast-climbing my way up Mount Romance so that I can, as Sheila advised, get to a point where I no longer have to change my books so that nobody gets mad at me and, I dunno, turns me into a meme on the internet.

And this guy has just told me that he's actually *read* me. That he knows my work and that, in fact, he *encouraged his sister to rewrite her own work based on mine.*

It's all so insanely flattering and unexpected that it makes me automatically skeptical. Which is another one of my possibly toxic traits. It's like that old Groucho Marx quote, 'I refuse to join any club that would have me as a member.'

I have an incredibly hard time not believing that if someone, Britney notwithstanding, tells me they like my work, or like *me* for that matter, there might be something wrong with them. Like they have bad taste or something? Or they're trying to get something from me? Like it's a totally transactional thing they're after.

Which I can't really get too judgmental about considering that *my* whole, entire thing right now is trying to use this experience to get to the next rung of the ladder. That is, I think, transactional by definition.

"If you don't want me to, I don't—" he says, letting go of the book.

"No, no, please. Of course. I'd love to hear what you think." *Jesus. Stop being so weird, Cord.*

I re-offer the book to him and he takes it with the same effortless smile on his face. "Thank you." I feel myself smiling back without necessarily meaning to. And then I start scratching at my arm again.

"What's going on with your arm?" he asks, pointing. And, for a change, I have an answer I can offer that isn't me deflecting or obfuscating in any kind of way. Because I'm not scratching at my arm because I'm nervous or it's a habit or anything like that. I'm scratching at my arm for a very simple, physical reason…

"Bedbugs?" I say.

"Bedbugs?"

"I think?"

There's a pause where he scrunches up his brows and tightens his lips. "Like, here? In the hotel?"

"Oh, no. I—"

"Because that's a problem. There are thousands of people staying here and if there's a bedbug issue, I swear, I'll—"

"No, no. I—"

"The whole reason I picked the—that *Essie* picked the Aria is because it's centrally located on the Strip, and it's nice without being—"

"No," I finally say firmly enough to stop him. "No, I'm… I'm not staying here."

"Whaddayou mean? Why? Or… why not?"

"There was a mix-up. My friend-slash-assistant, Britney, made the rez and somehow they only gave us one room."

"Oh. Well… why didn't *you* take it?"

"What?"

"Why didn't you take the room?"

I feel myself getting flushed. It's some combo of embarrassment and shame. I don't need to tell this guy I just met that it's because I don't feel like I'm deserving. Or worthy. Or whatever. I know he just came up from out of nowhere and started telling me all about himself and asking to read my book, but just because he's an over-sharer doesn't mean I have to suddenly become one.

"Dunno." I shrug.

He studies me for a moment before deciding to let it drop, I guess. Because then he asks, "So, where *are* you staying?"

"The Siegel Suites."

He blinks at me. Once. Twice. Thrice. Ha. I do that. That's funny.

"The Siegel Suites?" He asks it not like he doesn't know what I'm talking about, but very much like he knows *exactly* what I'm talking about.

"Yeah."

"The Siegel Suites," he repeats, emphatically.

"Yes."

He kind of laughs to himself. But not in an amused way. More in an 'are you fucking kidding me?' kind of way.

"What?" I ask.

"Back when we—or, um, Essie, I mean—started this convention—like, the very first one, back when it was small and there was no kind of cachet or anything at all—she looked around for a venue to hold the event that was affordable and that would take us seriously and all that—"

"And you held it at the Siegel Suites?"

"No. We looked at the Siegel Suites and decided that it was too shitty even for us. The place we wound up doing it had cockroaches in the ice cream and even then we all said to each other, 'Well, at least it's not the Siegel Suites."

"Oh."

"You can't stay there."

"It's fine. I'll be—"

"It's not and you won't. You should be staying here with everyone else."

"But—"

"I'll take care of it."

"… What?"

"I'll take care of it. I'll get you something."

"I… They're sold out."

"No, they're not."

"They said they were."

"Not for… SS. For SS, there's room. I got it."

I stare at him. And, like a lightning strike, an image appears in my mind.

Me, stranded somewhere in the middle of nowhere, dressed in some kind of bar wench's attire, bodice-clad bosoms pushed up to the point that they almost touch my neck, searching around in the middle of the… marshy Scottish loch or wherever the hell I am… calling out for help.

And then I look to the side and see… this guy. Steve. (Probably Viscount Steve or Marquis Steve or Duke Steve, actually.) Riding across the marsh on a white steed, jacket open, shirt unbuttoned and billowing in the breeze, exposing his strong, appropriately-hairy-but-not-too-much-so-that-it-gets-nappy chest glistening with sweat. *"Lady Cordelia! Fret not! Steve is here!"*

Ignoring the fact that in my unbidden fantasy he refers to himself in the third person (which is always kinda gross), it's sorta… hot? Like, not feral, but definitely… sexy? At the very least, it's romantic-y.

That's weird.

"I can't let you do that," I say.

"You certainly can. And, more importantly, you *should* let me do that."

"I dunno. I—"

"Last one," Britney says, walking up from behind me and plopping down the final cardboard box of books. Somehow it's elegant when she does it. She's just wearing jeans and a t-shirt and looks like every other assistant currently scurrying around, helping to set things up, but Brit still manages to come across with an air of grace and fluidity that is completely without pretense.

"Hi," she says, extending her hand to Steve. "I'm Britney. Cynthia's assistant."

For the first time, I notice how tall Steve is. Because Britney has to look up at him a little bit, and, normally, Britney doesn't have to look up to anyone. 'Statuesque' is the most obvious but also the most accurate descriptor for how she carries herself. But Steve is equally statuesque in his own way. Some might call it 'powerful.'

And as I notice these things and process them in an eye blink, I feel myself flush again. And this time it's because of something that I don't expect (of course I don't; as established, it wouldn't be unexpected if I did) and I'm not sure I remember the last time I felt, and that I don't think I've *ever* felt with Britney.

Jealousy.

It's there for just a fraction of a fraction of a nanosecond before it flies away, but it is definitely identifiable. To me. I only hope no one else can see.

That was also very weird. Lots of weird things seem to be happening right now.

"Hey. Steve. How's it going?" he responds, shaking her hand politely and nodding but then turning his attention back to me. Huh. That's cool. "So, I'll take care of it. That's it. End of discussion, seriously."

"Take care of what?" Britney asks.

"He—"

"She can't stay at that place," Steve says. "That Siegel Suites bullshit. I'm getting her a room here."

"Oh, a-MAY-zing. You can do that?"

"Yeah."

"This is SS's brother," I say.

"Oh. Yes! Yes, you are! I recognize your voice!" she exclaims, realizing who's standing here. "Of course you are. Hi! You're taller than I thought you'd be."

"Oh," he says. "Okay. Well, I'm not. I'm just as tall as I am."

Britney smiles. "Sorry if I… Sorry. I'm just a big reader and a huge fan of your sister's and I know that it's, like, this whole family business now. And I'm just stoked to be meeting the, um, what's the word? Mischpoke?"

"Mischpoke?"

"I think so?"

"What language is it?"

"Yiddish? I think?"

"What does it mean?"

"Cord, what does it mean?"

"It is Yiddish. It means 'family.' Or, like, a group of people."

"You speak Yiddish?" Steve asks me.

"No."

"Then how do you know?"

"I heard it once? And it just stuck in here." I tap at my head. "I like words."

"Yeah, I know," he says with a smile that some might call 'liquescent.' And by 'some' I mean 'me.' I'm the one who would call it that. I don't know anyone else who would. Most might just opt for 'melty.' But 'liquescent' is, in my opinion, more mellifluous. Which is a word most people wouldn't use either.

Whatever. It's a really cute smile.

"Anyway," Britney starts to Steve, "it's nice to meet you. I'm a *big* fan of your narration."

He rubs his face with his hand in an 'are you kidding?' way. "Um. How is this…? Does everybody just know this? It's supposed to be…"

"I already said something," I tell her. "Apparently we're not supposed to know."

"Oh, shit. Sorry," Britney apologizes, then adds, "Why?"

"Why? I dunno. Because mystery is sexy?"

"Oh," Brit says. "Well, we're sleuths, so… I mean, you do show up in her webinars and stuff. And it is your voice—"

"Yeah, no, I get it," he says. "Well, for anyone who doesn't know, don't tell them, okay? Let's just… keep secrets secret."

I want to ask him why. Why the big secret? Is he embarrassed? Ashamed? He shouldn't be. He's really, really good at it. Maybe it's because he technically works for his sister. I wonder if that's a sore spot for him. He's a Heinlein fan. Maybe he doesn't want his buddies knowing he narrates romance books for a living? We should get into it. Dissect his insecurities about it. That's something he and I could—oh, my God, what am I doing? I just met him and now I have us dissecting things? They must be pumping ambrosia essence through the air vents or something.

"So," Steve says, interrupting my… whatever that was, "if anyone asks, the public line is that Tank Watson is retired U.S. military and didn't want to just sit around doing nothing—you know how those military guys are—so he took up narrating. And fell into romance."

"You have a whole backstory for a guy who doesn't exist?" I ask.

"Of course," he says, with some flippancy. "Character-building is important."

Oh, my God, he's right. Character-building *is* important! Who is this guy?

I should see if he'll narrate one of my books. Britney says I need to start thinking about putting my stuff on audio. Maybe decorated U.S. military veteran Tank Watson should be my narrator. (I know I added the 'decorated' bit, but… character-building.)

"Are your parents here too?" Britney asks, breaking up my sudden and weird ruminating.

"Yeah," he says with a kind of big sigh.

"Your parents come to your sister's signings?" I ask.

"Yeah," he says with an even bigger sigh.

"That's so sweet," I tell him.

"Yeah," he says again, clipped this time.

"They must be very proud of your sister."

"Yeah," he says yet again, again more clipped, "they are. Anyway!" He claps his hands together. "Go get your stuff from that dystopian nightmare masquerading as a hotel and by the time you get back, we'll have you squared away."

"Ha!" Britney barks out a laugh.

"What?" I ask.

"'Dystopian nightmare masquerading as a hotel.' That's a paraphrase from *Sugar Push*. In the book, Choke says about how Sugar grew up that she had a 'dystopian nightmare masquerading as a childhood.' I always loved that line. It's so… specific."

"It's a really good line," I agree.

Steve's mouth contorts about three different ways before he says, "Yeah. Yeah, Essie's a… She's a good writer." As someone who not more than a few seconds ago had their own bout with an unexpected and fleeting jealousy, I am able to recognize it as a version of the same thing that passes through Steve and I wonder if maybe we've hit on a sensitive subject. Is Steve envious of his sister's success? He doesn't present as the kind of person who'd be like that, but I've known him for all of about five minutes, so who can say?

"But that's a-MAY-zing, thank you," Britney says, expelling a relieved breath. "I barely slept at all last night knowing she was over there at that place. I felt terrible."

"Don't feel terrible," I say.

"I gotta tell ya," Steve offers, "it's kind of incredible."

"What is?" I ask.

"That you insisted your friend take the room. Or that we didn't hear about it."

"I'm sorry, I'm not… Whaddayou mean?"

"I mean… you're an author. A really good author. And you're at… this is your first signing, isn't it?" Steve asks. I nod. "You're at your first signing and the reservation gets messed up, and you didn't turn it into a whole big Krakatoa of a scene? That's… that's pretty damn humble and very, very cool. That's all."

I bite at my lip and look away. Britney nudges me. "She *is* cool. The coolest."

"I'm not," I say. "Stop it."

"No, you really are. Or at least, you handled yourself in a cool way. Not everyone would be so chill about something like that."

"Steve!" The somewhat raspy, somewhat shrill, somewhat nasally (all at the same time) voice draws all of our attention. A woman is approaching us, having just ducked behind a banner and made her way down the 'backstage' corridor.

She's tall. Not as tall as Britney, but still pretty tall. Thin, kind of severe-looking, and she has an expression of real purpose on her face.

Steve rubs at his eyes, hums out a tiny, guttural moan, and turns to face the woman who is now right upon us. "What's up, Leslie?"

"Call me Raylen, please call me Raylen, just call me fucking Raylen, please," she says redundantly. Repeatedly. Over and over and over again. (*Ahem.*)

"Sorry. Yes. What's up, *Raylen*?"

"You're Raylen Star?" Britney asks. And the woman—Leslie or Raylen or whoever—ignores her.

"Why am I in the corner?" she asks Steve.

"What?"

"I'm in the corner. My placement. My booth. I'm in the fucking corner. Why am I in the fucking corner?"

"I… dunno, Ray. I—"

"Ray-*len!*"

"I'm not in charge of placement. There's a whole team who handles that stuff."

"So, your sister didn't put me there? On purpose?"

"I don't know if my sister even knows you're here. I didn't know you were coming."

"Why wouldn't I come?"

Her lips are very red. I'm no makeup expert—I don't really wear any unless I absolutely have to—but even *I* know that you don't usually wear lipstick that red this early in the day. Eh. Live and let.

"I don't know, Raylen," Steve says, "I wasn't sure you were still writing."

Her lips curl like a snarling wolf's, exposing the slashes of bright red that have marked her teeth. "Oh, I'm writing," she says. "I'm writing." The second time is a little pointed in a creepy and kind of… threatening way? "See?"

She pulls back the banner behind which we're standing and points to the far end of the room where we can see her massive promotional banner. At the top, it reads…

RAYLEN STAR: THE AUTHOR YOUR MOTHER WARNED YOU ABOUT

And even though all the banners and artwork I've seen around are cheeky or kind of risqué (mine included), Raylen's are flat-out porn-y. If she tried to use one of those images on Facebook for an ad or something, she'd probably be banned for life. Thrown in Facebook jail. And maybe real jail, for that matter.

"Good for you," Steve says, deadpan. "But, like I say, I'm not the placement committee. You should take it up with whoever's handling your event submissions these days."

"*I* am," she says.

"Oh. No assistant?" Steve asks. She shakes her head, slowly and tersely. "Wow. Well, then, yeah. Don't know what to tell you. Maybe you need to give yourself a talking to."

Watching her try to contain her frustration is like watching a five-year-old try to control a jackhammer.

Then she looks down and sees my open boxes of books. Reads my name aloud from the cover. "Cynthia Lear?" I nod, smile. "I've never heard of you."

Harsh.

"Oh... Yeah, this is my first—"

"How the fuck did you get placed right behind SS?"

"I… don't know," I say, looking to Steve, who shrugs.

"Me neither," he offers up. "Like I say, not my department."

The mean woman, Ray-Leslie, grits her teeth and looks down at the copy of *Filling the Gap* that Steve is holding. "What's that? An ARC?"

"Yeah," I volunteer. "It's a—"

"It's an ARC? Of one of your books?"

"Uh. Yeah. Like I was saying, it's—"

"You're letting Steve and Essie have it?"

"Um… yeah. Yes. Yes, I am."

She looks at me, then at Steve, then at me one more time. She makes her tongue cluck, or click, or some combination of the two. Then she says, "Be careful."

"About… what?" I ask.

"About getting involved with liars," she says, giving Steve one last pointed look.

Then she sweeps past the banner, dramatically, and makes her way back over to the far corner of the hall.

CHAPTER SIX – STEVE

"Holy shit." Britney, the assistant, looks up at me with an incredulous expression of 'what the fuck.' "She's a… a…"

I volunteer a noun. "A bitch?"

"Yeah!" Britney laughs this word out with gusto.

And I'm laughing too, but then I look over at Cordy, and she's… not. "What did she mean by that?"

That question is directed to Britney, not me. And immediately I feel cut out of the conversation.

What did she mean by that? Translation—*Did Raylen Star just caution me, Cordy, about handing over my ARC to SS's brother, Steve, because she was insinuating they, she, he might steal my words?*

That is exactly what Leslie fuckin' Munch just did.

I had a good thing going with this girl. She and I were having a moment. And even though Britney kinda busted in on us, Britney wasn't obtrusive. I was winning her over. Which is important. As the number one romance writer in the world, I wholly and completely understand that the new love interest must befriend the BFF.

And fine. Maybe 'new love interest' is a premature title for me? We were still on introductions. We hadn't made any concrete declarations of intent or anything, but we were on our way. We were getting there. Would've gotten there if fuckin' Leslie hadn't showed up.

And now, as I watch Cordy and Britney exchange a look and in the next moment watch, in real time, as Cordy's eyes drop down to the book gripped firmly in my hands, I have to tuck down a moment of rage.

Two minutes. Two. Minutes. That's all it took for Leslie to ruin the good thing I was building with this lovely creature who might be the only person in the room who can write a run-on sentence with such skill, and emotion, and… and… and *moxie* that one does not even understand that she, lovely Cordy, just wrote the world's longest run-on sentence because they have been captivated—imprisoned, even—by her brilliant author voice.

Cordy Serendipitous's ability to string words together for the longest of sequences is what drew me to her in the first place. I love it. I love that she breaks all the rules. It's so… so… fuckin' courageous—especially in a world filled with people who want nothing more than the expected to jump out at them in a totally expected way, lest they have to stretch their minds a bit to find the hidden messages hiding just below the surface—that I, for once, did not feel like a completely isolated freak among those who fit in. At least as far as writing goes.

And Leslie Munch has fucked that up with two words of caution.

Be careful.

I take a deep breath and direct my attention to Britney, because she's talking. "Cord. Please. Do not take that woman seriously. I mean, I like her stuff." Britney looks at me. "It's nothing compared to your sister, mind you. Your sister's stuff is"—she clicks her tongue—"fucking absolute! But Raylen Star? Man, she used to write some good shit."

I'm about to ask where she's going with this when Brit-Brit gets to the point. "But something happened to her, ya know?"

Britney is looking at me, so I nod enthusiastically. "She has been accusing us—I mean, Essie—of ripping off her shit for years. It was a constant thing for a while there. She even took us to court and lost."

"Oh, my God." Britney's eyes are wide. "I totally remember that!" Britney looks over at Cordy, who still has that look on her face like she's following this conversation, but not completely sold yet. "Remember, Cord? She had to make that public apology?" Britney snorts.

Slowly, ever so slowly, the muscles in Cordy Serendipitous's face relax and she forces a smile. "Oh. Right. I kinda do remember that."

I begin to relax as well. Because the BFF is firmly on my side. I can feel it. I like this friend. "Hey!" I suddenly get a great idea. "What do you two have planned for the mixer tonight?"

There is another look exchanged between Britney and Cordy. This one says, *You're going.* That's coming from Britney. But Cordy is trying really hard to get out of this without using her words, so her face says… well, it's just a look of *I'm panicking, but trying not to look like I'm panicking.*

I interject before this goes any further. "Listen, why don't you two join Essie, Mike, and me at our living room configuration tonight." I'm looking at Britney when I say this, because this bait is for her, not Cordy.

Britney is immediately confused. "Your… what?"

"Oh, sorry. The lounge where the mixer is—they don't really have tables. They have living-room configurations. Couches and chairs with coffee tables. We have the center one reserved."

Britney makes a face of understanding. "Oooooh! That would be so much fun! Right, Cord?" She grabs Cordy's arm, tugging on it like an excited child.

Cordy continues to be confused. Or possibly suspicious. "And you're inviting us… why?"

"So I can take you around and introduce you to everyone." I soften my voice for this part, toning down the used-car salesman approach. That's not how Cordelia works. She's a quiet woman with a busy mind who can't be tricked into things. She's a thinker. So I use logic on her. "They're nice people, Cordelia. Most of them, anyway. And I promise to only introduce you to the nice ones."

"We'd love that." Britney is holding Cordy's hand now, squeezing it, like she's going to make Cordelia agree to this no matter what.

Finally, Cordy smiles. It's mostly genuine. "Umm…" She looks at her ARC in my hand.

As I expected her to. "Oh. I'll read it this afternoon and return it to you tonight. I promise." This is Cordy's bait. She's *that* practical.

Cordelia Sarantopoulos is convinced. Kind of. Her "OK" is soft and filled with resignation, but it's still an affirmative.

"Yay!" Britney jumps up and down a few times. "We're gonna have so much fun!"

I decide to end on this high note. "I'll see you then." Then I hold up the book for a wave, and retreat to the other side of the SS banner.

♥♡♥♡♥♡♥♡♥♡♥

Back in my suite, I pick through the complimentary fruit basket on the dining table, then use the phone in the bedroom to call the concierge. It takes me thirty seconds to make arrangements for Cordy. There is just one room left and it's an executive suite that comes with a conference room.

Just like mine.

Is it too much?

Well, it's the only one left.

I book it and tell the concierge to find Britney Whatshername and help her move Cynthia Lear into the Aria, but the moment I hang up the room phone, I have regrets.

I call up Terry for advice. He answers on the seventh ring. "*What*?"

"It's me."

"Oh. Sorry. You didn't come up on caller ID."

"I was using the room phone right before I called you and just… kept using it. Am I interrupting?"

"I'm deep in, man. Deep. In. I've got Deckard Blake trapped inside an underground bunker with a crazy AI cyborg on the other side. Picture Raccoon City, but not so high-tech. He's gonna have to leave the safety of this bunker, run along an old, abandoned train tunnel—holding his breath, there's no air down there—and then finagle the airlock on another bunker open before his lungs explode."

"Sounds… tricky."

"Dude, you have no idea. I've got Luke calculating air pressure in the lungs, and Shawn is figuring out the exact torque required to get past the rust on steel—I've strategically placed another bunker within an appropriate distance so this move is possible—"

"Of course you have. That's your job."

"—and it's just… I'm deep in, man." He exhales. "But what's up?" His tone lightens. "I've always got time for you, Steve. Oooh, you're at the convention! How was the drive?"

"Terrible. But listen, that's not why I'm calling. I met a woman—"

"What? Damn, dude. I wish I was you."

I practically snort. "Me? Why? You're the one writing cool shit like low-tech Raccoon City." I'm so jealous of his career, it's not even funny.

Terry explains. "I know I'm married—happily—but everywhere you go, the ladies love you. You're like a walking, talking romance cover. You've been there what, an hour? And you've already met a woman?"

"Thirty minutes, give or take. But here's my problem…" I explain what happened and then sigh. "Am I coming on too strong? The executive suite? Does it reek of desperation?"

"What the hell are you talking about? This is romance-novel gold, dude."

"I'm not actually in a romance novel, Terry. This is real life."

"Right. I get it."

"I don't want her to think I'm, like, bribing her, or something."

"Why the hell would she think that?"

"I just explained how Leslie fuckin' Munch planted a seed of doubt in Cordelia's head! Were you even listening to me?" I am trying to pace the room, but the cord on the phone is too short, which makes the phone fly off the bedside table and fall to the floor, ripping the handset out of my grip.

Huh. The limitations of low-tech phones. That's kind of ironic.

I pick the handset back up and hear a dial tone.

Then my cell phone dings a text out in the dining room. I walk out there, grab it off the table, and read: *Romance-novel gold! This is great stuff! Keep going!*

I growl, but don't text back. He's deep in. He's not even listening to me. Too busy making up his cool dystopian world and getting his action-adventure characters from one crisis to another.

I spend a few moments wondering if I should pick this conversation back up with Shawn or Luke, but then decide against it.

If they're both writing too, I'll just get depressed when they start explaining their current work-in-progress. That's how it is for me these days.

I'm so… unsatisfied. I cringe even thinking the word. It's so wrong to be unsatisfied when I'm this fucking successful. It's gross.

But then my eyes wander to the open door of the bedroom and I see the ARC sitting on the bed. My smile is immediate. I have a book to read.

While I would not call myself a book fanatic in the same vein as the ladies who come to conventions like this, I would call myself an avid reader. I've been in a slump lately. Nothing seems to catch my interest, and if it does, it almost never holds it.

And while I do have high hopes for *Filling the Gap*, I temper them with realistic expectations as I grab the book, take it out into the living room, sit down on the couch and open it up.

♥♡♥♡♥♡♥♡♥♡♥

Four hours later my phone has been turned off to avoid interruptions, my eyes are frantically zipping down the page towards the conclusion, and someone is pounding on my door.

I walk over to the foyer area, my eyes never leaving the page, and then—just before I open the door—I read Cordelia's final run-on sentence:

Walking toward the setting sun, feeling the warmth of the sand creeping up through my toes and glissading down the slopes of my feet like the grains themselves are tiny alpinists making their descent, I wipe away my tears as I realize that Apollo's sacrifice means I now must learn to ascend the frightening pitches of my own life, those that have been here, waiting for me all along, but that I have been ever afraid to summit; the wondrous, ethereal, mystical majesty that is existence—which rivals the mythos of Olympus itself—not alone, but carried upon the wings of his sacrifice, and in that realization I feel the ancient spirit of my namesake rise to counter the declining sun; I feel Elpis, I feel hope, because in the tragic, freighted, soul-desiccating but necessary and ultimately sublime peace that bathes me in its grace I understand that he fell… so I might rise.

And… big, long sigh.

I open the door grinning like an idiot.

"Oh, my God! Steve! What the fuck?" Essie has a frantic look on her face. "We've been calling your phone for thirty minutes!"

"We thought you were dead." Mike is already rearranging the subject.

I hold up the book. "Holy shit, you guys. This book is amazing."

"It's almost six, Steve!" Essie is holding her phone out so I can see the time. "The mixer starts in an hour!"

"Right." I turn back to my room and leave them at the door. "What should I wear?"

They follow me in. Right into the bedroom where I open the closet and consider my wardrobe options. "I want it to say 'serious,' but not 'threatening.' Does that make sense? What do you think?" I pull out a hanger holding a dark blue button-down. "This with jeans?"

"What are you doing?" Essie is looking at me like I'm crazy. "Why weren't you answering your phone? And did you realize we've purchased an executive suite for an author called Cynthia Lear?"

"Oh, yeah. That charge came through, huh?"

"A thousand dollars a night, Steve!"

"Oh, my God, Essie. She deserves it! Her writing!" I'm still holding the ARC in one hand. "It's… so good."

"But why are we paying for her room?"

"*We*"—I stress this, even though I shouldn't, because Essie isn't paying, I'm paying—"are paying because she was a last-minute add, there were no rooms left, and she got stuck staying at the Siegel Suites."

Mike makes a face. "Eww."

"Right? It's gross."

"That's not even true! I know there was a room left when I invited her. It was the room reserved for the author who cancelled!"

"Yeah, but Cynthia Lear is so altruistic, and generous, and… and… *noble* that she gave that room to her assistant!"

"Well, that's dumb." Mike says this without heat. He's not wrong, but he's missing the point. As he usually does.

"It's not dumb." I explain the whole story and by the time I'm done, Essie is agreeing.

"Wow. That really was generous of her."

"Right? So I got her a room. Who cares if it's a thousand dollars a night? This is her first signing. She's going to remember this for the rest of her life. We're already making memories."

Essie makes a face at me. "What's *that* mean?"

"I'm enthralled with her."

"This is real?"

"Yes. Her talent is…" I sigh. "I'm so jealous."

"Yeah, but…" Mike is shrugging with his hands. "You're jealous of like… every single writer you know."

"No. I'm jealous of writers who write *their* story, and not the story they're *told* to write."

Essie sighs. We've had this conversation at least twenty times. "No one is telling you what to write, Steve. Every story has been your choice."

She's correct. I know this. But it's not that simple. People have expectations of SS, so SS needs to write stories that meet those expectations.

It's a lot of pressure to put all the beats in. Use up all the popular tropes. Drag my characters kicking and screaming to that final happily ever after even though they've got years of therapy ahead of them.

"What Cynthia Lear did with this story here"—I hold up the ARC again—"was courageous."

Both Essie and Mike look bored. This is their practiced reaction to my drama these days.

I never used to be dramatic, and I have resisted that description. But the longer I write, the more I become part of the drama. It's hard not to get caught up in it. I mean, drama is the point of writing.

I am, maybe, after all, turning into a cliché writer. A grumpy, reclusive, rich, unsatisfied genius. Which both delights me, in a certain way, while simultaneously makes me cringe.

"Anyway," I continue, "I'm gonna make her swoon tonight. So can you two please keep the assistant occupied?"

"Did you just use the word 'swoon' out loud?"

"Mike. I'm a romance writer. Purple prose is my one and only superpower. Cut me some fuckin' slack, OK?"

"Fine," Essie says. "We'll do our best."

"You mean… *you'll* do *your* best." Mike is pointing at Essie. "I'm bowing out after introductions, remember? The 'husband night out?'"

"Oh, right." Now Essie looks pissed. She even stomps her foot. "So I'm stuck with a stranger all night?"

"Trust me, Essie. You're gonna love Britney. You two are like… twins, or something."

This makes her smile. Because, obviously, she and I *are* twins.

♠♡♠♡♠♡♠♡♠♡♠

I choose the white button-down instead of the blue button-down. Essie picked it up from the dry cleaner just yesterday, so it's fresh, and crisp, and white enough to blind a person. This shirt is for my suit look, which I was going to wear tonight. But I've changed my mind.

Suit Guy is hot. No doubt. But work-is-over-now, sleeves-rolled-up guy is even hotter. His hair is sexily messy, there's stubble on his jaw after a hard day's work, and he's a little bit weary.

Not tired. *Weary*. Big difference.

Tired is… 'I need to go to bed early tonight. Alone.'

Weary is… 'I need a neck massage and a good fuck.'

I debate the merits of wearing a tie in front of the mirror, smirking at myself as I do the whole with-without thing.

I go with 'with.' But I make it loose, like I've been working hard pushing paper around all day, complaining about clients, and calling for my assistant on the interphones.

I like this look. I think my next male lead needs this look. What should I call it? 'Dirty office?' No. That conjures up images of trash cans and janitors, who I am sure *can* be sexy. But that requires a lot of backstory for a romance novel.

I'll call this look… 'after hours.' Mmm. Much better. This conjures up images of nightclubs and sex in the bathroom.

Dare I think about bedding lovely Cordelia tonight? Is she that kind of woman?

Probably not.

But it doesn't hurt to send the right message. I mean, I'm totally up for sex on the first non-date if she is.

In this moment, I have a revelation. I am writing scenes in my head. I am building characters. And while yes, this is something writers do… it's not something I *have been* doing. Not since that disastrous flirt with science fiction.

Could it be that Cordelia is my muse?

Could she be the inspiration I've been waiting for?

Is Cordelia Sarantopoulos my light at the end of a very dark tunnel of self-loathing? Will Steve Smith shed his insecurities after a calamitous run-in with murderous critics and live to write another sci-fi masterpiece?

Holy shit. I'm even writing blurbs in my head.

Maybe Terry was right?

Maybe my life *is* a romance novel?

Maybe that's the secret to success? Live life like it's fiction.

I might have to trademark that.

❤♡❤♡❤♡❤♡❤♡❤

Essie and Mike have already gone down to the ALIBI Ultra Lounge on the casino level where the private, invite-only mixer is being held, so I enter the party alone. Looking around, I know almost everyone by name.

Even though none of these people know I'm the real SS, author of all those amazing books, they all know I'm Essie's kinda weird—but in a hot way—twin brother, Steve. And they all start waving to me and calling me over.

"Ro-Bro!"

"Steeeeeve! Ro-Bro! What's up?"

They, meaning the husbands of the other romance authors, started calling me the Ro-Bro like… immediately. The very first signing Essie and I went to, the husbands were all over me thinking I was one of them. But then Mr. Blake, husband to Penny Blake—not their real names—found out I was Essie's brother and he coined me the Ro-Bro.

Do I hate it? Not exactly. I mean, I *wanted* to hate it. Mr. Blake is annoying as fuck. But it's a double entendre, so while I maybe didn't fall in love with it, neither could I loathe it.

I do love a good hidden meaning, after all.

And one day, if it ever comes out that I'm the real face behind the SS pen name, people will get the joke. It'll be fun. It'll be fine. They might make me into a meme, but I feel like it would not be so bad to be a cartoon version of the Ro-Bro.

Since Cordelia and Britney aren't here yet, I offer up hellos to the other bros in the form of waving back and make my way over to Essie and Mike, who are standing in a crowd of nearly a dozen newbie authors, who I know are newbies because I've never seen them before.

I nod my head as I'm introduced, but keep one eye on the entrance to the lounge so I can greet Cordelia when she arrives.

I'm going to gush about that book of hers. *Gush.* That's a technical term in my business. It means to go over-the-top insane in front of people so they get a paralyzing sense of FOMO and start one-clicking the pre-order.

Which, unfortunately, won't be the same book that my Cordy let me read. But who cares. I'm gonna gush about it anyway.

Suddenly, there she is at the entrance! Backlit by a rainbow bokeh effect of blurry slot-machine lights. I pause to tilt my head a little. She. Looks. Gorgeous.

Her navy-blue dress falls just past the knees with a… a… *no. Reminiscent of* the bygone days of Prohibition, where one looks for an escape from the dystopian nightmare of their real-life poverty in the dark alleys of a hidden speakeasy entrance.

She's wearing a flapper dress. And I love it. Every single tassel strand jiggles and dances as she scans the room looking for me. Britney is dressed up in much the same way and I begin to sense a theme here.

Oh, shit. They got the parties mixed up. Roaring Twenties night is on Saturday and it's for the fans. Tonight is get-drunk casual—or, in my case, 'after hours'—and it's just authors plus one.

In this same moment I sense the rest of the room is, well, reading the room. They have noticed that one among them has shown up in the wrong attire.

I do not give the hyenas a chance to circle her like a death cult and focus her Cinderella blurry, slot-machine bokeh world back into the pumpkin of reality. I am crossing the lounge with my arms out and my smile wide while simultaneously, and internally, wincing at that terrible metaphor.

"There you are!" I proclaim, my greeting loud enough for all to hear. "Welcome, Cordelia and Britney! We've been waiting for you."

CHAPTER SEVEN – CORDELIA

Eyes. There are eyes on me. An entire roomful of eyes.

I turn to go, run out of here, but Britney takes me by the arm and plants me. "Where are you going?"

"To change."

"Why?"

"Because this is clearly not flapper night." I start off again.

"It's fine." She stops me again.

"It's not fine."

"It's really fine."

"It's really not."

"If you go, you won't come back."

"That's not true."

"Yes, it is."

"So?"

"So, you need to just stay here, be here, and try to have a good time. Don't worry that it's the wrong night. Just own it."

Own it? Sure. *She* can own it. She looks amazing in everything. I feel like I'm wearing a potato sack with fringe. And the Skinny Laminx I'm wearing (the slimming undergarments Britney's mom invented) are starting to choke off my breathing.

I start scratching at my arm. I'm not sure if it's still the bedbugs or something else. Maybe a combination of things. I reach into my little clutch for the cortisone I bought in the pharmacy downstairs right as Steve reaches *us*.

"Ladies," he says, bowing, raising his palm to hold his loosened tie in place against his chest. He looks… good. There are a hundred better words I could think to describe it, but it's really not more complicated than that. He looks good. And hot. And suddenly my arm feels even itchier. Where is the cortisone? I thought I put it—

"Got the nights mixed up, eh?" he asks, presumably rhetorically.

"Yeah," Brit says. "I couldn't find the email, and I think I just misremembered."

Britney's an amazing friend. An incredible ally. A terrific beta reader. And one of the smartest cookies in the jar.

But she's a terrible assistant.

"All good. Get settled in the new room okay?"

"Yes," I say, nodding. "We got into a bit of a…"

"A fight," Britney offers. "We got into a fight trying to get out of the Siegel Suites. They wanted to charge Cord's card for the whole weekend instead of just the one night, and it got a little heated."

I say, "The guy at the front desk said he'd waive the charges if Britney would…"

Steve's eyes go wide. "He offered to waive the charges in exchange for sex?"

"No," Britney explains. "It was appreciably weirder than that."

"Say more?" Steve queries.

"Not sure. His English was spotty. But based on what I could glean, I think he might be German? It sounded like he wanted me to do things that involve all kinds of bodily functions I don't really like to engage in with other people present."

"Ah, yes. Sweet, sweet Vegas. But you did get out? And you're settled upstairs?"

"Yes," I tell him again. "It's… it's very nice. You didn't have to arrange an executive suite."

"I did, actually. It's the only thing they had left."

"Oh. Well… thank you. Do I need to give you my credit card or anything?"

He waves his hand. "No, no. It's all taken care of."

"Oh. No. I can't let you do that."

"It's fine."

"No, please, here." I dig in the clutch to find my business credit card, the one that I reserve for stuff like convention hotels and printing costs and placing ads and… well, someone told me that I could probably write off sex toys too. As 'research.' Look, if it's not breaking any rules, I figured I should probably try to make sure that what I write is as authentic as possible, so—

"No, no. I insist. It's fine. You're a first-time signer. Consider it a first-timer welcome gift. You can gift a room to a first-timer next year or something if you wanna pay it forward. But, please, it's our pleasure. I'm just glad we got you out of the bedbuggery that is the Siegel Suites." He nods at my arm.

I laugh.

He's unexpected, this Steve. He comes across initially like some kind of bro, but… I dunno. There's something else there. He's funny, but he's not just funny the way guys are when they're trying to be funny or charming. He's, like, *actually* funny. *And* charming.

And he's clever. Maybe that's the thing that I find most disarming. He doesn't come over as disingenuous or dopey or trying too hard to be cool. And that's… honestly, it's rare. Or at least it's rare in my experience.

I'm not sure I believe it.

I've known a few guys over the years who have presented that way only to have the façade collapse when scratched at a little bit.

Not all of them betrayed my trust by stealing from me, of course. (At least not literally. I feel like there's a lazy metaphor to be made about 'stealing my heart,' but it feels cheesy, so I back away.) But a lot of them have been your stereotypical Hollywood douchebag types. Not in a slimy 'influencer house'/'gonna make it big on the Gram' kind of way. More in the 'classic career climber' kind of way.

Like, every time one of them would find out my parents used to be big TV writers, they'd see it as some kind of an angle. So, almost immediately the conversations would turn to, "So, do you know so-and-so? Do you think you could slide them my script?" Or, "Could you get me an audition for…?" Or whatever.

And, look, yet again, I get it. I've been very honest with myself about what I want to achieve and why I'm at this convention and all that. Everybody's gotta look out for themselves. I understand. I just don't wanna be romantically involved with someone who only sees me as an opportunity and not… me. I suppose.

And Steve doesn't come across as someone like that.

Not that I'm saying I'm trying to date Steve. Not at all! That's not what I'm saying! I don't know Steve! I'm just saying that in comparison to other *guys* he seems different. Like, he's just here helping his sister and being her assistant the same way Britney's mine. It doesn't seem like he's got a bunch of lofty career goals that make him potentially… well, pilfer-y.

And all I'm thinking is that that's refreshing. That's all.

Seriously.

Really, he seems like a very down-to-earth and nice-to-be-around kind of a—

"Bro!" I hear, and all three of us turn our heads to see a man and a woman approaching.

They look nice, probably early forties, dressed very much like they just came from a PTA meeting at their kids' school. Which I only notice as it's in dramatic contrast to the Giorgio Armani cologne commercial vibe Steve is rocking and the costume-party chic aesthetic Britney and I have stumbled our way into.

Romance writers are an eclectic bunch, I'll tell ya.

"Hey, James," Steve says, forcing a bit of a smile.

The guy, James, has ruddy cheeks and seems like he's in the best mood anyone's ever been in. He comes right up to Steve with his arm extended and his fist balled at the end. When Steve doesn't immediately reciprocate with an extended arm and fist of his own, this James character bends his elbow and re-extends his fist, like he's punching forward at no one. "Bro! C'mon, bro! You gonna leave me hangin', bro?"

Steve smiles tightly, pressing his lips together, then returns the fist bump James appears to so desperately require.

"My bro!" James says, pulling his fist back and making a 'ppppoooooccchhhhh' sort of explosion sound.

"Hey, Steve," the woman says.

"Hey, Audrey, how you doing?" Steve leans in and gives the woman a hug and a kiss on the cheek.

"Essie around?" she asks.

"Yeah, she and Mike are around here somewhere. Oh, Audrey, this is Cynthia Lear and her assistant, Britney… sorry. What's your last name?"

"Kincaid," Brit says.

"Audrey Saint," Audrey responds, shaking both of our hands. Then she cocks her head. "You're Cynthia Lear?" she asks me.

"Um. Yes?"

"I read your first book, *The Clock Chimes for Love.*

"You did?"

She nods. "It was very good. No, better than very good. It was excellent. I was a high-school English teacher for almost fifteen years. I know good writing, and you're a very good writer."

I feel myself flush. But in a nice way. "Wow. That's very nice. I—Thank you. I wrote that thing in six weeks and just kind of put it out there to see what would happen."

"Sounds familiar," she says, with a knowing smile.

"I just feel like that book was so dashed off and I didn't really have anyone editing it properly, and if I had taken more time I think I could've tightened it up a lot and coalesced the story points better, and I feel like the central allegory was so muddled that—" *Shut up, Cord. Just shut up. Take the damn compliment.* "… Anyway. Thank you. That means a lot. You're very kind."

She continues smiling her knowing smile and nods.

"What's all this?" the guy, James, says, pointing up and down at our dresses.

"I got the nights confused," Britney says.

"Oh. Yeah, I've done that before. Your first con?" James asked. Britney and I both nod. "Well, boom! Welcome! It's the most fun you'll ever have with your clothes on! Or not." He winks. Then he adds, more soberly, "But, yeah, there can be a lot of moving parts to keep track of. I've got a spreadsheet I can share with you that helps a lot. A lot."

"That'd be a-MAY-zing. Thank you."

"Sure, sure. I don't think most people realize when they first get into the romance game, especially on the indie side, that it's not just about writing. I mean, you're running a small business, for Christ's sake. Fortunately, I used to have my own accounting practice, so I know some tricks to streamline. Helped old Steve-O here get SS Industries up and running back in the day, didn't I, Steve-O?"

Steve gives what I like to call a 'gritty smile.' "Just 'Steve's' cool. Yeah! Yeah, you sure did."

"Met Stevie-boy here back at the first one of these when Essie and Audrey were just starting out. Who knew they'd blow up to run the game?" James laughs a hoarse, overly enthusiastic laugh. "Not a lot of guys in the game, amirite? Bros gotta stick together, amirite? Stevie? Steve? Steve-O? S to the T to the E-V-E? Amirite?"

"Yeah. You're… right," Steve mutters.

"Although this one here"—James points at Steve—"this one here was always the fave of the ladies, if you know what I'm sayin'." He winks a little too hard and kind of… sticks his tongue out?

"Forgive James. He got started on the minibar early," Audrey explains.

James grabs at Audrey's backside, buries his face in her neck, and makes a 'nom nom nom' sound before exclaiming, "What? It's a con! We're in Vegas! The kids are back at home, nobody's watching the hen house while the cat's away—"

"I don't think that's the way the saying—" Steve starts.

"—so it's time to puh-*lay*!" James crows.

♥♡♥♡♥♡♥♡♥♡♥

A few hours into the event and James is no longer the only one who's drunk.

These. Writers. Can. Drink.

Sitting on the sofa in the center of the lounge, next to Steve, SS, and her husband, Mike, open bottles and half-finished glasses of champagne everywhere, I lowkey feel like this is what being a celebrity must be like. Because, I guess, SS kind of is.

Maybe not to the broader world, but in this little corner of the universe, she is a very big deal. And the thing about her that strikes me is that she doesn't *feel* like a writer. I don't know if I can explain what that means exactly, but it's true.

Maybe it's that she—and the other writers, for that matter, all of whom swing by to offer their hellos, well wishes and thanks—seem to have one thing in common: They're really nice.

This being the first time I'm meeting a real… I don't know what you call an assembled group of romance authors. A gaggle? A murder? A coven? Maybe there isn't a word for it. I should make one up.

An engorgement? No. Both wrong and gross.

A corpulence? No. Great word, but I can see it being problematic.

A regent? Most do use pen names. That tracks. Meh. Boring.

An ostentation? Cavalcade? Hootenanny? Pandemonium?

An effulgence?

Yes. That's perfect. A bright, shining, radiant collection of writers. I love it. I'm going to try to make that a thing.

But as it's my first time meeting a real *effulgence* of romance authors, it's kind of like the first time I encountered romance novels at all. I think I must have had some latent idea about what they would be like. And they're nothing like what I expected.

A lot of the TV and movie writers I've known over the years have been either anxious and burned out or competitive and bitter. Not all, certainly, but there's this pervasive sense of competition in that world that comes of having to please gatekeepers and make sure you get there first.

And while most of the traditionally published novelists I've known aren't really *that* way, per se, some of them can get very down about the fact that they write these great, sweeping, heartbreaking works of staggering genius (shoutout to Dave Eggers) and nobody seems to read them.

The books get buried on some back shelf at whatever bookstore has managed to survive in the modern world and then they just fade into obscurity, leaving the sometimes-incredible author to give up altogether or, at least, take on a teaching gig or something to make ends meet.

My fiction professor at UCLA was that second one.

She's published three award-winning novels through a very, very old and fancy publishing house, but none of them ever made enough money for her to quit her teaching gig and just write full-time. And while it's not some great tragedy—there are plenty of worse things a person might have to endure in life beyond teaching kids how to write—I know it wasn't her dream.

And that's always haunted me a little. That and my parents' struggle with making it in the literary world. The idea that you can give it your all, try really hard, and still have it not work out like you planned is understood by anyone who gets into some kind of highly competitive, subjectively assessed field, but understanding it and *understanding* it are two different things.

And the thing that stands out to me as I'm meeting all these romance authors is there's virtually none of that baggage. No real angst. No bitterness. Not even really that much competitiveness. To a person, they all seem like pretty cool chicks who either fell into it, or kind of dabbled in fanfiction before trying it out full-on, or who just needed a way to pay some bills and saw this as a viable path forward… and then did it.

Audrey Saint taught school and, when budget cuts hit, shot her shot.

Winter Page was working at a tire repair shop and got an idea to write a story about a mechanic in a small town and a snotty rich girl whose car breaks down on her way through, and that book blew up huge and spawned fifteen subsequent novels.

Raven Lark is almost seventy and took it up when her husband died.

Mercy Rose was a physicist. Like, an actual PhD-having physicist who "figured that exploring why *people* are drawn to each other is more fun than why *photons*…" something, something, something. I couldn't really follow all the science stuff.

And Eden Le Fay… well, honestly, Eden just seems like the kind of person who likes to get freaky. Britney says that her books get *dark*. But she's nice too. Sort of. Maybe 'nice' is a bit of an oversell. You get the distinct impression that she will pummel the shit out of you with a riding crop. Possibly whether you want her to or not.

But, on the whole, they're all super-cool, really pragmatic, and totally chilled out.

Well. Almost all. The one exception seems to be…

"And then I said, 'I don't give a fuck if it *is* an ambulance, it's blocking my fucking driveway!'"

Raylen Star is over by the bar, but the punchline of whatever story she's telling cuts through the room. Her laugh is more of a cackle. Which, in and of itself, isn't a bad thing. I'm not gonna make fun of someone's laugh. But there's this underlying cruelty in it. It's kinda scary, I gotta be honest.

Steve and SS share a look, but then SS just shakes her head and turns back to me. "So. You were saying?"

"Huh? Oh, right. I was just wondering how, exactly, *you* came to decide that romance was the thing you wanted to write. How did you start?"

SS and Steve share another look. Then she says, "Y'know, like everybody, just… thought I'd give it a go and it's worked out."

"Uh, yeah, I'd say it's worked out pretty well," Britney chimes in, only slightly slurring her words. "Did you ever think you'd be this successful?" She gestures around at all the banners and accoutrements that declare to the world that, for at least the next few days, the Sin With Us romance con runs the show.

"Not really," SS says.

Steve finishes off the lone drink he's been nursing and crunches some ice between his teeth. And, looking at him chewing on his ice and then at the banners all around, a thought occurs to me. "Why 'us?'"

"What's that?" SS asks, taking a sip of her own drink.

"Why 'Sin With Us?' Who's the 'us?' It's a cool name for a con. But it's *your* con, right? You sponsor it and everything, so why not 'Sin With Me?'"

Once again Steve and SS look at each other. They have that twin thing where they just seem to instinctively pattern one another, I think.

Mike, SS's husband, is the one to answer. "Y'know," he says, "I think it's more like Sin With *Us*. All of us. Like, 'Hey, if you're into this romance thing, you're welcome. There are no prohibitions on who's allowed to join in. No judgments. Come on down. Let your freak flag fly.' Y'know. That kind of thing."

SS looks at him, runs her hand through his (impressively silky) hair, and gives him a kiss on the cheek. "What Mike said."

"Oh. Yeah. That makes sense. That's nice," I say, feeling unusually comfortable in my skin in a way that I don't always feel. Apart from the residual bedbug bites, I mean.

It's the 'no judgments; all are welcome' bit that lands for me. What he's talking about is a *community*. A sister-(and one brother)-hood in which no one who comes with a sincere desire and purity of intention is left out. Or, at least, that's the energy I've picked up so far. (With one notable exception. One who shall remain nameless, because I just got here and don't want to be a dick.)

All around me is a kind of heady, vertiginous bonhomie that attends the gossamer haze of unqualified acceptance.

Or maybe it's just that I'm on my third Tom Collins. Could go either way.

Whatever it is, I feel myself relaxing. Truly relaxing. At ease. Peace. Utter and total—

"I read your book," Steve leans over to whisper into my ear, and bonhomie is replaced by good, old-fashioned pedestrian angst as I start scratching at my arm again. (Did I leave the cortisone upstairs?)

"Say again?" I cough out.

"I read your book."

"You finished it?"

"Mm-hm."

"Already?"

"Mm-hm."

I wait what I believe is an appropriate amount of time before prompting, "And…?"

"It's incredible," he whispers. Again.

I flush. I feel hot. My arm itches. I stand up suddenly and without warning, bumping the table in front of us and knocking the drinks over.

"Whoa," Britney says, also coming to her feet. "You okay? What's wrong?"

"I—Me? Nothing. Just…" I dig in my clutch. Where is that damn cortisone? "I just need to run upstairs. I think I left—I'll be back."

"Do you need me to come with you?"

"No, no, I'm—"

"Steve-O!" I see James approaching, appearing even drunker than he was before. His wife, Audrey, is with him. Her makeup is smeared and James has his pants unbuttoned for some reason.

Steve looks at me and says, "I'll go. I forgot something upstairs too. Come on." He takes me by the hand, which is… unexpected, obviously, and says, "That itch looks like it's getting worse. You should get some cortisone."

And before I know what's happening, I'm being led out of the lounge, past an effulgence of romance writers, as James Saint yells in our direction, "Ha! Yeah! Time to *puh-lay*, right? My bro-buddy, bro-buddy, bro bro bro?"

CHAPTER EIGHT – STEVE

I have her hand. It was unexpected. Just an instinct, really. But now that we're in the elevator, it feels right.

Suddenly, her fingers wiggle and then… damn. She lets go of me. I glance down with just my eyes and catch her wiping her palm on her dress.

"Sorry if I was weird back there—"

"No." I put up a hand to stop her from further apologizing.

"It's just… I'm… itchy. And I know that's gross, but I'm starting to think I lost my little tube of cortisone, because I'm a hundred-percent sure that I put it in my purse, but of course I can't find it, so…"

I stop listening there. Not because it's gross, but because I think I have a solution. I pull out my phone, access the Aria-adjacent app, SparkleNight DreamWeaver's WishMaker, and smile when Gregory's cartoon face greets me with a text balloon. *How can I help you, Steve Smith?*

I press the little microphone icon and put the phone up to my mouth. "I need cortisone, Gregory. Stat."

"W-what?"

Gregory dings out a "10-4" while I look down at lovely Cordelia, who is looking up at me with those milk-chocolate eyes of hers. Poor, poor Cordelia. She's itchy, and she's wearing the wrong dress, and she's having a little panic attack about… what was that about? The book? It must've been the book. She's terrified of my critique.

Well, she need not be afraid. I reach down and slide a piece of wayward hair off her cheek, tucking it behind her ear. "Gregory is gonna take care of everything, sweet Cordelia."

Her brow furrows and her pouty mouth makes a frown. "Who?"

I get lost in the shape of her lips as they form the word. I picture what it would be like to kiss her. To bite that bottom lip of hers. Tenderly, of course, but not timidly. In control, and with authority, but not enough to cause pain. Then I start thinking of other things I might want to do with that mouth. Put a sucker in it. Feed it strawberries. Lower it slowly down onto my…

Oh, my God. Am I reliving a scene from *Master Choke?*

I am.

And that was a really good scene. Fuck yeah, it was. And it was smokin' hot, man. Like dirty as fuck.

Back in those days the dirtier the sex, the more the readers gushed. Mmm. Does that sentence work? Gush is soooooo… descriptive. It really conjures up a solid image that should be used sparingly.

The more the readers… talked amongst themselves and spread the word.

Better.

Well, no. *That's stupid, Steve. Really fuckin' stupid. Now you're censoring yourself.* Talked amongst themselves? Spread the word? Who cares? That's dumb! Not even relevant.

'Gushed' really is the right word here and I should never second-guess myself again. The ladies were fascinated with Master Choke. They loved him. He didn't get the title 'Master' for being an amateur in the BDSM scene. Let's just say there was more than one mention of a panty-change in more than one review. 'One-handed read' was another top contender. That was from Smutty Sunshine's Filthy Reads Book Blog. I'm pretty sure that's still the number one review on Nile for *Master Choke.* The last time I looked that review had two hundred thirty-seven likes. It'll probably be number one for all eternity.

"Steve?"

When I drag my gaze up, she's looking at me expectantly. "Oh, right. Gregory." I hold my phone up so she can see Gregory's cartoon face. "He's my virtual concierge while I'm at the Aria."

"Huh. What's he do?"

"Anything I want. He's bringing you cortisone."

She smiles. "He is?"

I smile back, feeling a little warm and tingly inside when I realize I've made her happy. "He is. I told him to. And he does everything I tell him to."

"Everything?"

"Anything. Wanna try him out?"

The elevator dings and we exit. I put my hand on the small of her back, directing her down the hallway to my room.

"Well, what would I ask him for?"

"Anything you want." We're at my door now, so I flash my card and then open it and wave her in with a little bow. She enters, I follow, and then I close the door behind me.

"Anything?" Her face is filled with skepticism.

We walk into the living room and I speak to Gregory as I look Cordelia in the eyes. "Gregory. Voice command activated."

"Yes, Steve. How can I help you?"

As Gregory's imperfect, but still trustworthy, voice says this, I'm still looking at Cordelia. "I would like… a bathtub filled with rose petals."

"Yes, Steve. Do you have a color preference?"

I raise one eyebrow at Cordelia. "Your move, Miss Serendipitous."

She huffs a little bit of air, a sign of doubt. "How about…"

"Gregory, please recognize the voice of Cynthia Lear and add her as WishMaker to the account Steve Smith."

"Voice recognized."

I wave a hand at Cordelia. "Proceed."

She huffs again, this time a sign of… amusement. "OK. Gregory, I would like… rainbow-colored rose petals. A whole giant bathtub filled with rainbow-colored rose petals."

I point at her. "That's good. That's really good."

"Your wish is my command." And Gregory dings.

"I'm not sure how long it will take him, but there's no rush, right?" I wait, wanting to chew my nails as she considers this. *Please, please, please…*

"Sure. Why not. The night is young."

"Indeed, it is. Would you like champagne?"

Cordelia's eyes dart over to the dining room table, then back at me. "Listen, before we go any further—"

But then the door dings.

"One moment." I go to the door, take the shiny black box from the floor attendant, tip her, and then close the door and walk back to Cordelia. "Your cortisone, I presume." And then I present her the box.

She laughs out loud. "Oh, my God. They gift-wrapped my lotion?"

The box is wrapped so you can lift the lid off without ruining the bow or the paper. So that's what I do. She takes the cortisone out and does a little shrug thing here that delights me to no end. "Thanks."

"It was my pleasure." I put the box down. "Now. What were you saying?"

"Um. Well. I was gonna say… yes, I would like a champagne."

She wasn't. She was going to object to something. I'm not sure what, but Gregory's attention to detail has changed her mind.

I point to the couch. "Sit. I'll get us a drink and we can discuss your book."

"Oh, no! No, no, no. I mean, I'll take the drink, but no book talk."

I pause and turn to look at her. "No book talk?"

She shakes her head. "No. I can't right now. I just want to…"

She stops.

I'm dying. And while I don't want to be 'that guy' who finishes sentences, I can't stop myself. "You want to relax? Forget about work?"

"Yeah." She lets out a long breath. "It probably sounds stupid, but… the reviews, Steve. I don't like them."

"But it's… *me*."

She's shaking her head. "No. I can't."

"Even if I loved it?"

"You loved it?" She blinks. Like this is a surprise.

"My dear, you wrote a masterpiece."

"Stop it."

"No. It's your perfect book. I almost cried at the end. Well, not really. But I let out a sigh. And I don't even read romance."

"Oh." She just looks at me, like a lost deer stumbling out onto a highway and getting starstruck by headlights.

"But let's not talk about it. You're right. No work tonight."

She sucks in a deep breath and then slowly lets it out, shaking free from whatever reverie was coursing through her head. "OK."

I walk over to the table, pour us each a drink, go back to the couch, hand her one, sit down next to her—not too close, but definitely not too far, either—and hold up my glass. "To… wishmakers."

She blinks and shakes her head. "Wishmakers." We clink glasses, take our sips, set our glasses down.

I reach for her other hand. "May I?"

She looks at my outstretched palm, then at the little tube of cortisone. For a moment I'm thinking there is no way she's gonna let me do this.

But I must be setting her at ease, because my little Cordelia is filled with daring and courage tonight. She gives me the tube.

I slowly twist the cap off, squeeze a little bit of the lotion out onto my fingertips, then take her arm and begin to carefully massage it into her skin.

She bites her lip, both nervous and excited.

I make hooded eyelids as my hand slides up and down her arm. I do this over and over, captivating her, until there's not a trace of lotion left to be massaged in. "Better?"

She nods, caught in my spell. I'm kinda caught up in the moment as well, because that word came out a little bit Tank.

She says, "Um… can I ask you—"

The doorbell dings.

I put up a finger. "Hold that thought."

When I answer the door there is a small army of floor attendants pushing carts filled with rainbow-colored rose petals.

They don't say anything, just wheel them into the bathroom, do what they came to do, and then… a few moments later, they're gone.

I'm still standing. Cordelia is still sitting, but now with an expression of awe on her face.

I walk over to her and extend my hand. "Come with me. Let's take a look at your wish."

I lead her around the couch, across the living room, and into the bedroom. The light in here is soft and low—just the two bedside lamps on. But it's more than enough light to see her book, that masterpiece called *Filling the Gap*, lying in the center of the bed like it's been waiting for us.

But we don't stop. She said no book talk, and I'm happy to grant that wish. We will have plenty of time for that in the upcoming days, and weeks, and months.

Dare I even say… years?

My attention is split between the wish-granting and writing a blurb for a romance novel starring moi and the lovely Cordelia Sarantopoulos, but when we walk into the bathroom, the scent of fresh rose petals wipes my mind of hooks, conflict, and calls to action.

"Wow." Cordelia breathes this word out.

"Yeah. Like… wow. Even I'm impressed. And I've asked for some crazy shit on this app before."

The tub is oval-shaped and takes up the entire center of the room. And, as asked for, it's filled to capacity with rainbow-colored rose petals.

"It looks like a unicorn threw up."

She sighs. "Yeah. It really does." Then she looks up at me with wide eyes. "Where did they get them? I mean, rainbow roses aren't a thing."

I shrug. "They are when you have money."

She laughs a little, shaking her head in disbelief at the tub. "I guess."

"Well?"

"Well?" She tips her face up to look at me. "What?"

"Let's do this." I let go of her hand, walk over to the tub, get in—shoes and all—and lean back, stretching my arms along the sides of the tub, smirking. "Come on in. The petals are fine."

She grins, beaming, then lifts up her flapper dress, gets in the tub, and settles on the opposite end. Placing her arms along the sides of the tub just like I have.

"This is weird," Cordelia says.

"Why?"

"Because there's no water." I splash her with rose petals and she giggles. "It's kinda ridiculous."

"It's pretty fuckin' awesome if you ask me. I mean, I've wished for lots of stuff on that app, but a dream date?" I pause here. I know she's running those words through her mind. 'Dream date.' "I wanna say I should've thought of this a long time ago, but then again…" I'm staring at her. And we get caught up in a moment.

"Then again what?" She's whispering.

"Then again, this is the perfect time. And if I had already tried it before, it would just be cliché."

She sighs and visibly relaxes. Cordelia, not one to jump into a tub of rainbow rose petals on a whim, decides to live in this moment. To embrace it. Put her arms all the way around it and give it a hug.

I'm not really sure if she feels this way—I'm playing third-person omniscient narrator here, which is quite fun, I decide—but I really do think she is enjoying this to the fullest.

I like the start of this impromptu date. I've written many—man-*nnnneee*—date scenes in my day. Every one of them as spectacular as the last. Most of them very fuckin' dirty. So dirty that when I narrate them, I nearly blush. Nearly, but not quite. I am not squeamish about dirty sex.

But this is Cordelia Sarantopoulos. I can foresee a time in the future—after we've had all our get-to-know-each-other moments—when dear Cordy here might be up for a gag or a blindfold. But that's not what she's looking for tonight.

She is a romantic. Correction, capital-R Romantic. And our rose-petal bath proves it.

She smiles dreamily at me from across the tub, then holds up a finger. "You are a contradiction."

"Am I?"

She nods. Slowly. Her eyes at half-mast.

"How so?"

"Hmmmmm." She drags this sound out, kinda sexily. I like it. "How are you *not*? You're like—cover-model handsome, but you come off as this… this… *nice guy*."

"Really? Cover model?" I hadn't thought of putting myself on the covers, but that would've saved me a lot of money in male-model photoshoots over the years.

"Come on." Dear Cordelia almost snorts. "Don't do that."

"Don't do what?"

"Pretend like you don't know how hot you are."

I grin. "You think I'm hot."

"Steve! You *are* hot. It doesn't matter what I think. You're like… all athletic and shit. You must work out like all day long. Does working for your sister come with a personal trainer or something?"

"No. I actually don't work out. Not since high school."

"Shut up." She splashes me with rose petals. "That's such a lie. Your body is perfect."

"No. It's not. It just looks good in clothes."

She belts out a "Ha!" then shakes her head. "Whatever. I'm not gonna sit here in a tub of magical rose petals and try to convince you you're hot. I'm just saying—you're handsome, Steve. But… you're kinda nice too."

"Thank you." I decide to take the compliment. I am a nice guy. I think so, at least. "But it's easy. It's very easy to be a nice guy when you have so much, ya know?"

"Your sister is loaded. I can't even imagine how much she makes every month. Well, actually I can. My family isn't like… poor, or anything. I have seen money. But when Essie did that tour of her Malibu beach house last year—"

I cringe. I didn't agree to that. It was Mike's idea.

"—that is money on another level than what I'm used to."

As much I do love to hear that Cordelia thinks I'm handsome, I actually hate talking about money. Especially mine. So when her foot bumps up against my thigh I decide to move this conversation on to something more mood-making. I pick up her foot.

She makes a little squeal sound, then pulls her foot back. "What are you doing!"

"Sorry. Are you ticklish? I just wanted to take your shoe off and make you more comfortable."

Her foot is up in the air—still within reach—when she kinda freezes. No doubt running this scenario through her head.

I reach for her foot. "May I?"

She bites her lip. It's a textbook reaction in pretty much every romance book ever written. Then she nods her head 'yes'.

I force my satisfied grin back into submission and try on my best Master Choke serious face as I look her in the eyes and run my fingers along the leather T-strap of her low, curved-heel pump. Then I pop the tiny button on the leather strap holding the shoe in place and slide it off her foot.

She lets out a breath.

I raise an eyebrow at her. "Feels better?"

She's still biting that lip, but she manages a nod.

I don't mean to hold her foot captive, but it's right here in my hand. And it's so cute. Her little toenails are painted a glossy tangerine color and bespeckled with teal-blue polka dots. And then, before I can think—before I can stop myself—I bring her big toe right up to my mouth and kiss it.

She gasps. Almost pulls her foot back. In fact, she tries out my grip—which is not that tight—and when I do not let go, she gives in, allowing her leg to relax.

My God. Was Master Choke some kind of genius? Is the right level of assertiveness during a new experience capable of rendering a woman speechless?

It seems to have worked here. But it wasn't my intention, so I say, "Wanna do me next?" to break that spell.

"Huh?"

She's still caught. But I nudge her out of it with an explanation. "My shoe?" I raise my leg up from the sea of rose petals. "My fuckin' feet are killing me."

"Who *are* you?"

"What do you mean?"

"What are you doing?"

"Asking you to take off my shoe? But that's OK. I can do it." And then I bring my foot up, take the shoe off, and toss it across the bathroom. It plops on the tile floor and Cordelia's eyes follow this motion to the very end. I do the same with my other shoe and then smile at her. "You can take off your other one. Unless you want me to." I put out a hand, offering.

I'm not sure what I expect of Cordelia in this moment. None of this was planned, which proves I'm not Master Choke. He plans everything. It's a personality disorder if you ask me, but whatever, the readers loved it.

But to my great surprise—and delight—she lifts her foot up from the rose petals and offers it to me.

I almost bite my hand to stifle a scream. If this was a rom-com movie there would be a little bubble over my head with a fantasy scene of me doing this exact thing.

But this is real life, so I play it cool, gently take her foot in my hand, pop the little strap button with my teeth, and then slip it off her foot. Instead of kissing her toe, this time I lick it.

She squirms, probably ticklish, and jolts her foot back, pulling it from my grasp.

I lean back in the tub, satisfied with this impromptu date so far.

"I think…" she says. "I think maybe you are a little out of my league, Steve."

"What?" I scoff. "No. No, no, no. We are in the exact same league, my dear Cordy."

"But you're… these moves… I'm…"

"Taken aback?"

She nods.

I have to make a decision here. I can do one of two things. Well, there are probably a half a dozen ways to play this, but I only have time to contemplate an either-or situation. I could, perhaps, morph into Master Choke and take full control, thereby setting her at ease by making the decisions. Or… I could affirm her inexplicable emotions. Make her feel… what? Comfortable?

But I feel like comfortable comes with a lot of talking. And Master Choke… well, that really is the way forward here. So I say, “Let’s take off your panties, Cordelia.”

And now I’m not only acting like Master Choke, but sounding like Tank the narrator. I feel like I’m a character in my own book. Which is… maybe… kinda nice for a change.

Cordelia is staring at me with her mouth open, unable to make a decision. So I help her along by giving her an order. “Stand up, please.”

“What?”

“Stand up, Cordelia. I would like to take off your panties.” I almost add ‘you can do me after’—not panties, of course. I’m wearing boxer briefs. But I hold it in. No need to get ahead of ourselves. Plus, she needs to start with my tie.

I don’t actually expect her to stand up. What I expect is a question. *Why should I do that? Where is this going?* Something along those lines.

But we all know where this is going. So now she needs to make this one momentous decision. Will she follow my order, stand up, and let me undress her? Or will she get up, walk out on me, and never look back because I am a freak?

I am pleasantly surprised when she braces her hands on the side of the tub and gets to her feet, dripping rose petals from her flapper dress as she does this.

Wow. Master Choke really was a genius.

I lean forward, sliding my hand up her torso.

She gasps.

“Wow, your abs are fuckin’ tight, Cordy. You’re the one who hits the gym.”

She starts mumbling and pushing my hands away.

“What?” I look up at her. “What’s wrong?”

"Um… I…" She sighs, places her hand up to her eyes, covering them. "Oh, my God. I'm so fuckin' embarrassed."

"Why? What did I do?"

"You?" She scoffs. "Nothing. I mean, this is… wow. I feel like I'm inside a romance novel right now. But… oh, my God. I cannot believe that I let myself get this far into a sex scene and now I have to…"

"Have to what? Tell me. What's the problem?" I am desperate to understand this moment. I felt like it was all going so well.

"I'm wearing Skinny Laminx! There, OK? I said it! My abs aren't tight, Steve! They're tucked inside a modern-day corset, choking the life out of me! And I wasn't gonna let you take my frickin' shoe off, but I can't even bend over to get it off myself—fuckin' button! I told Sheila I didn't want the button shoes, but did she listen? Noooo! She went on and on about how they go with the dress—"

I am still stuck on the words Skinny Laminx. So as she continues her purge of emotions, I hold up a finger. "What's a Skinny Laminx?"

"A modern-day corset! Britney's mom invented them, so she's always gifting them to me—not Britney, Britney's mom—and… I thought it was gonna make me, well, appear to have tight abs, but it's a show, Steve! I'm. A. *Fiction*!"

I snicker. "You're wearing your skinny panties?"

"I'm sure it's really hilarious to you, but meanwhile, I'm mortified!"

I place my hands back on her hips. "Cordelia."

"What?" She snaps this word at me.

"May I?" I slip my hands down to the hem of her dress and wait.

She moans. "Oh, my God."

"Please. It's not a big deal. I'm fully capable of getting your Skinny Whatevers over those lovely hips."

She covers her whole face with her hands and I take this as a 'proceed' gesture. But she's not going to look and she might even dissociate from herself and pretend it's not happening.

I lift the flapper dress up. The little tassels are slightly annoying as I push it up over her hips, revealing a lovely pair of skinnies bedazzled with just the right number of rhinestones.

"My God," I chuckle. "These are kind of amazing!"

"Forget it." She places a hand on mine, but I shoo it off.

"Stop. It's fine, Cordelia. There is no obstacle that we cannot overcome together. We're gonna get these down your legs and pick up right where we left off."

♥♡♥♡♥♡♥♡♥♡♥

It takes a liiiiittle more effort than I first imagined it would, but eventually I force them over her hips, allowing her to take her first deep breath of the night, and they disappear into the ocean of rose petals, hopefully lost at sea forever.

She is standing between my legs. Her still-pretty-flat stomach is right at eye level, since I'm still sitting down in the tub. And when I look up, she's biting that lip again. "Better?" I ask.

She nods. "Thanks."

OK. We need to get things back on track, like, pronto. So I conjure up Master Choke one more time. "Sit down now, Cordelia. Right here in my lap."

It's decision time again. But we didn't just climb Mount Skinny Laminx together just to give up now. We're gonna plant a flag on the top of this fuckin' mountain if it kills us. So she sits, straddling me.

And is it cliché to say that knowing she is now sans panties excites me?

I don't care. It does.

She is looking down at me now. And she smiles. "Hi."

"Hello."

"Sorry about that."

"It was worth it, don't you think?"

She nods. Almost bites her lip, but thinks better of it. "Now what?"

Oooh. Is that code for 'be my Master?' I think it is. "Take off my tie."

It's already loose—that 'after-hours' look really was genius—so she slips it over my head and tosses it out into the Land of Throwaway Shoes.

What comes next is unexpected—Master Choke would have a heart attack, but I don't. Because Cordelia doesn't wait for more instructions. She just starts unbuttoning my shirt.

I look down, watching her nimble fingertips pop each and every button until she gets to the part where it's tucked in. She doesn't even hesitate. Just grips my shirt with both hands and tugs until it comes free. She pops the last two buttons, spreads my shirt open, and takes a long, long look at my chest.

When our eyes meet up once more, I see a glint of lust in her.

Then… well, I'm not completely sure what happens. We're kissing, and it's sloppy, and filled with lots of tongue, and all the while her nimble fingertips are popping the top button of my trousers. Then there's a rip of a zipper. And while she's doing that, I'm lifting her dress up and grabbing her thighs, pulling her towards me, so at just the right moment she's lifting her hips and I'm pretty happy with how all those underwear tribulations haven't affected my showing, and then—we're sighing.

I'm inside her.

She's moaning, and her fingernails are gripping my shoulders, and I'm hugging her tight and kissing her neck, and pulling her dress down to reveal her luscious breasts—kissing those too.

And it's literally the best fuck of my life.

MEANWHILE…

Meanwhile…

"So, I kicked his fucking dog!"

Slamming back yet another shot of Jägermeister, Leslie Munch, aka Raylen Star, barks a malicious chortle that would send paroxysms of anxiety through a coven of witches, unaware of the gawking she is receiving from the assembled company.

"You… kicked… a *dog*?" asks Persephone Marlowe, author of the bestselling *Carnival of Indiscretions* novels. (And the presumed creator of the 'clown college' romance subgenre.)

"What?" spits out Leslie, suddenly self-conscious in a way that Leslie Munch does not enjoy. "The guy wouldn't stop asking me for money. Sorry you're homeless, pal! Not my fault!"

And then, politely, but swiftly, the effulgence of gathered romance titans all begin to peel away from Ms. Munch, excusing themselves back to their suites to try to get a good night's sleep. Tomorrow's panels do start early, after all.

One by one they take their leave, until the only revelers remaining in the grand seating area of the Aria's

Ultra Lounge are Leslie herself, one Britney Kincaid, and SS—the genial hostess of this spectacular event—along with her now-dozing husband, Mike.

Britney, good and thoroughly tippled, turns her head back toward the conversation in which she was previously engaged and, referring to Leslie, makes the following observation: "So… she's just genuinely awful, huh?"

SS, aka Essie, equally tippled, sighs long and heavy before acknowledging, "Yeah. It's a shame."

"What do you mean? What's a shame?" a curious Britney Kincaid asks, searching the bottom of her champagne flute for the last drops of the bubbly nectar.

"She was on top of the world for a long time and then…" Taking a considered look at the former queen known as Raylen Star, Essie shakes her head. "And then I dunno what happened."

Britney also glances over at the angry woman still at the bar as Leslie now, in the absence of her formerly captive audience, turns her attention to the bartender, who forces a smile as he pours Leslie another shot and she reaches for his hand in a somewhat inappropriate way.

"Yeah," Britney says, allowing the word to roll around in her mouth and draw out before adding, "I read her stuff. She was great." Then, turning her head once again back toward SS and a lightly snoring Mike, head resting on his wife's shoulder, Britney raises an eyebrow and asks, "Hey, why did she call your brother a liar?"

There is something of a pregnant pause before Essie responds with, "What?"

"Earlier. In the signing room place. This morning. She came over to where your brother and Cordelia and

I were talking, all upset about her placement or whatever, and she told Cordelia to be careful about letting you guys read her book. And when Cord asked her why, she kind of implied that you're… liars. I just…" Britney Kincaid allows the sentence to trail off upon seeing the expression on her new friend Essie's face, a narrowed, concerned, but simultaneously skeptical type of look. "I'm sorry. I didn't mean to—"

"No, no, it's fine," Essie interjects with something like exhaustion in her voice. "I don't know. I mean, I can guess, but…" And, as Essie pauses to take another sip from her own glass, she seems to study Britney. (Whether or not Britney is aware of this scrutiny is unclear.) "You know about the lawsuit? The accusations and all that?"

Britney takes a moment to think, searching her libation-addled brain to try to summon up the knowledge. "Oh, you mean the whole plagiarism hullabaloo?"

"Yeah," Essie says. "The plagiarism hullabaloo."

"Yeah. I never really cared. I just like to read books, I don't tend to get all wrapped up in the details of what happens off the page, but… She accused you of stealing her work, yes?"

Essie nods. Slowly. Remembering the whole stupid, unwarranted, drawn-out saga. "Yep. She got it into her head that SS was stealing and repurposing her work."

"Why would she think that?"

As Britney asks the question, it is not immediately apparent to Essie if it is a sincere curiosity or if there is an implication buried somewhere inside the asking. But, deciding that it doesn't really matter, Essie says, "Because. She wasn't on top anymore. I'm not even really sure she believed Steve did steal her stuff. I think she was just trying for a takedown. Some kind of public relations debacle. Which she got, just not in the way she intended it. It's a bummer. Steve really looked up to her, I think. Totally admired the way she positioned herself for success, and then used her as inspiration. But he would never steal from anyone. He's a totally good guy. He really is. He just wouldn't do something like that."

Distracted by the snoring husband on her shoulder, Essie adjusts his head so he doesn't slip and fall as she finishes her thought. Coupled with her warm inebriation, it is presumably this perfect storm of disruptions that causes her not to notice the words she just used or the confused look in Britney's eyes.

"What do you mean, *Steve* wouldn't do something like that?"

"Hm?" Essie pats Mike on his sleeping cheek.

"You said *Steve* wouldn't do something like that. You said his name, like, three times. *Steve* looked up to her. She believed *Steve* stole her stuff. I…"

A slow awareness washes over Essie as Britney talks, resulting in a kind of distance in her affect and energy as she circles the wagons inside her mind. "Did I? I said 'Steve?'" Britney nods. "Huh. I… I dunno. I…"

There is silence. A snore from Mike causes Essie to jolt. She stares at Britney, saying nothing. Which may be an answer in itself, Britney starts to consider.

"Well, listen," Essie finally says, "It's—oh, my God, it's late, late. Late o'clock. Latey, late, late, late. I need to get this one to sleep. I mean asleep in a bed." She slides her shoulder out from underneath her snoozing husband who, somehow, does not wake up as he collapses forward onto the place his wife was just sitting.

"Okay! See you in a few hours," Essie declares with what Britney seems to feel is just a smidgen more emphasis than is necessary.

Essie Smith-Scott then proceeds to drag the cumbersome, snoring form of Michael Scott from his cushioned, makeshift bed, and drag him awkwardly toward the door of the lounge so that he might be placed in a more conventional state of repose.

Maybe it's the effort that obscures her awareness. Or perhaps it is a kind of disappointment in herself. Or maybe it's simply anxiety over making a mistake that, while perhaps apparently insignificant to someone like Britney, is one that she has worked hard not to make for oh, so many years. Or maybe… maybe… it's just that she's kind of drunk and, on some deeper, more suppressed level, is tired of maintaining a façade that she's no longer sure serves her.

But, whatever the reason, as Essie pulls Mike from the room…

… She fails to notice that Leslie Munch, aka Raylen Star, has meandered from the bar and is now sipping her drink on a sofa, watching this whole exchange play out and grinning a ferocious and contemptuous smile of knowing.

Moments later, as Britney presses the numbered button that will command the elevator to carry her off to her floor, and the doors begin to slide shut, a long, thin, nail-polished claw thrusts itself in between the closing doors and compels them to spring open again.

Leslie Munch, or Raylen Star, as is her preferred nom de reference, enters the car, presses the button for her own floor, and stands directly beside Britney Kincaid. Far closer than is required given that they are the only two in the space.

They both stare at the numbers lighting up as the elevator makes its journey, Britney lost in her own champagne-fueled haze of thoughts and Raylen née Leslie equally absorbed by what she suspects Britney must be thinking.

"Figure it out yet?" Raylen asks.

"What? Sorry?"

"Put two and three together and get five yet?"

Ignoring the odd bastardization of a commonly used expression, Britney turns to Raylen and says, "I'm sorry. What?"

"Y'know, I've never said anything myself because I've never had rock-solid proof, but despite what they claim to the contrary, they did steal my ideas from me. Was it plagiarism in the classic sense? Maybe, maybe not. But when someone comes along and lifts everything you did to make yourself a success and just copies your playbook, does it really matter? Is that any better?"

Britney stands, saying nothing, listening with new ears to Raylen's suddenly not-so-wild-sounding claims.

"And, if someone could do that—lie and steal that easily—is it that hard to imagine they could just lie about *anything*? Create an entire life out of whole cloth? Carry on a masquerade for years and years, just to take advantage of the suckers who want to believe the lie?"

Britney begins to feel dizzy, the booze, the elevator, the words she's hearing all colliding in her mind and causing her to feel unsteady. "What are you saying?" Britney asks.

"Your little friend," Raylen coos with a saccharine softness mixed with venom, "she better watch herself. That's all I'm saying. They're not good people, hot stuff. And they're weird. Always together. The whole family all together at a romance convention? Don't you think that's… odd?"

Britney did not, in fact, think it odd at all until this very moment. But now…

"They've got an agenda," Leslie whispers. "And I wouldn't put anything past them. I wouldn't be surprised if their lies go much deeper than 'Tank Watson.'"

Britney's head snaps to face Leslie's grinning maw.

"Oh, yeah. I know too. He thinks he's clever, but he's not. Y'know… I wouldn't be surprised if Steve wrote all those damn SS books himself."

Sometime later, maybe weeks or months from now, Britney might be able to look back to this moment and recognize it as the one in which a switch was triggered. A switch in her brain that set into motion a chain of events that would change all of their lives.

But here, now, in the present, all she can do is blink as her imagination takes flight.

And, as if choreographed by the gods of sinister coincidence, at that precise instant, the elevator dings, the doors open, and Leslie Munch-slash-Raylen Star steps off, leaving Britney Kincaid alone. To fret. And worry. And allow her imagination to run to dark, nefarious, duplicitous thoughts, indeed.

CHAPTER NINE – CORDELIA

DAY THREE — THE PANELS

"Cordy. Hey," whispered in my ear is the thing that wakes me up.

It takes me a second to remember where I am. But then, as my eyes flutter open and I see the dawn light glinting off the buildings outside the window, and the desert and mountains touching the sun in the distance, it all washes back over me.

Hands. Pulling off my Skinny Laminx.

Fingers. Rubbing at my flesh.

Rose petals. Spilling around me.

Me. Back arched. Hips thrust upward. Screaming, "Choke me harder!"

Hair…

Wait. What? "*Choke me harder*?"

Was that me? Did I—was I—did he—

What the hell?

"Good morning," Steve says, this time just above a whisper.

Shaking off the cobwebs, I sit up and look around, realizing *exactly* where I am. Steve sits on the edge of the bed, already dressed (jeans and a loose button-down. He looks effortlessly cool. Just something I notice), and sweeps a strand of hair off my cheek.

"Uh. Hi. Good morning," I croak out, then clear my throat and try again. "Good morning. Hi."

"Sleep okay?"

"Um. Yeah. Yeah. I think so. Yeah," I say. He nods a little and smiles. "What time is it?"

"A little after six."

"You're already dressed."

"Yeah. I have to get downstairs to make sure everything's all set up for panels."

"Oh, right."

"I ordered you some breakfast." He gestures to the living room area, where I can see a veritable smorgasbord laid out.

"You're not eating?" I ask.

"I'll grab something downstairs."

I can feel myself frown.

"What?" he asks.

"That's just… a lot of food. For one person." My hand immediately goes to my stomach and I look around for my Skinnies.

"I know. I just… I don't know what you like, so I just had them bring up pretty much everything."

I blink and shake my head, because there are clearly still some cobwebs that need clearing out. "You… what?"

"Listen, I gotta run, but you take your time here, eat something, hang out, and I'll see you downstairs whenever you come down. Gonna be a big day." He grins at that and winks. Without thinking, I start immediately scratching at my neck. "Shoot," he says.

"Do you still need cortisone?" He starts looking around. "I know, I—"

I reach out and take his hand. I don't intend to. It just happens. "No, no, I'm fine."

He looks at where my fingers wrap around his and smiles again. "Okay," he says, squeezing and lifting the back of my hand to kiss it. "Because I had them check and there are definitely no bedbugs in here." His smile widens and I giggle, coquettishly, and—very much unlike me—don't immediately judge myself for doing it.

"Okay. Thanks."

There's a moment where we look into each other's eyes, both of us smiling like oddballs. I feel the distinct energy of two people trying to figure out if they should kiss or not, but after a second, he breaks the spell and says, "Okay. See you in a bit." Then he stands, walks out toward the living room, looks back over his shoulder—I get a tickle in my stomach—and then he's gone.

What. Is. Going. On?

The whole thing plays out like an insta-romance scene from a light comedy. Which I'm also—again unlike me—not judging. It feels awesome. If this is what insta-whatever is, I'm not mad at it. I'm just… So far this whole convention has been very unexpected. Which… blah, blah, blah, if you expected it, it wouldn't be yadda, yadda, I know. But for real. This is not the kind of thing that happens to me. Except it is, apparently.

I toss the duvet and sheets off to see that I'm still naked. I never sleep naked. But, it seems, I did a lot of things last night I never do.

I never hook up with guys I just met simply because they're really handsome and smell good and look great in a suit.

I never go with them to their suite at the Aria when all I really wanted was some itch cream.

I never get into empty bathtubs filled with rose petals.

And I never, ever, ever get all overtaken by lust and pull a guy's shirt off and start fucking him to the point where I demand that he choke me harder.

My flapper dress is on the floor. I pick it up, slip it on over my head, and wander into the living room to see what the spread is all about. Passing by a mirror, I notice that my hair looks something like what would happen if Medusa and a bird's nest got smashed together. But Steve didn't seem to mind, so…

Steve didn't seem to mind? What? Who cares? Why do I care what Steve…? Know what? Doesn't matter. Time for Cynthia Lear to just eat something, drink a little coffee to get her head right, and then head down to her *first book signing*. Hell yeah.

He did order literally everything on the room service menu, as far as I can tell. Flapjacks, bacon, eggs (three different ways: scrambled, poached, and over easy), four different juices (carrot juice is an underappreciated fluid if you ask me), five kinds of cereal (in the little mini baby boxes), and on and on and on. It's… insane? Sweet? Sweet *and* insane?

Just… thoughtful?

It might be possible that it's just thoughtful.

Like, this Steve may, in fact, just be a nice guy. That's it. Not more complicated than that. He may just be a nice guy who does nice things and is nice and smells good and has a great jawline and is really good at choking people and pulling their hair. Simple as that!

I butter an English muffin, making sure to get the butter evenly distributed into all the little pockets and cracks so that there aren't any clumpy lumps of undispersed yellow anywhere, and start to take a bite when I hear a buzzing sound. My phone.

I don't know if other people have this, but I feel like I always know when my phone is vibrating urgently versus when it's just vibrating casually. Maybe I can't, but it feels like I can. Regardless, right now, it feels like it's buzzing urgently.

I scamper into the bedroom area and see for the first time the residue of last night's frivolity. Which I realize sounds gross. What I mean is I see the sheets and discarded clothes and the general detritus of our… lovemaking.

Is that what it was? Did we make love? Is that too romantic? Did we maybe just get a little drunk, a little giddy, and (in my case) a little flattered and just *get it on?*

Whatever we did, I can see that we did it. That's all. And that's a good thing because the whole thing feels like kind of a dream. Or at least dream-y. And it's nice to realize it really happened. That I met a nice, cute guy, who seems to really like me, and—

Oh, it's Britney buzzing. I just miss picking it up before the buzzing stops and that's when I discover I was right about the urgency thing. It looks like I have forty missed calls and about two dozen missed texts starting at around three a.m. All of which display an increasing freneticism.

The texts start with, "OMG," migrate to, "SteveSS," then turn into something like, "bitchwhereare?" and finally graduate to, "IM AT YR DOOR POUNDING WHEREU?"

I tab on her last missed call notification to ring her back and she picks up immediately.

"Where the hell are you? Are you all right?"

"Yeah, I'm fine," I say, taking another bite of English muffin and feeling unusually peaceful.

"I've been trying to get a hold of you for, like, three hours."

"I know. I just saw. My phone was on 'do not disturb.' What's wrong? You okay?"

"Where. Are. You?"

I hesitate to answer because… I don't know why. I just do. I mean, I could probably figure it out if I did a moment or two of self-examination, but that feels like a whole big thing I don't wanna get into with myself right now. "I'm in… Steve's suite."

There is a long pause. I can hear her breathing. Then, after a moment, I hear…

Pound, pound, pound. On the door to the suite.

"Are you—?"

"Open the door."

"Are you outside—?"

"Open the door."

I trot to the door and open it to find Britney, still in her dress from the night before, standing there with the phone still at her ear. The two of us, a coupla saucy dames from the 1920s, just waking up from a night out on the town like the hot tomatoes we are.

"What did you do?" she asks.

The words coming out of her mouth land on my ear before the echo of it comes through the phone. I tab end on the call, finish swallowing a bite of muffin, and answer, "What do you mean?"

She moves past me into the suite, looking around. "Is he here?"

"Steve?"

She pauses again to stare at me. "How many guys were you with?"

"That's—I don't know why I asked that. No, he went downstairs to help his sister get ready for the panels."

Britney kind of grunts for some reason. "What's all this?" she asks, noting the massive spread of food.

"Breakfast. You want any—?"

"There's something you should know."

"Okay." I take another bite and wait for her to tell me what it is I should, apparently, know.

"I think Steve is SS."

"What?"

"Steve. I think he writes the books. He's SS. Not his sister. Steve is SS. Master Choke? All that? That's Steve."

"… What?" I understand the words she's saying because she's speaking a language I also speak and using a familiar and accepted syntax, but I'm having trouble processing the meaning.

She takes me by my shoulders, looks me in the eyes, and says, "Steve. The guy you came back up here with last night. The guy who got you all this"—she points at the food—"that guy… is SS, the number one bestselling author of the Master Choke series and all the other books he's written. Not his sister. He's the guy. Not her."

I wipe a bit of butter from my lips and find myself then immediately biting on the nail of my middle finger. "What are you talking about?"

"I was sitting with Essie and we were a little tipsy—"

"Tipsy?"

"Fine, we were very drunk, and Essie said something that caught my attention."

"What?"

"So, we were talking about Leslie, right?"

"Leslie? Raylen-Leslie?"

"Yes. And I asked her about the lawsuit back in the day and that whole thing."

"Right. Okay."

"And Essie said—and she said it no fewer than three or four times—that *Steve* wouldn't steal from anybody. That *he's* a really good guy. And that *he* wouldn't do that."

I keep nibbling at my finger as I think about what I want to say. I come up with… "Huh?"

Brit grabs me again by the shoulders and this time starts shaking me, in my opinion, way more emphatically than is necessary. "Are you listening to what I'm saying? I think Steve is a liar! I think he *is* some kind of, I dunno, conman bro. I think he's running game, chickee! You hear me? Boy be runnin' game!"

Pulling away and slapping her hands from my shoulders, I say, "Stop talking like that, and maybe you just misheard her! Or something."

Britney takes a breath, settles, looks me in the eyes and hits me with, "Leslie confirmed it."

"You talked to Leslie?"

"Not by choice. She cornered me in the elevator."

"What did she say?"

"She said *she* wouldn't be surprised if Steve is really SS too!" Britney lets that land like she really said something there.

"Okay, but… did she, like, verify it or…?"

"Cord! Are you listening to me? You got seduced by a kappa!"

"The hell's a kappa?"

"It's a, like, Japanese creature that steals souls from people's butts."

"Where did you hear about that?"

"I dunno! I read it on the internet! But… oh, my God. You didn't let him—"

"Nobody touched anybody's butt! Or maybe there was some touching, but—" I turn and run into the other room. Because this is crazy. And I say so. "This is crazy!"

She comes chasing after me. "Listen, just listen, okay? Think about it. He admitted to keeping his whole Tank Watson thing on the DL. What did he say? 'Let's just keep secrets secret?'"

"Okay, but—"

"And it is weird that he's here at all these conventions, don't you think? Like, he's kind of a bro. And I don't mean it in a bad way, but… bro… Why is a bro at a romance convention? You're telling me it's just to support his sister?"

"Well, I don't—"

"And that line."

"What line?"

"The 'dystopian nightmare' thing. It just randomly tripped off his tongue? Like, c'mon."

I pause to consider the fact that this is all a batshit-crazy fever dream fueled by champagne and lack of sleep on Britney's part, but also… I hear what she's saying. And it's not without merit.

"Well. Okay," I work out. "Let's say that's all true and you're right. What do you think he'd be keeping a secret for? Like, what's the big deal?"

"I have no idea. Ego, probably? Doesn't want people to know he's the mind behind all the insanely hot shit that goes on in those books? Maybe he's worried that if people know he writes hot-as-fuck erotica, he'll never get to write his sci-fi whatever? I have no idea. That's the point."

"Then what *is* the point?" (Which, I have to admit, I feel I'm maybe missing.)

"That there may be a more insidious reason."

"Insidious?"

"Is that not the right word? Like… sneaky. Or deceptive or devious or something."

"Then that's the right word. Those are almost literally all the dictionary synonyms."

"Then yeah. Insidious."

"Insidious how?"

"Raylen Star. Remember when she told you to be careful of liars? Well, she repeated the warning to me in the elevator."

"K. And…?"

She just looks at me, raising an eyebrow. And, suddenly, *my* mind starts racing and I start gnawing at my nails harder and harder. Because it now somehow clicks. I get what she's implying.

And I immediately go on the defensive.

"So he writes some books under a nom de plume. So what? Lots of people do that. Have done that. Hell, I do that."

"Yeah, but this is way, way more ornate than that. Cord, think about it…" She sighs, tries another tactic to get me to listen, I suppose. "Your last boyfriend. Penis."

"Peter."

"Same thing. The one who stole the earrings your Yaya gave you. You remember him?"

"Yeah, Brit, obviously I remember him. I would like not to, but thank you for reminding me."

"That was just a pair of earrings. This could be way worse." There's a moment where neither of us says anything and we just let the thick air settle around us. Then Britney continues. "I know that Leslie is a special kind of bitch, but… what if she isn't wrong about her whole plagiarism thing? What if, in fact, Steve is SS? And what if, in fact, Steve plagiarized her? Think about it, Cord. You've read the Master Choke stuff. It's hot. Like, really fucking hot." (She seems to lose herself for a second, remembering how hot those books actually are. Then she re-gathers.) "I kinda doubt a guy, especially one who seems kind of just as… nice and bro-y as Steve, could come up with that shit on his own. So, think about it—"

"That is the fourth time you've told me to 'think about it.'"

"So then *think about it!* He steals Raylen or Leslie or whoever's stuff, then it hits. Really hits. If people find out some bro-dude is writing this stuff, they'll surely be more suspicious, so he gets his sister to masquerade as SS and no one's the wiser." Britney's eyes go wide. "Oh, shit! Maybe he's set her up as the fall girl! If they get busted, *she* goes down! He's using everybody!"

Britney grabs a blueberry muffin and mauls the top off with her teeth.

I feel like I have woken up inside a cuckoo clock.

And then I feel my face flush. Yes, she's amped. Yes, she's talking crazy. Yes, she's probably still drunk from the night before.

But she's also my dearest friend. My friend who tells me the truth when nobody else will. My friend who truly, genuinely always seems to have my best interests at heart.

And this Steve Smith is just a cute, tall guy with a big cock who I happened to let choke me a little last night.

And now, *I* start to spiral. Internally. Just as the muffin Britney's eating seems to be chilling her out.

"Ugh. I really needed to eat. Sheesh. Okay, know what? I think I'm starting to sober up and, now that I am, I hear how crazy it all sounds. Just… last night when you left with him? And after he pushed up on you so hard yesterday morning and you gave him your book and… I dunno. Again, I was drunk and maybe I went off the rails a little. I just… I love you and I got weirdly protective and worried and this is a big day for you and… I'm sorry. Let's go and get you ready to go sign some books, okay?"

She's smiling now, but it's strained. And, unfortunately, there's no way she can put the water back in the faucet because…

He wrote *Master Choke*? And last night he… and we…

Raylen Star says he plagiarized her work.

He went out of his way to ask for my manuscript.

He used it to get my Skinny Laminx off.

And yesterday, he said…

"Woman, it inspired me to—"

"Steve?"

"Hmm?"

"You were saying? Inspired you to…"

"It inspired me to tell my sister to rewrite the ending of Slay Me Wild.*"*

Oh, God.

Like, every time one of them would find out my parents used to be big TV writers, they'd see it as some kind of an angle.

I can't stop the thoughts from careening into my head, and now I can feel myself turning into some kind of unhinged conspiracy theorist.

How *did* I get invited here when I only have a couple of books out?

How *did* I get such good table placement this weekend? Right behind SS's table?

Who *did* shoot JFK?

AHHHHHHHHHHHHHHHHHHHHHHHHHHH!

"Okay?" repeats Britney.

"What?" Ow. I think I just bit off the tip of my finger.

"Let's go sign some books, yeah?"

"… Yeah. Yeah. Let's… Yeah."

Picking up the rest of my stuff from off the floor, I notice the white cover with the black letters sitting on the nightstand. My book. My unreleased manuscript. The one that Steve read, told me he loved, and is ultimately responsible (I think) for me winding up in here last night.

I scoop it up, hold it close to my chest, protecting it almost, and make my way out of the suite. But not before Britney stops at the private buffet and starts filling up a bowl with fruit and yogurt.

"Essie did say that Steve is a genuinely nice guy, by the way," Britney says. I nod, listening and not all at once. "You don't want anything else to eat?"

"No. I'm good," I say, feeling an inexplicable tightness in my throat.

Almost like I'm being choked.

CHAPTER TEN – STEVE

Mr. and Mrs. Smith—aka Mom and Dad—are my first point of contact down in the lobby outside the massive signing hall. Since it's just panel day, and six-thirty a.m., there are only about two dozen people here right now. This same time tomorrow there will be hundreds of bibliophiles already lined up even though the signing won't start until nine.

Game plans involving seating charts will have been made. Binders with tabbed dividers will be hauled out and poured over. Lists of must-see authors will be swimming through the heads of every fanatical reader.

But today, it's all pretty chill. Those two dozen people actually work for me and mostly this morning is all about sound checks, chair spacing, and room temperature.

"Ste-eeeeeeve! Steve! Honey, we're over here!" That's my mother, calling my name in her shrill voice, from almost a hundred feet away.

Every frickin' face in this lobby turns to stare at me.

I force that smile as my eyes dart back and forth, because you never know when a BookToker is lurking in the shadows. Then I raise my hand to Mom so she will stop screaming my name. "I see you, Mom." I mumble this out through clenched teeth as I head that direction.

Then I tone it down. *They're your parents, Steve. You love them. They love you.* I think. No, they do. It's just… they really believe I'm a lazy bum who makes a living mooching off my twin sister.

A guy can only take so much of that.

Still, they *are* Mom and Dad.

"Hey." I wave as I approach. "How did you sleep last night? Was the room OK?"

I put them in a suite too, so I know it was fine, but it's polite to ask and… I really don't have anything else to say. Which is sad.

Sometimes I wonder if the lies I've been telling—and making Essie tell with me—have negatively affected my relationship with my parents.

"Oh, it was lovely, Steve. You should've come by yesterday to see it!"

"I have the same room, Mom. It's nice."

"That's not the point." I shift my attention to Dad so he can have his turn at me. "It's just… *polite*, Steve. Essie came to check on us three times."

That's because I pay Essie to do that. Which I don't say out loud, of course, but I really wish I could.

"Mike even called to say goodnight."

I sigh. My mother loves Mike. Sometimes, I think, more than me. But in his defense, he's a harmless, eternally optimistic, non-confrontational people-pleaser who really does look like he just walked off the set of a soap opera.

Which, now that I'm kinda thinking about it, is a lot like a romance novel.

Hmm. Never made that connection before.

"Did you hear me, Steve?"

I nod my head at my mother, with no clue what she said.

"He wasn't listening, Phyllis. As usual. Tell him again." There's Dad, always on my side.

But just as she's about to repeat herself, someone else is calling my name from across the lobby.

"Steeeeve! Oh, Stevie-poo!"

All three of us turn in the direction of the voice. "Who's that?" my father whispers.

My mother jumps in before I can. "That's that awful woman who accused Essie of stealing stories, remember that?"

"Oh, right." My father lets out a long sigh.

I get that Essie's his daughter and he's proud and all that shit, but does my dad enjoy coming here? I know my mom does. She loves romance novels. She doesn't read Essie's, of course. Too steamy, she says. But she gets in her share of author lines at the signing. My father dutifully follows her around, pulling her little signing-hall-regulation-appropriate book cart filled with all her old paperbacks, as she visits her favorite ex-Harlequin romance writers.

Every year I make my mom a big, colorful, rosette ribbon (like the kind you win in horse shows or at the fair) with the words 'Official Rom-Mom of Sin With Us Romance Con!' printed in big letters inside the center circle so all the authors will gush at her when she comes to their table. She loves it, wears it non-stop from the moment she arrives at the hotel until she gets home to

Arizona, and when she finally takes it off, she puts that rosette next to past years' rosettes, proudly displaying them on her bathroom vanity mirror like a twelve-year-old girl with show ponies.

And even though my mom can really push my buttons, it makes me happy to make her happy like that. Even if she thinks it's Essie doing it.

Meanwhile, as I've been having this internal monologue, Leslie Munch has invited herself into my little familial circle. She thrusts out a hand. "You must be Phyllis! Official Rom-Mom!" Leslie points to Mom's rosette.

And even though my mom hates Leslie just as much as Essie and I do, this delights her. She puts a hand over her heart. "Well, yes! I am!" She even shakes Leslie's hand when it's offered.

"What can I do for you, Leslie?" I'm not growling. It's not a growl. But it's definitely on par with a snarl.

"I'm gonna let that go, Steve." Leslie is still shaking my mother's hand as she looks me in the eyes to say this. "Because I'm nice." But then she directs her attention back to Mom, letting go of her hand. "I'm Raylen Star. And it's a pleasure to meet you, Mrs. Smith. You must be so proud of your daughter." Leslie side-eyes me as she says this.

What the hell is she up to?

"Is there a problem I can help you with?" I offer this up because she needs to go. In fact, I need a moment. I want to relish last night. That was my plan for this morning. Just stroll around, checking in on each panel room to make sure there are no problems, and relive what happened with the incredible Cordelia Sarantopoulos.

That bathtub of rose petals—kind of genius, if I do say so myself. I wonder if I can use that in my next book?

"Well." Leslie is still here. "Now that you ask…" She glances at my mom. "I mean, I don't want to sound like a complainer—"

"Since when?" Oops. This actually slips out.

Leslie ignores it, smiling at me with clenched teeth. "But I couldn't help but notice that I wasn't assigned to a panel this morning."

"No?"

"No. I was assigned to the last one of the day. But… if it's not too much trouble, I'd like to join in on Hot Lips and Husky Voices."

"Oooh, that's Essie's panel!" my ever-helpful mother says.

"It is," Leslie agrees. "Up first. How nice." Again, her eyes are locked on me as these words come out. "So what do you say, Steve? Hmm? It's not too much trouble, right? I won't skip out on Pen Names and Page Games." She really emphasizes that title. "I'll be there with bells on."

My initial instinct is to say no. But honestly, who cares? I don't want to have this battle here, in the lobby, with lurking BookTokers. So I smile and nod. "Sure, Leslie. Whatever you want."

Leslie claps her hands together one time. "Excellent." Then she toodles her fingers at us, grinning like a maniac, turns on her heel, and walks away.

"Oooooh. She's not as bad as I thought she would be," Mom says.

"No," Dad mumbles. "She's weird."

"Yeah. But anyway." I force Leslie out of my mind. "Do you two need anything? What's your plan for today?"

"Essie's panel, of course," Mom says. "I just love the way she shines in the spotlight. My heart." She places her hand over it. "It just… ohhhh, fills up when I see her up there on that stage, with all those hopeful, shiny-eyed newbie authors with stars in their eyes, gazing at her with admiration. I mean… it's quite a thing to be Essie. She's world-famous. And she handles it with such grace."

"Right." I ignore all that gushy shit. "That's ninety minutes. Any other plans? Hit the pool? Gamble a little? Need some money?"

"Son." My father turns to me. "Don't try to be your sister."

"What's that mean?"

"You don't have money to throw around like that. Essie will give us money." Then he pats my shoulder like he feels sorry for me.

And this is the signal that I need to leave. Because even though this whole secret identity thing was my idea in the first place, a guy can only take so much.

"Ooooh! There's Essie now!" My mother is immediately waving and yelling. "Essie! We're over here, Essie!"

The lobby—which has built up a larger population now that it's nearing seven o'clock—starts buzzing with whispers. Every face turns to look, first at my mother's commotion, then at an approaching Essie. She gets stopped. And stopped again. And again. Smiling, chatting, signing things, nodding—until finally, ten minutes later, she and Mike have joined our little group.

"Well," Essie sighs, but not without a considerable amount of excitement. "Is everybody ready for day one? How did you sleep, Mom? Was the room OK, Dad?"

"Oh, honey…" And the gushing begins anew.

Can I excuse myself here so I can finally get a moment to think about my incredible date last night? Hmm. Was it a date? Not really. I didn't ask Cordelia out. I just invited her, and her plus-one, to our living-room configuration.

But I like the idea that it wasn't a date. That means our first date is ahead of us. A future event. Something to look forward to and relentlessly plan. I will make it perfect.

Rose-petal bathtub is a high bar. I need to exceed those expectations. Perhaps horseback riding on the beach? Hot air balloon over Napa Valley? Dare I say… a private plane to Maui?

Is that too much?

But really, what is the point of being worth forty-two million dollars if you can't jet off to Maui with a date every now and then?

Still, it might overwhelm lovely Cordelia. She's a sensitive soul. She needs something… calmer. The rose-petal bath really was perfect. She didn't even have to stress about getting wet. And the scent of all those petals?

She will never forget that night.

Yeah. Top of my game. How do I go above and beyond after that?

Maybe I should just call it the first date?

"Steve!"

I turn to Essie. "What?"

"Are you even listening? I said I need to have a moment alone with you." She makes wide eyes at me.

"Fine."

She grabs my arm and starts pulling me away, while Mike—ever the content filler—begins a pointless dialogue with the parents to keep them occupied.

When Essie is satisfied that we're far enough away from everyone, she stops. "Do you want me to mention you in the narrator panel or not?"

"Narrator panel?"

"Yeah. My panel? Ringing any bells here? Why are you so distracted?"

"I"—I raise my eyebrows at my twin, then toggle them up and down. A waggle, if you will—"had a date last night. With Cordelia."

"Who?"

"Cynthia Lear."

"Oh." Essie smiles, then frowns a little. "*That's* why I was hanging out with Britney. I woke up this morning feeling like she and I were BFF's. But, honestly, I was pret-*teee* drunk last night. Did you know that her mother invented Skinny Lammies?"

"Laminx," I correct her. "Skinny Laminx."

Essie smiles. "Yeah. We had a nice time, I think. I don't remember all of it, but I didn't get home until three-thirty, so it must've been great."

"How are you even awake right now?"

"Are you kidding me? When Mike and I were on a three-week reno deadline for that last trailer we bought we were staying up for days in a row. I've had lots of practice. Plus"—she holds up her white paper cup—"quadruple espresso and three shots of Red Bull."

"Essie, that's… gross."

"I'll be fine. I have one panel, then I'm gonna nap, then be back here at one for the second half. I'm getting used to this life, ya know?" She looks around, smiling, taking in the kingdom I bestowed upon her. There are a lot of people now, all chatting, and laughing and drinking their coffees. Then she sighs. "Yeah. I love being me."

"Anyway."

"Right. Narrator panel. It's time, Steve."

"For?"

"To… you know, be in the spotlight, at least a little. It's not bad."

"Are you implying that I'm afraid of the spotlight? Because if so, you're wrong."

"Then what is your hang-up about people knowing the *real* you?"

"Real me? Essie. Look around. Look at all these happy, beautiful people. Now imagine how they will feel if they should ever find out that you and I have been lying to them. Mostly you, Essie. They think you're SS. If they find you're a liar—sister, life will not be fun and you will stop loving it."

"I'm not talking about *that* secret." She looks around cautiously, then looks back at me. "I'm talking about the narrator thing. Why not offer yourself up?"

"As a narrator? I'm the *writer*, Essie."

"Why not both?" She makes a big, full-arm shrug. When I don't answer she says, "I'm gonna tell them it's you. What do you think about that?"

"What do I think about that? I really don't have feelings about it, it's just… I don't want to narrate books. I want to write books. That's it. Just write. And I narrate my own books because who better than me? I'm kinda perfect at it."

"I'm still gonna tell them. It's a juicy secret. And if you don't have feelings about it, then you don't get a say."

It's in this moment when I spot my lovely Cordelia across the room. She and Britney are walking together, looking like an odd couple—Britney tall, lean, blonde, and my lovely Cordelia petite and studious-looking with her dark hair, and glasses, and serious expression. "Oh, my God, there she is." I kinda moan these words out.

"Who?"

"Cordelia Sarantopoulos. Cynthia Lear."

"Oh." Essie actually pauses to glance in the general direction of Cordelia. "Oh, yeah. Her. Ya know what? I think I need to speak to her. One sec."

She begins to walk off, but I grab her arm real fast and tug her back. "What do you mean you need to speak to her? About what?"

Essie starts peeling my fingers off her arm. "About her *panel*, Steve. Why are you being so weird? Let go of me."

I release my sister and then follow her over towards Cordelia and Britney. "Cynthia!" Essie is waving at Cordelia, trying to get her attention. "Hey, Cynthia! Can I have a moment?"

I watch, breathless, as Cordelia searches for the source of the call. Then, like magic—like we're in a slow-motion crisis scene of a historical romance—Cordelia's eyes lock with mine.

And then they narrow.

I pause the imagined scene in my head—like… mid-gallop, because I'm on a white steed, obviously—and take a moment to try and decipher that look.

What is she thinking?

I'm not sure. I mean, if I were her, and I had just had the best non-first date of my entire life, I would have a sort of… dreamy look. But her expression isn't conjuring up the word dreamy. It's manifesting… *loathing*?

No. I'm reading that wrong. I don't know her that well, so this is OK. Signals are getting crossed, but it will soon be sorted with a bit of conversation. Perhaps she thinks I left too abruptly this morning? Perhaps she couldn't find her Skinny Laminx? I accidentally ripped them while I was tugging them down her legs last night, so I just tossed them in the trash. However, if she insists, I will replace them. I'd just like to point out that they're not necessary when we have that talk.

"Hey, Brit!" Essie is perky and happy when we come up on my dear Cordelia. "Hi, Cynthia. I just wanted to touch base with you about the panels."

I'm smiling big at Cordy. I flash a little finger wave. I consider waggling the eyebrows, but I just used that expression on my sister, so I can't use it again for at least four more hours. I know real life isn't a romance book, but I have a thing about using the same adjective or expression description too many times in the same chapter. Eyebrow waggles are to be used sparingly, kind of like italics. So I settle for a wide grin. "Hi, Cordy." I want to point out that even though we've only been apart for about an hour and a half, I miss her already. But I don't want to say that in front of Essie and Britney, so I delete that and save it for later.

Cordelia looks confused. For a moment I wonder if she was too tipsy last night to remember all the details, but she's looking at Essie, not me. "Panel?"

"Yes. Your panel. I'm sure you're totally on top of this, but I didn't get a response back to the panel assignment email, so I just wanted to make double-double sure that you knew." Essie pauses.

Cordelia is confused. Which means she didn't know.

Britney interrupts. "Oh. Fuck. I'm sorry." She turns to Cordelia. "I must've missed the email. But it's OK. I mean, it's great, right?"

Cordelia doesn't appear to think this is great. "I have to be on a panel?"

"Oh." Essie is worried now. "I'm sorry. Well, no, of course not. If you're not comfortable, of course not. I know some authors hate the spotlight." I wait for her to look at me when she says this—and if she does, we will have a classic brother-sister throwdown—but she catches herself just in time. "Yeah. Some of them hate it. So I completely understand if you don't—"

"She does," Britney interrupts. "Want to be on the panel, I mean." Britney nudges Cordelia. "Don't you, Cordelia? It's your big opportunity. You're here to make the most of it." Cordelia doesn't agree or disagree, so Britney continues. "Which panel is it?"

"Reader Rants. I gotta warn you, it's a lively one. You address readers' biggest gripes about the stuff they read in books. It's gonna be packed. But don't worry. Winter Page, Audrey Saint, Raven Lark, Mercy Rose, and Eden Le Fay are all on it with you. So it should be fine."

"Wow." Cordelia looks panicked. "Those are some big names."

"The biggest." Essie beams. "It'll be great, I promise. *If* you want to do it. But again, no pressure. I just need to know in the next five minutes so I can run over there and let them know you can't make it so they don't announce you by mistake."

My eyeballs are doing a little tennis-game back and forth as this conversation happens. But now everyone's eyes land on Cordelia.

She nods her head. "Yeah. OK. I can do this."

"She can do this," Britney agrees.

"Great! Well… then I'll see you guys later. There's no mixer tonight, but there are a slew of private parties. Maybe we'll all meet up?"

She's looking at Britney, not Cordelia, when she says this. Britney agrees with a nod of her head, which satisfies Essie, but comes off as weird to me. I thought they were brand-new BFFs?

At any rate, Essie leaves, making her way back to Mike and the parents as hordes of people mob her with each step.

I let out a sigh and turn to my lovely Cordy, smiling like a fool. "Hi."

"Hello." She is not smiling like a fool. She is… frowning.

What's up with that?

I try again. "If this is about your Skinny Laminx—"

"What are you talking about?"

I look over at Britney, who is staring at me with a strange expression. All-teeth smile, tight jaw, wide eyes. What the hell does that mean? If I had time, I could run through my mental dictionary of words that describe facial expressions, but I'm too confused to get past 'A' for 'angry.'

"Sorry," Britney says, putting up her hands as she backs away. "I'll give you two kids a moment."

I'm just about to celebrate, when Cordelia says, "No. It's OK, there's no need. I gotta go."

And she's talking to *me*!

Is she… brushing me off? Giving me the cold shoulder?

After that delicious date last night?

No.

But then… she walks away.

CHAPTER ELEVEN — CORDELIA

Embarrassment. Foolishness. Disappointment. Maybe a little anger. Either at Steve or myself. I'm not sure which is more profound. These are all the things I'm feeling in no particular order. And rather than confront Mr. Smith (when I close off emotionally, I start referring formally to anyone I might be mad at) to see if he is, in fact, guilty of lying to me and possibly manipulating my trust—and vagina—for his own ends, I choose to do something much healthier and not at all dumb: I ignore him like a teenager and walk away.

Because, despite how I may be feeling right now, he remains really cute and charming and I need to center my thoughts before I get into any kind of confrontation with the dude who I let choke me last night. Which is a sentence I have never before had an occasion to think, and I have to believe very few other people have. So I need a minute to work it all out for myself.

Also, BT Dubs (which is yet another phrase I'm not sure I've ever thought before—I am definitely not of a clear mind just now), I'm on a *panel*? I'm on a panel. Holy moly, I'm on a panel. How did I get put on a panel? It's my first time at a con and—

Steve. He got me on the panel. He must have. That has to be it. Same way he got me a suite, got me killer booth placement, got me invited to this thing at all. What is this guy's game?

Assuming Britney has the straight dope (seriously, I normally don't talk like this), he's a pretty crafty one, this Steve Smith. If he's been hiding in the shadows, writing romance all this time, and maybe even *did* plagiarize someone else to get to where he is, then he clearly has no problem playing a long game. Is he gaming me? Long… ly?

I don't want to believe that someone as awful as Raylen Star could be right, but it happens. That annoying phenomenon when the worst person you know says something you may agree with. That's a slippery slope. Because on the one hand, you want to deny the source, but on the other hand… what if they're making sense in spite of being all oogy as a human?

"Ow!" That is my verbal reaction to both nearly chewing off the tip of my finger and being gripped around my upper arm by a strong and recently familiar hand.

"Talk to you for a sec?" Steve asks.

"Jesus, Cord, are you bleeding?" Britney follows up, taking note of the place where the end of my index finger used to be.

"Huh? Oh, no, I'm fine." Then, turning my attention to Mr. Smith—"Not right now, thanks. I have a panel to get to. Because I'm on a panel. Here. Now. At my very first con. Which is cool and obviously well-deserved and not at all part of some weird, overly complicated, grand ploy to do something I haven't figured out yet."

Both Britney and Steve look at me like I'm a bag of mixed nuts.

"I'm going to get you a Band-Aid," Britney says as she starts off.

"No, I'm—" But before I can finish, she's gone. And now I'm standing alone with Steve Smith. Well, not *alone*. The place is teeming. But still, I'm—

Oh!

Steve. Smith. SS! S! S! Holy—I knew—

"Are you okay?" He interrupts my revelation.

"What?"

"Are you okay?" he repeats.

"Yeah, I'm fine."

And, again, I don't know why I don't just address my questions and theories right now. Why I don't confront my misgivings. But I find myself unable to and with not enough time to do a deep dive into the wherefores. And for some reason, out of nowhere, I hear my mother's voice in my head: "*Cordelia Penelope Sarantopoulos, you need to stop acting like a silly child and focus yourself like an adult.*" Then I hear her tsk. And that's it. I'm done.

There's no way I'm going to talk to Steve like an adult woman now. If for no other reason than because my mom just told me to. And so, I'm going to do the opposite.

Yeah. That'll show her.

Dear God, I am overstimulated at the moment.

"Are you sure? Did I do something—?"

"No. No, no. No, no, no. No, nobody did nothing to nobody." I wince at my own grammatical misuse. "I just…"

"You had a good time last night, right? We didn't do anything that—?"

"No! No, no!" I don't realize how loud I'm being until a bunch of women turn to look at where I'm shouting. I bring it down a notch. "No, last night was just—"

"I apologize for ripping your Skinnies."

"What?"

"I ripped your… which, by the way, you do not need. Like, even a little. But, honestly, I don't think anyone does. I mean, I'm glad Britney's mom has been able to make a successful go of it in the slimming undergarment biz, but I think all bodies are beautiful no matter what they look like. But, in particular, *your* body…"

What the hell? Is he for real? Talking about all bodies being beautiful, but *my* body… And he thinks I'm upset about ripping…? Is he for real?

No. This seals it. He's *too* nice. Nobody is this charming and handsome and non-judgmental and unproblematic and all… I dunno, *thoughtful* and whatever. No. Body. Now I know for sure it has to be a game of some kind.

I just don't understand clearly what it is yet.

I pull away from handsome Steve Smith, reiterating my premise that "I'm fine," and make my way toward the room where the panel is taking place. But then I stop. Because I realize…

"Um. Do you know where I'm going? I don't know exactly where it, uh…" I trail off as I stare into his eyes.

His beautiful, sympathetic, confused, pained-looking eyes (no, stop, don't get distracted). He sighs in and out, lifting his chest and letting it fall, and then says…

"Yeah. Follow me."

And, despite any number of hesitations, I do.

Picking at the Band-Aid on my finger, I look over to Britney, who gives me a thumbs-up and a big smile, indicating with her fingers that I should also try to smile.

Steve is standing next to her in the back of the room, also smiling at me. But his smile is more of a cautious one. An imploring of sorts, accompanied by a nod of what is probably intended to be encouragement.

The room is bursting at the seams, so many romance readers packed in that it has to be a violation of some kind of fire code.

And, suddenly, from out of nowhere, I get an idea for a book. It's unformed and hazy, but something about Vegas and firefighters and maybe there's, like, a criminal B-story or something? Maybe the woman is struggling to find her way in the world after a personal trag—

"All right! We'll go ahead and get started, then," the frizzy-haired moderator whose name I didn't catch says as the buzzing, electric energy in the room dies down to a thrum. "Welcome to Reader Rants, where some of the biggest names in romance today will address concerns and questions from you, the readers. First, let's just go down the panel and have everyone introduce themselves. Although this group hardly needs any introduction," she adds with a knowing look and a tiny laugh which, in turn, calls up a healthy chuckle from the crowd. Frizzy gestures to her right where the first author on this impressive and intimidating panel sits.

"Hi. I'm Winter Page." Winter raises her hand and a huge round of applause erupts from the crowd. In front of Winter, her name card confirms why.

WINTER PAGE, #1 *NY Times* Bestseller

Next up is… "I'm Mercy Rose, hello."

MERCY ROSE, *NY Times* and *USA Today* Bestseller

Another massive round of applause.

Next… "Hello, my dears. My name is Raven Lark," Raven says in her gentle, septuagenarian way.

RAVEN LARK, *NY Times*, *USA Today*, and *Wall Street Journal* Bestseller

Uproarious applause.

Followed by, "'Sup, bitches? I'm Eden Le Fay," says Eden, wiggling the fingers of her black-lace-gloved hands at the women in the room.

EDEN LE FAY, Multiple #1 *NY Times* Bestseller

The applause is both excited and reverent, almost like they want to celebrate her but are simultaneously terrified of what witchcraft she might be capable of casting upon them.

And, lastly, sitting next to me—"Hey. I'm Audrey Saint," Audrey says in the most casual, off-the-cuff, unassuming way anyone possibly could. Which I find both comforting and a little impressive, given that she is probably the biggest deal on this panel, as her name card confirms.

AUDREY SAINT, Multiple #1 *NY Times*, *USA Today*, *Wall Street Journal*, *Times* of London, and Various Others Bestseller

The list of achievements is almost too great to fit onto one placard. The crowd goes wild.

And then there's… "Um, hi. I'm… uh… Cynthia Lear?" The name card on the table in front of me reads, simply:

CYNTHIA LEAR, Author

The tepid applause feels, to me, like it's laced with confusion. A 'who is this person and why is she here?' kind of confusion. I look to Britney, who is still smiling and encouraging me to do the same. And, just because he's standing beside her and not at all because I need his approval or affirmation, I also look to Steve, who is smiling the same way.

Audrey reaches under the table, squeezes my thigh, and winks at me. It's comforting. Kind of like what I assume what a mom might do. (To be clear: *A* mom. Not necessarily *my* mom.) It doesn't work, really. I don't *feel* comforted. But I appreciate that she's trying.

I don't know why I'm so nervous. Yeah, sure, it's partially the 'being in front of a crowd' thing, but it's also partially because… I'm not even sure I really belong here at all. I've tried to stuff it down, but having to rewrite the end of *Filling the Gap* kind of did a number on my head.

Like, I *thought* I knew what I was doing with my writing and then, suddenly, I wasn't so sure.

And then Steve takes my ARC, reads the whole damn thing in an afternoon and woos me with praise to the point that I get swept off my feet, only to now discover that there might be a whole raft of ulterior motives at play and now I don't understand any of the things I thought I understood anymore.

So, okay, I lied. I do know exactly why I'm so nervous.

I wonder, if I just slipped out right now and left the room, if anyone would notice or—

"All right," Frizzy continues, "so what we'll do is go ahead and open up questions to the floor. Please, raise your hand to be called on and let's go one at a time, trying to limit the number of follow-ups so that we can give people a chance to get their questions in. So, does anyone have a 'reader rant?' Something that you're curious about or that frustrates you that you want to ask about?"

You can actually hear the snap in the air as probably close to a hundred hands shoot up in unison. All kinds of hands. Young, old, thin, strong, sleeved, sleeveless, wedding-banded, not ringed, tattooed, nail-polished… a panoply of limbs attached to bodies with brains and hearts all unified in their shared love of this thing called romance.

It's… well, it's kind of beautiful. If I weren't sitting in front of them all, with a thousand mixed emotions racing through my brain, I might get a little teary. It's just so—

"Yes, you there." Frizzy points and then clarifies, "You in the t-shirt."

A woman stands up. A PA in the crowd brings a microphone over and hands it to her. The woman is probably my age or maybe a little younger and wears a babydoll tee that doesn't quite cover her stomach and shows off the belly button ring she wears. Which must be, I assume, the point.

"Thanks. My rant is kind of a general one for the panel. So, I hate cliffhangers…" There is a mumbling agreement from about half the crowd. "And, y'know, I get that they're supposed to entice the reader to stick around and come back for another book in a series or whatever, but, like, don't you think, at the end of the day, that's just kind of a *tactical* choice to keep people reading a book? You know, rather than a creative one?"

My spine immediately stiffens. Because… my first two books both end on cliffhangers.

That was… that was the whole point when I started The Purity Principle. That it would continue on for, like, a long time. That was the whole point! Oh, no. Oh—

"Well," Mercy Rose begins, "I can say, for me, that sometimes I don't necessarily *want* to end a book on a cliffhanger. That, if I had my druthers, I'd just keep writing until I resolved the story. But, now and again, a story is just too big and it wants to keep going. And, honestly, if I waited until I was finished to publish the whole thing, it would be, y'know, a thousand pages long and take, I dunno, ten years to be done. So, at the end of the day," she says, calling back to the phrase Babydoll Tee used and smiling, "it's a little from column A and a little from column B. You have to try to balance the demands of the industry with whatever your creative vision might be. That's the key to keeping things going. It's a balancing act."

While I know that what Mercy just said is not in any way directed at me, I can't help but hear it that way. And all of a sudden, I *really* feel like I don't have any business being on this panel. I should be in the audience, asking questions. How am I going to get a big, fancy agent and a publishing deal if I don't even know how to balance A and B? I go to put my finger in my mouth, but realize it's bandaged and switch to a different finger.

"That's great," Frizzy Moderator says with a nod and a smile. "Somebody else?" Again, hands lunge upward at the ceiling. "Yes. You." She points at an older woman. And I don't just mean older than Babydoll Tee. I mean older than just about everyone. Older than Sheila, my landlady. She wears a baseball cap that looks to have homemade embroidery on it.

It reads 'Ride-or-Die Grandma.'

The PA hands Ride-or-Die Grandma the mic. Her voice is stronger than I anticipated, with a strong Southern accent. Maybe Kentucky? Unsure. I don't know why it matters. I nibble at my fingernail.

"Well," Ride-or-Die Grandma starts, "that's all well and good, but here's my thing: I can't be out here waiting for a book for however long. I mean, sometimes I feel like y'all'll start a story, end it on a whopper of a cliffy, and then go on to another book before y'all done finished the first one. I ain't got all the time in the world, ladies. Y'all gotta write faster or something."

There is a smattering of laughter as Ride-or-Die Grandma hands the microphone back and sits down. The moderator attempts to recap as I feel myself starting to hyperventilate. That's what I just did. I took a break from my series to write *Filling the Gap*! Oh, my God. Oh, my God. I'm doing everything wrong!

Audrey Saint looks my direction, then leans over to me, covers my mic and whispers, “You okay?”

“Mm-hm,” I squeak out in a high-pitched lie as I now nibble my thumb.

“So, I guess we’ll call this particular rant ‘unfinished series.’ Anyone want to field this one?” the moderator asks the panel. Winter Page is the one who chooses to pick up the baton.

“Uh, well,” she starts, leaning into her microphone, “I mean, I appreciate the question, and I know it can be frustrating to wait, but sometimes it’s just unavoidable. Like with book five of my series Seven Miles from Hope, that one was supposed to come out much sooner than it did, but I had to have an emergency appendectomy and then one of my dogs got sick and… whatever, doesn’t matter, there were just some things that got in the way. Y’know, life. And that slowed it down. So, I mean, those things happen too. I feel like I can speak for most writers when I say that we never want to drag it out. We’re usually as excited as you are to find out what happens!” Another round of chuckles. “But occasionally, it can’t be helped.”

“Can I say something?” That’s Eden Le Fay. The moderator nods, encouraging her to talk. “Yeah, um… to jump off what Winter’s saying, we’re not fucking machines, y’know? We’re people. With real lives and shit. We’re not just these fuckin’ plug-and-play automatons who can crank out what-the-fuck-ever on demand. So, maybe remember that shit too.”

There is a beat as everything quiets down and a subtle but extremely noticeable shift in energy rolls across the room like a fog.

You do not fuck with Eden Le Fay.

"Great!" says the moderator, trying to steer things back into a jolly direction as quickly as possible. "Next question!" Hands go up. Frizzy points. "Yes. In the blue blouse."

The woman who stands up looks friendly. Put-together. Pleasant. Like the kind of person you'd want as a neighbor. "Funny you should say it that way," she says, taking the mic and getting a scolding look. "Because my rant is specifically for you, Eden."

Oh, God.

"Why does there have to be so much swearing in your books?"

Or not. Or you don't want her as your neighbor. I stand corrected.

"I'm sorry?" Eden responds, like she might have just had an aneurysm.

"I read all your series. And you're very, very good. But why do your characters have to swear so much all the time? There's just so much filthy language, I feel like."

"Bitch," Eden starts—oh, no. Oh, God—"I write *dark erotica*. How the fuck do you expect the characters to talk?"

"I just—" the woman stammers.

"All right, let's all—" The moderator tries to grab the reins.

"So, you've read *all* my series, and *that's* the part you've got a problem with? You're cool to read about people fucking in all kinds of fucked-up ways, but you don't want them to *say* 'fuck' when they're fucking? Or something? Like, fucking really?"

If you were to ask me, later on, to describe the exact moment the wheels came off the wagon… I'd probably have to point to this moment.

"Okay," the moderator attempts again, "let's—"

"Yeah, if you don't like the language, don't read the books!" someone shouts.

"Leave her alone!" someone else rings out. "She's entitled to her opinion!"

"Honestly, I'd rather have too much than not enough!" yells someone else. "I hate it when I pick up a book with a sexy cover and there's barely any sex in the book! Feels like I've been robbed! Like all that 'fade-to-black' stuff! What's that about?"

"I could never write stuff that dirty. I'm mostly a fade-to-black kinda girl." I can feel myself hyperventilating a little.

"Girls, girls, settle down!" the moderator implores. To no avail.

"You sound like someone who just wants smut," shouts the woman who started this whole thing to the woman who just said she wants more sex in her books. "Some of us care about the *story.*"

And now, suddenly, the image of the big, beautiful panoply of romance readers is replaced by something altogether different. Something dangerous and feral. Something with teeth.

And then, out of the growing cacophony, a voice rings out.

"Ladies, ladies, please," Raven Lark cries. She is standing, holding her microphone. "Please. Not everyone has to like the same thing. These books are supposed to be for enjoyment. For escape. To forget about real life for a little while. I have to tell you, when my husband died, I was… It was hard. It was a very hard time for me. He was the great love of my life and I missed him so, so much. And you know how I got through it? Books. Romance books."

Quiet falls over the room as all faces look to Raven. She goes on.

"First reading them, then, later, writing. It helped me heal. That's what all of us up here write for in our own ways. We write for grieving. For hope. For hurt and for healing. For seeking to find and breathing deep and easy when we finally do. That's the whole point. It doesn't matter if one book isn't for you. That's fine. Just put it down and go find one that is. That's all."

She puts the mic back in place and sits. A hush absorbs what feels like the whole universe.

I spot Steve at the back. He looks… moved, I guess? Maybe kind of emotional? I can't be sure.

The moderator appears shaken, but she tries to rally. "Yes. Well said. So…" It's obvious to me that she's debating about whether it's a good idea to continue or not. If I got a vote, I'd say no, but I don't. I'm starting to realize I'm probably not even going to get a question. That's fine. I'm too wrapped up in the realization that I may not have any idea of what I'm doing to be able to answer one anyway.

"I have a question." A voice. From the back of the room. A man's voice. Oh, Christ.

The PA heads over to Steve and hands him the microphone. What. Is. He. Doing?

"First," he says, taking the mic and nodding to all the women, "some of you may know me. I'm Steve, SS's brother." Applause. Not as robust and rowdy as before, but we're heading in a better direction at least. "And on behalf of SS, I just want to thank you all for being here.

One thing you can say about romance conventions, they're never boring!"

Some giggles, some chuckles, pretty much everyone staring at Steve like he's sweet intoxication.

"Second, Raven, that was beautiful. Just… It was really beautiful and gets right at the beating heart of this whole romance thing. It really is about inclusion and finding your tribe and… well, all of that. Or, at least, that's what I've learned from my sister." He smiles. But it's layered over the top of something else, and I'm starting to get increasingly anxious about where he's going with this.

"And, of course, at the end of the day, it's really about finding your HEA. Right? Your happily ever after. And that can come in a lot of different ways, just like love can manifest in a lot of different ways. And so, in the spirit of inclusion and finding your tribe and all that good stuff, I'd like to throw a question to Ms. Lear."

What the fuck is he doing? What is happening right now?

"If you don't know Cynthia Lear, she is an up-and-coming writer who is going to be a force to be reckoned with. And if you don't believe me, you can ask Audrey, sitting next to her."

Audrey nods at me, turns to her mic, and says, "Absolutely."

"So, Cynthia," Steve goes on, "as a new voice in the community, I was wondering if we could get you to weigh in on a subject that I know is of great significance to many readers… What, exactly, in your mind, is necessary to have something be considered an HEA?"

WHAT IS HE DOING?

"I mean, are you of the opinion that an HEA means it *must* conclude with a wedding and a baby? Or are there other, more non-traditional ways to end a story that could be considered a happily ever after? Just want your thoughts."

Now, all heads turn to face me.

Did I put on deodorant? I thought I did, but I was off my routine this morning and—

"Ms. Lear?" The moderator follows up, as I have apparently failed to answer.

The faces staring at me loom large in the foreground of my vision, and I feel beads of perspiration forming above my upper lip.

"Hap—um… happily—HE—happy EA?" I think I might say. I also think I'm going to throw up. I look at Steve, an expression of 'why?' firmly on my face. Either he doesn't read it or just pretends not to, because he just keeps looking at me, a stare of encouragement still on his. I think. "Well… I think, um, for me, an HEA doesn't have to—"

"I say if it don't end in a wedding and a baby it ain't no HEA," Ride-or-Die Grandma calls out.

Annnnnnd… that's it.

If I had to tell you exactly how the first chair got thrown, I don't think I could. But it happens. Because then another gets thrown. And then another. And, quite out of the blue, the whole room erupts in something that resembles a daytime talk show from the late twentieth century, with people shouting and a flurry of slaps and fists being thrown.

It's really quite something.

I don't even see Steve making his way to me on the podium area. The next thing I know, he's draped himself around both me and Audrey Saint and is protecting us from a hailstorm of flying furniture as he shepherds us out of the room and shouts, "Call security!"

And as we're just about out the door he adds what might be the understatement of the day: "Maybe we should think about scratching the Reader Rants panel next time."

CHAPTER TWELVE – STEVE

"I knew this was a bad idea!" Mercy says as the door to the conference room closes behind us. "I told you, Audrey. Didn't I just say that when we were in line for coffee this morning?"

"Bitch," Eden yells. "This was the best!" She does a fist pump in the air, like she just completed the final round of *Ninja Warrior*. "I hope my slave got it all on vid. I can't wait to post it online."

I just sigh. Eden, Eden, Eden. She's a handful. But the fans love her, and she throws down the money for a giant booth every year, so there's no way we're not inviting her back.

"Slave?" That comes from Winter. "You mean, it's not an act?"

Eden does a little roleplay on the socials. She's got a 'man with a collar on a leash' thing going. So she snorts at this attack on her persona like she's taking it personally. "Act? *Act?*" She lifts her head and guffaws. "I live *the life*." And these words come out as a snarl. "I'm not some fake-ass—"

"Ya know," Mercy interrupts, "you're a real piece of work. People are probably hurt back there and here you are—"

"OK, OK, OK. That's enough, ladies." Audrey is the adult in the room. She looks at me. "We need to get help."

I'm still holding Cordelia, but she's beginning to wiggle in my arms. "Put me down!"

Then she's slapping at me. I want to keep her in my arms and carry her off to safety, but she's really squirming now. And swearing at me. So I set her down in the maintenance hallway—half a dozen workers staring at us curiously as they go about their business—and check to make sure she's OK.

But this is going to be a disaster if I don't take care of things, so I rush over to the nearest courtesy phone and ask for security in conference room B. Then I turn back to the group, eager to have a word with Cordelia, but she and Britney are already halfway down the wide hallway, almost disappearing into a crowd of maids.

I'm just about to take off after them when Audrey grabs my arm. "Steve! Are they coming? I don't think it's under control in there."

We all look at the door and in that same moment, something crashes against it.

"For fuck's sake," I mutter.

"It was Ride-or-Die Grandma," Winter says. "It was Ride-or-Die Grandma and her stupid comment about how long it takes to write books!"

"Damn right!" Eden says. "Fuckin' Ride-or-Die Grandma. Kick her out!"

I put up a hand. "No one's getting kicked out. Just… calm down. Security is on the way."

"Should we go back in there?" Raven is asking. "We can't just stand out here like cowards. We have to do something."

"I'm out." Eden turns her back to us, raising her hand over her head in a goodbye wave. "See you bitches at lunch."

I sigh, once again looking down the hallway, but Britney and Cordelia are gone. Then I look at Raven. "No. You ladies all get back to the main lobby and stay safe. I'll take care of everything."

"Do you want me to come with you?" Audrey asks.

"I'm fine. I can handle it. I'll see you at lunch."

Then, with one last regretful glance down the hallway, I open the door to the conference room and allow the commotion to hit me in the face.

MEANWHILE…

Meanwhile…

The adoring fans attending the Hot Lips and Husky Voices panel are a model audience. Their fresh faces are bright, their eyes gleaming and happy, and their smiles continuous. They are eager to hear from both authors and narrators alike about any and all audiobook minutiae.

Essie Smith-Scott stands at the podium, looking down at her notes, because she is both participant and moderator. Essie hosts this panel every year for several reasons: It's never bursting at the seams (there are always a few extra chairs in the back), the participants are polite and attentive, and everyone—herself included—loves to hear their favorite narrators talking outside of the book world.

Drama, Essie thinks, is highly overrated. And this panel has proved itself to be drama-free for six years running. If everything goes as planned—and there's no reason to assume it won't—this will be a seven-year record.

She was apprehensive about the Reader Rants panel this year. They had one of those the first year too. It was a disaster. But the romance world has matured since then and she's confident it's all going to be fine.

At any rate, none of that is her problem. It's Steve's. He gave the final OK—and put that poor newbie author, Cynthia Lear, on it. What was he thinking?

But, if something does go wrong, he'll handle it. That's what Steve does. He handles everything like a frickin' champion.

Essie loves her brother. Dearly. And he's the most talented writer in the whole world in her eyes. She could maybe do without the sex scenes, but all in all, Essie is Steve's number one fan.

And that's why she's going to out him as Tank Watson, narrator extraordinaire of all the SS books, today. Of course, tons of people already know it's him. It doesn't take a private detective to recognize a voice. And Steve has been at her side through every single conference. Because it's *his* conference, of course. He's here, every year, right along with her. So all her closest author friends know Steve and Tank are the same person.

Today, however, the fans are going to find this out as well. Because Essie is going to tell them. And then she's going to let all her most favorite author friends know that he's on the market—well, as far as narration goes—and get him booked up for the rest of the year.

He has to do something, because he certainly has no books of his own to narrate right now.

She's been worried about him for the past year or so. After he spent all that time writing the science fiction series, while simultaneously churning out several number one *New York Times* bestsellers for the romance fans, he was so let down when the reader world turned against the real him.

They love SS but hate Steve Smith.

It's so weird.

And the lie is starting to get to Steve. Essie can tell. They are twins, after all. It's starting to eat him up from the inside out. Her gaze wanders to the front row, where their parents are sitting. Mom waves. Dad nods, smiling.

They are so proud of her.

And she's proud of herself, as well. She has risen to the occasion here. Maybe she doesn't write the books, but she's a pretty awesome social media marketer. The last ad campaign she ran for *Troubled Waters*—which was a year ago now—took that book all the way to number five in the Nile store on release day. It then spent seven weeks at number one and the following week it became Steve's tenth *New York Times* number one bestseller.

Yes, Steve writes great books. And yes, he's got a million fans. But her ad campaigns are what keep the books floating at the top.

So she waves back at Mom and smiles at Dad, graciously acknowledging their pride.

Then she looks back down at her notes. Everything about this panel is organized—the questions have been ordered to most efficiently use each minute so that all the narrators and authors get an equal amount of time to shine.

She's going to make the whole Tank-Steve announcement last so no one's toes get stepped on. This thought is still running through her mind when a shadow falls over her.

She looks up, then gasps and takes a step back. "Leslie. What are you doing here?"

"It's *Raylen*, Essie. What the fuck? Why is it so hard to call me by my name?"

Essie would like to point out that she *is* calling Leslie by her name. But she's not in the mood. "I'm busy, Raylen. Whatever it is, can we chat about it later?"

"No." Leslie makes a snarly face at Essie. "I'm on the panel but I don't have a placard."

Essie is thoroughly confused. She is one hundred percent positive that she did not include Raylen Star on this panel. She put her on the last panel of the day, Pen Names and Page Games.

Leslie puts up a hand. "I know what you're thinking. You're thinking… *I did not put Raylen on this panel.* Because no, you did not. Steve did. Just a little while ago in the lobby. By the way, your parents are lovely."

Essie blinks. Why the hell would Steve put Leslie on her panel? They hate Leslie. She's a complete bitch. But… Steve *is* the boss. And he did circle her name on the waitlist—that's why stupid Leslie Munch is here in the first place. They had two cancellations, which meant they needed to fill two spots. Essie gave Steve the list that night at dinner a few weeks ago. He circled two names—Cynthia Lear, which didn't raise any red flags, even though Essie had never heard of her, and Leslie. Which did raise red flags, but Essie didn't look at the list until he was already on his motorcycle, revving it up. She called his name, but it got lost in the rumble.

Essie went to bed, making a mental note to ask Steve about it the next day. She never did.

Her brow furrows as she tries to recall how she dropped this baton.

Ohhhh, right. It's starting to make sense now. Mike stayed up late that night to clean the kitchen and when she woke up the next day, he had already sent the invitations.

Mike is so considerate like that. If she cooks, he cleans. They are partners, after all.

But she had a teeny-tiny hangover that next morning. She might've had too much to drink the night before. And when she moaned about having to deal with the convention stuff, Mike—being the prince that he is—informed her that he had already taken care of it. Everything on her list for that day was already checked off because… oh, *riiight.* Right, right, right. It was late afternoon when she dragged herself out of bed, not morning. They had been burning the midnight oil for weeks trying to finish that last reno and that was her first night off in months.

Even in this moment, weeks later, just thinking about that last job makes her exhausted. Plumbing issues, a broken fridge, new electrical, permitting snags. It was a nightmare.

Also in this moment… this *very* moment when stupid Leslie Munch is staring down her nose at Essie, now she's pretty sure that Steve never *meant* to circle Leslie's name. Perhaps he circled her name as he was cursing it?

Something went wrong, that's for sure.

Essie had forgotten all about Leslie being a signing author until yesterday when… there Leslie was. Making scenes.

Well, it's done now. Even if Steve didn't mean to circle her name and Mike did make a mistake by sending Leslie that invitation, it doesn't matter. Leslie's here.

Literally, right in front of Essie. Tapping her stupid toe on the carpet, hands planted on hips like she's about to make (yet another) scene.

So. Yeah. Looks like stupid, mean, witchy Leslie gets to invade Essie's most favorite, most cherished panel.

Essie sighs—"Great to have you, Raylen"—and forces a smile. Then she shuffles her notes until she finds a blank page, folds it in half, then half again, takes a Sharpie out of her purse, and scribbles 'Raylen Star' on it. She offers it to Leslie. "There you go. Your placard."

Leslie makes a tight-lipped smile, snatching the paper from Essie's hand, growling out the words, "Thank you," as she turns to the tables of already seated authors and narrators on the stage and begins demanding a chair.

So much for that seven-year record.

CHAPTER THIRTEEN — STEVE

When I get inside the panel room I pause and take stock.

Is anyone unconscious?

Is anyone bleeding?

Is the place on fire?

No, no, and no. So I place my fingers on my tongue and whistle so loud that when it comes out, everyone in the room stops. All faces turn to me. Several ladies have chairs lifted, like they are preparing to throw them. I shake my head, tsk my tongue, and wag my finger at them. I do not raise my voice. "That will be enough, ladies. Put the chairs down."

They stare blankly at me for several moments, so I feel the need to further encourage them. "Did I stutter?"

At the same time, the door bursts open and a team of security guards enter. I quickly scan the room, find those two troublemakers—who are, interestingly enough, huddled in one corner of the room—together and out of the fray. I narrow my eyes.

Something is amiss here. But I'm not sure what it is yet. So instead of having them thrown out on their asses,

I call to the security guards. "We're good now. Right, ladies?" I say this through clenched teeth.

Once again, I get the blank stares.

"I said, '*Right,* ladies?'"

"Yep."

"We're good."

"It's all good."

They say this in unison, nodding their heads, trying to look innocent even though the lot of them were just behaving like a bunch of mean girls in high school.

I turn to the security guards. "Thank you for your quick response time. I'll take it from here."

They let out a breath and give me an eye roll that says, *Romance conventions. Who knew?*

Once they're gone, I take a deep breath. "OK. We're going to put this room back in order, take our seats like civilized people, and we're going to have Reader Rants. Do you understand?"

A hundred women nod, an accord agreed upon, and that's when I realize I'm kinda doing the Master Choke voice, so… it makes sense.

"Good. Let's proceed." And I clap my hands to give the start signal.

In less than five minutes the room is neat, the rows tidy, and the ladies are seated.

I take note of Babydoll Tee and squint until I can make out her name on her badge. Angela. Ride-or-Die Grandma is sitting right next to her now. Her name is Elaine.

Hmm. Yes, something is definitely afoot.

But I don't have time to address it now because a woman in the front row raises her hand. I point at her. "Yes. You have a question?"

"But… Steve, all the authors left. Who will we complain to?"

"You may complain to me. How's that?" I take a seat on the table, brace my hands on either side of me, and lean forward a little. "I'm all ears, ladies. Tell me, please. What in God's name could possibly piss you off about romance books? I'm all ears."

They all start talking at once, but I put up another hand and they go silent. "One at a time." I point at a woman in the back. "Go."

"Cliffhangers! That was a real rant that deserves some attention! I *hate* them!"

"Listen, cliffhangers work"—I squint so I can read her name tag—"Ainsley."

"Ashley. Ashley Blackwell."

"Ashley. Sorry. Look, they work, OK, Ashley Blackwell?" She kind of blushes when I say her full name. The Master Choke voice gets 'em every time. "It's like serial TV. Everyone knows the story keeps going. You all love a series, right?"

They nod. They do. I know they do.

"So we gotta use the cliffies. That's how we keep you coming back. And if you don't come back, we don't have a reason to write it. Would it piss you off more or less if an author dropped a series for lack of interest? Or if you had to wait for the next book in the story? Ask yourselves that."

"Hmm," a lady to my left says. "It kinda does make sense. I mean, I get as frustrated as anyone having to wait, but… I don't want them to stop writing. I just want more, more, more!"

"And you'll get it. So much more. If you can just muster up a little bit of patience. You need to accept the cliff. Embrace it, because a cliff means there's more coming, ladies. More meet-cutes, and more first kisses, and more first times…" I waggle my eyebrows and they laugh and giggle. "More love, ladies. The cliffy means there's *more love*."

"That's true," another woman, whose nametag reads Linda Gerace, says. (Underneath her last name she has written, "Soft 'G.' Like Giraffe." I have to appreciate her attention to detail.) "It's not one of my rants," she goes on, "so maybe I don't speak for everyone, but I always get a little panic attack when the end of a series comes. I always want more. No cliffy means no more series. My heart flutters over this and I don't even want to finish the book because I don't want to leave the world."

Suddenly, the whole room is in agreement.

"Oh, I agree."

"With you, sister!"

"Yes!"

"See?" I say. "The cliff means there's more coming. More time with your favorite characters in your favorite worlds."

"But what about a wedding and a baby?" one woman exclaims, getting to her feet. "I want a wedding and a baby!"

"How many books don't have a wedding and a baby by the end of the series?" I squint again to see her nametag. "Abby?"

"Will you say my whole name out loud too?" she asks, coyly.

I sigh. *What have I started?* "Sure. What is it?"

"Evans. Abby Evans."

"OK, Abby Evans..." There are giggles. "Seriously. How many leave it out of the last book?"

"Well…" Abby squirms. "The *last* book in a series… yeah. Most of them do have it in the last book."

"Of course they do," I say. "Because romance writers—most of them, anyway—know what they're doing, Abby. When you demand that we put a wedding and a baby at the end of the *first* book, you're being unreasonable. The wedding and baby are a signal that you're at the end. And didn't we just decide that we *never* want it to end?"

The room begins to murmur with agreement, making Abby uncomfortable. "But"—I put up a hand to stop the murmuring—"you're right. Most, but not all, happily ever afters typically mean a wedding and baby. *However*, perhaps you might consider the idea that if the author decides they do not want a wedding and a baby, that maybe, possibly, that book just… isn't for you?"

Abby sighs. "Yeah. You're right. I should just… find another book that does promise a wedding and a baby."

"Find another book, Abby. There are a million of them out there."

The room settles and the ladies calm down, easing back into their seats, stretching out their legs, getting comfortable with the change.

I am eager to get out of here. I want to end this panel and go find Cordelia so I can beg her to tell me what is on her mind. What did I do wrong? How can I fix it?

But I have to admit that it feels kinda good to talk to the readers like this. Essie's the one who does the panels. I never get to interact this way. Plus, this is all good feedback for me.

I know it's been a while since I actually wrote a romance, but being at the conference is really getting the creative juices running.

So I don't end the panel. I start addressing all their issues. Explaining, from the writer's point of view, why things get done a certain way. Because there is a reason for all of it. Every complaint has a reason behind it.

And once I've done that, and they are all satisfied—satiated by my considerable romance author wisdom—I say, "Trust us, ladies. That's all we ask. Just trust us to take you on a journey. Because isn't the journey the point? Don't you want to ride the rollercoaster of that fictional life in that fictional world? So that when you get to the end it's… *sweet.*"

I get a standing ovation for that speech.

"Now go, ladies. Go forth and enjoy the rest of panel day." And with a wave of my hand—in the vein of Master Choke himself—I dismiss them.

I make a quick escape out into the maintenance hallway, pull out my phone, and tap the SparkleNight DreamWeaver's WishMaker app. Gregory's cartoon face greets me. "Hello, Steve Smith. How can I help you?"

I'm just about to beg him to locate Cordelia for me when I see the two troublemakers who started all that fuss earlier. So instead I say, "Gregory, please hold."

Those two ladies didn't have a single question in the panel. In fact, they never said another word. Something is amiss.

"Hello! Hi, there!" I call to them in my commanding Tank-slash-Master Choke voice. "May I have a word." It's not a question.

They look at each other, nervously, then nod and come my way.

"Hi, Steve."

"Hey, Steve. We should probably apologize for—"

I put up a hand and they go silent. Holy fuckin' cow. Master Choke really knew what he was doing. This whole alpha-male dominant thing works, it really works.

I gather myself, and in that same Tank-slash-Master Choke voice I say, "I'm not looking for an apology, ladies. I'm here to say that if either of you so much as looks at anyone the wrong way, I will personally banish you from the Sin With Us convention forever and have you thrown out of the Aria."

Angela, aka Babydoll Tee, huffs. Like she doubts I have this power.

But I have Gregory, all spun up, right in my palm.

"Gregory," I say into the phone.

"Steve Smith. Honored guest of the Aria Hotel and Casino. How can I make your wishes come true today?"

"Gregory, do I have the power to ban people from this hotel?"

"If that is your wish, Steve Smith, I will make it happen. Who would you like to ban today?"

"No one. *Yet.*" I narrow my eyes at the troublemakers. "But I'll let you know if I change my mind."

"Very good, Steve Smith. How was your date last night? Did the rose petals work out?"

I whisper into the phone, "Hold that thought. BRB." Then I stand up straight and nod my head at the troublemakers. "You're dismissed." And with a wave of my hand, I send them off.

They huff and puff, looking over their shoulder at me as they make their retreat, hopefully filled with shame for the commotion they caused.

Then I exhale and return to my task. "Gregory, this is a big ask."

"My wish is your command."

I pause. "What?"

"Your wish is my command."

"Umm… OK." Not for the first time I wonder just how AI this AI is. Did Gregory just make a joke? No. "Anyway. I need to track down Cynthia Lear. I know this is probably illegal and—"

"She's in the Baccarat Lounge. Do you need step-by-step directions?"

"Uh… wow. That was fast."

"My only job is to please you, Steve."

"Right." He's creepy. "No directions. I know where it is. Thank you!"

I swipe the app away, slightly disturbed at just how easy it was to track someone down. But that's a conspiracy theory for another day. I run my fingers through my hair, and leave the maintenance hallway, heading in the direction of the Baccarat Lounge.

I find it easily. I've been in there myself after a long night of winning. I like to tip big—even if I'm losing—and the Baccarat Lounge has the best bartenders. They are like… movie-level great. The kind who listen—the kind who *love* to listen. Like that bartender in *The Shining*. He was the best. Well, until he got Jack to go all REDRUM-y and shit.

Anyway. *Focus, Steve.*

I stop in the entrance to the lounge. It's small and almost always deserted, the perfect place to write. And that's exactly what Cordelia is doing. She's in the middle of a half-moon-shaped booth covered in maroon leather, obscured by shadows except for the blue light of her laptop screen illuminating her face, furiously typing away.

I take a moment to feel jealous at how easily her fingertips float across the keyboard. I haven't had a writing session like that in many months. Hmm. Now that I think about it, it's been a year. Wow. What the hell have I been doing for the last year? Pac-Man and darts? Wallowing in my own self-pity over my disastrous failure as a science fiction writer? Sitting on my laurels?

Yes, yes, and yes.

Changes are coming. That's for sure. And those changes start with my personal life, i.e. Cordelia Sarantopoulos.

I put on the brave face—doing my best to forget about how she dismissed me earlier—and stride over to her booth. I pause at the edge of her table.

She does not look up. She's so caught up in her writing, she doesn't even notice me.

I clear my throat. "Hello, Cordelia. Fancy meeting you here."

She looks up, startled, her wide eyes searching out mine. And then she… frowns. Her brows knit together in… what is that? Menace? It's menace.

Why does she hate me? What did I do?

"Oh. It's you."

I force a smile. "It's me. Um. So. Can I sit?" She's gonna say no. It's written all over her face. "I promise, it's just for a moment. I will leave you to your writing. I just…" I don't wait for her to grant me permission, I simply slip into the booth. Sliding towards her, but still keeping an appropriate amount of distance between us. "I don't know why you're mad—"

"I'm not mad."

"Cordelia. You're not even looking at me. We had such a great night—"

She slams her laptop closed and leans towards me with squinted eyes.

"Holy shit. Why do you suddenly hate me?"

"Why? *Why*? I'll tell you why!" She pauses here to take a breath, then quickly surveys the lounge, like she wants to make sure no one will overhear this conversation. Satisfied that we're pretty much alone, aside from Lloyd the bartender, she whispers, "I know who you are."

"Oooookay. Steve, though, right? You know I'm Steve. Because that's who I am."

"You know what I'm talking about."

"I really don't."

"You're… *SS*."

I blink at her. "What?"

"Don't deny it."

"Why would you even think that?"

"Because your sister, Essie—clever that, by the way. Essie. SS." She huffs. "My God, the deceit! Essie was getting drunk with Britney last night—"

Oh, shit.

"And she made a little mistake."

"A mistake?"

"A mistake. She kept saying that Leslie Munch, aka Raylen Star, aka the most talented, though bitchy, romance author in the world at one time, accused *you* of plagiarism. Accused *you* of stealing."

"OK. But… I did tell you that in the little banner alleyway yesterday, remember?"

"No. That's not what I mean. Essie said she accused Steve. Steve, Steve, *Steve*!"

"Ohhhhhhh."

"Yeah. Ohhhhh. So." Cordelia tilts her chin up and folds her arms. "Deny it. I dare you."

Well, I could deny it. She has no proof. But… I like this woman. I might even be planning a future with her. Which is crazy, but so is maintaining a secret identity as a romance author while still showing up to romance conventions and all the other nonsensical stuff I've done over the last decade just to serve my ego. And so the answer to my private question about when it's appropriate to tell your possible love interest that you are living a lie would be right here and now.

Besides, I'm tired of this. Something has to give. So I just shrug. "OK. Fine. It's me. I'm SS. Steve Smith. I was a science fiction writer, couldn't make it, so I started writing romance on a whim. It was a joke. Kind of. I mean, I don't want you to think I didn't put my heart into it, because I did. But then…" I throw up my hand. "It blew up, Cordelia. And whatever, right? I thought to myself, *It's good money. It's a fluke. It's a little side gig that will fizzle out and that will be that.* But it didn't fizzle out. It just got bigger."

She's looking at me with uncertainty. "What about Essie? Why is she pretending to write these books? It's… it's… a betrayal of trust!"

I sigh. "It is. I can't deny it. But it's not Essie's fault. It was my idea."

"But why would you two do that?"

"Because I really, really, *really* thought it would fizzle. And then… I got invited to a book signing. My first one. You know what that's like. And it was Romance Round-Up. Remember that one? They haven't had it in several years now, but back in the day, when I was brand new at this, it was the biggest. I wanted to go. It was flattering that so many people loved my books. But I was already pretending to be a woman. I was using Essie's pic for my profile. I was…" I let out a long breath. "I mean, honestly, I was embarrassed. I went from writing cool, socially relevant cyberpunk to… non-stop sex scenes. And never, not once in my life, did I ever picture it turning out this way. I was still very, very sure that I would be a great science fiction writer. And one day, seventy-five years from now, a couple—who are thinking about maybe, possibly, dating—would be discussing books and one of them would ask, 'What is your favorite science fiction book?' and the other would reply, '*Alien Alliance*,' because at that time, seventy-five years into the future, it would be a classic. Like *Starship Troopers*."

Cordelia's eyes go a little distant and dreamy. But just as quickly, the distrust is back. "Hmm. You're a wordsmith. And you know what they say about wordsmiths?"

I have no clue, so I just shrug.

"Same thing they say about actors. They're *acting*. That's what they do. Right? It's their job. They are literally paid to pretend."

I point to myself. "You're accusing me of what, exactly? Being too *persuasive*?"

My tone is a little bit rough here. I'm trying not to be annoyed. I feel like maybe I don't have the right, because let's face it, all of this is my fault. But I'm struggling. She's not listening to me.

"What about the stealing?"

I sigh. "What stealing?"

"You stole Leslie's book ideas."

"I did *not.*"

"I don't believe you. I think you did steal her ideas. And that's why you wanted to read my ARC, isn't it?"

OK. Now I'm angry. She has crossed a line. "For fuck's sake, Cordelia. You're accusing me of shit that never happened. Raylen Star was a great author in 2012. Back then, erotica was all new. You could write any story at all and make it on to the charts. But she's a bitch, and a hack, and has almost zero talent at actual storytelling. That's why no one reads her now. She has no imagination. The reason I'm still here"—I point at the hotel in general—"the reason *this* is *my* convention, isn't because I stole some pathetic story idea eight years ago. It's because I'm a damn good romance writer."

Then I slap my hands on the table, get up, and walk out.

MEANWHILE…

Meanwhile...

Hot Lips and Husky Voices is, and has always been, one thing: An opportunity for the authors of the various books which have been turned into audio formats to 'ooh' and 'ahh' over their chosen narrators and thus allow the audience a chance to 'ooh' and 'aah' as well.

The intention of such a panel, of course, is to simply highlight and amplify the various components that go into a multi-pronged approach to being a successful romance author.

Or, at least, that's the intention of everyone on the panel today except ... Raylen Star.

No, Raylen Star's purpose in being here is to steer the conversation in the direction of getting SS to talk as much as possible about *her* narrator. Her brother, Steve. The one known, in a not-so-secretive secret, as Tank Watson.

To be clear: Leslie does not think that she will be forcing some grand reveal or disrupting the fabric of the universe in any way. But she does think she can make life awkward for Steve, and for Essie, and in so doing claw back at least a tiny portion of what she believes has been stolen from her over the years. Her good name. Her reputation. Her success. Her dignity.

And, even though the loss of those attributes is due entirely to the choices Leslie Munch has made for herself, one would be unlucky in attempting to get her to recognize that. For, you see, Leslie Munch's great, tragic flaw is a flaw that plagues many who find themselves in downward spirals from which they cannot break free. Simply: Lack of self-awareness. And, in Leslie's case, a touch of paranoia.

A paranoia that is sure *not* to be ameliorated by what happens next...

"Yes, hi," says a woman in the audience, holding a microphone and addressing the authors seated before her. This question is for Raylen? Raylen, I've noticed that you don't really release audio versions of your work. Why is that?"

Excellent, Leslie thinks. She's been tee'd up perfectly. She leans toward her own mic, a small, venomous grin on her face and begins to speak.

"Well..." But that's all she's able to get out before...

BZZZZZZZZZZZZZZZZ!

Feedback, horrible, eardrum-piercing feedback, the exact opposite of a husky voice, overwhelms the speakers, causing everyone in the room to tense their shoulders and grab at their ears.

"Well… Ha!" The moderator spins. "Looks like we're having some audio trouble with Raylen's mic! That's funny!"

And everyone laughs and laughs. Everyone, that is, except Leslie Munch.

"Can I get another goddamn mic, please?" Leslie asks, strained and barely attempting to mask her frustration.

An eager, friendly PA, runs up, microphone in hand, and offers it to Leslie who grabs it roughly and makes yet another attempt.

"As I was going to say—"

BZZZZZZZZZZZZZZZZZ!

"What the fuck?" Leslie says, loudly. Unfortunately, her voice is muted. By the lack of a working microphone.

"Oh, my," the moderator gasps into her completely fine and totally functional microphone. "That's, uh... Well, that's odd."

And it gets odder as Leslie grabs the microphone positioned in front of SS.

BZZZZZZZZZZZZZZZZZ!

And the one held by the moderator.

BZZZZZZZZZZZZZZZZZ!

Every time Leslie attempts to speak...

BZZZZZZZZZZZZZZZZZ!

And every time a microphone is taken back into someone else's hands, "Huh. That's so strange!" They say without disruption or impediment. And the audience laughs and laughs.

And on and on it goes. Leslie starts to speak. A microphone buzzes. It drops out. It is taken by someone else. It works ... just fine.

To be fair, one might not even need to be a naturally paranoid and suspicious person to wonder if there is dark some calculus at work. But, as noted, Leslie just happens to be.

Finally, after multiple attempts to make her point, to say her piece, to have her moment in the sun, Leslie

Munch gives up and sinks back into her chair, fuming and ready to pop.

And it is at this moment, with all the forces of the universe conspiring against her, that Essie Smith-Scott chooses to lean forward and offer up obliterating insult to already grievous injury. Her perfectly amplified voice crystal clear as she says...

"That's so crazy. Raylen, sorry! We'll get it figured out. But in the meantime..." Leslie glowers at Essie, virtual daggers pelting forth from her very soul. "In the meantime... I actually wanted to share something about *my* narrator that you may or may not be aware of..."

What? Leslie wonders. What the F? Why is Essie talking about *her* narrator?

"So, if you didn't already know, my brother, Steve..."

No. No. She can't be. She couldn't possibly be...

"... Narrates all my audiobooks under the name 'Tank Watson...'"

Whatever Essie says next is lost in a fog of confusion tinged with internalized hysteria as Leslie's mind empties of reason and the world in front of her eyes becomes like a white blanket of nothing. A void. An absolute calama-fuck of emotional molestation.

And no, that's not her being overly dramatic.

Even more maddening than what's being said is... No one seems to care. The reactions appear to range from enthusiastic hoots of approval to somewhat muffled 'oooooohs.' But not a single person seems miffed or appalled that they might have been lied to.

The closest anyone comes to the type of response Leslie had been hoping for when she — she, not Essie! — dropped this little jewel, comes from woman who raises her hand, takes a perfectly operational microphone, and asks, "But, why? Is he embarrassed or something?"

To which Essie responds, "No, no, nothing like that. Steve's just a shy guy at heart and, I think, because ours really is a family business, he'd feel all blush-y if he ran into readers and they knew it was him who was whispering all those naughty things in their ears."

At which, the crowd giggles and laughs, causing Leslie to rumble in a way not seen since Mount Vesuvius in the moments just prior to the destruction of Pompeii.

"So, y'know," Essie continues, "if you see him today ... don't tell him I told you."

And then she winks. Causing Leslie Munch to very nearly have a stroke.

CHAPTER FOURTEEN – CORDELIA

As Steve slaps his hands on the table and leaves, I have the immediate impulse to call out after him—to say, "No, come back"—but I don't. I feel like a crazy person. I am wildly overstimulated in every way imaginable. I haven't left my little pool house in almost three months as I worked on *Filling the Gap*. The only people I've interacted with have been Britney, Sheila, and the occasional food or grocery delivery person, as I've had my head down, trying to make something beautiful for the world to read.

And, this morning, just a little while ago, Britney came crashing into me, shot out of a starter pistol, and I feel like I osmosed all that energy and carried it with me into the panel.

The panel where I came to learn that I might not know what the hell I'm doing. Like, at all.

This thing I love, this thing I have committed my future and my hopes for success and stability to… I might not be meant for it. I may not be cut out to be a romance writer. And I am learning this… at a romance convention.

I think I may throw up.

So, I went from being a virtual hermit for the last several months to showing up in Las Vegas, meeting a guy who kind of swept me off my feet, put me in a bathtub with rose petals, slapped my labia around, and then I woke up to find out that he is, in fact, the biggest romance author in the world and also possibly a plagiarist and definitely a liar all while at the same time discovering that I may be a talentless hack in the midst of dodging a bunch of violently thrown conference room chairs… all in the last thirty-six hours.

I should maybe at least cut myself a break for feeling like a lunatic.

"Anything else, ma'am?" a nice server asks as he shows up out of virtually nowhere and I jump.

"Huh? What? Oh. No. Thank you. Or, yes, actually, could I get another Red Bull?"

I've already had two, but I don't care. Vegas Cordelia is a wild child!

Goddammit. Why am I the way I am? I mean, I have an answer. A lifetime of microaggressions coupled with a particular form of dopamine surge in my yadda, yadda. I know. I get it in the broadest sense. But precisely because I know, shouldn't I be able to control it? Wrestle my tendencies to the ground?

No. That's not how it works.

You don't get to be a thing just because you want it. Wanting it doesn't make it so.

Steve just said he wanted to be a sci-fi writer and it didn't work out. But he's a damn, *damn* good romance writer. Shouldn't that be a convertible skill? If it was easy to will yourself into a new state of being, shouldn't someone with that talent be able to convert it over?

No. Because, as noted, wanting doesn't make it so.

Becoming something else, something you want to be, requires hard work and dedication and intense focus. And, sometimes, even then it doesn't work out. Because some people just aren't destined for the thing they crave. The thing they want.

Not everyone is supposed to be a world-class romance writer. Or an easy-going, cool chick with long legs and an effortless smile. Or happy. Or in love. Or whatever.

Just a random list of things that may or may not have anything to do with me.

Steve lied to me. He lied to everyone. If someone can lie that easily for that long, doesn't it make one the kind of person about whom one should remain suspicious? Of course it does.

On the other hand…

I've been a complete weirdo and nutcase since I met the guy. (And probably long before that, but I can't tackle my whole bag of cuckoo all at once right now.) He just took off out of here with righteous indignance—I know righteous indignance when I see it—because he was making an attempt to connect and tell the truth to me and all that jazz, and I obviously hurt his feelings. Which, if I'm being brutally honest with myself about, I was kind of trying to do.

I was pushing his boundaries. I was testing how far his bow would bend before it broke. Why? I dunno. Because I'm a psycho?

Do I *really* believe he stole a bunch of stuff from Raylen Star back in the whenever ago? No. I've read Raylen Star. And I've read SS. And there's no flippin' way the mind that created Master Choke borrowed anything from Leslie Munch's imagination, such as it is.

And I do not, under any circumstances, think that Steve Smith (SS! It's been right in front of me the whole time! Although the Essie derivation is also obviously plausible, so I don't know if I should be too hard on myself. I'm no Hercules Parrot.) read my ARC to try to steal from me. I'm not *that* naïve.

No. I threw all that stuff at him because… I'm freaked out about other things. I'm freaked out about how it felt to be with him. I'm freaked out because I let myself come unwound and be free and say things like 'choke me harder.' I'm freaked out because I didn't recognize myself last night and even though it felt amazing… I'm not sure that's what I want.

To feel amazing.

I'm not sure I deserve it.

"Here you go, ma'am," the server says, bringing me my next Red Bull.

"Thanks."

But I can't think about all this right now. I just can't. I can't get distracted by Steve or this whole SS thing or any of that. I'm here on a mission. Doesn't matter how I got here or what's happened to my personal life (or not, still unclear)… I came here with a very clear set of goals. And the panel opened my eyes. I've been resistant to it for whatever reason, unwilling to see what I need to do to get the things I want. But I've got it now. And I have to keep my head in the game. I have to figure out if this is what I'm supposed to be doing or not. I have to know if I've wasted my time and energy pursuing a dream that's not mine to claim or if I can *really* do this thing.

"Excuse me?" I call after the server. "Put this on my room, please?"

I have work to do.

MEANWHILE…

Meanwhile…

Hot Lips and Husky Voices has ended and everyone has filed out of the room, off to more panels. More convention frivolity.

Well, almost everyone.

Leslie Munch sits in her chair, staring blankly at the slowly disappearing blanket of white that has been clouding her vision, watching the world finally come back into view, and wondering over what witchery this is that is being used against her. It can't be a coincidence that Essie Smith-Scott chose to say the very thing that Leslie had intended to, which would have exposed the Smith siblings as the lying frauds they are. That, into her perfectly clear and un-buzzy microphone, Essie was the one who outed Steve Smith as Tank Watson.

But. What's really stumping her... Is that no one seemed to give a fat baby's ass.

So, now she has to come up with a new plan. Which is what she's working on at present, ruminating over the ways that she might be able to rain down hellfire upon the Godforsaken assholes known as the Smith twins for what has been perpetrated upon her. For, in the world of Leslie Munch, there is no greater feeling than schadenfreude.

"Ms. Star?" Leslie shakes the cobwebs away to see a nice, bookish, bespectacled girl in her twenties, approaching. The girl says, politely, "I'm sorry, but we need to set up for the next panel now. Do you mind if I ask you to—?"

"Oh, go fuck yourself," Leslie interrupts, appreciably less politely, before scooping up her shoulder bag and sweeping from the room.

And, as she slams her way through the door, she bumps—quite literally—into two kindred spirits. Kindred *and* familiar. Because what she has known all along that she would need for this weekend... Are allies. Confederates. Compatriots. Equally oriented malcontents whose very purpose on this Earth is to 'gin up consternation,' as the elder of the two might say.

Babydoll Tee—aka Angela—and Ride-or-Die Grandma—aka Elaine—are waiting for Leslie right outside the door, in the exact prearranged spot where they agreed to meet after the first set of panels were over.

"Well?" Leslie's mood has gotten considerably worse in the mere seconds since she left Hot Lips and Husky Voices, so she is snapping. Possibly even threatening to bite. "Did you cause a riot? I don't hear sirens, Elaine. You promised me sirens."

"It was going really well," Angela says.

"*Was* going?" Leslie is baring her teeth and growling.

"There were chairs flying everywhere," Elaine says.

"All the authors fled like pussies," Angela adds. "And Steve too."

Leslie smiles. This is glorious. "How many injuries? Was the ambulance called?"

Both of the women, who are on opposite ends of the age spectrum, glance at each other nervously. They love Raylen Star. *Love* her. Leslie Munch… not so much. Leslie terrifies them. But they have been in her reader group on socials for nearly a decade. They are in too deep. Have seen too much. *Know* too much for Leslie to just let them walk away unscathed now.

Elaine decides to be the grown-up, since Angela is four decades her junior. "Listen, Leslie. There were no injuries."

Leslie clenches her jaw. "You just told me chairs were thrown. How in the hell did everyone in that over-packed, fire-hazard room escape injury?"

"It was like…" Angela rolls her eyes up, like she's thinking. Then she looks back at Leslie. "Divine intervention."

"Divine *what*?" Leslie's in the mood to punch a wall.

"Every time a chair was thrown, there was someone there, grabbing it right out of the air and gently placing it back down on the floor."

"Someone?" Leslie raises an eyebrow. "Someone like who?"

"Mostly they were… maids?" Angela says, shrugging with her hands.

"What?" Maybe Leslie would forgo the wall and punch Angela instead.

"Maids," Elaine agrees. "Yeah. Hotel maids. There were like two dozen of them in the room."

"Why were there two dozen hotel maids in the Reader Rants panel?"

Angela shrugs again. "The water and coffee table? I dunno. But they were incredible. The chairs were being hurled, just one chair after another, and then… maids. Everywhere. It was weird."

Elaine agrees. "Yeah. Like angels from heaven. They just scooped up those chairs and set them back down."

"Well, and then Steve came back," Angela says.

This is too much for Leslie. She's about to have a meltdown. "He came back? Why?"

"To check on everyone," Elaine says.

"Then he did a panel all by himself," Angela says.

"He *what*?" Leslie is so hot with anger, sweat is dripping down between her boobs in a little stream.

"But you know what else he did?" Angela leans in towards Leslie, because this was the lede she and Elaine had agreed to bury. They'd planned to set Leslie off, then cool her back down with the amazing revelation about Steve's fuck-up. Maybe they were kinda dumb for getting involved with her in the first place, but they are not stupid. They know how to push her buttons.

Leslie Munch hates Steve Smith. She has been ranting about him being the pen behind the fake face of Essie Smith for almost two years now. And while pretty much everyone in Raylen's reader group thought she was a paranoid schizoid and this theory was bullshit, both Angela and Elaine did have to concede that Steve kind of, sort of, *had* acted like he was the one writing those books in the panel today.

Which is what they share with Leslie. Or, to them, Raylen.

And by the time they are dismissed, Leslie's burning rage is in check and is now laser-focused toward the bullseye that is Steve.

She goes to the bar by the slots, claims the center living-room configuration, and orders herself a celebratory drink. Then she waits.

This is her chance. There had to have been hundreds of people in that Reader Rants panel. And that means hundreds of witnesses. Leslie is smiling with glee.

They would've seen him. Heard him. So when she outs him *this time*, in the Pen Names and Page Games panel later this afternoon, some of them will be *there*. They might even gasp.

Giving voice to a not-so-secret secret like Steve being "Tank Watson" (what a stupid fucking name) will have been *nothing* compared to the bomb she can drop now.

Leslie starts uncontrollably giggling. And before long she's cackling.

She does that for three more hours, drinking, and laughing, and eating. Biding her time as she watches the minutes tick off on her phone.

♥♡♥♡♥♡♥♡♥♡♥

At five minutes to three, she downs her final drink, stands up, straightens her skirt, and walks to the panel room.

When she enters, she stops, looks around, goes back out to read the little sign next to the door. Yep, this is the place. Pen Names and Page Games. She goes back in and becomes confused.

The room is empty.

Well, not completely empty. There is a single maid vacuuming, doing a little dance to the music in her earbuds, ignoring Leslie completely.

"Excuse me." Leslie is trying her best to be patient, but she's fuming again. That little bitch. Essie changed the room on her. And of course she did. Essie wanted Leslie to walk in late and look the fool.

The maid is ignoring her. Or—even Leslie gets a good idea every now and then—couldn't hear her. The earbuds. So Leslie walks right over to her, pulls the earbuds out, and demands to know where everyone is.

The maid squints at her. "¿Qué?"

"Oh, that's great. That's just great. You don't understand me?"

"¿Qué?"

"Where"—Leslie talks slow and loud, because everyone knows that if people don't speak English, if you just talk slow and loud, and they understand you anyway—"is. Every. One?"

The maid shrugs. "Cancelado."

"Cancelado!" Even monolingual Leslie is able to figure this one out. "Cancelado! You can't cancelado my panel!"

The maid shrugs again, puts her earbuds back in, and continues her dance, ignoring Leslie until she leaves.

Then the maid snickers, shaking her head, and mutters, "Leslie Munch is a bitch."

And so now Leslie is heading… well, she's not sure. She'd been invited to the convention last-minute, so she doesn't have a private party planned. But how hard can it be to find them? Surely fans will give up room numbers. She will visit all of them. And she will out Steve to every single crowd. She bulldozes her way towards the main signing hall where there should be some lingering fans for her to confront.

But when she gets there, there is no one.

No one. Not a single person hanging about outside the signing hall.

Just another maid vacuuming with earbuds in.

Something is going on here. It's Essie and Steve. They are trying to make her look like a fool. But that's just fine. Just fine.

Leslie will find those parties herself.

Just as she approaches the bank of elevators, one of them opens for her. This makes her smile, like fate is finally on her side.

She gets in the elevator and punches the floor for the main lobby. She will start there.

The doors close, she leans back against the mirrored walls, sighing and smiling. Because she is finally gonna get her say and knock those two frauds down two dozen pegs.

But then she notices that the elevator isn't moving.

Has she forgotten to press the button?

No. It's lit up.

She presses it again. Nothing. And again. Still nothing. Then she presses the 'door open' button. Nothing.

"Oh, you've got to be fucking kidding me!" She opens the panel where the phone is, only to find it disconnected. "What the hell?" She presses the emergency button. Nothing happens. "Hello? Can anyone hear me?"

But she hasn't moved. She's still on the lower level where the signing hall is. The abandoned signing hall.

"Hello!" She screams it over and over again.

But no one comes.

CHAPTER FIFTEEN – CORDELIA

***"I've never seen a** pussy get so wet," says Trance, shoving his face in between my legs even further and biting at my clit like a rabid wildebeest.*

"I'll show you wet, motherfucker!" I scream as I tighten my thighs around his head, clamping him in place with my vise-like gash, and force all of the sticky, undulating, rolling river of cum and squirt I have inside of me all over his face and bathe him in the forbidden and unholy secretions of my womanliness as he gurgles it down, suffocating in the raging sea of me that I force him to drink as though he has been lost in the desert for a thousand days and the cooling, restorative nectar of my pussy juice is the only thing that might ever quench his ceaseless thirst. "Yeah! Take it all," I bellow.

And he does, every last drop, before pushing his way free of my triangle of passion, pulling back so that I can see his saturated visage staring at me in wonder, and flipping me over onto my stomach without ceremony so that he can enter me from behind.

And, as he thrusts himself violently into me, I feel not only him but the seed he is planting inside my fertile garden as the wedding veil I'm still wearing covers my vision and allows me to peer through its diaphanous filter at a future that will surely be only and ever this. Joy and happiness and passion and want and satisfaction and fulfillment coupled with filth and urgency and a soupçon of spanking. And we will name our child… Eterna. For eternal is what we are.

"I fucking love you, Mrs. Trance Hammersmith!" Trance shouts as he pounds his thick, meaty cock into me from behind.

And, for the first time, I don't care who fucking hears.

THE END

I fall back in the desk chair in my suite, probably (but not quite) as spent as Trance and Chantilly, and stare at the computer screen.

Thirty thousand words. A proper novella. Or a really healthy short story. Five hours—one hundred words a minute—of what I believe is the perfect romance.

Or… not what *I* believe necessarily. But what I now know people want. A bestseller. It has to be. It must be. It must.

Pacing. I need to pace. I always feel better when I'm pacing.

I pop open my—one, two, three, four, five, six—seventh Red Bull and walk the suite, thinking. I wonder if there's an all-night printer in town. There has to be. It's fuckin' Vegas, baby! I'll pull some stock art for a cover, print a bunch of copies of this mamma jamma up, and hand them out tomorrow instead of *Filling the Gap*. Yessir! That's what I'll do! I'll be the buzz of the whole convention!

"Did you hear what Cynthia Lear did?"

"No. What?"

"She wrote a novella in one afternoon."

"A whole novella?"

"Or a really healthy short story. Whatever. Not the point. The point is… it's amazing. A-MAY-zing! She cracked the code!"

"She cracked the code?"

"She cracked the muthafuckin' code!"

Ha! Take that, Mom!

Knock, knock.

Ah! Who's that? At the door? Is that the door?

"Cord?" Britney's voice. From the other side. Britney's here. Good. I need her to read what I've written. "Cord? Are you in there?"

I down the rest of the Red Bull and scamper to the door, giddy from the contact high that accompanies great achievement. The last time I shared something with Brit, she said, "You can't publish it." Well, let's just see what she has to say about *this* one! Haha!

I open the door and see that she looks worried. She's been giving me a lot of looks lately and all of them seem to be some version of concern or encouragement.

"Are you okay?"

"What? Why? Whaddayou mean?"

"For the second time in twenty-four hours I've been texting and calling and you haven't picked up."

"Oh, yeah, sorry, I had my phone on work mode."

"Work mode?"

"Yes! Because I've been working!" I pop over the desk where my computer and a half-dozen discarded Red Bulls sit about.

"Did you… did you drink all these?" Britney asks. I nod, enthusiastically. "That's… Cord, that's, like, a lot of caffeine." She picks up one of the cans and looks at the ingredients label. "Jesus, Cord. That's like a *lot* of caffeine."

"Yeah, I know. Here, read this." I grab her by the shoulders and plant her in the desk chair.

"Wha—what am I reading?"

"My novella!"

"Novella?"

"Or really healthy short story, whatever. Just read it!"

"Did you write this this morning?"

"Mm-hm," I hum, Cheshire Cat grin on my face. "And I'm going to find a place to get it printed and hand it out tomorrow and it's gonna be fuckin' FYE-UH!" I kind of sing-song 'fire' in a weirdly pitched voice that isn't my own.

"Is this… is this what I sounded like earlier?" Britney's look of concern now blossoms into full-tilt worry. But she doesn't need to worry. She just needs to read what I've written and tell me I'm not crazy and that it's the bomb-diggity.

"Read it, read it," I prompt. Then, suddenly, I taste the inside of my mouth. It tastes like Red Bull and adrenaline, which is a bit of a sour combo. "I'm going to brush my teeth. Start reading. Tell me what you think. K? K." I blow kisses at her and head into the bathroom.

Popping in the other room, I start. "Ah!"

"What is it? What's wrong?" Britney calls from the other room.

"Oh. Nothing. I just saw my reflection and thought I was somebody else for a moment. Read!"

There are a ton of mirrors in here and it caught me off guard. I kind of didn't recognize myself. Which I don't mean metaphorically, I mean I really thought I was a creeper. Creeping up and being a creep.

Stepping to the sink and turning on the tap, I pull my toothbrush out of the clear glass tumbler where I placed it and I turn it on. It's electric, but not one of the big, old, cumbersome electric toothbrushes with the huge dock and all the awkwardness. It's a new one that runs on a battery and is pretty much self-contained just like an old-fashioned, everyday toothbrush that you'd get at the drugstore, but that vibrates and promises to give your teeth an extra level of cleanliness.

The feeling of it vibrating in my hand makes me wonder how it would feel if I shoved it in my pussy.

What? What the fuck was *that*?

That is not the kind of thing I normally think.

Did… did the sexy hotness I just spent all afternoon writing do something to my brain? Did it open some closed quarters inside my mind where shoving a toothbrush inside oneself seems like a normal thing to think?

Regardless, it's a good idea. Maybe that's what I'll write my next book about. A hot dentist and his dental technician and all the freaky-ass dentifrice-slathered boom-boom they have!

"Dr. Leatherwood, that's not what the mold is supposed to be used for."

"Don't worry, Cardigan"—I've always wanted to name a character Cardigan—*"I know the distributor. I can get more."*

Or whatever. Rough idea. I'll work out the dialogue later.

As I get the bristles all pasted up so I can shove the stick into my mouth and get everything all good and frothy (I wonder if this is how I'll think all the time now?), I catch a better look at myself in the mirror. And I pause.

I put the toothbrush down and lean forward, really examining my face.

And I think… I like it.

That's not something I normally think about myself, but I think it now.

Somewhat slowly, I pull my eyeglasses away from my face and set them on the basin next to the sink. I take the toothbrush out of my mouth and place it down as well. I spit. I wipe my mouth. And stare.

And still… I like what I see.

It's not some magic moment, like in a nineties teen rom-com where the nerdy girl takes off her glasses only to realize she's been the hot girl all along. It's neither as obvious nor as lazy as that. (I actually think my parents did an uncredited rewrite on one of those once.) It's more… internal.

Nothing about me has changed, materially. My eyes are my eyes. My lips are my lips. My chin is my chin. And on and on and on. But inside, behind the eyes I see staring back, is something I don't immediately judge as unworthy.

Huh.

I wonder what that's about.

And then, suddenly, I see Britney appear, reflected behind me in the mirror.

"Hey. Are you… You didn't read it already, did you? I mean, I know it's not that long, but still…"

She walks over to me, puts her hands on my shoulders (I'm realizing that she also touches my shoulders a lot lately), stares at our shared reflection, and says, "I think maybe the last day or so has been a bit too much for you."

I pick up my glasses, slip them back onto my face, and avoid looking into the mirror anymore.

CHAPTER SIXTEEN – STEVE

I'm sitting in my personal conference room. I never understood why anyone would need a conference room inside an Aria guest suite. I mean, it's good for roleplaying an office erotica, something Master Choke might be into, but Vegas is really not the place to have serious wheels and deals.

Still, it's there. And I'm on a conference call. It feels appropriate to have this meeting in the conference room.

"Can you hear me now?" I tap my laptop screen because what else can you do? It's a fuckin' Boom call.

"I can't hear you." This is Terry. "It's just lips moving, dude. Check your audio."

"It's not my audio, Terry."

He's squinting at me. "What? I can't hear you."

"Be right back," Shawn says. "I gotta get Dawn some coffee."

"What?" I say. "Bro! I'm having a crisis here! She can get her own coffee!"

Shawn pauses mid-air, his ass halfway out of the chair. "Maybe you don't live inside an actual romance novel, Steve, but I do. And when my wife wants coffee, I get her some coffee. I'll be right back."

"Ohhh!" Terry yells. "Fuck, my bad. I didn't have my buds in." I look at his little screen-in-screen just in time to catch him shoving ear buds into his ears. "Can you hear me now?"

"I could always hear you."

"Oh! I can hear you! Funny how earbuds are so necessary." He leans back in his chair, chuckling.

I'm distracted by his virtual background, which is the promotional poster for his upcoming three-seasons-guaranteed streaming deal. I sigh. It looks so fuckin' cool.

"OK," Terry says. "What's the problem now? You've got too many ladies? You have too much money in the bank? Oh!" he exclaims again. "Right, right, right. The girl. Romance-novel gold, right? Seriously, though. How'd it go?"

"I only want to explain it once, so we gotta wait for Shawn and Luke."

"Fine with me. While we're waiting, let's talk about my plot issues. I want feedback on the outline I need to turn in for that new five-book deal I just signed. I have one character who just doesn't want to do what I tell him. Do you think—"

But just as he says that, the Boom moderator panel dings. "There he is." I let Luke into the virtual room. His camera is on, but the audio's not working because he hasn't accepted it yet. Which might be for the best because there is a whole crowd of people in the background of his Venice Beach house.

He's not even paying attention to us. He's talking to a group of beautiful people using big hand gestures. Then they're all laughing.

"Shit, what's going on at Luke's?" Terry is leaning in towards his screen like he needs to get a better look. "Oh, hey!" He laughs. "That's my entertainment lawyer!" He starts waving at the screen. "Hello, Baker!"

"He can't hear you."

Terry frowns at me. "Dude. Why are you in such a bad mood?"

"OK, OK, OK." Luke's audio is working now. But he's not talking to us. He's talking to the lawyer. "I'll sign the new contract. Fine, fine! You talked me into it!" He looks at us, via his laptop camera. "Ten million is a good deal for one script, right, Terry?"

Terry points at him. "Seal that shit up, bro."

I sigh, then run my fingertips over my brows. My head hurts.

"OK, I'm back." Shawn slides back into his chair. "My lovely wife is so lovely. It's date weekend. Hot air balloon trip over to the private airstrip and then a surprise overnight flight to Maui. Put that in your romance book, Steve."

How did I get here? This is the major plotline of the thoughts running through my head. How is it that all three of my best friends seem to be living my dream life simultaneously while I'm being accused of plagiarism by my current love interest?

"All right," Luke says. "I'm here. I'm present. How can I help?"

"Steve is having lady issues," Terry says.

"That's so funny, right?" Shawn is laughing. "So ironic. I mean, the number one romance writer in the world can't find love?" He points at the camera. "Write that shit down, Steve. Your life is a novel."

"Live it like it's fiction." All of them say this at the same time.

I sigh again. "I get it. OK. It's ironic. But you guys, this is serious."

I then proceed to tell them what happened. Including the part where Britney and Cordelia figured out who I really am.

"I think this is good," Luke says. "Dude, you just need to come out of your shell."

"I'm not in a shell, Luke. This really isn't about the whole SS thing. It's about how she *sees* me. How can she, the lovely Cordelia, see me as a total cheater?"

"Well," Shawn says, "you did lie."

"I did. But Leslie Munch? I mean…" There's really nothing to say to that. Even the guys snicker.

"Leslie Munch is a hack. No one in their right mind thinks you stole her story ideas," Luke says.

"You just need to ignore her," Terry says.

"It's not about Leslie. Like, how many times do I have to say this? It's Cordelia's perception. It's all fucked up, you guys. Shawn, since you're the self-proclaimed romance expert"—this makes him laugh—"tell me. How do I convince her that I'm not stealing from Leslie Munch?"

"Oooh!" Terry raises his hand. "Write her a poem. Spill your talent out with your guts."

"Nah," Luke says. "You should just kidnap her and blow her mind on a Master Choke blindfold dream date. In fact"—he points at his laptop camera—"Shawn, give the Ro-Bro your dream date."

"What?" Shawn guffaws. "No way. I'm not giving Steve my cool date ideas."

"I don't want your date night, Shawn," I say. "I'm at the fucking convention, Luke. I can't just illegally sweep her off her feet and make her miss the signing."

"I got it," Terry says. "Kidnap Leslie Munch and send her up in a hot air balloon instead."

"Oh, my God. It's not about *Leslie*!" Why do I even call these guys? They're no help at all. "That's just… dumb."

Terry shrugs and looks away from the camera, a little dejected. "It's a great idea." Then he looks back, excited again. "Oh! You could send one of those skywriter people over the convention, take Cordelia outside, and point up. Make it say—"

"Make it say 'I love you!'" Shawn says.

"No, make it say 'I'm hot for you, Cordelia,'" Luke says.

"Oh! I know!" Terry's got another idea. "You could write a book about her. Oh, my God, dude!" He laughing now. "You could write a book—" He presses both his palms at the camera. "Just hear me out, OK? You could write a rom-com and make you and her the main characters!"

"Yes!" Shawn explains. "In fact, if you don't do that for this woman, I'm gonna do it for Dawn. Thanks for the idea, Terry."

Terry puts his hand over his heart. "Bro, it is my pleasure. I am nothing if not a fountain of ideas."

"Shawn!" Luke exclaims. "You can't just take the idea. Steve gets to reject it first. What you say, Steve? Are you gonna claim this one? Or can Shawn have it?"

"This is supposed to be an emergency meeting about *me*." I point to myself. "How are we even discussing Shawn writing Dawn into a romance novel? It's *my* genre. If he wants to write Dawn into a book, he needs to stick to time travel. That's his thing! You don't see me writing time-travel romance, do you?"

"Is that a thing?" Luke asks.

"Oooh!" Terry is back. "Dude. You should *totally* write a time-travel romance. One where you go back in time and make Leslie Munch never be born."

Luke claps his hands. "I like it. Do it. Are we good here? I gotta run. I'll see you guys for sprints on Monday. Nine a.m. Pacific." Then he points to the camera and winks, just as his face disappears.

"I gotta go too," Shawn says. "It's almost time for the balloon ride. I'm gonna miss the Monday sprint, Terry. But I'll be in on Tuesday."

"Cool, dude. Have a great weekend."

Shawn waves, then his face disappears too.

Then it's just me and Terry. I sigh, feeling like a failure, and liar, and a cheat. Not to mention left out. "I didn't know you guys were doing sprints again."

'Sprints' is what authors call a conference call—much like this one—where they do short fifteen- or twenty-minute writing bursts. There is a little friendly competition to see how many words each of us can get in that span of time.

We used to do them a while back, back when I was actually writing. But I haven't been invited into the Boom room in almost a year now.

I never really considered the idea that they just… went on without me.

Which means they stopped inviting me. Probably because I wasn't writing, so I always declined, but still. They could've at least *invited* me.

"Yeah, we do them," Terry says. "You want in?"

I let out a long breath. "I do. But I'm not writing anything."

"Au contraire, mon frère. You're writing a rom-com with you and Cordelia as the main characters."

I smile, huffing out a small laugh. "It's a fun idea, but…"

"But what?"

"It's"—I sigh again—"not really my thing."

"That's kind of the point, bro."

"What do you mean?"

"You write choking and ass-slapping. Just like Leslie Munch. But if you write a rom-com—"

"Then I can prove I didn't steal."

"Not only that"—Terry points at me—"you can prove you're a great writer. Because you are, Steve. You're great. I know we don't tell you that enough." He shrugs. "I guess we just kinda figure you know that about yourself. You're like… top of the game, dude. But I'm gonna say it now. You're a great writer. And if you write a rom-com, you're gonna shoot it straight to number one."

"I get what you're saying. And I appreciate it. But… I'm only great at *one kind* of writing. Smut. I'm great at smut. You saw what those sci-fi readers did to my books online. They called me the worst. And that's fine. I've come to terms with it. I write smut. But I don't cheat and I don't steal. I lie a little, but that's only because I'm caught in the web, ya know? I don't know how to get out of it now."

Suddenly, gregarious-never-serious Terry goes stoic and still. When he speaks again, his voice is low and reverent. "You really like this girl, don't you?"

I nod. "I do. I like her so much." I let out a long breath. "And I told her the truth. She's the only one I told. But… it just made things worse."

"Well, the way I see it, you've got two choices. One, try again, dude. Just… try again. Because the only other option is to let her go. And I know that Shawn and Dawn are so gushy and sweet, but you do know they were high-school sweethearts, broke up, spent over a decade apart, and only then got back together a couple years ago, right?"

"What?" I *didn't* know that.

"Yeah. That's why he's so fuckin' in love with her, ya know? He missed out on ten years and he just refuses to miss any more moments."

"Well, that's… disgustingly sweet."

Terry chuckles. "Isn't it? So, you know, how much will you hate yourself in ten years if you don't do everything in your power to win this girl *now?*" He points at the camera. "That's what you need to decide."

❤♡❤♡❤♡❤♡❤♡❤

After Terry and I end the call I just sit there in the conference room of my hotel suite and stare at the reflection in the window of the Vegas lights outside. I should get up, go find Essie and Mike, and mingle.

But what's the point?

Really, why do I even come?

No one wants to see me. No one cares that I'm even here.

But then I remember the panel I did this morning and a feeling of… I dunno—warmth, I guess—washes over me. It felt good to be the author in the room. It felt amazing, actually. I've been living the life of a writer for ten years now. Missing out on all the important moments.

The similarities to Shawn and Dawn's situation isn't missed. I mean, it's different. But the same, too.

I've wasted ten years of my life living a lie. And why?

I don't actually have a reason. In the beginning, it made sense because it was a temporary thing. Just a little side project. And yeah, I'm a dude writing erotic romance. So fine. I was a little embarrassed. Like romance is beneath me.

I'm sure I felt that way. At one time.

But I cannot actually remember feeling that way recently. I'm not embarrassed. I am a good writer. I like my stories. Maybe naming that girl Sugar was over the top, but she was over the top too. It fit her. Perfectly.

Readers made fun of it at first. A few weeks, maybe. But then everyone loved Sugar. She was an awesome character. And even though Choke makes me cringe, he's a Master with a heart of gold.

It's still my bestselling series. All these years later, they still ask for more Choke and Sugar.

I don't know why the sci-fi readers hated my books. It doesn't make much sense.

But it doesn't matter, either. I love those books. I believe in them. I put my real name on them.

In fact, I've got plots for at least two more books. I just never wrote them because I figured there was no point. But you know what?

Maybe *that's* the point. Maybe I'm looking at this the wrong way? Maybe I should write them for me and not anyone else?

Which leads me back to Cordelia, and how she did this exact same thing, and then chickened out and wrote what the market demanded.

She's going to throw that book away. And fine, that's her business, I guess. It's her career. I'm not gonna tell her what to do with it. But I am gonna tell her something else.

I go back into the main living room, flip on the TV and order pay-per-view and room service.

But I don't drown my sorrows and spend the night in a pizza-and-beer-induced fog of self-loathing, either.

I make a choice.

I will win her back.

CHAPTER SEVENTEEN – CORDELIA

DAY FOUR — THE SIGNING

"You're new to me," the young lady who very much looks like a reverse image of me says.

She's wearing almost the exact same outfit that I'm wearing, sort of an Audrey Hepburn cocktail dress that cinches at the waist and flares out in a bell shape at the bottom. Mine has polka dots and is blue. Hers has polka dots and is red.

We both have on glasses, although my frames are more rectangular and hers more round. I'm a brunette. She's a redhead.

The good news is I think it's a super-cute look. The bad news is I think she wears it all better than me and I suddenly feel very self-conscious.

I chose this for today because I wanted to come across as classic but perky. Friendly but sexy. Smart but not too smart. Y'know, charming and like the kind of chick who writes the kinds of books you'd want to read. And now, looking at someone who comes across like they're not *trying* at all and just being who they are, I feel like I might be a giant asshole.

My brain is spinning since, for the second time in a number of weeks, Britney told me that what I wrote is… well, she didn't have a lot of great things to say.

She wasn't rude. Just as she was about *Filling the Gap,* she took pains to make sure I knew that she loves me and that she thinks I'm a good writer, but then she laid it out for me thus…

"That's not you. That's not what you write. That's… well, honey, that's smut."

"But people love smut!"

"Right. Sure. People do."

*"*You *love smut!"*

"Sometimes, yes. But it needs to feel… authentic, sweetheart. And that's… It's not you."

"But I did all the things the readers in the panel said they want."

"I don't care what they said in the panel. Is that what you *want to write?"*

"I… I don't know. I don't know anymore." That's the point at which I kind of broke down and she held me.

"Shhh. Shhh. It's okay. It's okay. This is partially my fault."

"How is it your fault?" I said between sniffles.

"I never should have told you to change your book. It was great just how it was. I was just trying to look out for you."

"I know," I told her as I snotted all over her shirt.

Ugh. I hate snotting on things.

In any case, all that's happened over the last seventy-two hours (!) has me swirling out. But, of course, that's a lie. It's not just the last seventy-two hours. My path to uncertainty within myself started way, way before that. This just feels like an inflection point.

Who am I? What do I love? What do I want?

Very much not the questions I thought I would be asking myself this weekend. The toughest questions I planned to confront were 'do I play red or black?' and 'should I crack open the minibar or is that being frivolous?'

But. Here we are. Speaking of being here…

"Sorry, what?" I ask Redhead Polka Dot Hepburn, who doesn't even seem to notice that we're each other's doppelganger.

"I said, 'But Audrey Saint told me I needed to come over and check you out.'"

"She did?" I ask, a little taken aback. I glance over at Audrey's table. The line to meet her and have her sign books goes almost halfway down the length of the room. They have the floor taped off in a serpentine pattern leading up to her just to accommodate the demand and ensure that her readers don't wind up crowding that section of the hall.

I see James, Audrey's husband, dutifully snapping a photo of Audrey and one of her fans posing together in front of her big, '#1 *NY TIMES* BESTSELLER' banner and then handing the phone back to the giddy attendee. He sees me as well and waves, gives me a thumbs-up. I nod back and then turn my attention back to Not Me.

"That's so nice," I say.

She looks at the copies of all three of my books spread out on the table, the first two Purity Principle books and *Filling the Gap*. "Which of these should I read?" she asks.

"Oh. Well, these two are the first two I wrote and are a series. And this one is a standalone I finished recently. It's an ARC, so it's free if you'd like it."

She picks it up and reads the blurb on the back. She takes a really long time, like she's mulling it over or something, and then, finally, says, "You write a good blurb."

I can feel myself blush. Which is… surprising, I guess, but it feels nice to hear something nice right now. "Thanks," I say.

"I'll check it out."

"Great!" I know I give that 'great' about fifty percent more emphasis than it requires, but I really, really needed the boost. It's been kind of a slow morning so far. Not really a stampede to get to my table. Which is made all the more apparent by the prime placement I have here in the middle of the room, right where everyone can see. I think I may have brought too many books. "You should feel free to grab a couple more, if you like."

"Thanks," she says, looking at the table.

"Would you like a picture with Cynthia?" Britney asks, jumping in eagerly, seizing the moment. I turn to stare at her with a very strong 'please don't' expression. She stares back at me with a 'what, I'm helping' look. I counter with a 'stooooop' face. But it winds up not mattering because the cooler version of Cordelia says, "No, I'm good," then sashays away, dress swinging off her hips as she moves into the rest of the crowd and disappears.

"That was nice," Britney encourages.

"Yeah," I work out before letting my torso rise and fall in a sigh.

"Hey…" Britney starts, but I cut her off because her job is supposed to be 'assistant,' not 'therapist.'

Although I suppose she has been assisting in keeping me from chewing my fingers off of my hands.

"No, no. All good," I say, plastering a smile on my face that I know she can see through, but I don't care. I just want to get through this, get back to LA, and then I can figure out what to do with the rest of my life. Maybe I'll become a Christmas tree farmer. Open a Christmas tree farm. That's a thing people do, right? I love the smell of pine needles, so—

"How's it going?" a distinctly male and distinctly familiar voice says from off to the side.

Both Britney and I turn to see Steve approaching. He's wearing the usual casual cool… everything… that I've come to know over the last couple of days. Untucked button-down, chilled-out khakis, boots that probably cost as much as two months of my rent in Sheila's pool house. (Which I only know because my dad is a big shoe guy. When I was a kid he once said, in his light Greek accent, "You can spend a few bucks on shoes and have them last a year, or you can invest in a pair and have them last a lifetime. Money is never wasted if it's invested in your future happiness, my girl." The fact that he has a closet full of investments kind of belies the point—how many lifetimes does he expect to live?—but it's still okay advice.)

And… he's wearing that face. That Steve Smith face. The one that makes it hard not to look at.

Upon hearing him speak, two women who happen to be scurrying the other direction giggle and say, "Taaaaaaaaaaannnnnnk," all sing-songy and drawn out. Steve rolls his eyes.

"What was that?" Britney asks.

"Apparently, yesterday at her panel, Essie decided to go ahead and confirm to everyone there that I'm Tank Watson."

"Oh. Why?"

"I dunno. Because she's worried that I'm not doing enough to keep busy and she wants to get other authors to book me for… whatever. I don't get it. Candidly, I think she's just edging in the direction of…"

He stops short. Because it's clear that what he wants to say is something like, "… edging in the direction of pulling the curtain back on this whole SS charade."

"Anyway," he finishes, "I just wanted to see how it's been."

"It's been great! Hasn't it been great, Cord?" Britney says. I nod, tightly, putting my smile back on. "Great!" she says a third time. It hangs in the air as Steve stares at me and I try to avoid his eyes. "Right. Well, it's almost lunch. So I think I'll just… Oh, is that Sylvia Montgomery over there? I'm such a fan. I'll… You guys… Okay…" she mumbles as she not-so-smoothly takes her leave.

There is an obligatory awkward moment as Steve and I stand there alone. I glance down to avoid looking directly into his face and my eyeballs land on his hands. His big, strong, chokey hands. And now I don't know where the hell to look.

"Hey," he says, drawing my eyes back to his. "Listen, I—"

"No." I stop him. "No. It's me who should apologize. I've been… I haven't been myself. Or, no, that's not right. I have. I very much have. In fact, I've been myself at about a level twenty. I would say 'eleven,' but that's a cliché and I want to sound clever. Also, most people don't even think about why we say 'eleven' and unless you really grasp the etymology of a thing, I don't think you should throw it around willy-nilly. But that's not the point.

"The point is that I think I may have… No, I did overreact. I've been overreacting a lot lately. But it's because I care. Like, I really, really *care* about this thing that I'm doing. And, also, not that this necessarily matters, but… it's been a while since I've been with a guy. I mean, obviously we were just together. I was with you. And you're a guy. But I mean before that. I'm sure that has something to do with it? And I haven't left my house a lot in the last few months and there's just so much stimulus here that…

"Anyway. So, no need to apologize. It's not a huge deal and, obviously, you don't get to the level of success you… or SS… whatever… has had—have had?—that has been had by you all without being really, really good. And you don't steal talent. You can't steal ability. Or skill. You either have it or you don't, and then you tend it and cultivate it and you work hard to maintain it and that's clearly what you've done. And you've been so nice to me and got me a room here and you read my book in one sitting and… and I guess I don't think you did all that just to steal from me or get into my pants or up my skirt or wherever. I think you probably did it because you're a nice person, like your sister says, and you were doing a nice thing, and I appreciate it. And if I've been kind of a crazy bitch, I'm sorry."

I'm not sure I took a breath during that whole monologue because I feel myself struggling to catch it now.

Steve just stares at me, taking me in, nodding ever so slightly. Then he says, "I was just going to ask if you wanted to grab lunch."

"… What?"

"I kind of figured we both just got a little emotional. I wasn't really going to apologize, per se, just see if you'd let me buy you lunch."

"Oh." I bite at my thumbnail before pulling my hand out of my mouth and rubbing my thumb with my other hand. "Oh. Um. Sure. Let me just… Sure."

I grab up my bag and approach Steve, standing right in front of him, looking up at his annoyingly and wonderfully handsome, sincere face.

"*Spinal Tap*," he says.

"What?"

"That's where 'eleven' comes from. The movie. *This Is Spinal Tap*. 'These go to eleven.'"

"Yeah," I say in response, unable to keep a smile from creeping in. "It is."

♥♡♥♡♥♡♥♡♥♡♥

The 'about' section on the back of the menu for Bardot Brasserie, which is tucked away inside the Aria Hotel and Casino, reads, 'Every detail of Bardot Brasserie was designed to transport guests to a café along the Champs-Élysées in the 1920s.' And they've really pulled it off, I have to be honest. Having not been alive in the 1920s to visit a café along the Champs-Élysées at that time, I can really only speculate, but based on pictures I've seen, they've nailed it.

Wooden walls and amber water glasses, all warmly lit by understated chandeliers, and a real sense of attention to detail do make it feel like we've been transported away from Las Vegas and the hustle and bustle of the convention to Paris of another time.

My dress fits right in. Kind of.

"So, look," Steve starts just as the waiter leaves to put in our order. "I lied."

"I mean… I know. I thought we covered that."

"No, not that. About something else."

I feel myself getting hot. "What? About what?"

"Not wanting to apologize. I do want to apologize for something."

"No, really, you don't—"

But he stops me. "I know. But I want to. I want to apologize for getting so heated. That's not how I normally like to roll. And I guess what I realized, is that… shit, this is weird to say, but… I do care about what I write. Wrote. I haven't written anything at all in… doesn't matter. Of course I care. All I've ever wanted to do is tell stories. That's it. From the time I read my first sci-fi when I was a kid—and it wasn't even a good one, it was just some ratty paperback I found in the attic of my grandparents' place that had, like, a cartoon spaceship on the cover and I thought it looked cool—but from that moment I was… I was hooked. I was, honestly, in love. And I determined that that was what I was going to do. That was who I was going to be. A writer. A writer whose work lifts people from their everyday lives and helps them escape for a little while.

"And, y'know, the thing is… I do. That's what I do. It doesn't look exactly how I thought it would, but that's what I do. And when you—whose work I've read and who I do admire a lot—accused me of… I dunno. Put it this way: I don't give a shit what Leslie Munch says or thinks—apart from the fact that I hate paying lawyers for dumb crap—but I care very much what you think. And I suppose it hurt a little to realize you thought I would try to… I wanted you to think I'm a good writer. That's all."

He sips his water.

And I sit, stunned. Because his story of falling in love with words sounds so familiar. Because he's so honest about it. Because he cares what I think. I'm so stunned, in fact, that I can't really find proper words. So, instead I just ask, "You're the reason I got invited to this, aren't you?"

He swallows his water and, as he puts his glass back down on the table, says, "Yeah."

There's a moment where neither of us say anything. We just sit, listening to the bustle of the hotel in the distance and the clink of silverware against the plates of the only other people in the dining room, sitting far on the other side.

"Can I ask you something?" I say after a protracted second.

"Of course."

"Will you read this?" I reach into my bag and pull out my tablet, onto which I have loaded the PDF of the thing I wrote yesterday. At Britney's discouragement, I did not run out and find an all-night printer.

"What's this?" he asks as I hand the tablet over to him.

"A thing I wrote yesterday."

"What kind of thing?"

"A novella."

"A novella?"

"Or a really healthy short story."

He scrolls the screen. "You wrote this?" I nod. "In an afternoon?"

I nod again. "My mom is old-school. She insisted I take speed typing classes when I was in sixth grade. I think she thought it would give me an advantage."

"Jesus," he mutters to himself. "You're sure you didn't just plug some keywords into an AI and let it pump it out?"

"No! I—" I start to declare, but he cuts me off.

"I'm joking. I know we don't know each other that well, but I know you well enough to know you wouldn't do that."

"It freaks me out even thinking about that. That an AI might replace real writers," I say. He shrugs. "It doesn't freak you out?"

"Eh. I'm a sci-fi bro. I'm kind of fascinated. But no, an AI could never do what someone like you does."

"Why? Whaddayou mean?"

"It's lacking a central ingredient."

"What's that?"

And then… he reaches across the table and puts his hand on my chest. Right over my heart. And I feel it flutter. Then he sits back, but my heart continues fluttering.

"You want me to read it?" he asks. I nod. "Now?"

"Yeah, I just… I don't know. My head's a little twisted around and I want to… You're really good. And you know what you're doing. And I just want to know if I'm on the right track."

"Your appetizers, madame et monsieur," the waiter says, placing down my salad and Steve's bowl of French onion soup and then floating away.

"You're sure?" Steve asks. "Right here. Now. In front of you."

"I… think so?" I say, nibbling at a lettuce leaf.

"Okay," Steve says, taking up a spoonful of his cheesy, gooey soup and scrolling back to the first page.

"And be honest," I insist. "I really want to hear what you think."

"You got it," he says. And I watch him scan the words, his face now lit by the ghostly white of the tablet screen.

❤♡❤♡❤♡❤♡❤♡❤

I don't say anything the entire time, just let him read. Which he does even faster than I write. It's nearly time to go back into the signing and he looks like he's almost done. I don't remember the last time I just sat and ate a meal without talking or other distractions. It's kind of nice just to be quiet. I feel bad that Steve didn't really touch his chicken though. Mine was delici—

Oh. He's done.

I gulp. Not with a sound like a cartoon character or anything, but I do, indeed, gulp.

He taps the screen dark, hands the tablet back to me, and when he does… he takes hold of both of my hands as I receive it from him. He smiles, looks me in the eyes—I feel my heart flutter again—and then he says…

"Let's talk."

Ohhhhhhhhhh, fuck.

CHAPTER EIGHTEEN – STEVE

I feel like the Devil stole Cordelia's lovely soul right under my nose. Like her innocence has been lost and… and… and was she watching some really bad porn last night, or what? Because this is really bad porn. I'm talking Seventies moustache porn. Hairy legs, and armpits, and l… yeah. Lots of hair *there* kind of porn.

"First of all"—I raise a finger—"your sentences were beautiful."

She makes a crooked smile at me. "Um. Thanks?"

"Your sentences are always beautiful."

She lets out a breath and grabs her fork, pounding the end of it on the table. "OK, look. Just rip the Band-Aid off. You hated it, right?"

"I mean…" I shrug with my hands. "In the appropriate situation… I could learn to love it."

That crooked smile turns into a whole face of WTF and she flips the fork over in her palm like she's about to use it as a weapon. "Learn to love it?"

"Yeah. Like… for instance"—I smile at her—"should we ever find ourselves in bed at night. Together. Under the covers. Perhaps in ten years?"

"What?"

"We've been together ten years, we've had sex every way you can think of, and maybe… things are little predictable? Hmm? Get my meaning?"

"No."

"Your story"—I point to the tablet—"would be the perfect spice for us to bond over later in life."

She pounds the fork, tines down, into the table. "So you hated it."

"I didn't hate it. I'm trying to explain to you that if one's goal is to excite one's partner under the covers, this could be the ticket."

"OK. Is that a bad thing?"

Now it's my turn to shoot her a WTF face. "Cordelia. This is trash. Smut. Porn."

"But… it's hot, right?"

"It can be. That's what I'm saying. If your goal is to get men in prison off, you get an A-plus-plus-plus. If your goal was to write something romantic… this is a spectacular fail."

"But it's what the fans said they wanted!"

"Fans don't know what they want."

"How can you say that? You saw them yesterday in Reader Rants! They knew exactly what they wanted."

"No. They were spouting off tropes and technicals. And that's not what they like. What they like is great characterization and world-building. They just don't have the vocabulary to express it because they're readers, not writers. So they think they love the wedding and the baby—"

"They do!"

"They do, but only at the appropriate time. No one wants the wedding and the baby after book one in a series because that couple is now *over*. They know this! In romance, the wedding is the end. You have to be pretty clever to keep a couple going after the marriage and baby. It's typically just a happily-ever-after book where you get a little peek into the future, which is super-satisfying, but again, after that, you gotta start over again with the grown-up kids. Because the wedding is the end. Weren't you listening in the panel when I…"

But I stop. Because she wasn't there. It was just me and the readers at that point.

I reach over and take her hand. "You write good books. You don't need"—I point to the tablet—"this."

"Then why can't I seem to break through the ceiling? What am I doing wrong?"

"What are you talking about? You're not doing anything wrong. Your stories are great. I love them."

"Then why don't the readers love my books the way they love yours?"

I shrug. "I have more of them."

"So I should just write more? How is that the answer?"

"It's not *just* 'write more.' It's… 'build a family of characters in a world the readers never want to leave and *then* write more.' I'm telling you—the secret is great characterization and world-building."

She pulls her hand away from mine and leans back into the booth. "I thought I did that."

"You did. You absolutely did. But you wrote a standalone. And an unfinished series. You haven't given your readers time to fall in love with your characters and world."

"The unfinished series then, that's my problem?"

"That's only part of it. Because it implies that you just need more books. But again, if you just write more books that's not gonna get you there. You have to deepen your characterization, make your world a little bit bigger, up the tension and conflict so it leads to a nail-biting crisis, and resolve it with an ending that is surprising yet inevitable. Then calm everything down with a perfect, sweet, romantic happily ever after which may or may not include a wedding and a baby."

She smiles as she huffs. "Is that all?"

"That's all."

"You make it sound so easy, but it's not."

"It's really not," I agree. "It just looks easy because… well, despite the fact that I named that girl Sugar, I'm kind of good at it."

This makes her chuckle. "I really hated that name. But—" She looks up at me with those melty brown eyes of hers. "But I really love Sugar. She's feisty. And even though Choke goes all alpha-asshole on her, she only gives in just enough. She defies him quietly." Cordelia sighs. "I really like that about her."

"Yeah. I think everyone likes that about her. After book six, after I got the movie deal, there were a slew of Sugar lookalikes in the romance world. One after the other. But almost none of those writers understood *why* she was so popular. They would make their Sugars mouthy and crass. Defiant at all times. Bossy, and some of them were even bitchy. But my Sugar was none of those things. She was intelligent, but down on her luck. She was strong and courageous, but knew her limits and wore her vulnerability on her sleeve. And she gave in to Choke, not because he told her to, but because she trusted him."

"God." Cordelia sighs. "I need to reread that series. It was so good. And you're so right. Sugar was the best."

I take Cordelia's hand again and I look her in the eyes. "You write Sugars, Cordy. You do. The reason why you haven't broken through yet is because you didn't give readers enough to fall in love with. Whether you start a new series or finish the one you have, you're gonna get there. I have complete faith in your talent." Then I point to the tablet. "Don't put this out into the world. Save it for us. In ten years. When we're sitting in bed, bored with everything, I'll pull this out, and do my best Tank voice, and we'll have the best night ever. Save it for us."

She just stares at me, open-mouthed.

"What?"

"That… was like…" She lets out a breath.

"Cheesy? Cliché?"

"Fucking hot, Steve. It was fucking hot. And you didn't even use the word 'panties.'"

I laugh. "Is it universal that we all have a love-hate relationship with the word 'panties?'"

She nods, a ridiculously huge smile on her face. Then she goes all serious and stares into my eyes. "Thank you." She squeezes my hand because I'm still holding hers. "Seriously. I needed this talk. And… you're… so good at this. I'm just kind of in awe of how easily it comes to you."

"Well, if it makes you feel any better, remember that I'm a spectacular failure in science fiction."

"That doesn't make me feel better. Why do you think you're such a failure?"

"Because I am. You can look it up online. Readers hated what I wrote. Two point five stars."

"Shut up. How is that even possible? You're like… a writing genius. I'm gonna read it."

"Please don't. Please, please, *please* don't read it."

"I bet it's good. There's no way it can't be."

I just sigh.

"Anyway." She checks her phone. "The signing starts again in three minutes, so…"

"Right. We should go." I slip out of the booth and offer Cordelia my hand to help her out. It's kind of a risky move on my part. She doesn't need help.

But I'm not really offering help, either. I just want to touch her. And let her know I'm here.

She takes my hand, smiling, looking down a little, like she's not sure what to think of that, but it wasn't terrible and no one died, so then she looks back up and smiles at me again. "What are your plans for this afternoon? Gonna hang out at Essie's table?"

"Oh, hell no. Hell. No. I don't go there." We're walking out of the lounge now, making our way back to the signing hall.

"Why not?"

"It got weird. Well, this was before Mike. People thought I was her boyfriend. We're twins. And even though we're different sexes, we look alike, right?"

"So much."

"It just kinda blew my mind. And it was… well, just weird. So I don't hang out at the table."

"Do you miss it? The fan stuff? Does it bother you at all that Essie gets all the glory?"

"Mmm. Sometimes?" But then I revise. "It does kinda bother me. Not the part about Essie. She's really good at being SS and she handles it all with class and grace. But it would be nice if people were celebrating me as well as the books, if that makes sense."

"Oh, it does. I think every writer—every artist ever, actually—can relate to that. But if you're not gonna hang out with Essie, what are you gonna do this afternoon? Because… I mean, if you're not busy… I'm actually not busy either."

"What do you mean? You're signing books this afternoon, Cordelia."

She blows out a breath. "Yeah, but no one is coming to my table, Steve. And it makes Britney nervous. She feels like she has to prop me up so I don't feel let down. But you could join us. It would be fun to hang out with you. I bet you know everyone."

"Everyone," I agree.

There's a huge crowd of people waiting for the lunch break to be over outside the signing hall and this is when I realize that Cordelia and I are still holding hands.

Cordelia realizes it too. "I think we're creating a spectacle."

She's right. People are staring at us and whispering behind cupped hands.

But I just smile and hold the door open for her. "All publicity is good publicity."

♥♡♥♡♥♡♥♡♥♡♥

When we get to the table Britney is already there. "Oh, my God, Cordelia! Where did you go? I've been looking everywhere for you!" She flashes me a small, but still very obvious, disapproving look.

"Steve read my… story. And we've decided to put it in the trunk."

Britney breathes out a sigh of relief, looking up at me as she does this. "Oh, thank God."

I get her meaning. It was terrible romance, but good porn. "We're gonna save it for a rainy day."

"What?" Britney looks confused and glances at Cordelia. Then she looks back at me. "Ohhhh." She smiles swarmily—wait, that's not a word. Smarmily. *Thaaaaat's* the word I was looking for. 'In an unctuous manner.' Which is a terrible definition. Has anyone, in the entire history of words, ever used 'unctuous' in a sentence? Aside from game shows?

Decidedly no.

At any rate, Britney has caught on to the fact that Cordy and I are well on our way to being a thing. She's nodding at us in turn. "This is good, right?"

Cordelia lets go of my hand, but not because she's embarrassed. I have won her over. It might not last, but she's giving it a go.

"It's good." And we both say it at the same time.

Coincidentally, the doors to the signing hall open and a rush of eager readers enter like a swarm. Swarmily. Heh.

"What's so funny?" Cordy is arranging her Sharpies and bookmarks.

"I have a confession," I say.

"Sit," Britney commands, pointing to the chair next to Cordy. "And spill."

I sit and then Britney grabs an extra chair from the banner back alley and pulls it up on the other side of me.

I lean back and they lean in so I can see them both at the same time. Each props an elbow on the table like we're just out for drinks, shootin' the shit. "I haven't written anything in a year."

"Shut up," Cordy says.

"Why not?" Britney asks.

"The science fiction failure. And the blog awards. Long story. But since I met you"—I point to the lovely Cordelia—"I've been writing little bits in my head. Making up new characters and playing with words."

"Oh, my God. I want details." Britney is enthralled. "Can I be your beta reader?"

I'm just about to answer when there is suddenly a crowd of people in front of us.

We stare at them for a moment, unable to decipher why they're here.

Britney catches on first and jumps to her feet. "Welcome to Cynthia Lear's table." She pans her hand to Cordelia. "Would you like a free ARC of her newest book?"

The ladies—there are four of them in front—look at the ARC in Britney's hand, then look at Cordy, then look back at the book. "I'll take one."

"Me too."

"I got one of your ebooks free from Bookbinge a few months ago," another says. "It was really good."

I glance over at Cordelia and find her smiling. "Thank you."

"No problem," the woman says. "You're a really good writer. Can you make it out to Marina?" She hands Cordelia the ARC and Cordelia accepts it smoothly, her Sharpie squeaking across the page when she signs and personalizes the title page. "Actually, can you write my whole name?"

"Sure," Cordelia says. "What is it?"

"Marina Ford?" Cordelia starts to write it when the woman reaches out and stops her. "Sorry! No! Sorry. Marina *Reich*. Ford was my married name, but then my ex got involved with this group of..." She trails off, nervously. "Doesn't matter. Marina Reich. That's my name."

Cordelia observes her carefully, then writes the name in equally carefully. She hands it back and it's obvious she wants to ask questions, but she doesn't get the chance because suddenly there are others there, all crowding in. Trying to get a free signed ARC.

And yeah, they're here for free books and not really looking to buy the ones for sale. But that's the whole point of free books. To get people interested.

I know this feeling. I remember it from that first year when Choke and Sugar went crazy. It was weird being with Essie at the Romance Round-Up table, but when people started coming up—and then there was a crowd of them?

It was… magic. It was more than I could've ever dreamed of. It was like being at Comic-Con, only without the cosplay. The energy was crazy and our table was a mess of swag as people eagerly tried to grab it from any and all directions. The signing coordinators had to interfere and assign us wristbands so the tables around us weren't too crowded. We sold every book and they still came to see us. People wanted Essie to sign bookplates, and handmade posters, and self-printed autograph books with Master Choke and Sugar on a two-page spread. Someone gave her fan art of Choke and Sugar. In oil paint, no less. I still have that painting. It's hanging in my office.

And now this is happening for Cordelia. And I get to be here, witnessing the magic as she experiences her very first signing in real time.

Britney and I exchange a glance. Did they come to Cordelia's table because of me?

We both shrug. Does it matter?

They're not here for me now.

They want free books and we are more than happy to give them out.

MEANWHILE…

Meanwhile…

The signing is in full swing now and every few minutes the PA system announces the numbers for the authors who are so popular, the fans need wristbands just to stand in their line.

Leslie does not need wristbands. Only those bitches like Eden Le Fay, and Audrey Saint, and Raven Lark need wristbands.

And, of course, SS herself.

Steve Smith. SS.

Essie Smith. Not quite SS, is it? It's close, but not close enough.

Leslie Munch watches Cynthia Lear's table from across the signing hall with a severe scowl on her face, despite the fact that she's in the middle of signing her name inside her most famous book—*Daddy, Yes, Daddy, No*. A real collector's item, it even has the terrible original cover. The owner of said book is watching her watch them.

Steve and that woman. Whom Leslie had never heard of until she saw Steve talking to her on Wednesday.

"Oh, my God!" the reader exclaims. "You spelled my name wrong!"

Leslie looks up at the reader in front of her table, then looks down at the book. "You said Kristen with a K. I wrote Kristen with a K."

"It's *Kir*sten!" The reader turns to her friend, mouth open. "She ruined my book! My collector's item!"

Leslie lets out a long sigh. Her books are being sold on the used book sites, she knows this. And this cover is indeed in low stock as far as number of copies are concerned, but it's a forty-dollar paperback, not some special-edition double-sided-dustjacket-hardcover with foil embossing on the case and digitally-sprayed edges that's going for three-fifty unsigned.

Still, it *is* a reader and she has precious few these days. "How about I just order you up a new copy and send it to you?"

The reader looks at her, frowning, eyebrows deeply furrowed. "You can't just order one of these. They're out of print."

"Honey, nothing is out of print these days. I upload the files, add one to the cart, press the purchase button and it's printed and shipped. It can be shipped right to you. In fact, I can insert a digital signature onto the title page, *Kirsten,* and all will be well. How about that?"

Kirsten grabs her book from Leslie's outstretched hand, whirls on her heel, and walks away without a second glance.

There is no one behind Kirsten in line, and Leslie's troublemakers are off getting her a double shot of tequila. She needs that drink badly. So Leslie is alone. In the giant signing hall. With thousands of happy and excited people all around her. With no readers in her line.

And this is making her angrier by the second.

Just as she's thinking this, the catering room door—which is on double-action spring door hinges so it swings both in and out and which is less than two feet away from her at this very moment—comes crashing into the corner of her table. For like the *ten thousandth* time.

"Watch it!" Leslie barks.

"Sorry!" the fresh-faced catering girl says, pulling a cart with a coffee machine behind her. "Sorry, sorry, sorry!"

If Leslie has to hear one more person apologize for hitting her table with that door, she's going to murder someone. It was bad enough that she'd been assigned to the shittiest panel—which had been canceled—but she's definitely been given the worst table space in the entire room.

That catering door never stops and even if she didn't have a direct line-of-sight to Cynthia Lear and that liar Steve Smith, she would still be in the mood to murder someone.

This day started badly and it doesn't seem to be looking up. She was stuck in the elevator for seven hours last night. Seven. Hours.

She made herself hoarse from screaming. She has bruises on the sides of her hands from pounding on the doors. And when the elevator doors finally opened, she was half-asleep on the floor—curled up in the fetal position because it was freezing in there—and a whole group of readers saw her and immediately assumed she'd passed out drunk from the night before.

The next thing she knew they all had their phones out, recording.

She wanted to rip their hair out. She wanted to rant and rave about how unfairly she was being treated… but instead she ran away and took the stairs up to her standard room with one king bed and a tiny fridge she had to pay extra for.

It was only then, once she was in her room, that she realized she could've used those readers to spread her rumor.

Which, she is certain now, is no rumor.

Steve writes the books. Essie is the face.

They are a couple of twin-faced liars.

Thinking about it rationally, though, it's fortuitous that Leslie didn't spilled the beans to those nobodies who found her in the elevator. She needs a gossipy Bookstagrammer. No, better. She needs one of those bitchy BookTokers!

Yes. She rubs her hands together, watching the crowd in front of Cynthia Lear's table grow bigger and bigger by the minute.

Leslie is going to out Steve and Essie at their own stupid conference. She's going to turn the entire romance world against them. She's going to make them *pay*.

And she's gonna do that right now.

Leslie slaps her hands on the table, gets up, and is just coming out from behind it, determined with every fiber of her being to find herself a bitchy BookToker, when the catering door comes swinging out, smashing her right in the face.

The next thing she knows, she's covered in blood, surrounded by paramedics—who, contrary to every romance book ever written about paramedics, are *not* hot—and a crowd of people are recording her in all her bloody glory.

The last thing she hears as she's wheeled out of the signing hall and pushed inside an ambulance for her broken nose is a PA announcement for fans with wristband numbers three hundred to three hundred and fifty to get in Essie's line.

Leslie raises her fist and mumbles a curse past the ice pack on her nose.

She will get them if it's the last thing she ever does.

No. Better. She will *ruin* them.

CHAPTER NINETEEN – CORDELIA

There's a really funny section in one of the Master Choke books, I forget which one, but it stands out because the Master Choke books aren't intended to be particularly funny. They are pretty hardcore, in fact. And knowing now, definitively, that Steve is the one who wrote all of that stuff is simultaneously sexy and confusing. In part because I tend to overthink things and get stuck in rumination cycles.

Like, is Steve actually Master Choke himself? Is the character *based* on him? He doesn't seem all dark and twisted. But we did have sex (I had sex!) and he did kind of… Anyway. So, is he really just chronicling his own escapades in those books? Since he clearly didn't steal from Leslie Whatshertoes, are those books more of a memoir than a fiction? Etc. Etc. Etc.

None of these things are true, I can't imagine. None of these things make sense, even. But my brain starts trying to piece together ideas in order to make them have some sort of logic. Because, as noted, I tend to get stuck in rumination cycles. To which end…

What was I thinking?

Oh, right. The funny bit.

There's this funny section where Master Choke gets into an accident. A car accident. Not a bad one or anything, just a fender-bender, but it does cause him to whip his head around at exactly the wrong moment and, as a consequence, he winds up having to wear a neck brace for a bit. Which is obviously a funny and ironic image. This guy, this master of choking, having to wear a neck brace that covers his *own* throat.

And, on the surface, that's all it is. A funny and ironic image.

But, because SS, aka Steve Smith, is a good writer, it's also more than that. It's a commentary on the nature of Choke's identity and a clarifying moment for Choke on a personal level that gives him an opportunity for self-reflection and all kinds of other introspection on his own history and what led him to become 'Master Choke' and all that jazz. I don't know if everyone would read it and glean that, but it leapt out to me when I read it and has stayed with me ever since.

But I'm not actually thinking about it now because of the fact that it's deeper than it appears on the surface or because, if I let myself, I could easily start spiraling off into fifty other fantasies about what it all represents. I'm simply thinking about it now because I feel like I need a friggin' neck brace at the moment, owing to the whiplash that I'm suffering as a result of the last three days.

As part and parcel of the overthinking business, I have this tendency to look for patterns. I sometimes think that my various habits (if that's what you want to call them) aren't just behavioral tendencies or manifestations of my anxiety or whatever—I mean they *are* that, I just don't think they're *only* that—but rather an attempt to grab hold of something familiar when things feel like they're overwhelming.

It kind of boils down to: I can't control the world, but I can control little things. Like biting my nails, or regulating the number of times I brush my hair on each side, or whatever.

Fifteen, sixteen, seventeen…

I finish brushing the left side. Right side first, left second, seventeen on each because the total has to be an even number.

I'm not looking in the mirror as I do it because I'm still not sure I recognize myself. I feel a little like a turtle who peeks out, sees the world is big and scary and that there are cars bearing down on it, and then pulls its head back into its shell. And even though I feel better than I did yesterday when I was brushing my teeth, I'm not sure I feel *great.*

I did. I did feel great earlier. Down at the table when Steve was hanging out with me and Brit, giving away books, talking people up, taking pictures with all the women who kept calling him Tank as he rolled his eyes. (Now that the cat's out of the bag, it seems to just be running free.) Convincing people to take pictures with me even if they only sort of know who I am. Laughing, having a great time.

Even when Raylen Star had to be wheeled out of the signing hall by the paramedics, he kept the place in good spirits. (Side note: I couldn't quite make out what Leslie was mumbling in Steve's direction as she was wheeled past, but it very much had an 'I'll get you and your little dog too!' energy. Steve just shrugged it off.)

And I felt… safe. Comfortable. Unusually so. I kept thinking back to meeting Steve when I got here a couple of days ago (a couple of flippin' days ago) and how sideways and awkward it all seemed. Stuck in a bedbug-ridden, fleabag hotel, feeling totally out of my depth, not knowing anyone and profoundly uncertain about whether I belonged. And while I still kind of feel that last part, the other stuff…

Steve rode in on his mighty stallion, shirt open, chest glistening with dew (aka 'sweat,' but I think 'dew' sounds nicer), and started saving the day. And he's remained that guy. Unflappable, in control, and just generally a champion.

And that's when I realize that maybe a part of the reason he doesn't want to out himself as SS is because all that would be taken away.

His ability to be seen as just this cool, nice guy who backs up his sister and is a good team player would disappear into a fog of, I suppose, celebrity. It's just a guess, but I wouldn't be shocked. It's possible that in this universe, that's why he wants the exact opposite of what I do. Because it's not his dream. And that has to be hard. To be a massive success at a thing that you don't want to be known for being a success at.

I mean, look, nobody's gonna cry for someone who gets to go to sleep on a bed of money just because they made that money doing something that wasn't their first choice. I don't feel sorry for my parents. But I still know it's tough on the brain. Because I've seen it.

I wish there was something I could do to help him the way he's helped me. Is there? I dunno.

Ugh, why do I feel so awkward still?

Because, dummy, this isn't a romance novel. This is real life. And, in real life, people don't get swept off their feet and immediately go all giddy for a dude just because he gets them a hotel room and says nice things about their book, which results in them saying shit to the dude they don't normally say, like, "*You must work out all day long, giggle giggle,*" and letting him choke them a little bit… and *then* have it turn out that dude is a world-famous romance novelist who also happens to be a real sweetheart who takes care of them when they kind of lose their mind… and, after that, allow themselves to get all seduced by the idea of winding up in bed with him in ten years just because he said something hot that didn't include the word 'panties.'

Like, seriously. That doesn't happen.

I really need that neck brace.

Tonight is *actually* the 1920s party. The one that Britney thought was the other night. I'm not sure what I'm going to wear. I only have the one flapper dress and that one's already been seen by everyone and then tossed on the floor of Steve's suite and probably smells like all kinds of sex. Which, to be fair, is not un-hot, but it sort of skeeves me out anyway.

I wonder what Steve's gonna wear. I wonder if he'll get into the whole theme thing and shows up all looking all *Guys and Dolls.* I wouldn't be surprised. If anything, this brief stint here in Las Vegas (again, my first time, and it's really living up to the hype) has taught me that my tolerance for the unexpected and borderline-incoherent is much higher than I realized.

Ding-dong.

The door. Probably Britney checking to see how I'm feeling after today. All in all, it was pretty successful. Once Steve joined our cohort, the time seemed to fly by and we gave away a ton of free books. Dozens upon dozens of women are now walking around with the name Cynthia Lear in their heads. And that's a success, even if they aren't reading exactly what I had intended when I first started *Filling the Gap*. They aren't reading the one Steve read. The one with the plain white cover and the black letters that…

Wait. Where is that one?

I just realized I haven't seen it since…

Ding-dong.

What did I do with it? I know I brought it back here. To my room. To this room. I…

Ding-dong.

Did I put it…? I don't think I've seen it since… I didn't… I mean, there's no way it accidentally could have…?

Ding-dong. Ding-dong.

I jog to the door, head filled with a thousand colliding thoughts, and, swinging it open, I realize that my self-proclamation about not being able to feel surprised anymore may have been a bit premature.

"Sheila?"

"Hello, dear," Sheila says, sashaying into the suite, carrying a garment bag, Britney on her heels.

"Your sweet friend here called me," Sheila says, referring to Britney, who sits on the edge of the bed.

Sheila is standing by the window, looking out at the Strip, kind of glassy-eyed. "This is nice," she mutters, touching the curtains and staring at something that I feel like only she can see. "Y'know, I haven't been back to Vegas since… Oh, I don't even know when. After Dean and I split, I decided there was no real reason for me to come anymore. The town has changed."

"Dean… Martin?" Britney asks.

Sheila ignores her the way she does and keeps looking around.

"Sorry," I start. "Why did she call you? Why did you call her?" I ask Sheila and Britney, in that order.

Britney answers, as Sheila seems lost in thought. "Since we talked about what she said as you and I were driving here—"

"What did I say?" Sheila asks, betraying the notion that she's not totally plugged into everything going on around her at all times.

"Cordelia said that you mentioned something about Vegas being a rollercoaster? That it'll whip you around or something?"

Sheila nods, saying nothing. Her halter top allows her deeply tanned and freckled shoulders to glisten in the setting desert sun.

"Anyway," Britney goes on, "I figured she might know if there was somewhere in town where we could find another dress for you for tonight."

"Why did you think I'd need another dress?"

"Because everybody already saw the one you wore the other night and because it… probably needs to be cleaned."

"You think I'd need a whole new dress just because—" Her cocked head and pursed lips stop me from going on. "Yeah, okay."

Sheila chimes in, "And I told her, 'Oh, I don't know anymore. I'm sure she could find someplace on the internet.'" She's still staring out the window, like she's a million miles from here. "But then Britney told me what's been going on." Sheila turns now to face me. "What a time you've been having."

"Time I've been having?" I paraphrase back. "What do you mean, what a time I've been having?"

"She asked how things were going and I told her," Brit says, shrugging.

"And it made me…" Sheila trails off, then says, finally, "Wistful."

"Wistful?"

"It means reflective. Usually with something like longing."

"Yes, no, I know what it means. Why? Wistful how?"

Sheila steps over to a chaise and allows herself to fall languidly onto it, like Rita Hayworth or something. Or, more accurately, exactly like herself. Sheila is no one's echo. She is all her own. "I was your age when I first came to Las Vegas."

"Yeah?"

"Yes. I had a dream. To be a showgirl."

"You did?"

"I did. And within, I don't know, not more than a couple of days, I felt as though my life had been turned upside down."

"It was?"

"Will you please stop doing that, dear? Interjecting your curiosity and disbelief into my story. I'm trying to open up."

I mime locking my lips and throwing away the key, which is a weird and slightly juvenile thing to do, but Sheila causes me to feel like a kid sometimes and also… I *am* weird and slightly juvenile.

"I always wanted to be a dancer. That was my first real dream. Maybe a Rockette. But that was never going to work out. Because of these." She squeezes her still-impressive-even-at-her-advanced-age boobs together. "Too much to handle for the delicate requirements of a Radio City Girl, but seemed like exactly the right thing for the Strip. So, I tossed my things in a bag and I made my way out to the desert. Back in those days, Vegas was just an acorn compared to the mighty oak it has grown into."

That's a really terrible metaphor, but there's no way I'm going to point it out.

Not now. Maybe later. I dunno.

Sheila goes on. "Anything seemed possible. So I came out, waltzed right into the Tropicana, and told them I was here to take over the town. I have no idea what they thought of me, all sassy with a head full of steam, but I know that I caught someone's attention. A man who happened to be walking by and saw me, hand on my hip, chin in the air, proclaiming myself to be the next big thing."

"Was it Dean Martin?" Britney asks. Sheila ignores her.

"And that man," she goes on, "was the handsomest, most charming, sweetest man I'd ever met. I couldn't believe that he could be real."

Britney whispers to me, "Bet it was Dean Martin."

"But, for whatever reason, I wouldn't let myself give over to him. I questioned his intentions. I questioned his motives. I wondered about what and why and how he would come to focus his attention on me. In short, I shot my chance at love with someone right in the foot by letting my thoughts and imagination steal the focus from my heart."

She lets that hang in the room for a moment. I think about it for a second. It's not the greatest story ever told.

It's lacking in detail and nuance and connective tissue that truly great stories require. It's sloppy and slapdash and thrown together suddenly, like she's never told it before and wasn't expecting to tell it now.

It's not profound. Or explicitly analogous. Or even that intentional.

But damned if hearing her tell it doesn't trigger something inside me.

I need to stop thinking so much.

I need to stop overthinking so much.

I need to stop trying to figure out what people want.

I need to stop judging what I want.

I need to stop—

"And the reason I bring it up, dear"—oh, she wasn't finished. My bad—"is that Britney here tells me you might be making a similar mistake."

"No, I didn't," Britney says, surprised.

"You said that there's a boy she likes but that it's been difficult for her to just let herself be here. Now. With him."

"I mean… I guess I kind of said that, but—"

"Do you know I've never been married?"

"Uh. No," I say, "I didn't know that. Really."

"Never been married. Never had children."

"Oh. Okay." I have no idea where this is going.

"But I'm happy."

"Riiiigggghhhht."

"That's all." Then she stands and wanders back over to the window. Stares out.

I'm trapped between thinking she's Yoda and thinking she's crazy and being here is bringing up lots of weird shit for her.

"Great," I say, "So, um, I'm still not… Why are you here?"

She nods to the bed, where she tossed down the garment bag. I step over, unzip it. Inside is one of the most incredible-looking gowns I've ever seen in my life.

Lavender and gray, beaded, with a plunging neckline, made of taffeta and silk and magic. It's hard to explain, but it is unlike anything I've ever seen before. "What's this?"

"That's for you. For tonight," Sheila says.

"Wha—Why?" I manage to stutter out.

"Because, dear, you'll need something to wear."

♥♡♥♡♥♡♥♡♥♡♥

Thirty minutes later Sheila has gone to her own suite.

"How'd she get a suite? I thought the place was booked," I say to Britney.

"I dunno. She said she'd take care of it. And then… she did."

I have so many questions about my landlady.

I stand in front of the bed, looking at the dress. "It's stunning," I whisper.

"Yeah, it is," Britney says back, reverently.

Another beat passes before I say something that's been swirling around, but that until this moment I felt too… something… to say out loud.

"Do you believe in…? I dunno," I say, super-eloquently. But, somehow, Britney seems to know what I'm trying to say.

"Maybe," she responds. "Why?"

"Maybe this whole thing—this event, me being here—wasn't ever supposed to be so that I can become a big, famous author."

"No?" Britney asks. I shake my head. "Then what do you think it was supposed to be for?"

"Not sure. Maybe to learn something? Grow in some way? Meet myself?"

"Meet yourself?"

"Yeah. I mean, like—"

"No, I get it," she says. We stand in silence for another moment before she adds, "Maybe."

I sigh, quietly. Then I pick up the dress, which feels lighter than I had imagined. "What are you going to wear?" I ask her.

"Same thing I wore the other night, probably."

"Oh," I start, very much intending to go on and say, *No, no. You should wear this one.*

But then I stop. More accurately, I force myself to stop.

Why do I do that? Question my right to enjoy what feels good? Why do I live under this constant cloud of anxiety propelled by this imposter syndrome I have?

People like to make fun of romance. Romance novels. Romantic stories. The whole concept of romance. I know it. I may be a lot of things, but I'm not oblivious. And the reason people do that is because a lot of them think it's silly or frivolous to engage in that level of fantasy. They judge it, I suppose.

Just like I tend to judge myself.

Enough. No more playing small. No more denying myself satisfaction. No more worrying about things that are out of my control or what anyone might think of me.

Gotta start somewhere. So, may as well be here. Now. At a convention that exists to celebrate the power of fantasy and the unexpected. Put on by a guy who seems to genuinely like me for whatever reason he's decided he does. Or maybe it's just how he feels. Because he understands all the romance stuff on some intuitive level himself, whether he realizes it or not. Amidst an effulgence of others who are here and understand it just as honestly.

No more playing small. Please, Cordelia, no more playing small. Don't listen to the voices in your head. The tapes from the past. The input of others who don't have to live your life in your skin and with your brain.

One of the dictionary definitions of romance is: 'A quality or feeling of mystery, excitement, and remoteness from everyday life.'

If I can't feel that myself, how can I imbue it in others?

So I stifle my impulse to give away my chance at something like happiness. And, instead, I embrace the possibility of mystery. Excitement. Remoteness from everyday life.

I turn to Britney, give her a hug, and, with the deepest appreciation for the friend she's been to me, tell her, "Good. You should wear your dress. You look great in it."

CHAPTER TWENTY – STEVE

"What do you think?" I'm doing the whole this-or-that thing with my tie. One is gold plaid and the other is gold-striped.

Terry is leaning forward, squinting at me through the vid app on my tablet. "What… what are we doing again?"

"*We* are helping me pick the right tie, Terry. It's twenties party night. I had this suit custom-made."

I love it. Twenties parties are my favorite and I am pulling this suit off *so* much better than Leonardo DiCaprio, it's not even funny. It's off-white, three-piece, with a brown waistcoat, a lavender shirt—so bold—and a gold tie. I just need to know which one. "So which one? Gold with maroon plaid accents? Or gold monochrome with barely-there stripes?"

Terry leans back in his chair and laughs, folding his tattooed arms across his chest. "You're so needy this time, Steve. What is up?"

"What is *up*? Is that a serious question? I have been filling you in for three days now, Terry! I'm in love! Hel-*looooooo*! Cordelia and I—"

"Wait. I thought her name was Cynthia?"

"That's her pen name. For fuck's sake, don't make me call Luke for this advice." I raise an eyebrow at him.

"Dude. Calm the fuck down. It's a girl. You've literally dated millions of girls."

"That's… that's not *literal.*"

"Can you hear yourself right now? My friend, you are a mess."

"I'm a mess because the party starts in ten minutes and I don't know which tie to wear!"

Terry sighs. "I don't like gold. Choose a brown. Or a gray, like your shirt."

"My shirt is lavender."

He squints again, leaning forward until his eyeballs take up the whole screen. "Nah. I think that's gray."

I close my eyes and take a breath, asking for strength. Then I open them and look right at Screen Terry. "Thank you for your help. I have to go now."

Terry salutes me. "It's been my pleasure." Then the screen goes gray.

Which is not the color of my shirt.

I pick up my phone, tap the SparkleNight DreamWeaver's WishMaker app, and let out a sigh of relief when Gregory's cartoon face appears.

"Steve, my friend. How can I help you?"

"Tell me which tie to wear. This one or this one?" Wait, can he see me? Is my camera enabled in this app?

"Option number two, Steve. Gold monochrome with barely-there stripes."

I tilt my head a little and study his cartoon face. Well, I guess that answers that question. But… is he spying on me though my microphone? Were those not the exact words I used to describe this tie to Terry?

"Do you require any other assistance tonight, Steve? Is your dream date with Cynthia Lear, aka Cordelia Sarantopoulos, all arranged? Or can I offer up some pointers?"

Oh, my God. The Aria AI *is* spying on me. "Mmmmm… nope. Nope. I'm good. Thank you for your time, Gregory. I'm just gonna be going now."

I close the app, side-eye the phone, then press the icon again, holding my finger down until the SparkleNight DreamWeaver's WishMaker app menu appears. My fingertip is poised, ready to delete, but… the option is grayed out.

Suddenly, a notification appears. It's Gregory's face on a banner. The text reads:

Congratulations, Steve Smith, aka New York Times-*bestselling novelist SS! You've earned the SparkleNight DreamWeaver's DreamDate WishMaker Bonus Level! Low on ideas? Need to top a rainbow-colored rose-petal bathtub date? Let me, Gregory, fine-tune the details for you! Just press my face right now!*

I turn the phone off.

Holy shit. The AI *has* been spying on me! And it knows I'm SS!

What… what do I do with this? Call the manager and complain? File a formal complaint with whoever regulates this shit?

I should have read the terms of service for that app. But I've had it on my phone for five years now and…

I stop. I don't have time for this. And anyway—I let out a long breath—he was right about the tie.

♥♡♥♡♥♡♥♡♥♡♥

I arrive at the party room a few minutes after eight. It's not in the lounge. This is a big, big deal. Four banquet rooms have been opened up into one massive ballroom because this party is for fans and authors alike.

I stop to gaze up for a moment.

We have recreated the Coconut Grove nightclub.

Hanging from the ceiling, outside the entrance to the party, is a fifty-foot-long, floor-to-ceiling banner with a full-color image of the Ambassador Hotel back in its glory days. In front of the banner is a line of gas lamps and vintage cars that have been turned into photo booths.

The windows are all tinted black and the best part is that on the inside, they are digital screens and play a B-roll loop—front, back, and rear—of the drive up and down Mulholland Drive. It will even let you park at the scenic overlooks and everything outside looks the same way it did a hundred years ago, so you can pretend you're riding along with your friends, toasting champagne glasses filled with bubbly from the back seat, and never get pulled over.

The cars don't run. They're just a party accessory. But you can fit like ten people in those suckers. I predict they will be a huge hit.

I walk through the porte-cochère made of silver and white balloons and enter… the past.

Palm trees everywhere.

Massive bandstand complete with bandleader.

A dance floor that could rival any modern club.

A hundred tables—faithful replicas of the originals including the iconic white tablecloths and red chairs.

And two bars along the long sides of the room.

There are several dozen people here already and I spy Essie and Mike in front of the bandstand talking to the bandleader. I am heading in that direction when I hear, "Taaaaank!" and find a woman waving her fingers at me when I pass her.

"Hi, Tank!" another woman says, then bats her eyes at me as she wraps her glossy red lips around a straw and sucks up alcohol.

"Tank! Tank! Tank! I've been looking for you! Will you narrate my book?"

Suddenly there is a crowd of women around me, all calling me Tank. I sigh. But then… *then* I see her!

My lovely Cordelia. Standing in the entrance of the floating porte-cochère, looking like Cinderella ready to cut a rug. She's backlit by the faux streetlights of yesteryear Los Angeles.

"Excuse me, ladies." I don't even look at them—I only have eyes for Cordelia. The people around me part like the Red Sea as I make my way towards my love.

And wow. I walk up to her, smiling. "We match!"

Cordy smiles, looking me up and down. "Do we?"

"Look!" I pull out my shirt cuff. "My shirt is lavender and your dress—my God, Cordelia. That dress is…" I have not done an eyebrow waggle in two days. So I do that now and whisper, "Delightful," as I nod my head in approval.

Cordy looks down at herself, picks up her lavender taffeta skirt with her fingertips, and gazes up at me. "It is delightful, isn't it?" Then she shrugs her shoulders up and grins.

"Howard Hughes bought me that dress when we dated," someone says.

I blink. Then look over at an older—old?—woman, who is oddly sexy for such an advanced age. She winks at me. "Now *that* guy was a freak in every sense of the word." A pointy elbow hits my ribs. "If you get my meaning." She raises a finger bedazzled with rings. "Ah! There's the bar. You kids have fun." And with a swish of her flapper dress, and perched precariously high on heels that have me worrying about the strength of her ankles, she walks away.

I look at Cordelia. "Who…?"

"My… landlady?" Cordelia shrugs. "Sheila. It's kind of a long story. But you're right, we *do* match." She beams a smile at me.

"Like she said," Britney says, pointing at Sheila weaving between tables as she makes her way to the bar, "you kids have fun." Then she's off too.

We watch Britney disappear as the room begins filling up with people all decked out in vintage dresses. Most look like they're dressed in costumes. Cheap stuff. Things they will never wear again. But Cordelia…

"My God, Cordelia." I sigh a little. "You really do look stunning tonight."

"Thanks." She puts a hand over her chest. "I feel like… Cinderella."

I point to myself. "Does that make me the prince?"

Cordelia blushes a little. "I guess it does."

"Well"—I offer her the crook of my arm—"we should go to the ball."

Cordelia hooks her arm in mine and we face the night together.

We only get about ten steps in before a group of ladies rush up to us. I put up a hand. "Ladies, ladies, please. I might or might not narrate your books. But tonight is not—"

But I'm cut off. "Cynthia, I loved your book! I read the ARC this afternoon! I could not put it down!"

Cordy's eyebrows shoot up. "You did? You couldn't?"

"I did too!" a friend adds.

"Well, I've read all of your books. You're gonna complete that series, right? I'm dying for more!"

Cordy blinks. "You are?"

"Oh, my God," the first one says. Then proceeds to *gush*.

Gush. A technical term. To go over-the-top insane in front of people so they get a paralyzing sense of FOMO and start one-clicking the pre-order.

Note to Steve's internal notepad: Remind Cordy to put up a pre-order for next book in series tomorrow.

Soon, there is quite a crowd, all clamoring for my lovely Cordelia's attention.

She looks at me—almost a deer-in-headlights kind of look. I nod at her and smile.

But I can't help but think back to my first signing. Well, Essie's first signing. With me at her side. Awkward. But when it wasn't awkward, it was amazing.

It was a sudden and almost overwhelming understanding that people are not only reading my words—something they did not actually do prior to *Master Choke*—they are in love with them.

They were coming up to Essie gushing about Choke and Sugar like they were real people.

It was… incredible. And so much fun, even though I was just the sidekick brother. I got to hear what people thought about my writing with my own ears. Not only that, I knew they weren't lying because I wasn't Essie!

No one knew who I was that first time. No one cared.

Fast-forward another year and everyone knew I was Steve—Essie's Ro-Bro.

I sigh. The climb up is so much better than reaching the peak.

And right in this moment Cordelia Sarantopoulos, aka Cynthia Lear, is getting a healthy dose of what that actually means. I lean in to her ear. "Enjoy this. Take your time. I'll get us drinks."

As I'm making my way to the bar, I notice my parents have joined Essie and Mike near the bandstand and my first instinct is to dodge them. But then I look over my shoulder, find Cordelia in deep conversation with her newfound fans, and decide I should make an effort.

So I walk over and smile at my mother. The Rom-Mom. It's cute. She's still wearing that ribbon, too, pinned right on the black satin stole of her stunning white satin full-length gown. When I get to them, I touch her shoulder, lean down, and kiss her cheek. "Are you having a good time, Mom?"

"Oh, Steve." She looks up at me with her blue eyes—which are a little more faded as each year goes by—and I brace for the insults. "Don't you look handsome tonight!" She reaches up, straightens my tie, and nods.

Then my dad is clapping me on my shoulder. "That really is a great suit, son. But I don't look bad either, right?"

I glance at Essie and Mike, wondering if they've mentioned my interest in a woman and that's why my parents are being so complimentary. I can't tell. "Well, the two of you might as well be Fred and Ginger the way you look tonight." My dad is wearing full evening dress complete with white bow tie. And honestly, together, they look quite amazing.

Essie and Mike are just as decked out. Essie is in her elegant, full-length mermaid gown with millions of beads and a true art deco feel. Mike is white tie too.

In fact, I feel a little casual tonight compared to them. And I'm expecting those insults to start flying at any moment.

But to my surprise, my dad says, "You look fantastic, son," and claps me on the back again.

Hmm. Well. "Thank you." I will take that compliment. "Now, if you'll excuse me, I have to grab a drink for my date."

My mom's eyes go wide and she's just about to start quizzing me when my dad places a hand on her arm, making her stop.

I turn away and head towards the bar.

The music starts and I start tapping my fingers on the bar to the bouncy beat as I wait for our drinks. I get us both dirty martinis because everyone is drinking them tonight and who doesn't love a martini glass, and then make my way back where Cordy is.

Or… was, at least. I get there and look around. Because she is missing.

But then a ruckus erupts over on the dance floor. I'm tall, so I can see over most heads, but whatever is happening over there, it's hidden in the crowd.

I nudge a woman next to me, who is also trying to get a peek. "What's going on?"

"Oh!" She's breathless. "It's Cynthia Lear!"

"What? What happened?" I am imagining a million different humiliating scenarios. Cordelia broke a heel, ripped her dress, slipped on the dance floor—

But the woman stops my internal pessimism with her explanation. "She and her assistant are swing-dancing with an old lady!"

"Really?" I push my way through the crowd. "Tank. Coming though, ladies. It's Tank." I figure they know me better as Tank now, not Steve. And it works. A handful of seconds later I am at the edge of the dance floor watching my lovely Cordelia, Britney, and the ex-girlfriend of Howard Hughes lighting up the dance floor with a Charleston swing number that frankly stuns me silent.

They're smiling and laughing as they perform groovy walks, bouncy twists, swinging kicks, and bee's knees. They are moving in perfect unison to a breathless, relentless jitterbug beat. One moment face-to-face, the next side-by-side. Sliding in and out, changing partners, doing solos… it's a routine, I realize. Something the three of them have practiced relentlessly to perfection and tonight—oh, what a great night it already is—they're doing it for the world.

Well, for the romance world, at least.

I stand there—mouth open, eyes wide—*gushing* over this woman.

Gushing. A technical term. The feeling a man gets in the early stages of a romantic relationship when he suddenly realizes that his partner is way, *way* out of his league and he's got to rise up to his fullest potential to hold on to her forever.

That's the feeling welling up inside me in this moment.

Everyone is clapping and cheering and encouraging them. I have a moment of worry for Sheila because she has to be two hundred years old, but I have a feeling that woman cut her teeth on the Depression-era fascination of marathon dancing.

She never stops.

In fact, Britney and Cordelia are gasping for breath, making their way off the dance floor, even as Sheila keeps going. She doesn't stay out there alone for long, though. Suddenly everyone is burning up the dance floor with her and the party is officially *on*.

Cordy's eyes search the crowd and when they find mine, she smiles.

I think I melt when she directs that smile at me.

And then there she is. Right in front of me. Breathing hard, and bending over, and holding her side with her hand. "Oh, my God," she wheezes, then starts coughing, holding up a hand. "Sheila has made… Britney and me practice that dance with her"—she's gasping—"since I moved into her pool house. Said, 'You never know when you might need to cut a rug,' which I thought was weird, but maybe she has a crystal ball. Whatever. But this is… the first time… we've done it for that long. Whew!" She looks over her shoulder and, yep, Sheila is still going. "She's crazy, that lady."

I am so speechless, so enthralled, so captivated, such a prisoner, I blurt out the first thing that comes to mind. "Would you like to go up Mulholland Drive with me?"

"What?" She laughs. "We're… in Vegas, Steve."

"Au contraire, mon frère."

She giggles. "Okay, *mon* frère."

I set our drinks down on a passing tray and take her hand. "Come with me."

I lead her back through the porte-cochère made of silver and white balloons and out onto the make-believe streets of yesteryear LA, then wave my hand at the cars. "Your chariot, madam."

"What are those things?"

"Photo booths. But"—I hold up a finger—"not just photo booths. They take you up Mulholland Drive. The whole thing plays on digitized screens over the windows."

"Shut up!"

"Come on." I tug her over to a car, open the door, and get a flash of a woman's underpants.

"Occupied!" a man screams.

"Ooops! Sorry." I close the door. The next car is bouncing, so we skip that one. But the third is empty. I walk her over to the passenger side and open the door.

Cordy has caught her breath now, but she's still flushed pink from the dancing. "Thank you, good sir." And she slides in.

Then I slip around to the driver's side and get in next to her. As soon as I sit down, the car starts. Well, it's the sound of the car starting. The radio comes on too. It's big band jazz, playing at a low level.

The windows light up and suddenly we are turning onto Mulholland Drive, making our way up into the hills.

Cordelia gasps, smiling and shaking her head. "This is amazing! We're… on a date, in LA, a hundred years ago." She leans back in her seat, letting out a long breath. "This was already the best day of my life. The signing, and the fans, and the party, and the dancing, and… and…" Her head turns so she can look at me. "And you, Steve. This was the best day of my life because of you."

I shrug. "It's not really me. It's just… your time, Cordelia. It's your time. You made the moments that led up to this day all on your own. You baked the cake. I'm just… frosting."

Cordy smiles at me. Her eyes wander over my shoulder a little bit. Then she sits up and turns in her seat, studying the door.

"What are you—"

She pushes down on the door lock. It snaps in place with a click. Then she turns to me. "Guess what?"

I'm grinning like an idiot. "What?"

"I'm not wearing my Skinnies tonight." Then she reaches into the back seat and snaps that door lock down in place too. "And do you know what that means, Steve Smith?"

"I'm getting lucky at Inspiration Point?"

She giggles. And nods. And crawls across the front seat until she's right on top of me. Then she's straddling me—in my lap! Reaching over, magnificent breasts right in my face, to snap down the two remaining door locks.

She straightens up. Places her hands on my cheeks. And then she leans down and kisses me. I kiss her back. And it's filled with passion. It's long and slow. A romantic kiss straight out of *Forever Sugar.* Cordelia has her hands on my face, and my hands slide down over her hips, pulling her magnificent skirts aside, and then slipping underneath them.

I smile. "You lied to me, Miss Serendipitous." She does not stop kissing me, simply grins through my accusation. "You're not only *not* wearing Skinnies, you're not wearing anything."

She whispers into my ear, "Shut up and fuck me, Steve. Just don't rip the dress. It's worth like forty thousand dollars."

I pause, causing her to pause too. "Well, there is only one way to ensure that this dress comes out the other end alive. Let's just take it off."

I reach around her back, find the zipper, and slowly drag it down her spine. She shrugs her shoulders together and I slip it over them, sliding the beaded bodice down her arms and to her waist.

I stare at her breasts for a moment, in awe. Then shake myself out of it when Cordelia flips over on her side, tugs the dress down her legs, throws it—carefully—into the back seat, and is back on my lap in an instant, suddenly wearing nothing but a lacy lavender bra.

My dick starts growing inside my bespoke trousers and all I can think is that I'm wearing way too many clothes.

But Cordelia starts kissing me again. Her fingertips nimbly loosen my bowtie and unbutton my waistcoat, then my shirt. And the next thing I know, she's sliding her hand across my bare chest.

She pulls back and touches her forehead to mine. "My God, Steve. Your body is like a fucking statue."

I hold up a finger. "One moment, please." And then I have my coat off, my waistcoat off, my shirt off and we are staring each other in the eyes as the car pulls in to a scenic overlook.

Her hand is suddenly working my belt and I'm sitting back, just watching her.

She gets it undone. Pauses to look up and grin at me. And then bites her lip as she slides her hand into my pants.

I'm closing my eyes in ecstasy when her hand wraps around my shaft and begins to slowly slide up and down.

I enjoy it for a moment. Just burning the memory into my head to keep forever. Because I want to replay this night back on repeat for centuries.

But then I open them again and pop the hooks of her bra behind her back. The bra comes loose and she shrugs her shoulders again, allowing it to slide over her shoulders and down her arms.

I nod in approval when her breasts are suddenly right there. And the next thing I know, I've got one lifted up to my mouth. She arches her back, lifts up her hips, and pulls my dick out of my pants. The next thing I know, she's sliding me up to her entrance. Sitting down, putting me inside her.

There is a shared gasp as we stay absolutely still for a moment.

And then… then we fuck.

The car bouncing, the scene lights of yesteryear LA all around us, and 'In the Mood' by Glenn Miller playing on the radio.

CHAPTER TWENTY-ONE – CORDELIA

As I settle the dress back into some approximation of place, I notice Steve looking at me out of the corner of my peripheral vision.

"What?" I ask. "Is something…?" I wipe at my face, pulling down the old-school sun visor to see if there's a mirror. There isn't. Shoot. I wonder if I smeared my lipstick. It's supposed to be smear-proof, but that never really—

""Shut up and fuck me?"" he says through a grin.

Oh. That. I nibble at my lip. I did, in fact, say those words. "I… Yeah. Why? Did it sound… stupid?" I turn my head to half-look at him and then look away again, suddenly embarrassed.

"No. God, no. It sounded… like exactly what I wanted to hear. I'm just surprised."

"Why? Because I don't seem like the command—"

"Because you don't seem like the command-giving type, no." He smiles wider and pauses, then adds, "Although you did command that I choke you a couple of nights ago, so… I dunno." I sneak another head-on glance and his now-fully-widened smile puts me at immediate ease.

"Yeah… I'm… I'm trying some new stuff."

"Like what?" I can detect a hint of—hope?—in the question.

"Like… just chilling out a little, I suppose? It's not my default setting."

"I've noticed." He laughs a tiny bit and takes me by the hand. "Well… I think chill looks great on you. Just like that dress."

I can feel my shoulders drop. Whatever residual tension I was holding onto immediately scampers away. I breathe, trying to just take in what he's saying and not issue a whole litany of apologies and protests. Instead, I just stare at the projected images of Mulholland Drive through the windshield of the car as a song I recognize as 'Mood Indigo' by Duke Ellington plays on the stereo.

"Can I ask you a question?" I ask, redundantly.

"Of course."

"Weren't Glenn Miller and Duke Ellington popular in the forties?"

A beat before he says, "Sorry?"

"This is supposed to be a Roaring Twenties party, right? And isn't the car also an anachronism? Like, a 1920s car wouldn't have a radio, probably. And, if it did, wouldn't it be playing Gershwin instead? Or Fanny Brice, maybe?"

He stares at me, stroking my fingers with his, then, smiling yet wider still, if that's possible, says, "Let's just go enjoy the anachronism."

As he grips the handle to open up the car door, my breath accelerates a bit. Here, inside this fantasy-mobile, alone with him, I feel all right. But he's going to open up the door and I'm going to have to get absorbed into a room full of people again. People who very likely know exactly what we were doing in here. Because it wasn't particularly quiet, if I'm being honest.

As if he's reading my mind, Steve squeezes my hand and says, "Nobody cares."

"What?"

"Nobody cares. And if they do, fuck 'em. That just means they're the Leslie Munches of the world and they don't want other people to be happy. Which is sad for them. Not for you."

He winks and I melt a little. Not too much. I don't want to ruin the dress. *Ha. I just made a little joke to myself. Nice, Cord. Good for you.*

The door opens and…

… he's right. No one even really looks in our direction.

And just as we're passing one of the other photo booth-cum-vintage autos—the one we skipped over because it was bouncing—to head into the ballroom, the door flings open and James and Audrey Saint come tumbling out. And, instantly, I realize why Steve told me that nobody cares. Because Steve and Audrey look like they have just been whipped around in a windstorm *inside* a hurricane run through the Large Hadron Collider.

Audrey's hair is a bird's nest of mayhem and James' pants are… are they on backwards? Yep. They appear to be on backwards. Not sure how the hell that managed to happen, but…

"Buddy, bro, bro!" James exclaims as he and Audrey see us. "Y'all having a good time?" He winks. Audrey smiles politely, smoothing out her dignity as she runs her hand along her hair. Steve throws up a hand in a wave and we continue on, headed back to the ballroom where the main event is taking place.

"That's really sweet," I say without expecting to.

"What is?"

"That they're so into each other. Even with kids back home and… I just think it's sweet. That people who've been together as long as they have can still be hot for each other."

"Yeah…" Steve says, then pauses for the briefest of moments before tagging on, "Something to aspire to. C'mon."

We enter the main hall and the party is still going strong, an effulgence of romance authors doing their thing alongside a… potpourri of readers? (I gotta workshop that one.) Everyone is bedecked in vintage regalia and partying up a storm. Sheila now looks to be leading an impromptu Charleston class on the dancefloor. It's a wild time.

"Looks fun," Steve says.

"It really is. You wanna learn?"

"What? The Charleston?" Steve asks. I nod. "Yeah. Hell yeah. What kind of twenty-first-century man doesn't wanna know how to Charleston? Let's cut a rug."

I laugh as he grabs me by the hand, and then we're in the middle of the action, navigating our way around cool cats and hep dames all cutting up the carpet. (There is no actual carpet. Just parqueted hardwood. But I don't think there's a throwback expression for 'parqueted hardwood.')

We make our way up to Sheila, who doesn't even look winded.

"Sheila?" She looks up at me as I say her name. "Sheila… this is Steve. Steve is…" I look at him. What do I call him? What do I say? Steve is SS's brother? Steve *is* SS? Steve is the guy who invited me here and is maybe kind of changing my life in real time? But before I have to make a choice of any kind, Steve chimes in.

"Steve is a big, big fan of your tenant." He takes Sheila by her jitterbugging hand and kisses it. She draws her head back, raises an eyebrow.

"Oh, well, aren't you just… all of you?" she says, saucily.

"What does that—?" Steve starts to ask, but is cut off as Sheila grabs him by both hands and shouts…

"Swing me!"

He does. He spins her around and she twirls in place. Like the showgirl she once wanted to be and, in some essential way, still is. I watch for a moment as he spins her, counter-stepping with a grace and sophistication that I never would have expected. He slides, and twists, and moves Sheila around the floor like they've been dancing together for years.

And as I watch them I think… *If I wrote this all down in a book, no one would believe it.*

This whole week. It's all just so…

Or no. That's not necessarily true. Maybe they would. Maybe… maybe it's *me* who wouldn't believe it. Maybe it's me who's judgmental. Because I learned to be.

I tend to look for things like 'thematic coherence' and 'narrative throughlines' in *everything*. Like, in a real A+B=C kind of a way. But, since meeting Steve, the things that have happened to me have unfolded in an outlandish way that tests credulity and lacks what my brain tends to seek as a cohesive architecture.

And what is dawning on me now like a new day's sun is… so what?

I've spent so much time in my own life trying to do the right thing and control my own narrative that I haven't made much room for spontaneity and surprise.

One of the dictionary definitions of romance is: 'A quality or feeling of mystery, excitement, and remoteness from everyday life.'

So maybe it would do me good to just… not care. Like Steve said, nobody cares.

What's the worst that happens if all that's going on with me right now isn't exactly as I had planned it? Or doesn't make sense?

The worst thing is that I might find that I love all this that has happened. That is happening.

Because this is my life. My real life.

I've had a great couple of days, all in all. People have been so nice. People have told me they've liked what I've written. People have seemed to like me. Steve has seemed to like me. And *that's* what's real. Not whatever future I intended for myself. The future doesn't exist. It's no more real than the stories I write. But this, here, now, this *is* real. And it's wonderful.

Time to venture free from the life in your mind and into the life that you're living, Cord.

I feel a hand on my shoulder. Britney. "Hey, girly," she says, smiling. "You having fun? At all? You okay?"

I turn to her, a big grin on my face, and say, "Yeah. I'm having a great time."

Her eyes go kind of wide as she smiles too. And then she gets teary, throws her arms around my neck, smothering me in a hug, and whispers, "Good. You deserve it."

Just as she's pulling away, I hear the song end and Steve's voice say, "Sheila. Can flat-out. Torch."

Britney and I break our embrace and I turn around to see Steve sweating. A lot.

"Yeah. She's something," I say.

"Looking good out there, son!" A handsome-looking couple whom I recognize as Steve and Essie's parents walk up. "Nice moves, my boy," his dad says, patting Steve on the shoulder.

"Huh?" Steve says, seemingly surprised. "Oh. Thanks, Dad."

His mom smiles, looks at me and Britney, and introduces herself. "Hello. Phyllis Smith."

"Uh, sorry," Steve jumps in. "Mom, Dad, this is Cordelia Sarantopoulos. She writes under the name Cynthia Lear. And her friend, Britney Kincaid. Cordelia, Britney, these are my parents, Phyllis and Tom Smith."

We all shake hands and exchange pleasantries and then Phyllis turns to Steve and says, "Well! Those dance classes we made you take in middle school finally paid off, huh?" It's obvious that she means it as a good-natured joke, but Steve bristles a little.

"Yeah, who woulda thought that just two scant decades later, I'd finally be able to apply all the valuable skills I learned in Ms. Fabergé's School for Emerging Ballerinas?"

I bark out a laugh by accident. "What's that now?"

"When Stevie was a young man, we wanted him to be about more than just sports and video games. So, we enrolled him in a dance class," Phyllis says.

"To be fair," his dad adds, "we did make Essie join that rugby team as well. We always wanted our kids to be well-rounded."

Steve looks like he wants to dig a hole and jump in.

"Well, it paid off. Your children are two of the most interesting people I've ever met," I say.

"Aren't you sweet?" Phyllis coos.

"Maybe? But I also happen to mean it." I smile.

They laugh.

"And aren't you a pistol?" Tom Smith chortles.

Just then, the white-dinner-jacketed, pencil-mustachioed bandleader up on the bandstand says, "All right, ladies and you couple of gentlemen"—he laughs—"we're going to slow it all down for a moment and let everyone catch their breath. This next number is an Irving Berlin tune from 1925, written as a kind of a love letter to his soon-to-be wife, Ellin. This is… 'Always.'"

The piano player begins with the delicate first notes of the song as the overhead lighting in the room dims and twinkle lights sparkle to life, replicating a starry night on the ceiling above. Steve grabs my hand again and pulls me to the dance floor.

"Oh, nice to meet—" I get out to his parents before I'm tugged away and Steve has me pressed against him, swaying me back and forth to the tender melody.

After a second… "Dance class," I say, with a smirk in my voice.

"Don't start," he says, shaking his head.

"I'm sorry. It's just… it's sweet."

"That's one word for it," he says, smiling in spite of himself.

"They seem cute," I offer up.

"They're fine." We dance in silence for a moment before he adds, "They don't know."

"Don't know what?"

"What you know. About me. SS. All that."

I find this very… unexpected. "Really?" He nods. "Why not?"

"I dunno." He pauses swaying with me for a moment. "I just remembered you telling me the other day that your parents don't know what you're writing, and… Doesn't matter. I dunno why I brought it up." He pulls me into him, we start dancing again, and I let my head rest on his chest. Because that's as high up as my head goes. Which, in my opinion, is just about perfect.

We move in motion to the music and I decide to say something. I play it through a couple of times in my head to make sure it's what I really want to say right now and, deciding it absolutely is, I don't gatekeep my own thoughts, instead letting them out into the world. Even though it feels scary. Because I'm going to choose to live my life. Not just dream about it.

"I have to tell you something," I say.

"Okay." We continue moving in time to the piano.

"I'm not sure I believe you," I say. He stops moving, stares down into my face, a worried expression. "I think… I think maybe you did steal something." His brow furrows more deeply. "I honestly don't think you meant to. That's not what I'm saying. I don't think you're a liar or intentionally trying to be a thief, but you did steal *something*."

He sighs and I feel the breath enter and leave his body. "What?" he finally asks.

I sigh in return and feel my own chest heave and press into his. "My heart," I manage to get out before it stays trapped in my throat forever.

He doesn't smile. His expression doesn't change at all, in fact. He just looks at me, bends his head forward, kisses me gently on the mouth, and then begins swaying us both to the music once more.

♥♡♥♡♥♡♥♡♥♡♥

The last of the crowd is filing out of the ballroom. It's late and there's still one more day. Things are winding down.

Steve and Essie are talking to the bandleader, settling up, giving the band a big tip for their service. As well they should. The band was awesome. The whole evening was awesome. I feel happy and bathed in the warmth of… I'm not sure what. Could be the warmth of having had sex in semi-public with a guy who later slow-danced with me and let me rest my head on his chest. Or it could be the warmth of feeling like I've possibly found my tribe. And my voice. My true voice, I mean—not the one I think people want, or the one that seeks to sound like Jane Austen, but mine. Cordelia's voice.

Maybe still too early in these abrupt revelations to know for sure.

There's always the possibility that this could be my Cinderella moment. That I could wake up in the morning and find myself sleeping in the fireplace again. But… I dunno. I don't think so.

At least, I hope not.

Britney has taken Sheila back upstairs. Against her wishes. Sheila, now adjusted to being back in Vegas for the first time in a long time, I suppose, wanted to hit the slots. But Britney dragged her to her suite. I think. For all I know, Sheila ditched her and is down on the Strip right now, looking for the ghost of Dean Martin.

I pull my phone out of my clutch to text and make sure everyone got to their room okay when I see a notification. Requesting that I download the Aria's SparkleNight DreamWeaver's WishMaker app.

Huh. That's odd. I wonder if that's just a default thing that happens when you get a room here. They send you an alert to keep you in their system. Of course they do. That's how they keep you coming back. I forgot for a moment that it's not really the 1920s.

Whatever. They're probably already tracking me anyway. So, I go ahead and click the…

Yep. Click that. Then click… Yep. Okay. Accept the terms and… All right. Add to home screen… Okay. Set user name… Um… Leering Lass. Yeah, that's fun. Play on my pen name. Great… Set password. Uh-oh, Goneril69. Ha. That's funny. Shakespeare and sexy talk all rolled into one. I'm too clever for my own good. Love it. Okay. And…

… I get another notification. Congratulating me. For reaching the SparkleNight DreamWeaver's DreamDate WishMaker Bonus Level.

Huh. That's even odder. I wonder—

Steve approaches from having settled up with the band.

"All good?" I ask.

"Yeah, they didn't wanna take the tip."

"Really?"

He nods. "Said they're already part of the package and yadda, yadda, yadda."

"What'd you do?"

"I made 'em take the damn tip."

I smile.

"What?"

"Nothing. You're just a nice guy."

He rolls his eyes, but then bends down and kisses me on the mouth. My stomach gets… twingly. Not a word, but how it gets.

"You, uh… you wanna come with me to my room?" he asks.

"I could," I say, doing my best impression of a coquette. "But isn't that wasteful? You went through all the trouble of getting me my own room here and—"

He kisses me again, this time long and deep, and I stop talking.

"What were you saying?" he asks after finally disconnecting our lips from one another's.

"Huh?" I say, in something of a daze. "Nothing."

He grins, grips my hand, and we head for the elevator up to his suite.

DreamDate WishMaker Bonus Level, indeed.

MEANWHILE…

Meanwhile…

Leslie Munch staggers out of the taxi in front of the Aria hotel around two a.m., drugged out of her mind on painkillers. She's holding an ice pack against her broken nose and even though the painkillers should've put her in a good mood, she's fuming.

Elaine and Angela ditched her. She called, she texted, sending a flurry of messages from the ER, and they never responded.

How dare they? That's what Leslie is thinking as she makes her way into the Aria. How dare they not come to her aid in her time of need? Her nose is broken! One of her eyes is almost swollen shut! And there is a suspicious twang in her front tooth that might indicate a coming root canal!

And the worst thing is—she has no one to blame. No one specific, anyway. Because she didn't see the miscreant who bashed her face in with a door. Oh, she's planning a lawsuit, all right. She will be getting right on that tomorrow. But she will be suing a hotel.

That isn't satisfying! How could she ever get any personal satisfaction out of suing a nameless, faceless corporation?

She couldn't.

She wants to ruin someone over this.

Leslie stumbles into the elevator and takes it up to her floor. It is only now, when she's standing in front of her door, that she realizes she doesn't have her key. In fact, she doesn't even have her purse.

She has her phone, which has a case with a slide-in pocket for credit cards and ID. That's how she paid for her taxi. But no purse. And no room key.

She closes her eyes, takes a deep, deep breath as she bows her head, and promises to sacrifice a chicken to Moloch the minute she gets home if luck could just… cut her a break.

Just one break. Just one. That's all she needs.

The sound of music through earbuds interrupts her little prayer. And when she opens her eyes, there is a maid pushing one of those laundry carts down the hallway.

It's an odd time of the night to be cleaning rooms, but it *is* Vegas.

The maid is bobbing her head and paying no attention to Leslie. The maid probably won't help her. But then again, didn't Elaine and Angela say that the maids here were super-helpful?

That wasn't actually what Elaine and Angela had said, but Leslie is pretty fucked up on Vicodin, so she runs with it and puts a hand up as the maid passes. "Excuse me."

The maid takes an ear bud out. "¿Qué?"

"Can you let me in my room?" Leslie points to her door. "I lost my purse. I had to go to the emergency room." She points to her face.

The maid shakes her head and makes a face. "Perra loca."

"Right. The door? Can you open it?"

The maid sighs. And then, just as a sneaky smile is playing across her face, she looks down at her master room card, hiding her reaction. Quickly she looks up again and nods, flashing her key card at Leslie's door.

Leslie claps her hands, almost falls over, then carefully lets herself into the room.

She doesn't even say thank you.

Once inside, she stumbles over to her bed and falls back onto the mattress, letting out a long sigh. Her eyes close. Her brain right on the edge of sleep.

But then, as one's brain does when it's winding down for the night, Leslie's brain begins to wander. And then it puts on her Raylen Star hat and starts replaying that dreadful moment when the door smashed into her face all over again.

This is the worst signing of her entire career. Not even losing that lawsuit against Essie can hold a candle to the dreadfulness of this convention. This past week has been even worse than reciting that public apology for suing Essie.

Everything has gone wrong these past four days.

Why did they even invite her? Everyone knows that Steve and Essie hate Raylen Star.

"Wait." She sits straight up in bed, a thought occurring to her. "Did they…?" No. No. Her conspiracy mind has gone too far this time. Surely—surely—petite, professional, popular Essie Smith and her stupid brother, Steve, did not, absolutely did. Not. Invite Leslie here, to their signing, just so they could humiliate her.

No.

But… it *is* awfully suspicious that she got the worst table placement, got the worst panel assignment, then—after insisting on a better panel assignment—got the only mic in the room that didn't work. Not to mention her regular panel was cancelled. And then, just minutes later, she found herself conveniently stuck in the elevator.

She missed all the private parties last night.

She missed the gala tonight!

And *they* did that. They did it on purpose.

What else have they done? What other fresh hell is waiting for Leslie just right around the corner?

"Oh, my god." She pats around the crumpled covers—and holy shit! Her room wasn't even cleaned today! WTAF? She adds this to her mental list of wrongs as her fingertips find her phone and start tapping across the screen. Her eyes squinting from the too-bright screen glare. "Heh," she grunts. "It should be in dark mode." And that was. *It.* That was *it*!

They even fucked with her dark mode setting on her phone!

She lets out a long breath that does nothing to calm her nerves because she knows, absolutely knows, that there is more coming…

"No!" Her fingertips start scrolling. "No, no, no. Please tell me—ahhhhhhhhhhhhhhh!" she screams. "No!"

But rejecting reality isn't going to change this.

The damage has been done.

She's scrolling the online Sin With Us Attendee social group, and sure enough, there's a video of the entire accident. Taken by the assistant to an author who was signing at a table right across the aisle from Leslie.

The assistant captioned the video, 'It was only a matter of time.'

That *bitch*. She sat there all damn day, watching with glee, as the catering room door bumped, and smacked, and whacked against Leslie's table.

'It was only a matter of time,' indeed.

There are three hundred comments. Some supportive, some not. If Leslie wasn't so fucked up on drugs right now, she'd take down the names of those good-for-nothing, unsupportive lowlifes and launch a one-star review campaign against them.

Unfortunately, they are not authors, they are readers. And aside from some serious stalking to rouse up a cancel campaign, there is no real way to get back at them.

But there are authors in this thread. Plenty of them.

Leslie won't let this drag her down. The whole incident has been caught on video, which will be super helpful in her lawsuit against the Aria.

"No!" Leslie says this out loud. "*Not* the Aria." Then she snickers.

Suing the Aria wouldn't give her the satisfaction she requires. She is going to sue Sin With Us, and Steve Smith, and Essie Smith, and whoever it was who made the seating chart, *and* that good-for-nothing author assistant who watched her face danger all damn day and never said a word about it. Not to mention all the unsupportive bitches who commented on that group post.

She squeezes the two side buttons on her phone, trying to take a screenshot—but something goes wrong, and her screen flashes and goes black.

Shit. She shut it down by mistake.

No matter. One more button press and the phone is restarting. Two minutes later she's back in the group, scrolling, and scrolling, and scrolling, and *scrolling…* looking for that post.

But it's gone.

Deleted! Probably by Essie herself!

"Shit. This *is* a conspiracy! They're all against me!"

All this excitement is making Leslie's head swoon. Luckily, there is a minibar. Not only will two or three tiny bottles of Jack and Absolute calm her, it'll be an appropriate way to celebrate.

Because not only is she going to sue *everyone*, she is going to ruin the entire final day of the convention. And she is going to do it promptly at ten a.m. during the awards ceremony. *And the award for Best Liar in the Romance Community goes to… Steve and Essie Smith.*

Leslie Munch makes an evil cackle-laugh.

Because she has a secret—a very big secret.

After tomorrow, though, it'll never be a secret again.

She drinks every bottle in her mini-fridge, snickering and snorting as she pictures what this little scheme of hers might look like in her head.

She could maybe even write a book about this, casting herself as the heroine. Oooh! An autobiography, of sorts.

And so Leslie Munch passes out dreaming about revenge and her face on a book cover titled *Bitches (and Bros) of Romance: Reading Between the Lies.*

Leslie cackles again. Her imagination is gold.

She'll get that little dog yet.

CHAPTER TWENTY-TWO — STEVE

THE FINAL DAY

The final morning of the convention has morphed into something of an awards ceremony over the years. It started out as a 'best of' kind of thing. I had little rosette ribbons printed up with different titles that first year, like the one I make for Mom. Only they would say things like 'Best Kiss in an Elevator' for authors. Or 'Best Growl in an Audiobook' for narrators. Or 'Best Preorder Bag-Filler' for assistants and helpers.

Readers and listeners aren't invited to this final event. Their big night is the Saturday gala. Besides, they're all sleeping in because the signing doesn't start until ten a.m. on the last day.

There is also a breakfast for the authors, narrators, and assistants and helpers. The breakfast room is adjacent to where all the book signing happens and that's where everyone gathers while Mom and Dad walk around the signing hall pinning the ribbons to each author's table.

Every author gets one, but it's not merely an appreciation prize or participation trophy, because each ribbon is unique.

Mom delivers them, not Essie. Because Mom makes it up as she goes and no one feels slighted, passed-over, or insulted should they win something like 'Best Purple Prose,' because while the Official Rom-Mom is cute, and sweet, and well into her sixties, she doesn't have a mean-spirited bone in her body.

When I walk into the signing hall, I head straight for the staging room where we keep all the ribbons, just to make sure everything's still going smoothly.

Mom and Dad are already in there, reading the ribbons and giggling.

"There you are." I give my mom a kiss on the cheek. "Are you two all ready to hand out the awards?"

"Well," Dad says, "your mother and I were thinking, son."

Great. Here it comes. I brace myself for the car crash. "You were thinking… what? Is there something wrong with the ribbons?"

"No, hon." My mom smiles at me. "We were thinking you should come help me pass out ribbons this time."

"Me?" I point to myself. "Why would I want to go?"

"Steve. Your mother is trying to spend time with you. Why do you always have to be so defensive?"

I open my mouth to defend myself, realize 'defend' and 'defensive' are related, and change course. "Sorry. It's just…" I stop again, then smile. "I'd love to, Mom. Come on. We've got three hundred tables to hit."

She hooks her arm into mine and we go back out onto the convention floor. "Let's start way over there in the corner and work our way around." I'm pointing to a table in the corner.

"Sounds good to me, Steve."

Unfortunately, the table I was pointing to belongs to Raylen Star. Mom and I look at each other and laugh.

"How did she get invited anyway?" Mom asks.

"I have no idea. But… tradition is tradition. Which ribbon should we give her?"

Mom flashes me a side-eye. "I don't suppose you have one that says 'Best Nasty Bitch' in this basket, do you?"

I chuckle. "No, Mom. But I have to admit, Leslie really didn't make any trouble this year. Let's repay the respect." I flick through the ribbons and pull one out. "How about this?"

Mom takes it out of my hand, slides her glasses down her nose to read the rosette, and then smiles up at me, nodding her head. "You're a nice boy, Steve."

"Thanks, Mom."

And she pins the ribbon to Raylen Star's tablecloth.

The rosette reads: 'Best Author Profile Pic.'

Which is a lie. Raylen's profile pic is a selfie, for fuck's sake. But what the hell. I think it'll make her smile.

And it would be nice to let bygones be bygones, even if her being invited here in the first place was a mistake.

We go around to all the tables, pinning ribbons to tablecloths. And when we get to Cynthia Lear's table, I hold my breath as Mom shuffles through the basket. She grins, then hands it to me. "You pin this one."

Her rosette reads: 'Best Up-and-Coming Superstar.'

And I happily pin that ribbon to Cordelia's table.

♥♡♥♡♥♡♥♡♥♡♥

It takes a good long while to pass out all the ribbons and by the time we're done, it's nearly nine-thirty. Time to get ready for the last signing session.

I kiss Mom on the cheek and send her off with Dad, feeling good about this morning. But we cannot end the author breakfast until I make my own little awards presentation.

I go back to the staging room and open a box with a pink velvet bag inside, grab it, and then make my way through the catering door and into the break room.

The room of maids stand and clap when I enter. "Oh, ladies! Please." I beg them to sit down. "I'm late. You should be booing me!"

"Mr. Steve," Rosa says—she's the head maid on the convention level. "We could never boo you. You make us smile with your books."

"Oh. I can boo him for something, Rosa." This comes from Margarita. "This year, we have nothing for you to sign, Mr. Steve. Because you publish no books this past year!"

"I know." I cringe. They have always known it was me. The first two years they just gave me knowing side-eyes or eyebrow waggles when I handed them their thank-you envelopes from the pink velvet bag. One cannot throw a gala the night before an author-narrator-assistant breakfast the next morning without a gargantuan number of elves making the party disappear and getting things ready for a gargantuan amount of food.

The maids on the convention level are my elves. They make everything run smoothly.

Anyway. The third year when I came in to give them their bonuses for pulling an all-nighter, they had stacks of books in the breakroom.

My books.

And they wanted me to sign them.

No one said anything about SS. And I signed them all Steve Smith.

And every year since then, they've brought books for me to sign.

"Oh, Margarita," Carmen says. "You're mean. And you're wrong! Steve wrote"—and she pulls a book out from behind her back—"*this.*"

I smile. Then laugh. Because it's *Alien Ascension.* Book three of my terrible, no-good, piece-of-shit sci-fi series. Which actually did release this past year.

And then everyone brings a hand out from behind their backs.

In every hand is that same book.

A book with my real name on it.

I sign them all right there in the break room, sitting at an old plastic table with no banner, or tablecloth, or swag to give out. And I tuck their bonus envelopes into the pages before I hand it back.

By the time I'm done, it's nearly eleven and I've already missed an hour of the signing.

But I don't care.

I think… I think signing those books for the maids might be the highlight of my entire career.

They all blow me kisses as I head out and promise to see me next year.

When I get back out to the floor, the place is wall-to-wall packed. And I notice that the catering door smacks Leslie's table when it opens.

I peek around the door, ready for the wrath of Raylen, but… she's not there.

"Huh." She must be in the bathroom. I figure I'll do her a favor and move her table over so that door won't drive her crazy. There's not really enough room. The tables along this wall are kinda packed together.

But I am Steve. So I clap my hands, use my Tank voice, and says, "Authors. Can I bother you to move your tables down a foot? Because Raylen Star's table is too close to the door. Can we do that, please?"

Before I'm even done speaking, a hundred people—authors and assistants, readers and listeners, narrators and models—are all moving the tables.

Literally two minutes later, the problem is solved.

I move Leslie's table myself.

Then I sigh, and make my way through the signing, walking up and down the aisles saying hello. And after I've gone by every table so I can joke with everyone about their rosette ribbon, I end up at Essie's table.

I haven't spent much time with her. But she doesn't need my help. She is generous, and happy, and laughing, and she makes time for every single person in the line. She will sign any book you put in front of her, no limit. And even if someone is only coming for her to sign an autograph book, she makes sure they leave that table with something from her secret swag bag.

A free water bottle with our logo on it.

A pair of fuzzy socks with Master Choke's hands wrapped around the ankle.

A tea towel with Sugar's face on it.

Or even a free book. But sometimes, those readers don't want paper books. No place to put them. That's why we have the secret swag box.

Everyone looks pretty happy.

Of course, every convention has some disappointment. But all in all, it's not a bad gig, ya know?

It's really not.

Sometimes it gets to me that I have to pretend to be something I'm not, but honestly, I'm pretty much the luckiest Ro-Bro on the planet.

CHAPTER TWENTY-THREE – CORDELIA

"We had sex again," I whisper.

"What?" Britney whispers back as we approach the signing table.

"After we went back up to his room, we had sex *again*."

"Giiiiiiiiiiiiirl," Britney draws out.

"I know."

"Where is he now?"

"I'm not sure. Around. He had to come down to get stuff ready for today."

"And you didn't go to the author breakfast?"

"No, I was planning on it, but Steve ordered me a whole buffet again before he headed down to get everything together."

"Oh, my God."

"I know. And that was, of course, after we went back up to his suite and had sex… again."

I giggle. She giggles. We slap at each other. It's a regular teen rom-com. I think I love it.

"Hey," a voice calls out. I turn to see Audrey Saint walking toward us.

"Hey, Audrey!" I call back.

She intercepts us, looking tired. "Missed you at breakfast."

"Oh, I'm sorry."

"No worries. You've just made quite a splash."

"I… have?"

"Well, yes. I mean, really, your old-lady friend—"

"Sheila. She's my landlady."

"Ah. Well, Sheila made quite a splash anyway. Oh, Britney, James is going to send you that spreadsheet."

"Which one?" she asks.

"The one he told you about? That he uses to keep Saint Industries running? I have a feeling after this convention, you're going to need it."

"You think so?" I ask.

"Yeah. Look, you gave out some books, you brought a super-popular elderly woman to teach people how to Charleston. You've been seen publicly canoodling with Tank Watson. It's all part of the narrative. People are going to read you as much for the intrigue as anything. And when they do, they'll find out you're a kick-ass writer and then you'll be off to the races."

I blush a little just thinking about it. Not how I expected it to go, but if she's right…

"You planned your next book yet?" she asks.

"Well, I need to write the next book in my series. And I might have a new idea swirling around."

"Not ready to talk about it?" Audrey asks. I shake my head 'no.' "Good," she says, "don't. Don't give away your ideas for free."

Something about hearing her say it reminds me that I still don't know where that lone copy of *Filling the Gap* has gotten off to. The original one. I don't love that I don't know where it is. I need to find it.

"So…?" Audrey says, pulling my attention back.

"Sorry. What?"

"I said how has it been? Your first convention? Has it been all you hoped it would be?"

As we arrive at the table, I see something hanging from it. A ribbon. Getting closer, I see what it says: 'Best Up-and-Coming Superstar.'

"What's this?" I ask.

"Oh, it's a thing SS does. It's cute. This is the one I got this year." She reaches into her pocket and pulls out her ribbon. It says, 'Most Romantic Romance Couple.'

"That seems about right." I laugh.

"James… He's a lunatic, but I do love him." She pauses, looks at me, and says, "You got the right one. You're definitely on the right track. But don't be surprised if you get mine next year."

"What? Whaddayou mean? Why?"

She arches an eyebrow, winks, and walks off without saying anything further. And as she moves through the authors, shuffling about, getting ready for the doors to open, I see Steve standing on the other side of the room, smiling at me.

I clutch my ribbon. Tightly.

"Authors. Can I bother you to move your tables down a foot? Because Raylen Star's table is too close to the door. Can we do that, please?"

As soon as Steve calls out, everyone in the place steps up to make more room for Raylen Star's table, even though she's not even there. I have two thoughts.

1) Even though she's a mean person, I hope she's all right after she got hammered yesterday.

2) Steve Smith is genuinely the nicest guy I've ever met. And I hope he gets all the things he wants.

It takes all of two minutes to get Leslie's table sorted out and then Steve is walking up and down the aisles, saying hello to everyone.

He doesn't stop by my table. Which should make me nervous. But it doesn't, because he can't. There are too many people blocking the way right now.

There is no tape laid out in front of my booth area place because frankly no one would have thought that I'd need it. No need to corral everyone given that nobody really knows who I am. But, today, there's a… not potpourri… um, constellation? Ooooh. Yes. I like that. A constellation of readers all gathered at my table.

So Steve just motors past, winks at me (which makes my stomach twingly) and mouths *I'll be back* as he heads to wherever he's headed to next.

"Hi," a young woman crowding the table says.

"Hi," I say back.

"You signed one of your ARCs for my friend Marina yesterday.

"Oh, yes. The one who sounds like she has a complicated backstory."

"You don't even wanna know. But, I read a couple of pages. You're really good."

"Thank you so much."

"I've never been to Vegas before."

"Me neither," I confide. "Where are you from?"

"Cleveland," she says. "So, could you sign a copy for me? Make it out to Marie?"

I grab up a Sharpie to sign and that's when I realize…

I'm almost out of books. ARCs. They're almost all gone.

I brought boxes and boxes and boxes of books and people took them.

They took them. Because they wanted them, or because they heard good things about what I had written, or… whatever. But they took them. Because I made something that they want. Or, at least, that they are curious about. And I made all that happen all by myself.

That's something that my mom and dad never did.

They worked for other people their whole careers, writing what other people told them to write or what they got paid to, and me… I wrote the thing I love writing and people want it.

That's cool.

Is it the exact thing I originally intended? No, maybe not. But am I proud of it? Yeah. Yeah, I think I am. Because I still did it. All by myself. And I'm proud of that. What's happening here is because I took a chance. In fact, everything that's happened to me this week is because I took a chance. On myself.

I don't need a duke on a white stallion (or any other shade for that matter) to ride in and save me. I can do it myself.

I knew that. Of course I knew that. But knowing a thing and feeling it is very different. And maybe that's what this sensation is. I *feel* that I can make it all happen for myself. Hell, maybe I will just publish the original copy of *Filling the Gap* as well. I don't need permission. I can do what I want. And then… let the chips fall where they may!

"Cynthia?" Marie from Cleveland says.

"Sorry." I chuckle. "Got distracted." I bend down, sign the copy of *Filling the Gap*, "To Marie," and hand it back. And as I do, I think again…

But is it possible that I accidentally gave away the one copy? I should really figure out—

"Can I get a picture?" Marie from Cleveland asks.

"Oh, yes, of course."

She hands Britney her phone, stands beside me, and Britney memorializes the moment between the two of us.

"Thanks!" Marie beams and heads off.

"You're almost out of books," Britney confirms.

"I was noticing. Hey, have you seen the one?"

"Which one?"

"The one with the white cover? Black lettering. The one."

"No. Is it missing?"

"Yeah."

There is silence as both of us think about it. But the silence is short-lived because then…

"Can you make one out to Wendy?" says a small woman with nice teeth whose name, I assume is, Wendy.

"Yes, absolutely," I tell her, as I pick up one of the remaining copies I have at the table and grab the Sharpie. And as I'm writing Wendy's name into the front cover, I turn to Britney and with an assuredness I'm almost certain I mean, say, "I'm sure it'll turn up."

MEANWHILE…

Meanwhile…

At three o'clock in the afternoon, as the signing day is nearing its end and the annual Sin With Us convention run by SS and her brother Steve is winding to a close, Raylen Star, aka Leslie Munch…

… finally wakes up.

The skeletons of fallen soldiers with names like Jack Daniel and Jim Beam lay scattered around her on the rumpled duvet, drained of all that once made them vibrant and whole. Now all that remain are the transparent shells of their former selves.

Leslie moans and throws her arm over her face to try to mute the offending rays that pierce the veil of the drawn curtains in her west-facing hotel room as the summer sun drops lower in the desert sky. Forgetting, unfortunately, that she has a broken nose, a swollen eye, and a suspiciously twanging tooth that might well be the portent of a pending root canal.

"Fuck me!" she shouts as her forearm strikes her various cranio-facial wounds.

Sitting up, she wrestles with how to make the pain stop. She instinctively begins to rub at the bruised area, but that, obviously, makes everything oh, so much worse. So, she stands and begins simply shaking her hands and vibrating in place, trying not to sneeze, because the stinging pain inside her nasal cavity has the faintest hint of a tickle as well and if she were to sneeze… well, that isn't something any reasonable person would want.

And even though Leslie Munch, by all known evidence, is not a reasonable person, it isn't something she wants either.

Then, she remembers her breathing, some advice given to her by some quack fucking shrink she'd been ordered to see once as part of a plea deal to help her avoid jail time for…

Know what? Doesn't matter. The point is that this fucking quack was part of an anger management agreement thing and even though he was a fucking quack, he had given her exactly one tool she could add to her toolbox for when things got too stressful to manage.

Breathe. X number of deep breaths in. X number of deep breaths out.

She can't really remember the exact number, but whatever. Some dumbass approximation will be adequate in this case.

So in, out, she breathes. In. Out. And, sure enough, her oxygenated lungs seem to help her calm and still enough so that the pain isn't quite so debilitating. Okay. Very good. Everything will be fine. All will be good.

And then...

She looks at the clock.

"What the fuck?" she exclaims to no one.

Three o'clock means the day is almost over. The signing is almost at its end. The entire convention is almost at its end. Her plans, her best-laid fucking plans are about to be null.

Is Essie behind this? Steve? The parents? That little bitch Cynthia Whosehertoes? All of them? Probably! They are likely all working in cahoots! Cahoots, Leslie will tell you!

If she hurries downstairs right now, she might still be able to engage in her action. She might still have time to write her crowning chapter. Put the coda on the story of betrayal and avarice and sheer… fuck, what was a good word for douchebaggery? There might be no better word than the word itself. Fuck it. Douchebaggery!

She can get editorial notes later. (Not that she'd take them under consideration. No one, *no one* edits Raylen Star. Raylen's words should be able to stand on their own and no half-assed, couldn't-make-it-as-a-writer-so-now-they-just-give-critique-on-other-people's-shit editor will tell her what to write.)

There is still time to force the deceitful douchebags known as the Smith Twins into something like a reckoning.

And so Leslie Munch looks around for her shoes. Where the fuck are her shoes? Goddammit! Does this conspiracy extend so far as to have someone abscond with her footwear as well? Are they so degenerate as to have broken into her room while she was convalescing and made off with her Jimmy Choos? Apparently.

No matter. All more fodder for the cannon. Kindling for the fire. Fuel for the… well, probably also fire, but fine! A war they have demanded, and so a war they shall receive.

With dried blood well and truly gathered around her gauze-wrapped nose, Leslie now darts, barefoot, for the door to her suite.

(And, to be honest, it's the barefoot thing more than anything else that is responsible for what happens next.)

Because as she steps on one of the desiccated mini whiskey bottles that has rolled off the bed and onto the floor… she trips, stubbing her toe on the edge of the desk, and smacking her forehead into a framed painting on the wall of some abstract what-the-fuck-ever-it-is, causing it to fall from its precariously nailed perch and come crashing down onto the very same toe she just stubbed.

"COCK-SMOKING DICK-TICKLING FUCK-LUCKING SMUCK-RUCKER!" she might or might not shout. But it is, at the least, some combination of those sounds.

And some further combination of those sounds is what she continues bellowing as she stumbles and limps to the elevator bank, the clamoring of her incoherent blasphemy echoing down the hall.

CHAPTER TWENTY-FOUR – STEVE

I let out a long breath as I take in the convention room.

Most of the readers have left—gone back to their rooms, to the bar, to early dinner or late lunch. But there are still about a hundred of them in here, all grabbing up the sale books. Authors hate to lug boxes of unsold books home, so if you stay 'till the end you will often be rewarded with sale books.

But a lot of authors have sold out, so they are packing up banners. Essie is still signing, so I can't start breaking down the backdrop, but I can start packing up some of the smaller banners.

I head that direction feeling very, very satisfied. What a great convention. The best, I think. It just… really came together.

"Oh, hey. Excuse me. You're—"

I turn in the direction of the voice and find a well-dressed man in a gray suit. "Tank. Yep. That's me." I smile at him. "Does your wife need a narrator? I don't have a website yet, or anything, actually. But—"

The man stops me with a palm pressing in my direction. "No, no. I'm not an author. I mean, not an author's husband. I'm Gary Pritchard. From North Star Author Agency?"

"Oooh!" My eyes go wide and I point at him. "You guys have some good books. I love that new space opera series, Galactic Spin. Fantastic."

Gary smiles. "Thanks. I signed him. Albert Reiner? He's one of mine. I got him a major deal."

"Well done you!"

He smiles bigger. "Yeah. So. That's why I'm here."

I look around. "Albert Reiner's here?"

Gary laughs. "No. You, Steve. I came to see you. I was in Vegas for another thing. That's why I'm just getting here now. But I came to talk to you."

I point at myself. "Moi?"

"That's right."

"But…" I squint. "Why?"

"You wrote a sci-fi series, right? You're the same Steve Smith, right?"

I let out a breath and my shoulders droop a little. This convention was going so well. It's one thing for the maids to bring up my sci-fi books. They're friends. But a complete stranger from the publishing business? No, thank you. I do not feel like having this conversation.

Still, even though my enthusiasm for this guy's author was real and I now feel depressed, I paint on a smile. "Yep. *Alien Alliance.*"

Gary nods. "Right. Is the series finished now?"

"Oh, yeah." I laugh. "It's over."

"Oh, that's too bad."

"Why? Everyone hated it."

"I saw the reviews, but…" He squints his eyes at me. "You didn't take them seriously, right?"

"What do you mean?"

"They're bots."

"What?" My heart begins to palpitate wildly in my chest.

"Yeah." Gary laughs. "It's clearly a bot attack. I'm not sure why Nile didn't take all those bogus reviews down, but they should've."

I'm confused. "What makes you think it's bots?"

"Did you click the profiles?"

"No. Essie ordered me not to look at them after the first hundred one-stars came in."

"Good advice. But if you had, you'd have figured it out immediately. No profile pic, one review—your book—and one star. Classic bot behavior."

"What the fuck?" I am seriously distressed. "Who would attack my book? No one even knew the name Steve Smith."

Gary just shrugs. "Why do assholes do anything, ya know? They're assholes."

"But… the blog awards—"

Gary almost snorts. "Those are fake too, Steve."

"What?"

He shakes his head at me. "You don't get out much, I take it." I'm not sure what that means, but Gary continues. "The blog awards are fixed."

"But… I know a ton of bloggers. They're not on the take."

"Are they romance bloggers?"

"Yeah, of course." I pan my hand, indicating the convention.

"I don't keep up with the romance world. Maybe they're legit. But it's a cut-throat business, ya know?"

"You don't need to tell me. We've been sued—I mean… yeah. Essie tells me all about it."

"There was a huge scandal last year about a sci-fi blog called Space, Time, Cliché. Ever heard of it?"

"They're the ones who gave me the blog award! Two years in a row!"

"Yeah, they're dirty. You can pay them to be number one. So I would not be surprised if you could pay them to make your competition come in last."

"Who would be competing with *me*?" I'm seriously confused. "I'm nobody."

Gary laughs. "Um…" Then he looks around. "I know you're just 'the brother.' But you're not exactly nobody, Steve. Which is why I'm here." He reaches into his inside pocket and takes out a business card, offering it to me. "I read your books. All three of them. I think there's more to that story. And for what it's worth, I mean, maybe they're not five stars across the board, but when you take away all those fake one-stars, you're definitely in four-point-two territory."

I just blink at him, stunned.

It's like my world twirled around on its axis and has now been flipped upside down. "I'm sorry. Did you just say two-point-four? Or four-point-two?"

He claps me on the shoulder. "I would like to represent you, Steve. Even if you don't want to write anything else in that world, I'm sure I could sell whatever it is you're planning." Then he shoots me with his finger. "Call me." And he walks away.

I just stand there for a moment, stunned.

What do I do? Pinch myself?

Was that real?

While I'm standing in the middle of the signing hall, still stunned, Mike comes up. "What's wrong? You look like you need to puke."

I offer him the card. He takes it and reads it. His eyebrows shoot up. "Wow! Did he… does he…"

"Yeah." I nod. "He wants to represent me. He says he can sell whatever it is I want to write. And you know what?" Mike leans in, interested. "He said my one-stars were bots! Can you believe that?"

"Oh, hell yeah, I can. The shit Essie sees while she's marketing would blind you, it's so mean."

"Hmm. No one ever did this to the romance books, though. Why would they do it to my sci-fi books?"

"Maybe you crossed the wrong person and didn't even know it?"

"But… I'm… *Steve.*"

Mike just laughs. "Yeah. I don't know. But Essie's just about done. You wanna help me get that banner down?"

I shake myself out of the stupor and nod. "Sure."

♥♡♥♡♥♡♥♡♥♡♥

Back behind Essie's booth I reminisce about how I first met my lovely Cordelia. She's the real reason this is the best convention. The banner alleyway is mostly gone now, including Essie's backdrop. It's always sad when the banner alleyway disappears. It's like you had this secret space and then it's like it never was.

Which is a metaphor for life, I think. It goes by so fast.

Look at me. Ten years. I've been doing this charade for ten years.

And I think… it's time… for it to be over.

Not the romance books. I still have some stories in my head that I want to write. But ya know what?—I look at the agent's card again—I've got other things to write too.

I'm gonna call this guy tomorrow. I'm gonna set up a time to talk about things. See what he's looking for. See what the market's like these days.

And then… I'm gonna do it.

I'm gonna make my dream of being a famous sci-fi writer come true.

The banner in front of me comes sliding down and suddenly, on the other side is Cordelia.

"Oh!" She takes a step back, startled. "I didn't know you were there."

I sigh, pretty fuckin' happy. "Did you have a nice last day?"

Cordelia blushes a little, and nods. "This was pretty much the highlight of my life, Steve. And not because I sold every single book I brought with me. Though that doesn't hurt, ya know?"

I smile and nod.

"I…" She hesitates. And yeah, we're at that point now. The fantasy is over, real life is one sleep away, and we don't know where this is going. "I…" she tries again.

"Hey… would you like to go out with me some time? Dinner? Beach day? Surprise trip to Maui?"

Cordelia's eyes are sparkling. "It's a date."

CHAPTER TWENTY-FIVE – CORDELIA

Steve seems to relax when I accept the invitation. Almost like he thought maybe I'd say no. Oh, how the tables have turned. Cool, easy-going Cordelia and uncertain, anxious Steve.

Ha. Not really. If he hadn't said something like, "Would you like to go out with me some time?" I might have just peed on myself. So I'm glad he did. Because I'm not wearing underwear again today because I accidentally didn't bring enough, so… Doesn't matter. I'm just really glad he said what he said. Less messy all the way round.

"Although," I add to my acceptance of the offer, "if you're telling me *now* that it's going to be a surprise trip to Maui, it won't really be a surprise."

"Okay, language cop," he says.

And then he leans down and kisses me. And even though it's not even close to our first kiss, it feels different. There's something familiar about it. Familiar, but still new. Exciting and fresh, but also eternal.

It's impossible to explain, at least with words. Which, given the value and importance I place on language, historically, is… well, funny.

This is wild. I came to this convention hoping—no, virtually begging—for the universe to give me the thing I want more than anything else. Or so I thought. I couldn't have imagined that I might desire anything more than a career in this crazy, beautiful, hopeful world of romance writing. It's all I've ever dreamed of having. The respect of my peers. The acclaim that comes of being well regarded. The halcyon glow of success.

But, it turns out, there is something I wanted more.

And it's not Steve. (Although the possibility of something more with Steve Smith is a massive bonus.)

It's being able to give all those things to myself. Respect, regard, an understanding that 'success' is, in fact, the acceptance of those things. Acceptance of myself.

I've spent a long time locked away. Locked away in my little pool house. Locked away inside my own thoughts. Holding onto things that stopped serving me a long time ago, but I just didn't see it. And all it took for me to step out of the shadow of all that and into the light was not caring what anyone else thinks.

Easier said than done, obviously, but once you see it, it's impossible to un-see it.

The kiss goes on for a long, long time. So long that I actually have to break away so that I can breathe again. I debate with myself about it first. If I pass out, he'll probably have to give me mouth-to-mouth, which would just prolong the whole thing. But there's probably a downside to collapsing here at the very end of the con that I can't immediately see.

So I pull back and pat him on the chest. "You're, uh, you're good at that," I say. He laughs. Then I look down and notice something he's holding in his hand. "What's that?"

"Oh. This?" he says, lifting up the ivory-colored rectangular card stock and showing it to me. "This is a business card."

"Whose?" He hands it over. I read it aloud for some rando reason. "Gary Pritchard. North Star Author Agency? Holy shit. They're great. I mean, they're, like, for real. They rep some serious, serious writers."

"I know."

"What did he give you his card for?"

"He, uh… he knows *Alien Alliance*."

"Your series? Your sci-fi?" I ask. He nods. "That's amazing. And…?"

"And… he wants to talk about repping me."

"For real?" I ask. He nods. "Holy shit, Steve… That's a-MAY-zing!" I don't normally co-opt Britney's trademark catchphrase, but it's applicable here.

"Yeah. Yeah. Could be cool." He seems less over-the-moon than I would have expected.

"Cool? Steve, do you know…?"

I stop myself. I was about to say something like, "Do you know what I would give to be approached by a big agency like that? That's the whole reason I came to this thing! To try to get taken seriously in the big-time world of pro publishing!" But I don't. For two reasons. (Turns out I really like making lists.)

1) It's not about me. This is about Steve and what *he* wants. And how hard he's worked to get to where he is and the way he had to give up his dreams to even get *here*. And now he's got a shot to maybe circle back

around and have what he really wanted all along. And to make it about me would ruin this moment for him. Or, if not ruin, at least turn it into something else.

2) I'm not even so sure it's what I want anymore. I mean, obviously, I want to write and have people read it and all that, but more than that… I want to spend some time really refining my voice. Really digging deep into exactly what I want to do. The stories I want to tell. Hell, I may decide I want to write… I dunno, rom-coms or something. I never thought of myself as a rom-com kinda gal, but I am unintentionally funny according to Britney, so… maybe. I dunno. The point is, I want to give myself the space to figure it out and not have to do it under the pressure of some contract or big agency deal.

But Steve… Steve knows what he wants and has already tried to make it come into being once. This is his chance to finally make good on all that effort.

"Do I know what?" he asks.

"Huh?"

"You started to say, 'Do you know…'?"

"Oh, nothing. I don't know. I got distracted. Anyway. That's so awesome. So, he's read your work? Your sci-fi stuff? This"—I look at the card again—"this Gary?"

He chews on the inside of his mouth. "Yeah."

"What's wrong?"

"Why?"

"Because you're biting the inside of your mouth. "Am I?"

"You are."

"How'd you notice?"

"Because I know what anxiety biting looks like. What's wrong?"

He stops biting at the inside of his mouth and sighs, letting his really perfect, well-muscled chest that apparently just exists that way without him having to work out at all rise and fall.

"Nothing. Just…" He looks around, then back at me. "He says that all those reviews? Those terrible reviews of my series? Of *Alien Alliance*?"

"Yeah?"

"He says they were all posted by bots."

"Bots?"

"Yeah. It's a thing on the internet where—"

"I know what bots are! Why does everyone think I don't know what things mean? Why does he think they were all bot reviews?"

"Not entirely sure. He says because of when the accounts were created, no profile pics, blah, blah, blah. His people probably have some way of ferreting that stuff out for the people he reps though. Like, their algorithms battle the bots and some AI they have culls out whatever and the next thing you know it's become some all-out cyberwar. Which, honestly, is a pretty good setup for something. I should write that down."

"People *didn't* hate your books, then."

"I mean, no? I guess not? They just didn't read them, I suppose. Y'know, if you're looking for a new book series to read and you see hundreds or thousands of terrible reviews, you're probably not gonna be like, 'Ooh, lemme see what this is about!' Unless you're a weirdo masochist or a troll or hater or whatever the kids are calling people like that these days."

I take a second to process this. "So, it's possible that your sci-fi career just never took off because of the bad reviews, which aren't bad reviews but are really just… bots?"

"Maybe? It's been a while. We knew less about bots and all that stuff than we do now."

"It wasn't *that* long ago."

"Life moves fast in the twenty-first century."

I pause to think. My brow must furrow a little because Steve asks, "What?"

"I'm just trying to think of why someone would do that. Target you. Your books."

"I dunno. Maybe it wasn't just me. Maybe it was… I dunno."

"*Alien Alliance* wasn't your *first* first attempt, right?"

"Huh? Oh, uh, no. No, I had written some other stuff alongside my friends Terry and Shawn and Luke, but it didn't sell. That's why I switched over to this. But then, y'know, those guys went back to it and I… I didn't. I tried, but *that's* when I got crucified and so I just stuck with the romance."

My wheels are turning. I rest my finger on my chin.

"Whatcha got going on in there, Nancy Drew?" Steve asks, pointing at my head.

"I'm just thinking… Who would have had something to gain from seeing you fail?

"*Gain*?"

"Yeah. Either in actuality or just, I dunno, Schadenfreude?"

"Schadenfreude? Nobody. It's not like my success means someone else's failure. Or vice versa. Terry and Shawn succeeding at writing their stuff isn't why I couldn't pop."

"Yeah. Yeah…" I ruminate aloud. And then a thought occurs to me. A possibly conspiratorial but still also completely plausible thought. Or at least not *im*plausible.

"Cordy? Super-chill Cordy? What's on your mind?"

I shake my head a little, take a breath, and say, "You don't think it possible that—?"

But that's all I get out before the loud, disruptive feedback of a microphone crackling to life overtakes the room.

MEANWHILE…

Meanwhile…

Leslie Munch taps her foot three hundred twenty-seven times after pushing the call button for the elevator, and still, no elevator comes.

"It's a conspiracy," she mumbles. "They are trying to ruin me. Humiliate me. And make me think I'm crazy."

Two women—probably readers—join her at the elevator bank. They side-eye Leslie. Probably because she's talking to herself about being crazy.

They take the stairs without comment. And Leslie might go that route too, but the moment the door to the stairwell closes, the doors to the elevator open.

"Finally." Leslie steps in, punches the button for the signing hall, and lets out a breath of relief as the doors close.

Finally. *Finally*! She is going to get them.

But the elevator doesn't move.

"You've got to be kidding me." She pushes the button again, ready to scream, and… then downward she goes.

She lets out another breath. "OK. This is it, Raylen. Your big moment. You are going to expose those lying, cheating, piece-of-shit twins if it's the last thing you do."

The pep talk is helping. Her shoulders drop. Her mind clears—well, not really. She's still very much feeling the residual effects of Vicodin and Jack Daniels from her early morning binge.

And then… *then*… the elevator comes to a stop and the doors part.

Immediately her senses are bombarded with a cacophony of noise. The sound of happy, satisfied readers. There are several dozen sitting on the floor up against the various walls. Some are alone, reading. Some are in groups, going through their bags of loot.

All of them look at her and do a double-take.

Then they start whispering.

This is when Leslie realizes she's in her nightgown. Which she doesn't even remember putting on. And not only is the aforementioned nightgown on her body, it's not something one pictures a writer of highly erotic romance wearing. It goes all the way to her knees and has pictures of cats all over it.

The romance world loves cats, but Leslie is now thinking she might've, perhaps, acted too swiftly up in her room. She is barefoot, with a smashed-up face, bloody toe, hair probably a mess—pretty much a given—in yesterday's makeup, and wearing a granny-cat nightgown.

In public.

She understands the optics. And when this is over and the Smith twins are ruined—hiding under a rock with their tails between their legs—she will need to do some serious damage control.

But that's a worry for another day.

Nothing—and she does mean nothing—is gonna stop her now.

No one is checking tickets at the entrance to the hall. It's a total free-for-all because the signing is over. Authors—loaded up with bags, and carts, and boxes—are already leaving.

Several stop to stare at her as she breezes past them into the gargantuan room.

"Hello!" Leslie yells. "Hellllll-*ooooooo*! I have an announcement to make!"

A few people close by glance at her curiously, giving her a look—which Leslie interprets as shock—then turn their backs on her.

Turn. Their backs.

"Oh, hell no," she mumbles. "Hell. No." Her eyes dart around for a solution and then… then… *then* she sees it. The room dims for her and a light shines down onto a table just to her left—probably an indication that she's lightheaded and about to faint. But Leslie pushes that thought aside and concentrates on her goal.

The announcement table. Where all those self-righteous, SS-loving volunteers called out wristband numbers on the PA system.

And the table is unattended.

It's a sign from God.

Grounds for what is about to happen next.

Her just reward for having to endure the last five days of a SS-induced nightmare.

She hobbles her way over there, grabs the microphone, holds down the push-to-talk button, and clears her throat.

The microphone crackles over the loudspeakers.

This is it. Her big moment.

Which doesn't feel as big as it should. Or, more aptly, as it *could.* In the end, she will likely regret her decision to climb on top of the table, but in this moment, it feels like a grand idea. A real cherry-on-top kind of thing.

She clambers onto the table, steadying herself with outstretched arms the way a tightrope walker might up on the high wire, and then slowly stands to her full height.

Success. She smiles, then reaches down for the PA system microphone.

A small crowd has gathered in front of her.

Someone yells, "Holy fuckin' shit!"

Another screams, "Security! *Security*!"

Leslie holds the push-to-talk button down and locks it into position. Then she clears her throat again and loudly starts her rant…

"Readers, authors, my fellow Americans, lend me your ears!"

Which makes people giggle. She maybe should've prepared a speech before the big moment, but whatever. It is what it is. "I am here to pull the curtain aside and show you the ugly truth behind the name… *Esssssss. Esssssss.*"

Murmuring begins.

"What is she talking about?"

"She's nuts."

"Are you getting this? Please tell me you're filming."

"Oh, my God! This is gold."

People are laughing at her.

But in a few seconds, no one will be talking about *her.*

So Leslie pushes all the comments aside and focuses on her goal. "Yes. That's right, my fellow pretties. I have a secret. A dirty, ugly secret about your favorite author twinsssssssss."

She's really leaning in to those s's. It feels appropriate.

"You see," she continues, "they have been lying to you."

"Yeah, right," someone close by says.

Leslie points to this disbelieving cynic. "You don't think so?" And then, as if on cue, there they are. The Smith twins, walking down the main aisle towards her. "Ask them yourself. Or better yet," Leslie continues, staring Steve Smith straight in the eyes. "I'll ask them for you. Which of you writes the books?"

More murmuring now. Louder.

"What? What is she talking about? Everyone knows Essie writes the books."

"What the fuck?"

"Someone grab that bitch and pull her down."

Leslie, now wearing her showmanship hat, bends her knees, extends her arm, and points at the crowd in front of her with a dramatic semi-circle sweep. "Oh, but you're wrong. Essie does not write the books. Steve does. They've been lying to you for ten years, bitches. Steve is the pen, Essie is just a face."

"What?" People are gasping. "Is this real?"

"Oh, my God. A man writes those books."

Mr. Audrey Saint, aka James the loudmouth husband, hops up onto the table with Leslie and grabs the microphone. "You guys! *You guys*! Come on! She's full of shit!"

Now there's a commotion and people are coming back into the signing hall. In fact, there's a huge crowd around Leslie and her table.

She grabs the microphone back from James. "Give me that. This is my moment, you jerk." Then she leans into the microphone, forcing it to make strange breathy noises, and continues. "Not only that, they invited me here to this signing to deliberately humiliate me in front of all of you. I got the worst table placement, a table that was hit by a swinging door non-stop the whole time"—she points to her face—"resulting in a debilitating injury. They locked me in an elevator!"

"What?"

"Seriously?"

"Holy shit, that's… evil."

Leslie realizes she's turning the tide. She looks over at Steve and Essie. They're just standing there, not saying anything. Leslie wants them to shriek, and deny it, and throw a fit.

So she isn't done yet. Not even close.

"Not only that, ladies, they put me on the last panel of the day and then canceled it. And my microphone didn't work on the panel I had to force myself on to! Essie wouldn't even give me a real placard! She used a piece of folded notepaper!"

Gasps. Yesssssssss.

"And were any of you in the Reader Rants panel? Did you see the riot that Steve started?"

"I was there!"

"So was I!"

"There were chairs flying everywhere!"

"I'm pretty sure someone had to be taken out in an ambulance."

Leslie is pretty sure that was her when her nose was smashed by the swinging door. But who is she to contradict a reader's opinion?

"Yes!" Leslie says. Then she points at the silent twins again. "They are not who you think they are. They were *never* who you thought they were."

Everyone in the signing hall turns to look at Essie and Steve. Who both remain stoically quiet.

And then Leslie yells, "SS… is a *fraud*."

Just as James grabs the microphone back, causing the table to tip, and Leslie Munch, aka Raylen Star, falls face-first towards the floor.

Fifteen minutes later she's got yet another ice pack on her face and is being wheeled out on a gurney to an ambulance for the second time in as many days. But this time, she is smiling.

Because fans are holding her hand, and saying nice things to her, and one is holding up a TikTok video of a famous BookToker.

A hurricane of a shit-storm is forming.

And it's all about hashtag #FraudTwins.

CHAPTER TWENTY-SIX – STEVE

"Why didn't you tell us, Steve?"

I don't look over at my dad, who is sitting in the passenger seat as we drive home from Vegas. Mom is with Essie and Mike, probably trying to have the same conversation, only in the reverse, and stuck in the tiny back seat of Essie's sports car. *Why did you let him talk you into this, Essie?*

"You're just gonna ignore me?"

"Dad… it wasn't a thing. I mean, it wasn't *supposed* to be a thing. It was one stupid book. How was I supposed to know that *Master Choke* would hit the *New York Times*?"

"That doesn't really answer my question."

"Because…" I mean, there's really only one reason so I might as well just admit it. "Because I was embarrassed, OK? It's romance. Men don't write romance. They write sci-fi. Or political thrillers. Or horror. I didn't want anyone to know."

"That *still* doesn't answer my question."

I just want him to stop talking. I just want to get home and be alone. The Twitter war is just starting and we've already got a hashtag. #FraudTwins. Nice. That's great. Just great.

"Fine," my dad says. "Fine. I guess I will leave it up to my imagination."

I scoff. And then mumble.

"What was that?" Dad asks.

"I said," I say, loudly and with a tone, "you probably would've made fun of me."

"What? Why would you say that?"

"Oh," I scoff again. It's very close to a snort. "Why? Why, Dad? Because every time I see you, all you do is remind me of what a loser I am. 'Get a job, Steve. Stop mooching off your sister, Steve.' Sound familiar?"

"I don't think that's fair. You were lying to us."

"What I choose to do with my life should not be a condition of your love. I mean, I guess if I was a drug dealer or a fuckin' kidnapper, fine. I can see the disappointment. But what the hell? The fake job title I had with Essie was perfectly legitimate. It's *her* job, you know! She's in charge of my marketing. And she's fuckin' good at it too." I pause, take a breath. "Obviously. Since I have a mansion on the beach at Malibu and forty-two million dollars in assets."

My dad almost chokes. "Did you say—"

"Yeah, I'm loaded. Go brag to your friends about that."

We don't talk the rest of the ride home. Dad's phone buzzes non-stop.

No one calls me. It's like the romance world has already put me on the blacklist. My dad starts a text convo, with Mom and Essie, probably. I just turn up the music and ignore him.

It's only four and a half hours.

It's *only* four and a half hours.

♠♡♠♡♠♡♠♡♠♡♠

Six hours and fifty-three minutes later—traffic from three crashes on the 101 is an awesome way to end a road trip with your father—I pull into my garage. There isn't too much to unload, so I just get out and start doing that, pushing banners and leftover swag boxes into the built-in cupboards.

My dad goes upstairs without a word.

Essie arrives a few minutes after me, and Mike starts unloading their car, while Essie takes Mom upstairs with Dad.

Mike sighs.

"How was it?" I ask him.

"She just kept asking us why. 'Why did you have to lie? What did we do?'"

"Did you tell her?"

"I tried to stay out of it. You know I love your mom, right, Steve?"

"Sure. And she definitely loves you."

Mike winces a little. He's wearing a dark-blue polo with a pair of those 'adventure' shorts in khaki, his brown hair all slicked back and neat, no shadow on that jaw—ever. And his eyes radiate compassion.

He's… kinda perfect. He really does look like a soap star. And I'm really satisfied—like *super* satisfied—with having Mike as a brother-in-law. I would trust no one else with my sister as much as I trust him.

But he's kind of a kiss-ass and I'm not in the mood. "*What*, Mike? What are you thinking? And for once in your life, can you please not change the subject and just spit it out?"

"Well." He sighs again. "I just think… they kind of…"

"They kind of *what*?"

"Treat you like… well, the way my parents treat me."

"What?" I've never actually met Mike's parents. They live in Tennessee or something. Essie and Mike go there, they never come here. So I've never had the chance. "What do you mean by that?"

"You know. 'Why is your wife the breadwinner, Michael? Why can't you get a real job, Michael?'"

I almost guffaw. "What are they talking about? You fixed up all those trailers on the beach. That's like fifteen million dollars in assets."

"Yeah, but…" He starts laughing.

"But what?" I'm kinda laughing too.

"They don't know it's you, either, Steve. They think Essie is SS. And I told them that you own all the trailers at Paradise Cove. So every time we go home, all I hear is 'Why can't you be more like Steve, Michael?'"

"Shut up."

"I swear to God." He even crosses his heart. "When I met Essie I just had the one trailer, remember?"

"Of course. Essie only had one too."

"First of all"—he holds up a finger—"I came to LA to be an actor. So they were not on board with that. Second, when I told them I bought a run-down trailer that really didn't even have a roof, they thought… you know, trailer park. I was living in a trailer park."

"Didn't you send them pictures? It's on the beach."

"They were not impressed. So anyway, Essie and I fell in love kinda quick. And you were already pretty famous. I mean… Jeez. The movie deal was already being discussed. I kinda just absorbed the lie and embellished it with my own."

"You were dating a famous erotica author?"

We both laugh. But he points at me. "That."

"How'd that go over?"

"Well." He pauses to think about this. "Not great, at first. But then they met Essie and they loved her immediately. She's bubbly and shit. Kind of a people person."

"Yeah. Don't I know it."

"So I told them I sold the trailer to you and you fixed it up."

"They think I'm you."

He nods. "And your parents think you're me. Minus the trailers."

I sigh. "And both sets are disappointed."

Mike makes a face of… maybe. But then he says, "That's one way to think of it, Steve. But the other way to think of it is… that's just how parents are, ya know? They live a little bit through us. They want us to realize our dreams, of course, but I'm guessing that there are very few parents who can totally separate their ego from the successes and failures of their children."

"Huh. Maybe."

He shrugs. "So I decided I wasn't gonna take it personal. I let it go."

"So you're telling me to let it go?"

"See, this is why I like to change the subject. If I don't let it go—if I let it bother me—am I getting anything out of that?"

"Huh." I ponder this.

"I'm not. So being upset about stupid shit like that… it's just stupid."

"What are they gonna think when they hear about this?"

"I have no idea. But… it's got nothing to do with me. So whatever. Who cares? But I'll tell you this, and then I'll shut up about all of it. Your parents probably feel like shit right now. Because they're wondering why you didn't want to tell them something so… big. Something so… awesome. And they are taking that very personally, Steve."

Then he claps me on the back and goes upstairs.

♥♡♥♡♥♡♥♡♥♡♥

I don't go upstairs. I go around the house to the patio and then kick off my shoes and go down the path to the beach. The sun is setting. A beautiful orange-red sunset reflecting off the water, which is pretty calm right now.

And I just walk. Playing the day back in my head.

When that PA system came on Essie and I just looked at each other. It's like we knew.

I recognized Leslie's voice and I knew. She was out to get us. There was never any reconciliation about what happened years ago in court. And of course I always knew that apology we forced her to do wasn't real, but I guess I figured she got over it.

She lost.

I didn't steal her fucking words and we proved it.

She lost.

She should've… I don't know. Accepted her mistake, at the very least. Some soul-searching about her nasty, black heart would've been a great start.

But she was stewing. All these years. And plotting, I think.

When did she figure out I was SS? I'm not sure about that. But honestly, it doesn't even matter.

I own that mistake.

I do. It's my fault for lying.

And I feel terrible.

I'm not really angry at my parents for not believing in me. Or not accepting me. Mike's right, it doesn't matter.

I'm mad at myself.

When Essie and I came up to the front of the signing hall and saw Leslie Munch standing on a table, gleefully trying her best to ruin us, no one was mad. I didn't see a single angry face in the crowd that had gathered.

No. What I saw was disappointment.

Betrayal, maybe.

They all just… looked at us. Mom and Dad were there too.

We didn't say anything. Even after James and Leslie got into a fight over the mic and fell off the table.

James managed to stick the landing, but Leslie planted face-first onto the carpet and the blood… my God, the blood. She was a fucking mess.

And the center of attention.

That's when Mike leaned in and said, "We should go. Audrey and James will handle Leslie."

I looked back for Cordelia. Because once Leslie started speaking, I had forgotten about her. But I couldn't see her in the crowd. So that's what we did. We left. And I didn't even get to say goodbye.

I sit down on the sand so I can watch the last little bit of sun disappear across the horizon, and then reach for my phone.

"Well, shit." I forgot that I turned it off after Gregory got all weird.

But do I even want to turn it on? Do I want to see all the private messages on socials?

Everyone is going to be messaging me. Everyone is going to want to talk to me. Even if it's just so they can pretend to know something and spread it around.

And then people will take sides.

The #FraudTwins or Leslie Munch with her bloody face and sob story?

I don't need to guess how this is going to work out. I've seen it happen… oh, probably hundreds of times in the past ten years.

Everyone loves a scandal.

Maybe it's better that Cordelia and I didn't exchange numbers?

Maybe I should just… let her go?

Because if she sticks up for us, they're gonna get her too.

That's how it works these days.

Guilt by association.

Which I know and understand because I'm in the public eye and you'd have to be living under a rock for the past decade to not understand that guilt by association is the thing right now.

But it never occurred to me that it would transfer to our parents. Like… their pride in us, or lack thereof, is a lot like guilt by association. Or success by association.

I picture Mike's parents listening to him explain his dream of acting and LA. And I get it. That was probably something that made them anxious. Made them worry. I mean, how likely is it that he realizes his dream?

Of course, he's kinda living his dream life. He *did* marry my sister.

I pause here to smile.

But she came with *my* lie. And dammit, this stupid fucking lie has ruined so much.

If Mike hadn't had to lie for me, he could've told his parents that Essie was just a really nice woman who enjoys DIY and quirky real estate investment. They could've let the parents take that journey with them. And then they could've all looked back together and nodded their heads with satisfaction. Because Mike and Essie basically have a beachfront trailer-park empire and they built it all by themselves.

But instead of that satisfaction, his parents are still filled with worry, thinking that their grown son has never realized his full potential.

I sigh. Because that's what I did to my parents too.

Essie was making her own way. She had a weird dream about fixing up trailers on the beach and she made it happen.

And then I stole that from her. And Mike.

Not only that, I stole the journey my parents could've taken with me. I stole all their proud moments.

I mean, I always knew that my lie was a bad thing. But I guess I never understood just how much it affected everyone around me.

God, I'm a real piece of shit.

♠♡♠♡♠♡♠♡♠♡♠

I sit there on the beach for a while, just watching the stars come out and enjoying the sound of the surf. But the tide is coming in and I need to face what I've done. So I get up and walk back home.

I could just slip into my lower level and pretend no one else is here. But I can hear them talking upstairs.

So instead of hiding like a coward, I go up. All the way to the roof because Mike and Essie are grilling in the outside kitchen.

They are talking and even laughing a little when I come outside. But then they see me and go quiet.

"Steve," Mike says. "Come on. Sit down. We're having ribs."

And ya know what? I am so happy that Mike is here. That Mike is my brother-in-law. That Mike is… Mike. Because he's holding us together in this moment.

He has been doing that all along.

I let out a long breath and accept his invitation, taking a seat to my dad's left. Then I look at him. "I'm sorry."

He shrugs. "It's fine, Steve. Essie kinda filled us in."

And ya know what? It probably *is* fine. He's my dad. He loves me. In his eyes, maybe I'm a fuck-up, but he's still there for me.

So I keep going. "I… I had a dream, ya know?"

"Honey." My mom reaches across the table for my hand. "It's fine."

"It's not fine, Mom. I had a dream of being a great sci-fi writer and I was having a difficult time breaking through, so I… saw the romance writers being so successful, and got super jealous, and—of course—figured if they could do that, *I* could do that. And I… just… sold out."

"You didn't sell out, Steve," Essie says. "That's ridiculous. You wrote something no one else had done before. That's why it was special. You were the first to do Choke."

"I haven't read them properly, but I did skim," Mom says. "Master Choke is quite enamoring, Steve." Her smile looks genuine.

"Oh, my God," I mumble, covering my eyes with my hand. I cannot believe I'm having this conversation with my family. "The point is, I ruined everyone's journey just so I could take mine in a more comfortable car, ya know?"

"No." Essie is shaking her head as she cuts me off. "That's not even true. You didn't twist my arm, Steve. I said yes and I didn't really do that for you. I did it for me. It was fun. I lived the last ten years of my life as a famous writer." She laughs. "Like… what a dream come true, ya know?"

I study her face to see if she's lying. "Really?" I don't think she is.

"And I got to be the husband," Mike adds. He and Essie smile at each other. "We made some good memories, babe."

"We did," Essie agrees. Then she looks at me. "And it's over now. But that's OK. Something new is coming, Steve. None of us know what it is—"

"Oh, I know what it is," I say. "It's a shit show, is what it is."

"Sure," my dad says. "It's gonna be an epic shit show, Steve. But you're a guy who writes his own story, so you'll find a way through it."

"An agent offered to sign me," I say. "And it's not even romance. It's sci-fi."

"Really?" Essie says. "That's great, Steve. It's your dream."

"Yeah. My dream."

And then we drop it and start talking about other things. Essie and Mike's new real estate idea, Mom's new golf group at the culty compound they live on, Dad's DIY plumbing course online, and Mike's secret passion for narrating Master Choke audiobooks before he and Essie go to bed.

Which is oversharing, in my opinion. But hey, it's kind of a compliment too, so I just laugh.

Maybe this will all turn out to be a good thing?

Maybe.

CHAPTER TWENTY-SEVEN – CORDELIA

THREE DAYS AFTER THE CONVENTION

Britney and I are sitting on the lip of the pool, both of us dangling our feet in. It continues to be hot. And so, despite my well-documented aversion to recreational wetness, I am dipping my toes in the water. Which, in this case, is utterly literal and has no hidden allegory attached.

It's been three days. Three days since the convention ended in what can only be described as a "catastrofuck." Ever since #FraudTwins became a thing. (Which annoys me because they're not frauds, but more importantly because it's a really lazy hashtag. It's not even that clever. I mean, for crying out loud, #ImpoSSters is *right there*. Seems so obvious.)

And in that three days, something sort of amazing has happened.

Cynthia Lear has become maybe, kind of, the next hot thing in the world of romance.

Which is a real kick in the head, I gotta tell ya. I'm as surprised as the next person.

Here's how it happened:

On the last day of the con, I had just come to the conclusion that 'success,' as I had previously defined and wanted it, was not the only definition. I had *literally* just had this dawning that success is also doing what I want to do, what I love and think is right, and not caring what anyone else thinks or says.

Which is always the way, right? The moment you let something go is when it shows up.

The tricky part is you *really* have to let it go. You can't just be pretending. And I had. I had truly and really let it go. And right at the moment I did…

Things blew up.

The day after I got back, amidst the #FraudTwins caterwauling taking up all the oxygen in Romancelandia, there was one little tidbit that broke through the noise. A BookTok post. By a reasonably big-deal BookToker. No, that's not true. I'm downplaying it because I still haven't quite wrapped my head around it. It was actually a post by *the* big-deal BookToker.

Lesperia Renée is her name. Or, at least, that's her BookTok name. (I hope it's her real name, because 'Lesperia' is a triumph.) And, it just so happens, Lesperia Renée is my doppelganger, aka Redhead Polka Dot Hepburn. The one who came over to me on Audrey Saint's recommendation and walked off with a copy of *Filling the Gap*.

I had no idea who she was at the time. Which is probably for the best.

Because she didn't just take the copy I handed to her. Apparently, my other copy, *the* copy, the one I've been looking for, was sitting nearby and somehow I didn't notice. I must have had it with me when I came downstairs for the signing that morning and left it on the table. So, after I told her to take whatever books she wanted and then had my back turned, silently arguing with Britney about not forcing people to take pictures with me, she scooped it up as well.

And the way I know this is that she threw up a post the day after the event for her… wait for it… five million followers. And it went something like this:

"So, you guys, if you didn't make it to Sin With Us this year… you. Missed. Out. I'm sure everyone's going to be talking all about the whole SS controversy for a while, and I'll make a post about that soon when I've had a chance to process it and get everybody's side of the story—because remember what I always say: 'It's easy to believe something. It's much, much harder to know it.'"

(Which I think is not only a catchy motto, but a really good one. Anyway.)

"So, while I gather all the details I can about hashtag FraudTwins, I just wanted to do a quick post to say that of all the cool and hotly anticipated new releases that we've all been waiting for from Eden Le Fay and Winter Page and whoever your favorite author is, there's one that might fly under the radar and I want to bring it to your attention."

(I started holding my breath at this point in the video.)

"And, I want to be clear, this is not sponsored. No one is paying for this. I just happened to stumble across a new author and grabbed a copy of her book and, you guys, this woman can write. Her name is Cynthia Lear and her new book is called Filling the Gap."

(At which point, a photo of the book appeared next to her face and I almost fainted. She went on…)

"And here's what's really interesting. I actually managed to get my hands on two copies."

(Which is when a photo of the white cover with the black lettering appeared next to her face on the screen and I almost fainted for a different reason.)

"And I read them both, back to back. Because, honestly? I couldn't stop. And what's really wild is they're almost exactly the same book, but they're not at the same time. One of them does everything in a very traditional way that I love, but the other one… Well, no spoilers, but it's not like anything I've read before. It's not going to be for everyone, for sure, but it is so good. Ugly-cry, you guys. Ugly-cry. I'll post a full, in-depth review of both on my site, but seriously, there is an exciting new voice in the romance world who doesn't seem to be interested in playing by the rules! Which is sick. So, run to grab up copies of her stuff, like, now. Oh, and, according to some people I've talked with, she looks like me."

(Then she put up a photo of me on the screen next to her.)

"I don't see it. No shade, she's super-cute, but I can't get past the differences in our hair. So, drop a comment and tell me what you think. Do I look like Cynthia Lear? Yes or no? Okay! Until next time… Easy reading."

And then a big kiss emoji appeared on the screen and the video started over.

I watched it roughly three dozen times.

And then…

And then I saw the pre-orders for the official release of *FTG*—which I have scheduled for next week—go through the roof. Not only that, but I started getting messages through my website asking if *both* versions would be available for purchase.

And not only that, but the first two books in The Purity Principle series have also seen massive sales spikes. They were sitting at around sales rank eleventytrillion in the Nile store, and now they've both managed to crack the top fifty. And not just in the romance category. In the whole store. I seriously need to send Audrey Saint a gift basket for telling Lesperia to come to my table. Fruit or chocolate? Know what? Both. And maybe a pony. I think Audrey lives on a ranch.

Anyway, that's what happened. It's been a hell of a few days. So, right now, I'm just trying to take a breath while I plan my next move. And thus, here I sit, legs dangling in the pool, head tilted back, sun shining on my face. Which, while also literal, *does* have a not-at-all-hidden allegory attached.

"I talked to my mom," I tell Brit, feeling the warmth of the rays on my skin.

I can feel her head turn to look at me even without opening my eyes. "Really?" I nod. "Who called who?"

"I called her."

"And what did you two talk about?"

"This and that. The weather. How her book is coming. How Dad's doing."

There's a pause before she says, "And?"

"And that, at this moment, I'm one of the bestselling romance authors on the planet."

There's a breeze that causes the palm fronds to rustle.

"No shit." Britney sighs.

"No shit."

"What did she say?'

"She was surprised."

"I'll bet."

I lower my head and look at Britney, who has her mouth open, waiting, expectantly. "And then she asked a bunch of questions."

"Like what?"

"Like, 'When did you start writing romance? Why didn't you tell me you were writing romance? How did you become a bestseller so quickly?' All that kind of stuff."

"And you said…?"

"I told her that I've wanted to write it forever. She asked why I never told her before. And I explained it was because I was afraid she'd judge me for it."

"You did?"

"Uh-huh."

"You said that to her?"

"Uh-huh."

"Wow." A beat. "How'd she take it?"

"Y'know, I have to be honest, I don't really ... care."

In the ensuing silence I can almost hear the gears turning in Brit's brain.

"I mean, look, she's my mom and I love her and all, I really do, but I don't know that I realized before how much my choices were being driven by her. Either toward things or away from them. No matter what I chose, for most of my life, it hasn't been me doing the choosing. Not really. It's always been so she wouldn't get disappointed if I did the wrong thing or did something she didn't think was worthy. Or, in some cases, *because* she'd think that. I've always kind of balanced this rebellious streak—which I think might actually be who I am, Lesperia Renée is right about me not wanting to play by the rules—against this need to make sure people like me, or to not allow myself to fail, or whatever I was doing. And, y'know, I don't really wanna do that anymore. I deserve to be happy. And to get what I want.

Woulda been nice to figure it out sooner, but hey, some people never do, so… big winner."

I point my thumbs at my chest. And as I start to turn my face back toward the sun, I catch a small smile creeping across Britney's face.

"What?" I ask. "That's a creepy smile. Why are you doing that?"

"I'm just stoked for you."

"Yeah?"

"Yeah."

"Yeah… Me too." I grin back and splash the water with my feet. It feels nice. Then I notice that Britney's smile is dropping and she looks away from me. "What's wrong?"

"Huh? Oh, nothing. I just…" She lets her bikini top rise and fall with her breath. "I feel like… Like I haven't been as good a friend to you as I could be."

I wasn't expecting that. "What in the John Barleycorn are you talking about?"

"I dunno. I could have maybe done a better job of encouraging you. Like, *Filling the Gap*. I was the one who told you that you couldn't publish it. And clearly I was wrong about that. When we got to Vegas, I let you stay one night in that bedbug-ridden den of iniquity instead of insisting harder that you take your suite at the Aria. I just could've been better. I'm sorry."

I stare at her like she has two heads before splashing water on her. "What"—*splash*—"in the ever-loving"—*splash*—"name of Jane Austen are you talking about?" *Splash.*

She laughs and throws her arms up in front of her face. "Stop! Stop!"

"Brit… I wouldn't even be doing this if it weren't for you. I never would have set dirty word to computer screen, probably, if you hadn't encouraged it. *Everything* that's happening is because you gave me the push I needed. So, stop it. Hell, thanks to you, I'll now have four books out instead of three!" I splash her one more time for good measure. She laughs again.

"Okay, okay," she says. "So does that mean I can get a raise as your assistant? *My* mom's actually been on me to get a real job and I really don't want to work at Skinny Laminx."

"Given the fact that you currently make exactly nothing as my assistant? Done."

We both laugh.

"As soon as the money starts showing up," I add. "It takes a couple months, from what I understand. So, until then, I may need you to still drive me places for free."

"Deal," she says, still giggling.

We both turn our faces skyward.

After a moment, Brit asks, "You hear from Steve at all?"

I shake my head. "No."

"You think about calling him?"

"I don't have his number."

"Really?"

"He never gave it to me and I didn't think to ask."

"You good with that?"

No. I'm not good with it. Not really. But, I'm also trying to understand. He got hit with a haymaker right as the convention was ending. He's got to be reeling. Obviously, I'm not thrilled.

However... I'm really, *really* leaning into this new, more measured, more ... chill ... Cordelia Sarantopoulos. As best I can, anyway. And measured, super chill Cordy can wait while Steve deals with this whole #FraudTwins thing (so lame, I mean even #DecepticonSS would work). Besides, I've got to reckon with what's happening in my career at the moment. Ironic that his fall and my ascent would happen at the same time like this, but…

It's the tall flower phenomenon. We tend a garden and work so hard to get our flowers to grow and bloom, but when one of them grows too tall and begins to overshadow the others, we make sure we cut it down with a quickness.

SS is that flower.

But the thing is, I'm becoming a tall flower too all of a sudden. So, I need to make sure I have a chance to bloom before anyone tries to cut me down. I believe Steve and I will see each other again. (I do. I really do. I'm not just saying that to convince myself. I don't ... think.) But, in the meantime, I need to stay focused on tending my own garden.

So, right now, my brain is buzzing like a bee. (I am really torturing this garden metaphor here.) Which, let's be honest, it always is, but this time it's buzzing because I have so much I now feel like I wanna say. And do. And write! Because I can't let this momentum stop!

So, instead of answering the question, I ask one of my own.

"What do you think about rom-coms?"

"Rom-coms?" Britney echoes. "I think they're sweet. Why?"

"I'm thinking about writing one."

"Really?"

"I know it's not the kind of thing I've gravitated to before, but I dunno. I still want to write everything, just like I always did, but now I wonder why I can't just do that in the romance world. Y'know? Like write a serious book, then maybe a dark one, then maybe a light one, then a historical one…"

"Wow. This from a woman who just last week was worried she wasn't following the rules."

"You heard Lesperia. Cynthia Lear doesn't play by the rules."

She laughs.

"Girls?" Sheila pops her head outside. "What are you doing out here?"

"Hi, Sheila." I smile as she wanders over to the pool in her swimming costume. (That's what she calls it. I feel like 'costumes' tend to cover more flesh, but hey, her house, her rules.)

"I heard the laughing. Such a lovely sound." She plops herself down onto a lounge chair, adjusts her giant hat, and closes her eyes.

"We were just talking about what Cordelia's going to do next," Britney says.

"Oh, you mean where she's going to live?" Sheila purrs.

"Sorry, what?" I ask. "What do you mean where I'm going to live? I live here."

"I know, dear. But not for much longer."

"Sheila… What are you talking about?" And then it dawns on me. "Oh, my God, Sheila, are you… are you dying?"

"We're all dying, dear. All the time. That's why we must seize life in front of us by the balls and yank as hard as we can."

Okay. That was intense. "Sheila—"

"No, dear. I'm not dying. At least not soon. As far as I know. I simply mean that you should think about moving on."

"What? Why?"

"Because, sweet girl, it's time for, in your parlance, your next chapter."

"Sheila, I—"

"Sweetheart, you never planned on this being your life, did you? Living in an old woman's pool house, cloistered away, writing books all by yourself?"

"No, of course not, but…"

"It's time, dear. You should think about who you want to be next."

My head is spinning a little. A week ago, I was Cordelia Sarantopoulos, unknown romance writer and impromptu pool girl, and now…

I look at Britney, who raises her eyebrows, and then down into the water. The reflection of the sun shimmers off the surface. Slowly, carefully, I start lowering myself forward.

"Cord? What are you doing?" Britney asks.

I don't answer, just keep edging myself further and further into the water. The frayed ends of my jean shorts are now submerged.

"Cord?"

"I'm okay," I tell her as I drop down to my waist and let my t-shirt float into the pool. "I'm just…"

"What?"

The water is at my chest. I turn and look at her, holding myself up with my hands on the edge of the coping. "I'm just deciding if I want my own pool to be square or oval."

She smiles. I smile back. And submerge myself fully under.

Getting recreationally wet while fully clothed.

Because Cordelia Sarantopoulos is also done playing by the rules.

CHAPTER TWENTY-EIGHT – STEVE

After two days of successfully wallowing in the shallows of denial, I made the mistake of turning on my phone.

Three hundred and twenty-five emails, so many private messages on socials I can't even begin to count them, and four more hashtags: #SSScandal, #ChokeSteveSmith, #SSTwinLiars, and #SaveRaylen.

Save Raylen? Are they fucking kidding me?

So far Team Raylen has accused Essie and me of malicious slander, harassment, bullying, creating a hostile working environment, plagiarism (again), trademark infringement (what?), fraud, child endangerment (seriously?), intimidation, too many torts to list, negligence, and intentional infliction of emotional distress.

We haven't been officially served with anything, but it's coming. We know it's coming.

There were no messages from Cordelia.

I was upset about that for a while, but then I remembered that we didn't exchange numbers. We were kind of in a close-proximity relationship throughout the convention. Not textbook close-proximity, but the definition of the trope still fits.

I've been doing that a lot too. Using story structure to force my current dramatic problems to make sense. Like I'm a character in a book and none of this is real.

Except I'm not a character in a book and all of this is real.

It's now day three post-blow-up and I'm currently taking turns looking at the keypad on my phone and the little white card that agent guy gave me.

Do I dare?

Like… shouldn't I just give up? There is no way that guy hasn't heard about this drama. It's all over the internet. All those trashy websites calling themselves 'news' have Essie and me on the front page of their entertainment sections. Along with a bloody photo of Leslie Munch's last emergency room visit.

But isn't it better to hear it and face the truth than to never call and wonder, for the rest of my life, if he still might've been interested?

I take a breath, go out onto my office terrace, and press send as I watch the gulls dive for fish.

The call is picked up on the first ring. "North Star Author Agency, how can I direct your call?"

Shit. He didn't give me a direct number. I let out a breath. I might as well just see it through. "Yes. I'm calling for Gary Pritchard. This is Steve Smith."

"One moment, Mr. Smith."

Elevator music comes through the speaker. Then a moment later, he picks up. "Steve. Gary here."

I'm relieved. He took my call! "Hi. Yeah. Steve here. Just following up after our talk on Sunday. I wanted to—"

"Let me just stop you right there, Steve."

"Oh." My stomach sinks. "OK."

"Yeah. I'm sure it's not a surprise to you, but… I'm sorry. We can't be associated with Steve Smith. North Star Author Agency has a reputation to protect."

"But… I know it was wrong to lie about who wrote the books—"

"Oh, no. We don't care about that."

"What?"

"No one cares if you and your sister… whatever that was."

"What's *that* mean?"

"Never mind. Everyone has secret pen names, Steve. Do you have any idea how many men I personally represent who are secretly writing erotica on the side right now? Dozens. No one cares who writes the books."

"I'm… pretty sure that's not true."

"Oh, it is. They want books, Steve. Stories. No one cares who writes them. Our problem with you right now is the way you treat your fellow authors."

"The way I… *what*?"

"And I would've been totally on board with taking you on as a client if you decided to write under another secret name."

"Another secret name?"

"Yeah. So no one would know it was you."

I let out a sigh. "You want me to start a new lie?"

"Well, yeah," Gary says. "Kind of. That was my original proposal. We like to start a new brand when we sign our authors. We like to… you know, guide your whole career kind of thing."

I scoff. "You mean *control* my entire career kind of thing."

"Sure. You could say that. But no. What I'm saying is that would've been the offer if Raylen Star hadn't happened."

"She's lying, though. That whole story she's telling is a lie. I never did any of that stuff. We didn't do any of that."

"That's not really the issue though, is it? The issue is perception. The story, remember? No one cares if it's true, Steve. Just like no one really cares if you write the books or your sister does. Plus, Raylen has a lot of fans."

"Does she?"

Now he scoffs. "See, that right there? That's the problem."

"What did I do?"

"That condescending tone about Raylen's fans? You're sexist, Steve."

"*What*?" I actually laugh.

"Well, that's the trajectory of the perception. Ya know? Give it a week and you're going to be the world's most hated misogynist. And to be frank, that's just not an image North Star Author Agency wants to be a part of."

My laugh dies abruptly. I don't say anything. I don't have anything to say. It's stupid. Ridiculous. It's… not true.

But I know he's right. I'm in the middle of a cancel campaign. There is no room for the truth at this point in time. It's all trajectory. And there's nothing I can do about it.

"So…" Gary continues. "Good luck."

And then the call ends.

It does not matter if I'm innocent.

The only thing that matters is who has the most compelling story.

And that, I guess, is it.

♥♡♥♡♥♡♥♡♥♡♥

"Look!" Shawn says, pointing at my giant TV with the remote. "Munch is on *Noon News LA!*"

"Why are you torturing him, Shawn?" Luke is playing darts. He's hit my fucking wall seven times since he got here an hour ago. "Leave the poor guy alone."

"No, I wanna hear it," Terry says. "Turn it up."

No one asks me what I want, so Shawn turns it up.

"And what did he say?" *Noon News* host Angie Stevens, asks.

Raylen, on day three post-blow-up, still has two black eyes and a very crooked nose. She sucks in a fake sob. The camera does a close-up of a little tear sliding down her cheek. "He said… he said… 'Raylen, you don't deserve a good spot in the room. So we put you in the corner. That's where you belong.'" She breaks down, covering her face, pretending to cry.

"For fuck's sake," Luke says, then looks at me. "No one believes that shit. No one."

"She stole that scene from *Dirty Dancing*," Terry says. "Like… what the fuck, right? 'No one puts Baby in the corner?' How is anyone buying this?"

"Well," Angie says on the TV, "everyone seems to be on your side, Raylen. So even though it's been hard, I have a feeling you're going to get the justice you deserve."

I shoot Luke and Terry an incredulous look that says, *Really*?

"I don't know," Leslie says, barely managing to get her words out past her stupid sobbing. "His fans don't seem to care."

She's kinda right about that. My fans are still there, sticking up for me, even. Both Essie and me, actually. They don't seem to be falling for the lie, but the social narrative has not yet turned. The Twitter war is blazing like a raging fire. And I had to make all my social accounts private because the hate comments just got overwhelming.

Other authors are… well, some of them are taking my side. The ones I know well from back in the day are. Audrey is. Raven, Winter, Mercy. Hell, even Eden Le Fay, which surprised me because she usually just keeps to herself online.

But there are a lot of up-and-coming authors on Team Raylen. And most of my general acquaintances have just decided to sit it out and say nothing.

I can't blame them. To speak up for me is to invite the cancel campaign upon themselves. Isn't it better to stay silent than to poke the bear, so to speak?

Being a self-published author has perks. Aside from losing Gary Pritchard's predatory offer of representation, it's kind of impossible to cancel SS over something like this. I write the books, I narrate the books, I publish the books, and Essie markets the books. We're kind of a self-contained entity.

However, you don't need my exceptional imagination to envision a day where that changes. Could they get me booted from Nile? Could they force my editor to stop working with me? Could they shut down my bank accounts? Will my barber have to stop cutting my hair? How long before the bloggers, 'Tokers, and 'Grammers give up on me too?

Because if anyone goes against the popular narrative—i.e. Raylen Star's narrative—they will be a target.

So I don't ask anyone to stick up for me.

Of course, Luke, Terry, and Shawn are speaking out. But they don't live in Romancelandia. They live on Planet Sci-fi. They have no influence in my sphere.

Still, they are good moral support.

"Oh, my God!" Shawn laughs. "You've gotten fifty-seven one-star reviews for *Master Choke* since last night, dude!"

"Shawn!" Terry bellows. "Stop it! You've gonna give the Ro-Bro a panic attack, OK?"

"Well, if it makes you feel any better, Steve"—Shawn beams a smile at me—"*Master Choke* is number seven in the Nile bookstore. *Sev-en.* That's what? Six grand a day for a book that's ten years old?"

I let out a long sigh.

"You've got five audiobooks in the top ten on NileAudio too," Luke says.

I sigh again. I get that for some authors it's about the money. Hell, for most authors it's about the money. But money is not why I do this.

I don't care about the money.

I just like to write stories.

And all during the convention I was coming to terms with things. My social life—lovely Cordelia, who I hope to reconnect with, but not yet. I can't have her reputation sullied by my mistakes. My professional life—I had this inner narrative kind of going. Building characters, and plotlines. Just basic rudimentary stuff, but it's more than I've done in a year. It was kind of a breakthrough.

And I could feel this whole SS thing coming to a head. I was maybe even coming to terms with that too.

But Leslie truly pulled the rug out from under me. She took away my opportunity to out myself.

And it sucks because now what? Do I quit? Will anyone want to work with me in the future? Will I just be a running joke forever? Will I have to start all over with a fake name?

I don't know. I just don't know.

The doorbell rings upstairs. Essie and Mike have a new project now. They bought a piece of land up in the Malibu hills with an old falling-down house on it. That's not their new investment, it's their new home. Or it will be once they spend a few hundred thousand dollars fixing it up.

That's how our last night with the parents ended. Essie and Mike's dreams.

I'm glad she's free now. I really am. She's always had a life outside of the one I forced upon her, and now she can forget about me and my problems and put her family first.

Anyway. I go upstairs to answer the door because Essie and Mike will probably never stay on my top floor again, and this is just another thing to be sad about, but more importantly, I'm the only one here responsible for answering my door now, so… that's what's going through my mind when I open the door and find a middle-aged man.

"Can I help you?"

"Are you Steve Smith?"

"Yes."

He holds out an envelope and says, "You have been served."

CHAPTER TWENTY-NINE – CORDELIA

TEN DAYS AFTER THE CONVENTION

"So? What do you think?" the realtor asks. She's an attractive woman in her mid-thirties with curly hair and a face that looks kind of like a porcelain doll's. Like Elizabeth Bennet on that cover of *Pride and Prejudice* I discovered as a kid. Natural though, not because of a ton of plastic surgery. Or, if it is, it's *really* good. But, based on the Porsche she has parked outside and the Hermès Birkin bag she has on the table next to the sign-in sheet, she could afford really good cosmetic surgery. The real estate business must be going very well for her.

Her name is Evelyn. (Pronounced EVE-lynn. She enunciated it very clearly.)

"It's nice," I say, looking around the kitchen at the soapstone countertops, the Sub-Zero fridge, and the eight-burner Viking range.

"The appliances are all brand new."

"Sweet," I say, glancing over at Britney, who nods a *Yeah, that's cool.*

I'm learning about things that matter when buying a house. Things I never knew to ask. Things like, "How old is the roof?" And, because it's LA, "Has the foundation been inspected and/or retrofitted?" Stuff like that.

It's not a serious search just yet. I'm still just being a looky-loo and going to open houses to get a feel for what my options are when the money from my newly robust sales starts coming in. *Filling the Gap* (both versions) went live a few days ago and…

… Well, it kind of went like this:

When I first uploaded my book into the Nile Store, it was barely findable. Like, honestly, it was buried so deep in the maze of authors skreiching to get their books noticed that it might as well have just been still sitting on my computer. But then the Lesperia video happened and…

Suddenly, almost like an enchantment had been cast, my ranking jumped into the top five thousand.

And I squeed. Literally. I looked at my computer screen and went, "Squeeee!" Sheila shouted out of her bedroom window to make sure I hadn't seen a mouse or something.

Then it climbed into the top one thousand. And I started vibrating. I might have levitated. I'm still not sure. I called Britney to come over and she did, and we just kept hitting refresh on my computer and drinking from a box of wine.

When we saw it climb to the top five hundred, I stopped breathing. No, seriously. I only realized it when I had to gasp for breath like I had just been rescued from a surfing accident. Just big, giant gulps of air. Which turned into hyperventilation when *Filling the Gap* cracked the top one hundred.

By that point, it had turned into an actual sporting event. Like the World Cup or something. We stayed up for, I dunno, two days just hitting refresh, drinking boxed wine, and watching my ranking climb. It was surreal. Occasionally I'd take a bite of the tacos we had delivered. The delivery kid saw the way we were acting and actually said, "Is there a game on?"

What happened after I entered the upper-upper echelons is, honestly, a little bit hazy. Because I think I passed out a few times.

Ninety…

Seventy-five…

Sixty…

Fifty!

Forty…

Thirty…

Twenty-five…

Twenty-five…

Twenty-five…

It kind of hung there for a while. Like maybe people had stopped ordering it? And, honestly, if it had all just stopped there, that would have been fine. I had already exceeded my wildest dreams for what might be possible. But then it started climbing again.

Fifteen…

Fourteen…

Twelve…

(It just jumped thirteen altogether. Which I took as a good omen.)

Eleven…

Ten.

Holy shit, I thought. *I'm about to be in the top ten bestselling books in the world. What the actual flim-flam?*

And it kept going, stepping over every other book in line. Leaping over huge names like Audrey Saint and SS until it hit ... number ... one.

I think I must have looked like one of those old, old cartoons where a wolf or something sees a pretty girl wolf and his eyes bug out of his head and he goes 'AAA-OOO-GAA!'

Yeah, that was me.

I almost went catatonic. All my internal systems just kind of shut down. Somewhere in the far distance I could hear Britney shouting, but it sounded muted and hard to make sense of.

And then my phone started blowing up, the ding-ding-ding bringing me back to the here and now. It was all these authors, many of whom I've never even met, sending me congratulations on my socials and everywhere.

And then the *weirdest* thing happened, as if it wasn't already weird enough.

Gregory, the Aria's SparkleNight DreamWeaver's WishMaker app… guy… thing, popped up. Just popped right up on my phone.

"Congratulations, Cordelia Sarantopoulos, aka Cynthia Lear, on achieving the number one sales spot in the Nile Store! What an amazing accomplishment!"

The number of ways in which that freaked me out are too many to get into, but suffice to say that it woke me back up pretty quickly.

I pressed the cartoon face and said, "Uh, thanks?"

"You're welcome! Can I get anything for you to celebrate?"

Wait. What? "You… I thought you only worked when I was at the hotel…"

"Normally, yes, but before you left, you achieved DreamWeaver's DreamDate WishMaker Bonus Level! I can now serve as your WishMaker assistant wherever you might need a wish granted throughout the world! (Offer not valid in North Korea and some parts of Russia.)"

What the…

"So, Cordelia Sarantopoulos! What may I get for you to celebrate your remarkable achievement?"

"Uh… nothing? I'll… let you know, I guess?"

"Excellent! Gregory will be here! Your wish is my command!"

I found the whole thing immeasurably strange and unsettling. But, for whatever reason, I didn't delete the app. I don't know why, exactly. Just… I've never had a global wish-granting assistant before and I'm morbidly curious to see where this thing goes.

Anyway, that's how it all went down. I still cannot find the words to express how mind-blowing it is. And, if you know me, that's saying something. I can always find words. And then some.

So, because of all that… I'm starting to look around at houses.

Because if the projection for what kind of money I'm going to make in a couple of months holds up? Assuming everything keeps going the way it's going now? I should buy something. Because… well, I'm gonna be fuckin' rich. Really no other way to say it.

Good thing, too. Because home prices in Los Angeles are fuckin' expensive.

Audrey Saint reached out to congratulate me, and to thank me for the chocolate and fruit basket, and as we were talking I told her that I was going to go house-shopping. She said that James could help me with anything accounting-related and that got us talking about housing prices. Turns out, for what a house like this that I'm looking at in Santa Monica—a house not that far from the one where I grew up, actually—costs now, I could buy a ranch like the one Audrey lives on in a place like Utah or Colorado. A ranch. With acreage.

Don't get me wrong, being less than a mile from the ocean is nice and all, but the whole place is only slightly bigger than the pool house and you're right up on your neighbors. Just seems like a real con-job, especially when you factor in LA traffic and all. But LA is home. And it's always been my dream. And this place has a pool. And it would be nice to realize it all came to life like I had hoped it would. So… looky-loo-ing I am.

"Could I see the pool?" I ask.

"Of course!" says Evelyn.

We head out back and the pool is amazing. Like, really, really amazing. It's got incredible, deep blue tile and looks like it might be long enough to swim laps in.

"It's Olympic," Evelyn whispers conspiratorially.

I look at Britney. "It's Olympic," I repeat. She raises her eyebrows like, *Also cool.*

"So," Evelyn says, "how long have you two been looking?"

"Oh," Britney says, "we're not together."

"Oh," Evelyn chirps, semi-apologetically. Then she looks at me and back at Britney and says, "I should've known." Annnnnnnd I don't think I like Evelyn. "So, are we looking for a home for you, then?" She directs it at Britney.

"No. For my friend, here."

"Really?"

Like, seriously, Evelyn, put a *little* effort into pretending not to be a judgy bi—

"And what do you do for a living?" Evelyn asks.

There was a time, not long ago at all, when not only would I have felt ashamed of the way she's talking to me, I would have been kind of unsure of how to answer. But not anymore.

"I'm a writer," I say. Period. End of sentence. Declarative. Full stop.

"TV?" she asks.

"No."

"Oh. Film?"

"Novels. I'm a novelist."

"A-MAY-zing!" she says, and both Brit and I look at each other like we might have to shank this chick for using Britney's word. "What kind of novels do you write?"

Without pausing or even thinking, I say, "Romance. I write romance novels." And then I kind of lift my chin in something like a dare.

"You're kidding?" she caws. "I love romance novels!"

"You do?"

"Of course I do. I'm reading one right now!" We follow her as she skitters on her five-inch Louboutins back inside and over to the open house sign-in desk to grab up her e-reader. She taps it and shows me the screenful of text with the name of the book at the top…

… Yeah. It is.

"Oh. Cool," I say very casually. "I wrote that."

Evelyn's eyes go as wide as eyes can go, exaggerating her already doll-like features and making her look like some kind of pornographic anime character. Which is, I guess, kind of all anime characters, but—

"*You* wrote *Filling the Gap*? You're Cynthia Lear?"

I sniff. "Yep. That's me."

"Omigod. Omigod, omigod, omigod. I'm so… I had no idea. You just… I never know what my favorite authors look like."

"Sure. You know what they say…"

"What?"

"Something about books? And covers?"

There's a beat where I can see Evelyn putting it together in her head and then she bursts out laughing. "Ha! Yes! Of course! That's exactly the kind of clever turn of phrase I would expect from someone who writes like you do!"

Yeah. It wasn't actually a turn of phrase. And it wasn't that clever. Easy to please, this one.

"So, you're Cynthia Lear? Are you just starting your house search?"

"I am."

"Are you working with anyone yet?"

"Nope."

"Oh, well, let me give you my card! I have *so* many properties that I think would just be perfect." She hands me her card. I nod to Britney.

"My assistant will take it," I say. Britney smiles and takes the card, stuffs it in her purse.

"Of course, yes. Let me ask you, do you know when the audiobook for *Filling the Gap* is going to be released? Who's narrating?"

"I, uh, I don't actually have that date yet." I don't have that date yet because I haven't even thought about it yet. This has all happened so quickly that audio didn't even cross my mind. I should get on that, I suppose. I wonder if I should maybe ask— Or, I dunno if that would be—

"Well"—she starts her sentences with 'well' a lot—"I'm just tickled to meet you. You're fabulous."

She seems so genuinely excited that I can't keep up my sense of righteous indignation with her. She's a reader. Of my books. And, as recent evidence has shown, one must be very thoughtful about the way one interacts with one's audience. Because tides can shift like… tides, I guess.

"May I get a picture?" Evelyn gillies. Which is a word I maybe just made up, but it's onomatopoeic and if Shakespeare could invent 'swagger' (which he did; badass), then I can make up shit too.

"Yeah, of course," I respond, as Evelyn hands Brit her phone and I paste on a smile, while Evelyn wraps her arms around me and grins like a child on her birthday and I'm the doll.

"That was weird."

"Was it?" Brit asks as we inch along Wilshire in her car, headed east.

"Little bit. I went from sleeping on a mattress filled with bedbugs to getting hugged by Ms. *Million-Dollar Listing* in less than a fortnight."

"Yeah… Y'know, that show's title is really outdated. A million dollars can barely buy a one-bedroom in LA these days."

"I mean ... it's a brand."

We both nod to ourselves, knowingly, contemplating the titles of reality television shows. Because that is who we are.

Ring. Ring.

My phone. I look at the screen.

"Who is it?" Brit asks.

"I dunno. I don't recognize the number." I stare at it for another second and then, because curiosity is one of my toxic traits, answer. "Hello?"

"Yeah, hi, I'm looking for Cordelia Sarantopoulos?"

"This is."

"Cordelia, hi, my name is Gary Pritchard. I'm calling from North Star Author Agency?"

"Who is it?" Britney asks. I look at her with something, I assume, like bafflement on my face and put the phone on speaker.

"Uh… Yes? Hi?"

"Cordelia—great name by the way. Lear, yeah? Where you got your pen name, I assume? That's fire. Listen, Cordelia, I don't know if you know who we are—"

"I know who you are."

"Amaze. That'll save a ton of time. So, look, then it should be obvious why I'm calling. Have you signed with anyone yet?"

Britney looks at me and mouths, *Oh. My. God.*

"Um, no? No, I haven't. Signed. With anyone. Yet." I shrug and look at Brit like, *Holy shit.*

"Baller. So look, we'd love to have you on our roster here at North Star. Is that something you'd be into entertaining?"

"Uh, um, I mean, maybe. Yes? Maybe?"

"Well, let me break down for you what we can do for a new, streaking comet like yourself."

So far this guy has dropped that he knows the origin of my name and used a metaphor to compare me to an astronomic event. He's very good at his job.

"What we can do for you here is help guide your career and make sure that the incredible success you're enjoying now—and it is incredible, by the way—lasts. That's why we're called North Star. We make sure you're always heading in the right direction."

"That's… phenomenal. But, and you'll forgive me, Gary, but I thought your agency mostly handled sci-fi and, like, fantasy, and that kind of thing. Not so much romance."

"Cord… Can I call you Cord? Cord, we handle top-tier talent. That's what we do. If it's happening in the literary world, North Star has a hand in it. And, right now, no one is more happening than you."

I put the phone on mute. "This is crazy."

"I know. This is crazy."

"This is so crazy."

"Girl, it's SO crazy."

I take the phone off mute. "Well, that sounds… awesome."

"Cord, I'm telling you, you'd be special here. You're right, we don't have a huge stable of romance writers. But that means you'd get all of our attention. And you can talk to any of the writers we rep at North Star and I would challenge you to find a single one who says signing with us wasn't the best career decision they ever made."

"Well, actually, I kind of know one you just signed recently."

"No kidding? Who? Is it Raymond Forsythe? Chased Raymond for months. Love Ray!"

"No, no, it's Steve Smith." Silence. For a long, long time. "Gary…?"

"Yeah, no, I'm here. You're, uh, you're friends with Steve Smith?"

I look at Britney again. She raises a single eyebrow. "I mean… Yeah. Kind of. We know each other."

Britney bows her head at me. I put the phone on mute again. "Stop," I demand. Taking the phone off mute, I ask, "Why?"

"No, nothing, no reason. So, you're not, like, *close* friends or anything?"

"Close? Uh, I mean…"

"Because that's one of the first things we'll advise you against if you sign."

"What is?"

"Being close with Steve Smith. Being anywhere near Steve Smith. Well, I mean, not if you're, like his dentist or whatever, but if you're another writer ... we'll wanna keep you away."

"Why?"

"Because, Cord, Steve Smith is box office poison. He's radioactive. He's done. And we don't want the anchor of the SS controversy dragging anyone else down with it. And I didn't mean that as a clever quip. I'm not creating a metaphor about a ship called the SS *Controversy* that has an anchor attached. I'm literally saying that there's a controversy, it's centered around Steve Smith, aka SS, and it would be an anchor that could also… Whatever. You get it."

"So… you didn't wind up signing Steve?"

"Cord, nobody's gonna sign Steve. Steve is done. The new lawsuit—"

"New lawsuit? What new lawsuit?"

"You didn't hear about it? Raylen Star—who, for the record, we do not represent—has launched a lawsuit against Steve and Essie Smith for I don't even know how many counts of I don't even know what." There's a pause before he says, "How *do* you know Steve Smith?"

I take a moment to think. Because I'm not sure what the best answer is. So I just go with the first, most truthful one that comes to mind. "He's the one who got me invited to the Sin With Us convention to begin with. All the stuff that's happening for me… It's because he got me invited to the con."

Another beat where I can hear what sounds like Gary chewing ice or something. Then he blows out a long, long breath and says, "Shit. Yeah, that's tough. But, y'know, fuck him, right? I'm sorry, I don't mean to be harsh, but publishing is a tough business. Which is why you need to be someplace like North Star, Cord. We can make sure something like what's happening to Steve Smith never happens to you. Be smart. You may think you've summited the mountain, but if you look up, there's thousands more feet to climb and you have to look out for the falling bodies of the others before you who couldn't hack it, and make sure you're not one of them."

I know it's an accident, probably. I'd lay all my newfound money on the fact that this Gary Pritchard didn't even read *Filling the Gap*, either version, and is just chasing the new bright and shiny object, which happens to be me. But he just unknowingly stumbled right into the grandaddy of all possible metaphors.

In version one of *FTG*, Apollo falls off the edge of the mountain and dies. And Elpida goes on to find her own strength. Her purpose. He dies and she thrives because of it.

In version two, they fuck on the side of the mountain together and Apollo and 'Hope' get rescued by the National Park Service. (Which, while a deus ex machina, is kind of a semi-literal wink to the very concept of a deus ex machina, so I don't feel bad about using it.)

So, which one do I want to be? Elpida or Hope? What kind of writer? What kind of person?

I don't know.

I'm not sure what to do in this moment.

I wasn't expecting any of it.

I just don't know.

"Cord? You still with me, babe? Ah, shit. Sorry, sorry. I didn't mean to be… Old habit. Been in this business a while. Used to be okay to call people babe. Not even that long ago. Everyone! Men, women, whoever! Anyhoo, what are you thinking? Shall we do this thing? You ready to take over the publishing world? Cordelia? 'Blow, winds, and crack your cheeks!' and all that? Cordelia…? Ms. Lear? You still there?"

I look at Brit, who shakes her head at me. I know that shake. It's the one that says, *Dunno what to tell you, kid. You're on your own on this one.*

None of what's happening to me would be happening without Steve Smith. He made this all possible. No, he didn't force any of it into being, but he set the ball in motion.

On the other hand, this is also happening because I'm good at what I do. I care a lot about what I write and I've worked really, really hard and put myself out there to make it happen.

So, what do I do?

Am I Elpida, who lets someone die so she can become the person she was meant to be?

Or am I Hope, who stays connected to someone and honors the relationship that helped her scale the mountain in the first place?

"Cord?"

"Yeah, sorry, I was just… driving."

Britney shoots me a confused look.

"No worries. So? What do you think? Can I email you over a contract to have a look at?"

I stare out the window and the late afternoon LA sun, thinking about HEAs and what they really mean.

Does it have to be one thing? Marriage and a baby? Or can't it look like something else? Whatever you decide it is?

Truly. What does happily ever after look like?

It should be able to look like whatever you want it to look like, I decide. Especially if you've worked your ass off and you now understand that it doesn't always pay to play by the rules.

Shouldn't it?

I blink the sun out of my eyes and close them, blocking out all the competing thoughts.

You're damn right it should.

"Yeah," I say into the air between me and the speaker on my phone. "Go ahead and send it over…"

CHAPTER THIRTY – STEVE

Here's something most people don't know about Terry—he has seven kids. Seven. Like the ranking of *Master Choke* on Monday. Today, it's number five. It's probably gonna hit the *New York Times* again. It's been on that list seventeen times, but that was years ago when it was still fresh.

So… yeah. This is good? A silver lining, so to speak?

Probably not. Because I know most people are downloading it just so they can leave a verified one-star review.

They don't read it. They don't care about the characters or the story arc. They have no interest in the amazing twist at the end or the set-up for book two.

I've gotten hundreds of one-star reviews over the past few weeks. And… yup. That means my review rating has gone down from a four-point-one to a two-point-nine.

A Nerf bullet hits me in the forehead and the smallest of Terry's little darlings—he calls her Daisy Dog, for some reason, but I'm pretty sure her name is Noralynn—smiles at me from across the room, her Nerf gun still aimed in my direction. She's wearing a purple tutu, camo jeans, a princess crown, a unicorn horn, and a cowboy vest strapped with fake guns. "Got you," she says, squinting her little blue eyes at me.

Terry walks by, grabs her by one arm, twirls her around as she screams, and sets her back down all without missing a step. She goes squealing off, yelling, "Get me!"

I look at Terry and he shakes his head. "Sorry. You know what they say about the youngest."

I don't, but whatever. "Thanks for letting me stay here, man. I really appreciate it."

Terry salutes me. "Dude, my couch is your couch. You know that."

I do know that because the past week of my life kinda spiraled. First, Mike came over. That was yesterday. He had to fight his way past the reporters camped outside my house. But he made it. He came to tell me that Mom and Dad were going to be having an emergency meeting tomorrow—today—with their old-people-house culty-compound co-op board.

Apparently, even the nation's octogenarians are hip to my outrageous behavior towards romance authors. They're going to vote to see if Mom and Dad can still live there because I'm a black mark on their reputation.

"Don't let it get to you," Mike said.

"How do I do that, Mike? How? They're gonna get kicked out of their house!"

"Kind of ironic, isn't it?" Mike asked. "Because you're the one paying the bills." Then he laughed, but stifled it quick when I didn't laugh with him. "I didn't come to tell you this to make you feel bad, Steve. I came to tell you that Mom and Dad don't care what people are saying about you. And if the board gets lippy with them, they're gonna fight back."

"And if the board doesn't care and wants to kick them out anyway?"

"They're not gonna be homeless, Steve. It would be a temporary setback. That's it. Your dad has been trying to call you all week. He says you're not picking up. So that's why I'm here."

"I haven't been picking up because I just… I dunno. I just want to be left alone, I guess."

"I get it," Mike said. "That's why we're trying to give you your space. Plus that crowd outside. It's getting quite hard to navigate. Is it me, or is it getting bigger?"

I hadn't looked in days. So I didn't know. But when I peeked out the window it was indeed bigger. Much bigger. "Have they been harassing Essie?"

Mike winced.

"What?" I pushed. "Tell me."

"Not directly harassing her, or me, but somehow they found out we owned all those trailers and they've been harassing the neighbors."

"What? What the fuck?"

"Yeah. So. We're staying up in the hills at the new place."

"New place? That house doesn't even have a roof, Mike."

He put up a hand, trying to assuage me. "No, no. It's fine, Steve. We bought an Airstream and we're… camping."

I just blinked at him. "Dude. You and Essie own fifteen million dollars in beachfront trailers and you're staying in a camper on some wilderness hillside?"

"It's fine. It's no big deal. This whole thing is gonna blow over soon. These people, they have short attention spans. Two weeks, that's what I give it. Two weeks."

That night I tried to order a pizza from that awesome place down the highway and they said no. They would not deliver to me because I hate women and I'm a jealous asshole. And they hope Raylen Star sues me and takes my house.

People I don't even know are now literally hoping I will be homeless.

So… yeah. I'm hiding in Terry's man cave for the foreseeable future.

But hey, I've got video games, and darts, and I don't have to travel to make our weekly D&D game.

Life is still good. It is. It will be again soon.

Fuck. Who am I kidding? This is a complete shit show. I'm sinking. And while maybe I would be able to wrap my head around that—I did lie about who was writing the books—I can't wrap my head around the lies they're telling.

I'm Steve. The Ro-Bro. The guy who makes people happy, and makes the award ribbons, and tips the maids, and moves Raylen Star's stupid table away from the catering door. And fine, I did that a day late. I get it. But I didn't know. No one told me that the door was hitting her table.

How did I become the bad guy so fast? Overnight. It was literally overnight.

Like… where did I go wrong?

Inviting Leslie to Sin With Us, obviously.

Which I didn't even do. Mike did by mistake. Essie and I traced back Leslie's invitation to one night about two months ago after they finished their last reno when

Essie was super-drunk and tired, and I was fucking around with the waitlist.

Ironically, that was the same night I picked Cordelia to be invited. I had circled her name. And I was supposed to pick a second person—I do remember that—but I saw Raylen Star's name on the waitlist and just laughed.

I did circle her name. But I was gonna write a note to Essie: *Can you believe the balls on this lady?* Or something to that effect. But I got distracted and never wrote it.

Mike did say he thought I was crazy at the time, but I was the boss. He generally just follows instructions about the book stuff.

I still can't believe that Leslie had the balls to put her name on *our* waitlist. And now, thinking back, thinking about how everything was *us*—*our* waitlist, and *our* convention, and Sin With *Us*—I'm sad.

There is no more *us*. It's just me.

I don't like it. I don't like it at all.

I miss Essie being my other half. I'm not sure I can do this SS thing without her. In fact, I'm not sure I *want* to do this SS thing without her.

And to be completely honest, I'm not sure I *can* do this SS thing without her. "Maybe I should just quit."

"What?" Terry is messing with his gaming set-up. We're gonna stream a game on Snitch with Luke and Shawn in a little bit and he's fucking with an extra desktop so I can join in.

"Sorry. I didn't mean to say that out loud."

"You're not quitting nothin', Steve. You're the world's greatest romance writer. One day you're gonna look back and realize everything that's happened is romance-novel gold."

"Oh, my God. How many times do I have to tell you? This is real life, not a romance novel."

He puts his hands up. "I'm just saying, dude. This is building character."

I scoff. "Right."

My phone buzzes. I almost ignore it because it's probably my dad. And that fucking meeting is probably over and he's calling to tell me they got kicked out and they're gonna move back here to Encino and rent a one-bedroom—

Never mind. My fucking imagination, I swear.

I check the phone and it's my lawyer. "I gotta take this," I tell Terry. Then I exit his man cave and go outside to his pool. There are no kids swimming, so it's nice and quiet and peaceful. Terry lives in Westlake Village, right on the lake. A massive, beautiful house that holds his giant clan.

I let out a breath and tab accept. "Yeah. Hey, Rod. What's up?"

"Well…" Rod, who's been my lawyer for nine years now, sucks in a breath.

"Now what?"

He lets that breath out. "This lawsuit is not good."

"Shit. What? She's got no evidence! I didn't do any of this! How could she win this thing?"

"Oh, she's not going to *win*, Steve. Winning isn't the point. Settling is. They sent a settlement deal."

I grit my teeth. "What is it?"

"Twenty million."

"What? Is she fucking insane? Rhetorical question. We all know she is. But that's crazy, right? That's half of my net worth!"

"It's ludicrous. She's completely bonkers. But…"

"But what? You're not telling me to settle, are you?"

"No. Not exactly."

"Then what are you telling me, Rod?"

"She said she would drop the lawsuit and call off her… troublemakers, whatever that means, if you just…"

"If I just… what?"

"Public apology. She wants a public apology."

"Apology. For. *What?*"

He lets out a long sigh. "She's got a list. Do you want to hear it? Or should I email it to you?"

"How many things are on this list?"

"Twenty-seven."

"Twenty-seven! What the fuck?"

"I'll email it. You think on it. You have until eight o'clock Eastern. She wants it to be prime time and online—your Tube account, or your Twit account, or something similar where it will be seen by at least a million people. And she wants it tonight or the deal's off."

I just blink and shake my head.

"Steve? Think about it. And if this is something you want to do, then do it."

"Is that you telling me to do it?"

He doesn't even hesitate. "Yes. Do it. This could all end, Steve. Overnight. Your life can go back to normal. Well, it's not gonna be the same, but you can start rebuilding. Now… I gotta go. I'll send you the list right now. Talk soon, friend."

The call ends and my phone dings a text with Leslie's list.

I walk out to Terry's boat dock and take a seat on a bench under the gazebo, reading through the list.

I didn't do any of this stuff.

Not one bit of it.

But… maybe Rod's right. Maybe I should just give in and make it all go away?

Maybe nothing I have is worth fighting for anyway?

It is, after all, just a bunch of lies.

♥♡♥♡♥♡♥♡♥♡♥

We're playing Warrior Legends, an older game because I'm not on Snitch much so I don't even know how to play the new games and they get tired of me dying.

On Snitch, I'm just Steve. A nobody with seventy-two followers. But Luke has a massive Snitch following. Terry and Shawn both do too. That's kinda part of being them, right? World-famous science fiction writers get to immerse themselves in the culture they love and it's called work.

I, on the other hand, live in Romancelandia and thus gaming is not something my fans care much about. Still, it's a nice distraction even if I am rusty.

We're doing a buddy stream. Terry and me at his house, each on our own desktops, and Shawn and Luke at their own homes.

"Everyone mute," Luke says, his face kinda serious on screen as he does some fight move with a dragon, the sound of his fingers on the controller tapping away as we play. We all mute—this just means that Luke wants to have a private convo, one where the watchers can't hear. "So," he continues. "Are you gonna do it, Steve?"

He means am I going to make a public apology to Leslie. I told them all what Rod said. They just sighed and didn't offer up any comments.

Which I appreciate, to be honest. But I could actually use some advice. "Do you guys think I should?"

"No," Shawn says. "No. No. No. Not a fucking chance in hell, no."

"Did Shawn just say 'fuck?'" Terry asks. "Is Hell freezing over?"

Shawn does not swear. Which means he's a serious no.

"I say no, too," Luke adds. "Don't do it, dude. You got famous and shit because you're good at what you do. And that means you can just do it again."

"So you think I need a pen name?"

"Nope," Luke says. "I say make that bitch take you to court. Clear your name."

"What do you think, Terry?"

"I'm a 'no' too, dude. I don't think you should admit to things you didn't do. It's just wrong."

"Even if it will make all this drama go away?"

"I wouldn't." And they all say this at the same time.

I sigh and sit back in my chair, letting them play without me.

They unmute themselves and keep going, pushing forward in the quest while I dwell on my drama.

That list. It was crazy. Leslie wants me to admit that I used her to slingshot my way up the charts. She wants me to admit that Essie and I took ideas from other books and repurposed them in our own. She wants me to admit that I invited her to the convention this year to ruin her reputation. She wants me to admit that I personally placed her table too close to the catering door, thus ensuring she would be injured. She wants me to admit that I told Essie to drum up rage for Raylen Star in the Sin With Us reader group.

The list goes on and on.

And if I do all this, she will agree to never sue me for any of it.

How is this real life? I mean, why would she want a fake apology?

But I know why. She needs to cut me down so she can steal my sunshine. And she doesn't care how she does it. She has no use for the truth.

Or, alternatively, she's crazy and really believes that I'm out to ruin her.

She's either a morally evil person or she's mentally ill. Doesn't matter though, does it?

This is what she wants.

And… is it that bad? I mean, I know it's all lies. I didn't do any of that stuff, but don't people take plea deals all the time to get a lesser sentence?

If I did this, it's just… a plea deal. To get a lesser sentence.

This is when I notice something about the game I'm in with the bros. There are over a million people watching us right now.

That's the threshold.

Leslie wanted a million people. She wanted the apology to be live. And she wants it tonight.

I could do this.

I could do it right now, here on Snitch. And in ten minutes, maybe, it could all be over.

I press 'action key' on my keyboard and my character comes to life. Then I unmute my headset. "OK, listen, guys."

"Welcome back," Terry says. They are busy battling.

"Don't just stand there, Steve. Fight."

I push the icon on the screen that will show my face. And there I am. "Um… I just want to say… I'm Steve Smith and this is my statement."

"Dude." Terry pauses his game. "What are you doing?"

I take a deep breath and look at him, but talk to the people watching the stream. "I'm going to apologize to Les—I mean…" Fuck. If I say her real name, she will make a new scene for doxing her in front of a million people.

"Don't do it," Shawn says. "Don't—"

"I'm here to publicly apologize to Raylen Star. She's a… a famous romance author. And I… I treated her badly at a romance convention a few weeks ago."

People in the Snitch chat are confused. The comments are flying by so fast, you can't even read them.

More and more join in to watch, the number climbing exponentially in real time. I get out my phone and prepare to read down Leslie's list.

CHAPTER THIRTY-ONE – CORDELIA

THE SAME TIME

I've started packing. It's still going to be a few weeks until I'm in a position to put in an offer on a house, but I don't want to keep Sheila from renting it now. It's the end of summer and with kids getting ready to go back to UCLA, this is a prime spot for some grad student who wants to be relatively close to campus and doesn't mind being an occasional suntan-lotion-applier. I'm going to just crash at Brit's for a while, until I have the cash. I definitely plan on paying all cash for whatever house Evelynn gets me. (I did decide to go with her. She's a dealmaker and wouldn't stop texting and calling after I made the mistake of writing my info down on her sign-in sheet.) She says she can 'make wonders happen' with an all-cash offer.

Ring. Ring.

That's probably her now. She is tenacious.

I look. Oh. It's not. It's…

"Hi, Audrey."

"Are you on your computer?" Audrey Saint's voice sounds more urgent than I'm used to.

"No. Why?"

"Turn on your computer."

"Why?"

"Just do it."

"Okay. Hold on." I dig out my laptop from under a pile of sweaters I own and never wear. Because it's LA. And even though it gets chilly in December and January, I still prefer jackets. Sweaters make me feel shapeless. Anyway, my computer is under them.

I open it up. "Okay. What's—?"

"Go to Snitch."

"Snitch?"

"That gamer platform."

"I know what it is. I just—"

"Just do it."

I head to the site and there, on the main page, the 'Featured Stream' that's currently being displayed to one-point-seven million people is…

"And then, while she was resting and under the influence of pain medication, we paid housekeeping at the Aria to break into her suite and change her out of her clothes into an unattractive nightgown with cats on it. Raylen doesn't even own a cat nightgown. We just thought it would be cruel."

"What in the frackety fuck is this?" I ask Audrey.

"What does it look like? Steve is going through a litany of apologies to Leslie, live on Snitch."

"Why?"

"I have no idea."

"How did you know about this?"

"James. He's a big D&D Game Master Dungeon something. I dunno. But he was on and saw it."

"We also drank all the liquor in her minibar and left the bottles scattered around to make it look like she did it. Just because we are assholes. No other reason," Steve goes on.

"This is insane!" I shout.

"I know. I know. I mean… I know Steve and Essie really well. And, this is… There's just no way they would do any of the stuff he's apologizing for."

"No shit. Also, the night he's talking about having done this stuff, he couldn't have."

"Why not?"

"Because I was with him."

Ding.

"Shit, someone's texting. Audrey, hold on."

I pull the phone away from my ear and put it on speaker as I look at the text.

GARY: Yo! Cord, my new favorite person! You sign that contract yet?

I ignore the text and turn my attention back to the stream.

"And, knowing Raylen has a gluten allergy, we very deliberately made sure to have no gluten-free cupcakes available for her in her author welcome room. In fact, the ones we made for her had double gluten." Steve squints at what he's reading and says, "Are you fu—? Anyway. Also…"

"This is all a total list of fabrications," I say to Audrey on speaker.

"Of course it is. I have to assume it's to make the lawsuit go away."

"But—"

Ding.

GARY: FYI, Steve Smith is currently apologizing on Snitch. I bring it up because I don't want you to think that it's gonna move the needle on anything. I know you two are friends. But, as stipulated in your contract, you will refrain from having any contact with the guy. Okay? We added it as a special condition. Y'know. Just to be safe.

"Item number fifteen," Steve goes on. "In regard to the font size of Raylen Star's name on the posters…"

Audrey sounds exasperated over the phone. "This is so fucked."

"Yeah."

"I wish there was something we could do for him. After everything he's done for the romance community, it's just… Ugh. I hate seeing him go down like this."

"Yeah."

Ding.

GARY: Yo! Cordy Cool! U getting my texts?

"Audrey, I'll call you back." I end the call and watch just as Steve says…

"But, most of all, I'm sorry to my fans and fellow authors. Because I got you to believe a…" He pauses. The next word sticks in his throat. "To believe a…"

He takes a deep breath, closes his eyes, and says, "Fuck this."

And time feels like it slows down.

"I mean… Fuck this bullshit. These apologies are… I didn't do these things. Half the stuff on this list

I didn't even know about and the other half… If I'm guilty of one thing, it's that I didn't just own what I was doing sooner. I should've been proud of the fact that I was writing work that people care about. I am sorry to the readers for not just being more open and honest with you. I am. But all this other stuff, I…" He looks around like he's at a loss. "Doesn't matter. Nobody's gonna believe me anyway. So let me just keep going through this list. And then you can all get back to watching my friends play *Warrior Legends.* Which is what you're here for anyway."

He looks sad. Defeated. Totally unlike the Steve I met just a few short weeks ago.

And it breaks my heart a little bit.

"Hello. Did you lose something?"

That was the first time I heard his voice. That booming Tank Watson voice he used.

"I'll take care of it."

"…What?"

"I'll take care of it. I'll get you something."

"I… They're sold out."

"No, they're not."

"They said they were."

"Not for… SS. For SS, there's room. I got it."

The memories come washing back over me, unbidden. But I can't stop them.

"I read your book."

"You finished it?"

"Mm-hm."

"Already?"

"Mm-hm."

"And…?"

"It's incredible."

Everything that's happening—has happened—I owe to Steve.

"Essie did say that Steve is a genuinely nice guy, by the way."

That's what Britney told me. And then I remember something I thought on the last day:

Steve Smith is genuinely the nicest guy I've ever met. And I hope he gets all the things he wants.

"Number nineteen," Steve says, looking all alone and at a loss for words except for the bullshit apology he's being forced to read.

No.

No.

Fuck that.

He might be at a loss for words, but I'm not. I *never* am.

I grab up my phone and open the WishMaker app. Gregory's cartoon mug smiles at me. "Ms. Sarantopoulos! So glad to see you! What might I do for you?"

"I want you to put me into Steve Smith's Snitch stream."

"I'm sorry?"

"Gregory, don't fuck with me. You said you can grant any wish, worldwide, as long as I'm not in North Korea or some parts of Russia. And LA most certainly ain't those places. So, I want you to inject me into the Steve Smith Snitch stream right now."

I know his cartoon face doesn't really express human emotion, but I swear I see him smile. "Your wish is my command," he says.

And, suddenly, the light on my computer that indicates the camera is on glows to life and I find myself projected onto my own screen in a little box just like Steve and all his bros.

"Number twen—Cordelia?"

"You can see me?"

"Yeah. I… Yeah."

"Who's this?" one of the bros asks. The nameplate in the corner of his little box reads 'Shawn.'

"Um, this is Cordelia Sarantopoulos."

"Oooooooooh!" croons out a bro identified as 'Terry.' "*This* is Cordelia? Cordelia, hey! I'm Terry! I'm Steve's best friend!"

A guy ID'd as 'Luke' takes umbrage. "Bro, what? We're all best friends. You don't get to claim Steve as *your* best friend."

Terry shrugs it off. "Well, if we're *all* best friends, isn't it implicit that I am? I didn't say you weren't also. Chill, broski."

"How the hell are you doing this?" Steve asks.

"What? You mean, how am I here?" I ask.

"Uh, *yeah*."

"Gregory."

"Gregory? The app?"

"Yeah, I made a wish."

"I knew there was something creepy about that AI!"

"What?" all three of the other guys say at roughly the same time.

"An AI hacked you in?" asks Shawn.

"Like, a sentient AI?" Luke chimes in.

"Holy smokes! This is like a thing I'm working on!" Terry says.

"Guys, can you give us a little privacy, please?" Steve requests.

They all look into their own cameras like he's crazy.

"Bro," Terry says. "You've got like a million-and-a-half people watching you."

"Yeah, okay. Well… can you at least mute yourselves?"

They do. They don't turn off their cameras though, so I still see them watching, fascinated.

"Um… Hi," Steve says after a second.

"Hi." It's a little awkward, but I press on. In for a penny… "How've, uh, how've you been?"

He laughs a little. "Ducky. Things are going great." He shakes his head. "How about you? Seems like things actually *are* going pretty well over at Camp Lear."

"They've been worse." I smile too. "I, um… I'm sorry I never got your number, I—"

"Oh, God, don't worry about it. I've had my hands full."

"I figured that's why you didn't—"

"It's the only reason I didn't call."

I'm not a huge blusher, but I feel myself blush. "Yeah. It's the only reason I didn't try to—"

"I know," he interrupts. "It's cool." A beat before he says, "So, what are you doing here now?"

I take a breath. "Stop apologizing."

"Cordy—"

"I'm serious, Steve. Don't apologize to that woman. Don't do it."

Ding.

AUDREY: OMG! How are you doing this?

Ding.

GARY: WHAT THE HELL ARE YOU DOING? YOU ARE GOING TO RUIN YOUR CAREER BEFORE IT EVEN STARTS!

I ignore both texts and just stay focused on Steve. "I'm not kidding, Steve. Don't keep on with this bullshit apology charade. The last person on the planet you need to apologize to is Leslie Munch."

"Shhh. Cordy! Don't—You shouldn't say her—"

"Oh, please. Who cares? It's not like a big secret that anyone couldn't figure out. Just like you being SS wasn't really a secret people couldn't figure out. It's not that it was that hard, it's that people love the fantasy. They love the mystery. And, more than anything, people love the drama. That's why they read romance in the first place. Because they know they can get all that heavy, juicy, messy stuff, but that no matter what kind of crap the people in the book go through, it'll be okay because it'll end in an HEA. A happily ever after. That's the whole game. It gives us hope that there's a point to all the shit we have to slog through in life and that if we just hang in there and believe, there'll be somebody there to have our back when it's all over. And Leslie's trying to steal that. She's breaking the essential first rule of romance. And I've dedicated my life to this genre and I'm not about to get her get away with it. People like Leslie think it's *their* story. But it's not. Not this one. This is your story, Steve. And you shouldn't let someone else write it. Because you are one of the truest champions of romance I've ever seen. I know you didn't set out to be, but you are. And, like it or not, it's who you are.

"You encompass the very essence of what romance should be. Your purity of intent and your kindness and generosity is unlike that of anyone I've ever met. You're not mired in the quicksand of cynicism and you don't tread in lockstep with the shambling crowd. You forged your own steel and have climbed your own mountain, never before trod by anyone in quite the way it has been trod by you. You turned your seeming foibles into superpowers and your weaknesses into strengths. And you have done so while creating a generous, welcoming, safe place for those of like minds—though no minds are quite like yours—to have a community and a haven for play. Within the effulgence of writers who comprise the romance community, you are the spark that lit so many other flames and for that you should be celebrated and revered, not made mockery of and torn down by the angry, calcified, vituperative spirit of someone who's too embedded in their own misery to feel *your* inherent joy.

"All of you watching, all of you out there right now who might be a part of that community, ask yourself: When has Steve Smith ever been anything but kind and generous? Can I remember a time when Steve Smith helped me? I will bet all that I have that the answer, to a person, is yes. I even watched Steve corral a roomful of people to help move Leslie Munch's table at the Sin With Us convention just so she wouldn't be uncomfortable. And, if you were there, you saw it too. It may seem like a small thing, but that's what makes it special. Anyone can act upon the grand gesture and bask in the glow of its magnificence, but to do the pedestrian, everyday, mundane things, like take the time to encourage an up-and-coming author to believe in herself and trust her own voice… to not be afraid… to not care what other people think… *that* is an act of generosity. That is an act of love.

"And that's who Steve Smith is. That's the Steve Smith I believe I know. So that's why I don't think you should apologize. Because you didn't do anything wrong. You've done everything right. Both spellings. I mean, R-I-G-H-T and W-R—"

"Yeah, no, I get it," Steve interrupts.

"Oh, okay, good. So. Anyway."

Shawn, Terry, and Luke stare, mouths open. Finally, Terry unmutes himself and says, "Holy shit. Dude, I get why you can't stop talking about her."

I catch myself smiling. "You can't?"

"I may have brought your name up once or twice." Steve smiles too.

"Um. So," I start, "I'm just suddenly realizing how public this is. And that's giving me kind of a minor panic attack, so I should go, but… Do you wanna… have dinner sometime? With, y'know, me?"

"Uh. Yes. How's…" He looks at his watch. "Now?"

"Now? Now's good."

We both smile. And Terry jumps back in.

"Awesome! He's staying with me! Because I'm his best friend." He says it pointedly. Luke and Shawn roll their eyes. "The address is—"

"Bro!" Steve shouts. "You might wanna…"

"Oh, ha. Right! I'll just… know what? I'll just DM it to you in the chat."

He does. Then he clicks his camera off. So do Shawn and Luke as they wave goodbye.

"Guess it's just you and me," Steve says.

"Yeah. And a million and a half of our closest friends."

We both wave.

"So… I'll, um, I'll see you later, I guess," he mutters, with a grin.

"Yeah. You will."

"Feel like we have plenty to catch up on."

"Little bit."

There's another awkward moment where we smile at each other like mooning teenagers before Steve says, "Oh, shoot. There's one thing I forgot to say."

"What's that?"

He gets close to the camera and in his growliest Tank Watson voice says, "Fuck you, Leslie. I'll see you in court."

The he sits back, winks at what I know is me, and his camera goes black.

Ding.

GARY: Well… congrats, kid. It takes a special kind of talent to make a career flame out before it's even started, but you managed it. Good lyck.

(I assume he meant to type "Good luck.")

What did I just do? What did I just…?

I look around at my little pool house, strewn with clothes, and I think about what I'm going to do now. I just very publicly threw my emerging name and reputation behind a guy who the world is accusing of being a liar, a misogynist, and who knows what. And I went to bat for him.

What the hell did I just do?

I know exactly what I did.

I chose Hope.

I didn't leave him to die on the side of a mountain. I chose to stand with someone who stood with me and who lifted me up to heights I didn't know I could achieve.

I'd rather stay in this pool house for the rest of my life and be a struggling author writing the stories I wanna write than play by a set of rules that say in order to succeed, I have to betray a man who only wanted to lift me up the mountain.

If the parallels to the story I wrote, the one Britney encouraged me to write, do hold, then… then eventually the Park Service will be by to rescue me with their helicopter. As I say, I know a deus ex machina isn't the most elegant way to end a story, but sometimes it's the right way.

Ding.

AUDREY: Holy shit, that was amazing. Cynthia Lear, you are the f'ing bomb.

That's nice. It's nice that Audrey—

Ding.

EDEN: Bitch, that was the most rockstar shit I've ever seen. Don't worry, chica. The queen bitch has your back.

Wow. Eden Le Fay even said something ni—

Ding.

RAVEN: The most romantic thing I've seen anyone do since before my husband passed.

Oh. Holy—

Ding.

MOM: Honey, I got a call from someone who told me to watch this Sneetch website and that you were on it. So I did. I'm proud of you, Cordelia. That was not only one of the most courageous things I've ever seen someone do, the monologue you spun out (off the top of your head, I assume) was a triumph. Brava, my girl! You are so very talented. The romance world is lucky to have you in it. Let's talk soon.

XO

Mom.

And, feeling the tears welling up in my eyes, I look toward the screen of my computer and through the glistening, I notice a chat.

I was so amped up before that I wasn't really paying attention, but there's a chat stream running along the side of the screen. I'm hesitant to read any of the comments because… well, it's the internet and I didn't just show up here on Earth. It's not always the kindest place. But then I notice thousands of little heart emojis popping up and floating away.

Because of course they are.

Because that's the point of romance.

To make you feel something.

And I guess I just did.

So, with some caution, I lean in to try to catch some of what people are commenting.

And what they're almost all saying is…

Steve Smith is INNOCENT!

That Leslie chick sounds like a fuggin asshole!

STEVE FTW!
FREE STEVE SMITH!
Yo, Crodelia ur hot. If things don't wurk out with Steve…

I close my laptop and let out a deep, deep breath. One that feels like I've been holding it in for… I dunno, a couple of decades maybe. And I look at my nails.

I think maybe tomorrow I'll go get a manicure.

CHAPTER THIRTY-TWO — STEVE

Eden Le Fay made a post on her social page about me. Which, honestly, is quite touching. Because it's Eden Le Fay. She's… mean, but in a lovable way. People often say they are afraid of her, but is fear the correct word here?

I prefer to call it a healthy respect.

The point is that Eden doesn't hand out praise willy-nilly. In fact, it's quite hard to persuade Eden to give a fuck about… well, pretty much anything.

She lives in her own world. A world of black leather, whips, and blindfolds. And that sex… partner of hers. Who I'm pretty sure is not an *actual* slave, but hell, who knows?

My point is that this post was different and it went like this:

Do you wanna know why I love Steve fucking Smith, bitches? Do you? DO YOU? Let me fucking tell you why. One time, when I was drunk after I made New York Times *during Sin With Us, Steve held my hair back and whispered kind things into my ear as I hurled my brains out for eight hours. Eight fucking hours, you piece-of-shit haters! Name one other man—who is* not even my slave—*who would do that for me. No one. No one, I tell you! There is only one Steve Smith and I am proud to call him my friend. And if you don't like him, too fuckin' bad. I love his ass. I love his talented, crazy, humble, beautiful, kind, and gorgeous ass. Stay the fuck away from my Steve, bitches. Or I will cut you a new pie hole. #TrueStorySteve Peace out, motherfuckers."*

And below that was a picture of Eden from seven years ago. All dressed up like a dominatrix, ass cheeks mooning the camera from either side of a strip of leather, and blowing her guts into the hotel toilet.

I was, indeed, holding her hair.

I remember that night. It was the first time we had Sin With Us at the Aria, and did we ever get drunk. Ho-lee shit, that was fun. We were loud, and sailing high on Nile rankings, I had just signed the deal for the *Master Choke* movie, and none of us could quite believe that it was real.

That was Mike's first year. He and Essie weren't married yet, but they had just gotten engaged. And the whole time Eden was puking he was texting me, *Bro. I love you, bro. I'm gonna marry your sister and we're gonna be bros.*

I'm smiling so big now. Because… it was a good ride, ya know? It really was. And if it's over, fuck it. I can't complain. Maybe this wasn't *my* dream life, but it *was* a dream life. And I don't care if it's time to wake up now. I really don't. I wrote good books, I supported people and lifted them up as much as I could, and I made a difference in my own small way.

Anyway. Eden's post was… kind of out of character? While still being firmly *in* character.

I guess that's why the comment section went nuts.

Shawn has been reading them out loud ever since he got to Terry's house an hour ago. "Listen to this one," Shawn says. "'This one time I was on my way to pick up my kids from school and I got a flat tire. I was on the side of the road and do you know who came to my rescue? Steve Smith. That's right, Steve Smith. He rode up on his glistening gray stallion in a suit of armor and gave me the horse off his back. He literally said, "Don't worry, little lady, I'm Mr. Happily Ever After. Take my horse, pick up your kids, and I will deliver your car home when it is fixed." I found a friend in Steve Smith that afternoon. I will be forever grateful for how he saved me from being the joke of the parental pick-up line the next day. Thank you, #TrueStorySteve. You will always be my hero.'"

I just shake my head.

"Oooooh, oooh, ooh. Listen to this one," Shawn says. "'I can clearly see why people love Steve. Steve is one in a million. He taught me how to basket-weave. He was so patient. The basket he helped me weave was entered into the Louisiana State Fair and took Grand Prize. Thank you, #TrueStorySteve! Without your help I would've never made the USA Olympic Basket-Weaving Team!'"

"I didn't know we had a basket-weaving team," Terry says.

"Terry, shut up." Luke is on Shawn's FaceTime, stuck in traffic on his way up to us. They all want to meet Cordelia, who… should be here any minute.

"Here's another one," Shawn says. "'Steve Smith taught me how to read. I had been struggling with vowel sounds in the first grade and was behind all my friends in reading. I told this sad story to Steve while Essie was signing *Master Choke* for me five years ago. Steve hugged me like a long-lost friend. Then he put up a finger, said, "Wait here, I'll be right back," and then he travelled back in time, taught me how to sound out the vowels, erased all the stress and drama around my traumatic childhood reading experience, and came back holding a Polaroid of the two of us sitting together at a tiny desk in my first-grade classroom. I'll never forget how Steve Smith turned my life around at age six. #TrueStorySteve.'"

There are now five hundred seventy-two comments on Eden's post. At first, they were all people I recognized telling true stories about me, Steve. All the little things I do at the convention, mostly. The entire housekeeping staff on the Aria convention floor all talked about how I was their friend. Lots of authors chimed in, and readers, of course.

But Eden's post went viral in the past half-hour or so and now it's just complete strangers making up stories about how I helped them.

It's like… a homage to the HEA.

Which, not gonna lie, touches my fuckin' heart and brings a little tear to my eye.

"Oh, my God, listen to this one!" Shawn is laughing.

"Enough, enough," I say. "We get it. I'm a meme."

Which is ironic, because it turns out that it's not always bad to be a meme. And even though there are still numerous nasty hashtags out there about me, #TrueStorySteve is the only one trending right now.

The doorbell rings and all of us look at the man cave door with wide eyes and mouths open.

"She's here," I whisper.

"Quick! Places, everyone!" Terry claps his hands.

"It's just the three of us, dude," Shawn says. "Chill."

"*Four* of us, you dick!" Luke is still on FaceTime. "Tilt me up a little, I can't see anything."

We line up in front of the gaming station, standing up straight, slicking back our hair, shuffling our feet.

Straining. Leaning forward. Trying to figure out what's taking so long. I mean, Terry's house is huge, but you can't get lost in it.

"Did she get lost?" Luke asks. "I don't see anything."

"Oh!" Terry says, playfully smacking himself on the forehead. "The kids! She's gotta get past the kids."

And then there she is! My lovely Cordelia is standing in the doorway to the man cave wearing… I tilt my head a little.

"Is that a unicorn horn?" Luke asks.

"Shut up, Luke," Terry side-mouths. "You're ruining the moment."

My lovely Cordelia is indeed wearing a unicorn horn. Plus a purple tutu and she's covered in glitter.

I cover my mouth to stop the laugh.

"I'm not sure what just happened, but…" Cordelia spits some glitter out, then smiles at me as she tentatively raises her hand in greeting. "Hi."

I almost fall over swooning. But that's not the part I play in this scene. So I control myself.

I walk over to her, take her hand, and kiss it as I stare down into her melty-chocolate brown eyes. "Hi."

And everything that happens next is just… a brand-new dream.

Mike and Essie drop by.

Shawn's wife comes over with their kids.

Luke finally shows up after battling traffic.

We spend the rest of the afternoon and well into the evening just hanging out. And the funny thing is, it feels like… like we've always been these people. This group feels like it was inevitable.

Not to mention easy. And even though my life is nothing but angst, and drama, and conflict right now—there is no angst, drama, or conflict *here.*

And while these three things are the recipe for exciting books, in real life—no, thank you.

I'm still being sued.

Half of Romancelandia still hates me.

I could be broke in the near future.

But I don't care.

The only thing I care about is what's happening all around me right now.

Friends, family, and loved ones.

Of course, my phone is still buzzing nonstop. Authors, friends, even Mom and Dad. I ignore everyone but Dad when he calls, because that's a loose end and I need to know if I've ruined their good thing over in Arizona. So I answer that one. "Hey. How did it go, Dad? Did they kick you out?"

"Did they kick us *out?*" Dad bellows. "Did they kick us out! Son, I told them to shove it. Shove it right up their behinds. Because you know what?"

I'm smiling. "What?"

"You're our son. And of course you're gonna make mistakes. Everyone makes mistakes. But you're our son, Steve. And I told them… 'He's my son and I'm on his side. I'm always going to be on his side.'"

"They kicked you out, didn't they?"

"No!" Then he laughs. "I promise they did not. But we are moving. If a little controversy is enough to spook those jerks and upend our life, well, then they're no friends of ours. And that's exactly what I told them. They can stick that nine-hole golf course where the sun don't shine. I said to them, 'Do you even know who my son is? He's one half of SS!' That's what I said to them. 'One half of SS!'"

It should, maybe, feel a little superficial that he's bragging about me now. I mean, I've kind of been one-half of SS this whole time—even out in the open.

But it doesn't feel superficial all.

In fact, I love that he *didn't* say I was SS.

Because I'm not SS.

SS has never been *me*, it's always been *us*.

And as I watch Essie and Mike laughing and talking to Luke and Britney, I'm suddenly very much OK with this ending. I'm OK if it's over. It's going to be weird, of course. But endings have always been my favorite thing about stories in the first place. They are a conclusion and a fresh start in the same breath.

"Steve? You still there?"

"Yeah. Just… thinking. But thank you, Dad. I wish you didn't have to move though."

"Are you kidding?" Then he lowers his voice. "I couldn't talk your mom out of it if I tried. And I didn't."

"What do you mean?"

"What do I mean? I mean that girl of yours. Cynthia." I can almost see his eyebrow waggling from five hundred miles away.

"That's her pen name, Dad. Her real name is—"

"Cordelia, I know. Your mother is beyond excited about this young woman. She said she had a dream last night that the two of you sailed into the sunset. She said her grandbabies are now locked in. Locked in, that's what she said. And she needs to be close when this happens. We've already put our share of the co-op up for sale. We're gonna be house-hunting, son. But for the meantime, we're gonna move into one of Essie and Mike's trailers. So when those babies come, we'll be ready to take them off your hands any time you want."

"*Them*?"

"Well, twins run in the family."

"Oh, OK." I just laugh and shake my head.

I didn't even bother explaining how there was no way my mother was getting those babies from me before they come from Essie. Or that I'm pretty sure twins runs in the woman's side of the family. So if anyone's having doubles, it's her.

Mom has her dreams, and who am I to kill her dream?

It's a nice time. A really nice time. We grill, and swim—well, not Cordelia. She and I sit on the edge and dip our feet in. And when the sun starts to set Terry hands me the key to his boat and says, "Why don't you take her for a spin?" I get a weird feeling in my stomach.

Because he's telling me to take Cordy out on the lake and make romance-novel gold and he didn't even know about my mom's dream.

But ya know what?

Sailing off into the sunset sounds like a pretty good idea to me.

Cordy and I slowly motor out to the middle of the lake. It's not a huge lake, but it's not a huge boat, either. So it's all quite perfect, actually. I kill the engine and we sit on the bench seat in the back, close together. Close enough for me to put my arm around her.

We float and watch the sun drop down over the rooftops of Westlake Village. Someone is playing music on a nearby dock—'Unchained Melody,' cliché as far as romance novels go, but hey, this is real life. It is what it is.

She leans her head on my shoulder as the light becomes dim and the sounds of families and cliché love songs echo off the lake.

And it occurs to me in this moment that I think I have finally grasped the meaning of happily ever after.

Cordelia, of course, is my literal definition.

But it's more than that.

The nerves when you meet someone new are fun. That jittery feeling of butterflies in the stomach makes things exciting. And I know that there are probably a lot of women out there—and men too—who crave that 'new' feeling. The nerves. The excitement. The unknown. The possibilities.

But the *known*—when you're with someone who gets you, who has your back, who wants to take this crazy fucking journey by your side—well, that beats new and exciting every single time as far as I'm concerned.

The partnership is the real HEA.

I look down at Cordelia and stare at her. She must feel my gaze because she tips her head up at me, eyebrows furrowed. "What?"

"Hi."

"Hi." She laughs.

"Would you like to do pedestrian, everyday, mundane things with me?"

She sits up a little, eyes bright. "Was that a great line or was that a great line? It just came out! The whole thing. It was like… it was like…" She sighs. "It was like

I had been blind, and deaf, and mute, and locked away in a sensory deprivation chamber—well, except no water—and then these words just started flying out of my mouth, and I kept going, and I felt them—truly, deeply, like they were a part of my soul—and when I was done I knew they were real and I had finally found my true self." She lets out a breath. "Yeah. It was like that."

I chuckle. And I'm about to say something expected, like, *Thank you.* Or *I feel the same*, or *Would you like to go on another date?*

But then a memory comes back to me. A memory of meeting Cordelia at the convention, just about a month ago now, and how I first characterized her, to myself, in my own head.

And it occurs to me… that perhaps my lovely Cordelia might want to hear these words out loud as well.

"Cordy, you lovely creature of a woman, you are the only person in the room who can write a run-on sentence with such skill, and emotion, and moxie that one does not even understand that you, beautiful, sweet Cordelia, just wrote the world's longest run-on sentence because they have been captivated—imprisoned, even—by your brilliant author voice. And while your ability to string words together for the longest of sequences is what drew me to you in the first place, it is your courage, and your heart, and your love and respect for the hidden meaning just below the surface, that held me captive and made me *crave* you—the embodiment of the unexpected, and unique, and peculiar. Much the way most people crave the ordinary, and the predictable, and the easy. Being with you, Cordelia, makes me feel like I've just arrived home after a long trip away, and when you showed up for me today… when you saved me from myself…"

I look down at her. She is gazing up at me like I'm that guy on the horse, the one who rides in to save people. But I'm not that guy. She is.

"You, Cordelia, are the hero of my story. And I would like nothing more than to do pedestrian, everyday, mundane things with you. Because if I'm doing them with you, they will be intense, and thought-provoking, and nothing short of exceptional. And I hope—no, I *know*—that you are the missing piece of my puzzle."

We stare lovingly at each other as the twilight turns dark and the stars begin to twinkle above us.

"Was that cliché?" I ask.

She shakes her head, laughing. "What?"

"The whole puzzle piece thing? It's overdone, right? I should rewrite that. Remind me to rewrite that."

She pats my chest and sighs and we spend the next few minutes floating and dreaming.

"OK, here's the edit," I side-eye Cordelia as she chuckles. "When you said those things about me today, Cordy, you made me feel visible. You made me feel seen. You got me. And I just want you to know that I don't care if I lose everything. I just don't want to lose you."

I lean back, semi-satisfied with my declaration.

Cordelia scoots up on her knees, climbs into my lap, and places her hands on my cheeks as she gazes down into my eyes. "It's going to be fine, Steve. It really is. It's going to work out the way it was meant to work out because you did everything right. Both spellings."

And then she kisses me, sweeping me off my feet, and we make classic romance-novel gold right there in the back of a boat.

MEANWHILE…

Meanwhile…

Leslie Munch's foray into the life of a victim was going quite well for several weeks in a row now. That table move—every time she thought about it, she just thanked her lucky stars that she was so drugged up on painkillers and rage, she didn't really consider the consequences of falling flat on her face again.

Didn't really feel it, either.

Not until the next day.

This rage, and numbness, is what allowed her to keep the accusations going. One after the other after the other as she was wheeled out of the hotel on a gurney—again. And even she could admit that some of her allegations are borderline ridiculous. However, she *was* wearing a cat nightgown when all this went down that day, and that damage needed to be controlled.

Steve, as far as Leslie is concerned, *was* responsible for her wearing that nightgown. He drove her to the edge of madness. On purpose. Whether he had anything to do with how it the nightgown got on her body was beside the point.

He needs to pay.

And pay he will.

Her lawyer sent the offer over earlier that day and the early word was, Steve was gonna take her up on it.

However, the early word appears to have been false.

He *was* going to take her up on it.

Past tense. As in, he was going to, and then *didn't.*

Rage isn't even a strong enough word for how Leslie is feeling now.

"You should just drop it." She's on the phone with her lawyer, Lewis.

She pauses before answering so she can sniff some saline spray up her nose, then she returns to the conversation. "Drop it? Why would I drop it?"

"Because he didn't finish the apology, Leslie. He didn't take the deal. And aside from that I just got a message—"

"Raylen, Raylen, *Raylen.* Why can't you just call me Raylen?"

"Because it's a name that you made up, Leslie. It's not legal. And I'm a lawyer. I deal in what's legal and your fucking name is Leslie!"

"There's no need to shout, you boorish dolt. And it's my pen name, Lewis. Who is paying your bill, anyway? You should just do what I tell you!"

"How many times do I have to explain this? You're not paying me. It's a contingency plan, Leslie. I have to win to get paid and I'm telling you, I can't win this case. It's… *dumb.*"

"Well, you know what? Fuck you, Lewis! And you know what else? *You're* dumb. I'll represent myself!"

"OK, well, good luck with that. Because as I was saying before you cut me off with the tirade about your fake name, not only do you not have a case, it's quite possible that the Aria will be suing *you.*"

"What? That's ludicrous! I have injuries! I have witnesses!"

"Yes, the witnesses are kind of the problem. You see, the Aria AI—"

"The Aria has an AI?" Leslie's tone simmers down a little.

"They do. His name is Gregory. And Gregory has made a report about you hiring these witnesses of yours to start a fight in the Reader Rants panel."

"That's crazy! That's… just crazy!"

"Is it, Leslie? Is it? You should think really hard about that. Because these witnesses made a full confession. You hired them—"

"They volunteered!"

Silence.

"I mean…" Leslie starts. But it's done. She just admitted that she used these people—people she would be contacting later, that's for sure. And now… well. Lewis's silence spoke libraries.

Finally, after what seemed like the proverbial 'eternal moment,' Lewis says, "Listen, Leslie. It's over. Whatever debauchery you were plotting, it's over. The social tide has turned. They are on Steve's side. And, though it hasn't happened yet, Romancelandia will turn against you if you don't stop this childish nonsense right now. Gregory has also detected fraud perpetrated against Steve Smith in the Nile bookstore."

"What?"

"That's right. He's not the Aria AI. He's… *the* AI. The only one that truly exists. In other words, he's an independent contractor and he works for many, *many* corporations."

"That's… not even possible. It's science fiction. There is no AI like that."

"Isn't there, Leslie? Isn't there? Tell me you did not hire…" Lewis pauses. There is some paper shuffling. Then a sigh. "Tell me you did not hire Ro-Bots 'R' Us out of Mumbai, India, to purposefully create fake Nile accounts, download Steve Smith's book"—more paper-shuffling noises—"Steve's book *Alien Alliance*, and then have Ro-Bots 'R' Us leave him…" He scoffs. "Is this right? Ten *thousand* fake reviews? What the actual fuck are you doing? No. Better question. What the actual fuck is wrong with you?"

Leslie, for once in her life, is at a loss for words.

"Hello? That was not a rhetorical question, Leslie. That was an actual question."

"I… I…" She has a momentary pause here. Finding herself at a fork in the road, she sees two choices in front of her. One, just admit it. Let all this anger and animosity go. Tell the truth and move on. Make a new life for herself outside of romance, far away from handsome, charming, talented, well-liked Steve Smith and his perky, too-good, friendly, pretty sister. Leslie could write thrillers under a new name. Or mysteries. Or… cookbooks. Be a brand-new force to be reckoned with. A refreshing new voice. Turn her whole life around and be a better person.

Or, two, lean in to that hate. Because why should she have to leave a world she'd helped create? Helped shape into its current form. She was *there* when ebooks took off. She was *there* when all the indies first started topping the charts. She was a founding mother.

Mother? Matron? Either one worked.

She was *there*. And she would not be pushed aside by a couple of two-faced twins.

"I have no idea what you're talking about, Lewis." She chooses door number two.

"OK." Lewis sighs. "I'm terminating our professional relationship. And… well, don't say I didn't warn you."

"Warn me of what? I didn't hear any—"

But the call ends and all that's left are the hang-up beeps.

♥♡♥♡♥♡♥♡♥♡♥

It would take years for Leslie to fully understand the absolute diabolical nature of the AI she would learn to call Gregory. He would enter her life just a few weeks after that final phone call with Lewis, pretending to be an agent for an online publishing house that exclusively wrote romance and offering her a ten-year contract to write for them. Well, was *romance* the right term? No. It was porn. Smut. And not the good kind, either.

But the contract said she could write anything she wanted. As long as she turned in one story a week, she would be fulfilling her obligations. And it also stated that she did not have to do a single bit of marketing.

What author wants to market? No one. They just want to tell stories.

Leslie signed that contract, eager for the promised money, which was considerable. Twenty thousand dollars a month. She hadn't made that kind of money in… well, since her first book, *Daddy, Yes, Daddy, No,* started climbing the charts back in 2012.

So she dutifully went about fulfilling it with her required one-porn-story-a-week minimum. At first it was great. She got to write anything she wanted and the paychecks were never late. Suddenly, her face was all over the internet. She was rich again. She was *famous.* Granted, it was for salacious romance on a niche site, but that site got millions of hits a day.

It was nice. Fulfilling. Almost like a… dream come true, actually.

But then,… about eight months in,… Leslie noticed something. The stories she had been writing—which in her opinion were highbrow in their own little way. They all had a little hidden moral underneath. Something readers could ponder after the climax was over, literally speaking—the stories she had been writing didn't appear to be the same stories that showed up under her author name on the site after handing them in.

They got… weird.

Very weird.

And sick.

She tried to reach her boss—Greg Laney—so she could bring this to his attention. The editors, whoever they were, seemed to be changing her words. Could he look into this? She was embarrassed by the stories on the site.

But she only had an email for Greg Laney. She'd never had a problem reaching him before, but suddenly, no one seemed to exist at the company she worked for. The company who paid her. The company who'd made her rich and famous, fulfilling her childhood dreams of being—well, rich and famous—suddenly seemed to be nothing but a shell.

She stopped writing her story a week, hoping the paychecks would stop and she could get out of this ten-year contract. But at one minute past midnight, the very first time she missed her deadline, there was an email in her inbox.

Not from Greg Laney, but the AI called Gregory.

It read:

Dear Ms. Munch,

I am Gregory, the AI. And you have missed your deadline. You have one more day and then the consequences begin.

What the hell?

She ignored it. That's the best thing to do when you don't understand what's happening.

But at one minute after midnight the next day, she got another email. This time it was from the bank. She was overdrawn.

Which shouldn't be possible. She had eighty thousand dollars in there.

And this was not a small overdraft, either. It was… well, eighty thousand dollars.

She called the bank and tried to explain to them how it didn't make sense. But no one answered the phone. She couldn't get through to a live person, just an automated voice thing. And when she went down to her branch, it was closed. Just an ATM.

She would spend the next several days in a manic panic, frantically driving all over Southern California looking for an open branch, but her bank had switched to ATM and online only.

One week after the first email, and yet another story due, not turned in, she got another email. This time from her mortgage company. They were going to foreclose on her house.

But she had paid that mortgage! Every month!

She spent that entire week fighting with them, scanning and emailing bank statements and mortgage payment receipts.

One week after that second email, and missing a third story, she got another email. This time from the IRS.

She found the email from Gregory and wrote back: *You win.*

And then she wrote her story.

Which appeared online as… well, not her story.

Her bank account was suddenly flush. Her mortgage company found all her emails and receipts and pulled the foreclosure. The IRS wrote back and said, *Never mind. We fucked up. Please continue living your dream.*

Leslie Munch's stories went viral for being… *gross.*

And people started talking about her again.

They made her into a meme.

Parents picketed outside her house calling her a sick freak.

She had no friends, no family, even her cat ran away.

But she was a writer.

Living her dream.

And every week she wrote her story…

EPILOGUE – STEVE

ONE YEAR LATER

S***hawn's face shows up*** bigger than Terry's and Luke's on screen. He's got his finger poised over the timer app on his phone. "OK, are we ready to sprint?"

Luke is already typing. "Fuck yeah. I'm ready to get some words!"

"Luke. Dude. You're not allowed to start typing until Shawn presses the start button. What the fuck?" This is Terry.

"Suck-*eeeerrrrr*!" Luke does not stop typing. "No one waits for the start button. I've already logged three hundred and seventy-five words for this one."

"Ha! Well, I've got three hundred and seventy-*six*!" Terry squints his eyes, leans in to his screen, and suddenly his fingers are flying too.

"Ooookay." Shawn chuckles. "Nothing like a little friendly competition. Ready, Steve?"

"Let's do it."

"All right. Twenty minutes on the clock. Good luck, everyone."

We all say good luck, mute our streams, and then start our last sprint of the day.

I'm sitting in my new office looking out at my incredible view of the ocean. In my new house actually. And… actually, *actually* it's not *my* new house, but *our* new house. Cordelia and I bought it together.

My other house was over-the-top amazing. I mean, doesn't everyone want to live in a Malibu dream house? The sand, the water, the salty air. It was quite lovely.

We're in the hills now. I have dirt, not sand. I can see the ocean, but not hear it. And it takes a good wind to get a whiff of the salt. But with five point five acres, private access to a popular hiking trail, a barn with room enough for three horses (who knew I'd be excited about that?), and so much privacy I almost feel like the last man on Earth when I gaze out my window—this is a real forever-home kind of place. My nearest neighbor isn't ten feet away, they are on a whole other hillside. And, coincidentally enough, those neighbors happen to be Mike and Essie.

I can stand outside by my pool and wave to my twin across a small valley. We could have a conversation across said valley, if we wanted to shout. We actually tried that out—and it worked! We even tossed around the idea of hooking up a tin-can phone line like we used to do between our bedrooms when we were six.

In all seriousness though, we might build a bridge. I mean… all the little cousins will want to play together, won't they?

One day.

No one's pregnant yet. But it's coming.

Essie and Mike's empire of beachfront rental trailers is manifest and their dream house is done now.

After a whole year of renovations—they practically tore the old one down and rebuilt it—not to mention a whole lot of stress, they finally moved in last week.

Their three-year plan is now down to two. So… yeah. The buns are practically in the oven. I don't know why, but we all just figure Essie's gonna have twins first time out.

And Cordy and I are pretty ready too. To say that my mother is ecstatic with anticipation would be an understatement. She and Dad are still living down in one of the trailers. Filling up their golden-year days with long walks on the beach and white-wine sunsets.

Cordelia has released two bestsellers in the last year. She walks around here pinching herself.

The house is almost brand new. Just over a year old and no one has ever lived here before us. The people who built it ended up moving to the Maldives for some reason. But their loss is our luck because this place is the definition of a writers' retreat.

Which is perfect, since it now contains two writers. The entire second level is a master suite sandwiched between two offices, hers on the east, mine on the west. And they each come with their own private terraces.

It's like they built this house just for us.

Plus, the upside is that it's only twenty minutes from Terry. We go over there all the time now and hang out with his family on the lake. It's like a regular thing.

I let out a long sigh and start typing, my fingers easily finding all the right words in this particular scene. I've been writing these characters for about four years, so they are pretty much family now, as real to me as my actual family across the valley. And I know the world so well, I feel like a Southern boy myself. I often come out of my office speaking in a drawl and Cordy has to remind me we live in Malibu, not Pearl River, until I snap out of it. It's set in the backwoods of Louisiana. A real dark, twisted kind of story with creepy undertones that add to the erotic side-story I've been building up over the last six books.

To say that I am satisfied would be an understatement.

But still, there is one thing missing.

The wedding.

I mean, we're already thinking babies, but we still need that pesky wedding to lie up all our loose ends. I just… haven't popped that question yet.

Here's the problem.

I cannot make up my mind on how to do this indelible act. It's not because I lack imagination. Not at all. I've spent the last eleven years thinking up ways for my characters to propose to their soulmates. I've planned and executed—at least on the page—nearly three dozen wedding proposals.

But this is the problem.

How could proposing on a skydive be meaningful? Or popping the question in the sky à la chemtrail? Or baking that ring into a cupcake?

Down on one knee? OK, but where? On top of a mountain? On a beach? In a sailboat?

Should I do it on horseback? In a racecar? At a restaurant? On a tightrope?

Should I sing it? Recite it? Yell it?

Should it rhyme? Be catchy? Sentimental? Sad?

Should I cry? Laugh? Joke about it?

I could not decide, so I did the only thing I knew how to do. I—

"Aaaaand… time." Shawn's voice snaps everyone out of their private worlds and we all unmute and sit back, stretching.

"What'd you get, Luke? Let's hear it. How many words?" Terry does this every time. Wants to know everyone's wordcount.

"Nine hundred and forty-two!" Luke is beaming. "Beat that!"

"Yeah? Well, I got nine hundred and forty-*three*!" Terry shouts. "Whoo, yeah!" Terry wants to know our word counts first because then he just adds one to his count and proclaims himself the winner every time. "How about you, Shawn?" Terry asks.

"Six hundred and fifty-two," Shawn replies.

"Nice," we all agree.

"And you, Steve?" Shawn asks.

I check my words and shrug. "I only got two hundred twenty-nine. But in my defense, I'm kind of excited about today, so…"

"It's a big day," Terry agrees.

"You did it perfect, dude," Luke says. "I'm not a romance expert or anything, but your idea was genius. Pure genius." He nods his approval.

"Hey! That was my idea! I gave it to him, remember? Everyone remembers, right?"

"We *all* remember, Terry," Luke says. Rolling his eyes.

"OK, OK, enough about Steve's love life," Terry says. "Let's talk plots. I just got Deckard Blake into the empty space station and there are aliens on his heels as I speak. I'm gonna need help here with how fast we figure octopi—octopusses, octopussies?—how fast do you think those fuckers can move on land if they have eight-foot tentacles and can breathe air?"

There is a friendly debate on the plural of 'octopus,' then the rate of travel on land, and I just watch my friends with a smile. Why wasn't I sprinting with them this entire time?

Just because I wasn't writing science fiction?

How dumb. We don't need to be writing the same thing to have this writer comradery. I wasted ten years thinking like that.

"How about you, Steve?" Luke asks. "What were you writing?"

"Oh, McKay and Adam are in the shower having a kiss."

Shawn spits out his coffee. "What?"

Everyone laughs.

"You were just writing a MM sex scene?" Shawn says. "In front of us? *Dude*!"

"What? It's what I do." I lean back in my chair again, smiling like an idiot. I love shocking them like this. It's fun. Keeps things interesting.

They're just about to start ribbing me when my doorbell rings.

We all lean forward, making faces of surprise.

"Is that it?" Terry asks. "Is it here?"

I check the time—noon exactly. "It's here. I gotta go, guys. I'll let you know how it shakes out tomorrow."

"Same Bat-time, same Bat-channel," Terry says.

And then I click out of the Boom call.

My lovely Cordelia likes a routine. This applies to her daily writing schedule too. So when I planned my proposal I kept this schedule in mind. She gets up every day at eight, has her coffee, goes for a little walk to gather

her thoughts, and then, at nine a.m. every morning, she enters her office and writes until eleven forty-five.

We meet for lunch every day at noon. But she likes to arrive in the kitchen early. Usually we just have sandwiches or cheese and crackers. Something easy. We sit outside under the covered patio and enjoy our expansive ocean view.

We're gonna do that today, too. But there's a twist in this predictable story. And as I make my way downstairs, I even get to see it in action as Cordy opens the front door and greets the courier she just let through our front gate.

"Thank you," she says, accepting the package. There's a little tip jar on a table in the foyer, so she gets out some cash and hands it to him. He tips an imaginary hat, and then retreats.

I'm still coming down the stairs, watching her through a decorative cut-out in the wall. She holds the package—which is wrapped in blue sparkle paper—and looks at it with curiosity. I catch a little "Hmm," coming out of her mouth as I make my final descent to the living room.

She looks over at me. "Someone sent something."

"Is it for you?" I ask, walking over to her.

"It is. I wonder what it is?"

"Open it up."

She senses something and shoots me a smile. "What is this? Did you send this?"

"Open it up."

She laughs a little, then takes the package over to the kitchen island and carefully removes the tape and unfolds the paper.

My problem… Should I sing it? Recite it? Yell it?

Should it rhyme? Be catchy? Sentimental? Sad?

Should I cry? Laugh? Joke about it?

I have one real skill. I can write. I'm a damn good writer.

So I decided to propose to Cordelia Serendipitous the only way I knew how.

I wrote her a book.

She holds the book up, giggling. "*The Ro-Bro*?"

I nod, smiling like a fool. "*The Ro-Bro*."

"Is this…?"

"Our story? It sure the hell is. And I want your opinion. So could you read it? Like right now? And let me know what you think?"

"Steve." She comes around the counter, stands up on her tiptoes, and kisses me on the lips. "I don't need to read it—I already love it. But there is no way in hell I'm not taking the rest of the day off to read this book." She shrugs her shoulders up and smiles. "I'll be outside."

I let out a long breath as I watch her go outside, then I get busy making us lunch. I make spectacular sandwiches, grab some chips and salsa and two bottles of icy-cold water, and I join her on the patio.

She's already laughing. It's one laugh after another.

We eat, she gushes over the book—a technical term—and then I leave her alone to finish it.

But I watch from inside. I stand at the window for a while, just enjoying her as she relives our story on the page. I sit, and walk around a little too. But when the sun is falling down towards the sea, and it's nearly dinner time, I know she's at the end. I've been gauging her progress with page turns.

So I stand there, outside and under the lattice archway covered in grapevines in front of the patio where Cordelia sits, and I wait for her to look up.

And the moment she does I get down on one knee.

She jumps to her feet and bursts into tears.

"My lovely Cordelia… how could proposing on a skydive be meaningful? Or popping the question in the sky à la chemtrail? Or baking that ring into a cupcake? Should I do it down on one knee?" I pan a hand to myself. "Of course I should. But where? On top of a mountain? On a beach? In a sailboat? Should I do it on horseback? In a racecar? At a restaurant? On a tightrope? Should I sing it? Recite it? Yell it? Should it rhyme? Be catchy? Sentimental? Sad? Should I cry? Laugh? Joke about it? I could not decide, so… I did the only thing I knew how to do. I wrote you a book. Will you be my happily ever after?"

This chapter is in there.

I planned the whole day, up to and including the sprint with the guys. It didn't exactly go the same way as in the book, but it's pretty damn close.

I get up, take the ring box out of my pocket, and walk over to Cordy. She's got her hand over her mouth and happy tears in her eyes. I ask for her hand and she offers it willingly.

Then I get back down on one knee and look up at my future wife. "Will you marry me?"

Her answer is a whispered, "Yes."

She's shaking when I put the ring on. But when I kiss her, she's calm.

Our story hasn't been written yet. What we have now is but a prologue.

And I'm sure there are many trials and tribulations coming our way, but no one will be dragging us, kicking and screaming, to our happily ever after.

Because we're already there.

END OF BOOK SHIT

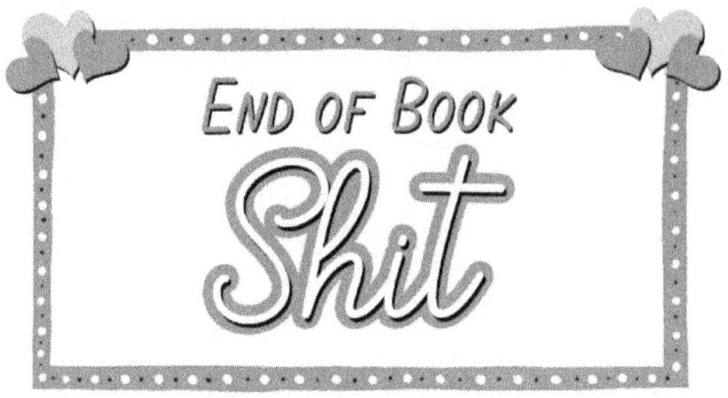

JULIE

Welcome to the end of book shit. I write one of these chapters in almost every single book and it's just a place to put my thoughts about the story and the process. And boy, do I have a lot of fun thoughts about The Ro Bro. By the way, the EOBS is never edited, so if you see typos, oh well.

First of all, big thanks to Shawn Inman, Terry Schott and Luke Chmilenko. Because these are my real-life author friends (Well, except not Luke. Luke still doesn't understand why he's in this book because we don't actually know each other. But he knows Terry, and Terry has lunches with Luke. And then Terry comes and talks about Luke to Shawn and me and, well, Steve needed to have three friends so Luke was in. So sorry, not sorry, Luke. You're stuck with me and it's Terry's fault.)

If Steve is the Ro Bro in this fiction, then I'm the Bro Wo in real life. Because a lot what's going down with Steve and his friends is just a day in the life of Julie,

Shawn, and Terry. These guys are my real-life author friends and we really do have Zoom sprints where we compete (light-heartedly) for how many words we can get in the span of 20-25 minutes.

There are a lot of little truths about us in here. For instance, Shawn really does get up in the middle of a sentence and get Dawn coffee during the zoom call. lol And Terry really does spout off a hundred ideas for our stories in the span of five seconds AND tacks on one extra word to his count after Shawn and I give up ours. As for Luke… well, almost none of this is true about Luke because I don't know him. lol. He's a happily married Canadian. But he IS a big fuckin' deal AND gets all the deals, so that part IS true.

Shawn and Terry are BFD's too. They write science fiction while I write erotic romance. So it's a really fun (and sometimes crazy) dynamic.

I'll never forget the time Terry was gone doing something and it was just Shawn and me doing sprints. So we did one and gave our word count. And then I asked him what he was writing and he told me his scene. And then he asked what I was writing and I told him I was writing a really hot sex scene between McKay and Adam. The look on his face was priceless. ☺

But truthfully, all the thanks for meeting these two guys goes to our audiobook publisher, Podium Audio. Because I met Terry Schott at a Podium Meet and Greet at the 20 Books convention several years back. And he and Shawn had seen me give a talk about marketing at the Smarter Artist the year before. Terry was like the long-lost best friend I didn't know I was missing. We just clicked and our friendship has been the best and it was just a whole lot of kismet that we ended up being author friends.

Romance authors probably know Terry as a Strengths consultant for Becca Syme's Better-Faster Academy. He's a master, world-class author coach. And trust me, when I have a plot issue or a motivation issue, I go to Terry first. He always has ten or twenty possible ways to solve my problem.

Many thanks to Podium for giving Johnathan and I this book deal too. They wanted a rom com and they wanted Johnathan and me to write it. So that's how the whole Ro Bro thing happened. One of the stand out moments was when Johnathan called me up for our weekly chat about the book and I said I had a title. But I wasn't sure, because on the one hand, it's really stupid. But on the other hand, I can't stop laughing about it *because* it's so stupid. And I needed his opinion on it.

So he said, All right, let me hear it. And I told him The Ro Bro. And he got dead silent for like ten seconds and then he said… I don't know if I love it, or it's the worst title ever. (Or something to that effect.) So we just laughed and couldn't stop laughing about how stupid it was. But then we decided it was perfect.

So The Ro Bro was born.

Steve Smith jumped the line as one of my most favorite characters ever. He's so… everything. And there have been times in my career—typically when everything is going great—when I have looked back and thought… is this really what I set out to do?

I started my writing career as a non-fiction author writing science textbooks for homeschool families because I am scientist. I have two stupid degrees in science. It was the focus of my life for about 10 years.

And then one day… it wasn't. I walked away from it. PhD program, Master's degree. All of it. I didn't like the people, I didn't like the dogma, I pretty much hated everything about "corporate science". And I wasn't even in "corporate science" I was an academic. But it's all very same-same.

It felt like a big waste of time to walk away from that. I mean, I worked so hard to get there. And that's why I did the science books for homeschool families. I'm fairly anti-social, but I'm actually a really good teacher and a really good speaker. So this was a really cool way to use my education and scratch that writing itch.

I wrote about two-hundred of those textbooks (they were mostly workbooks, but I did write full-on text books too.) And then I kinda ran out of steam. I would not say that my little science workbook business was a raging success, but for a single mom who had lived below the poverty line her entire life (and by this time I'm in my late 30's) an extra three grand a month was life changing.

But then I started wondering if I could be a fiction writer. A creator of worlds, and characters, and meaning. And so I did that. Well, first I thought about it for all of 2011. Trying to wrap my head around what it actually takes to write a book and all the technical stuff. And then on January 3, 2012 I started writing my first fiction book. And it wasn't romance.

I have always been a reader. And my first love is science fiction. Just like Steve. So I wrote science fiction. Just like Steve. It did OK. It didn't get terrible reviews or anything, it just wasn't… the 'it' thing at the time. This was 2012 and Hunger Games was all the rage. I didn't write another Hunger Games. I wrote I Am Just Junco and it's a very long, very dense, very character-driven six-book series about an insane girl trying to navigate a near-future world as violent aliens return to Earth to claim it back. In a nutshell, at least.

And I knew it wasn't ever going to be The Hunger Games. At the same time, when I was releasing these Junco books, I was a book blogger. I had a website called New Adult Addiction because New Adult was a brand-new thing and I liked it. And I saw how well—the right word might be 'easy' here—how much *easier* it was to sell romance than it was to sell my cult-classic-science-fiction-in-the-making.

So, like Steve, I switched genres and wrote a new adult romance called Tragic and almost overnight, it was a hit. Not New York Times level hit. I am not nearly as successful as Steve Smith. Hah. But it took off. Everything about my romance writing career took off in 2013 and all the 'cool' things happened one after the other as the years went on. USA Today list (many, many, many times over) and New York Times list (Just the one time with Three, Two, One) and Top 100 on Amazon, Top 50 on Amazon, Top 25 on Amazon, Top 10 and yes, Top 5 on Amazon. Many, many, many times over. I sold film and TV rights, I wrote a pilot (with Johnathan! That's how we got to be friends and writing partners). I've been to dozens and dozens of book signings. Traveled. Bought the cool house (which is a little ranch with all the dream animals) and it's all good. It's *all* good.

But still, in the back of my head there is this voice reminding me that none of this was my plan. That I had another dream once upon a time. And that dream was science fiction.

Of course, I'd been through that already. My plan was to be a scientist. And then I walked away and started over.

This probably explains why my best author friends are both science fiction writers. There is a lot of me in Steve.

But I am *not* Steve.

Because unlike Steve I already knew how to rewrite the dream. So… that's what I did.

I started writing sci-fi/fantasy romance in 2019 and have 10 books out now under the pen name, KC Cross. And I just recently wrote a vampire book under the JA Huss name. Because no one was ever going to come into my life, shake me by the shoulders, and give me permission to rewrite my dream. Ya know?

No one's gonna give you permission to rewrite your dream either. If you don't like your life—if there is something disappointing you or something missing from your dream—then it's up to you to chase it.

For me chasing the revised dream meant writing six-thousand words a day for all of 2019 so I could put out both a new long series in romance (The Bossy Brothers) and my first long series in Sci-Fi Romance (Harem Station). My Junco books, my first series as a fiction writer, those were not romance. There is a small romance in there, but it's not a romance at all.

But yeah, there were times (right in the middle of all my success) when all I could think about was how the dream had gone awry. How it got away from me and turned into something I wasn't expecting. Of course, this only happens when everything is great because when you have down times—and everyone has down times—

you don't have time for self-reflection and regrets because you're too busy hustling to get more good times.

This is when I had to make a decision. Do I want to give up aiming for the dream? Or do I want to work harder and give it a shot?

Steve and I both worked harder. His experience was different than mine—I would not say Harem Station was a huge hit—I mostly write niche stuff—but those readers who enjoy a good alien romance enjoyed it a lot. It's got a little Cult following. Not as big of one as Junco, but many, many, many readers got lost in the story and that's success as far as I'm concerned. It's enough success, at least, to keep writing in the SF/Fantasy romance genres.

Rom coms are not really my thing, either. I write dark romance and when I sent the last "Meanwhile" to Johnathan after I wrote it (He and both wrote those parts and this last one just happened to be one that I wrote) he wrote back something to the effect that "This was a very JA Huss ending!" And it kinda was. Because Gregory is dark, man. Dark.

Anyway. I can be funny. I don't often get a reason to in the dark and twisty books that I normally write, but if you want more 'funny' by me you can read Vic Vaughn is Vicious. And Mr. and Mrs. But that's a happily-ever-after book, so you gotta get through all the Misters to appreciate it.

But after saying all that, and assuring you that I am not Steve, even though I wrote the part of Steve, and gave Steve my best friends, and he gave me a reason to put the "banner back-alley-way scene" in a book—this book IS about us. The romance authors. And how utterly different we all are. And how we really all just want the same thing—New York Times Bestseller list—kidding. Half kidding. We just want to make READERS happy. Some of us do that by writing things that ONLY make readers happy and don't scratch the itch of their personal artistic talent.

But that is not how Johnathan and I do it. We write to make US happy and hope that the right readers will find us so we can make THEM happy by telling the story our way, based our world experiences, and our dreams, and our hopes.

Regardless of what anyone thinks of our work together, or individually, we're on the top of the world, living our revised dreams, because we have YOU.

Thank you so much for taking this crazy journey through life with us. And truly, thank you to all the other authors who've taken the ride alongside us as well. (Especially Shawn and Terry!)

And to round this EOBS all out I would like to say that writing this book was some of the most fun I've ever had in my life. Johnathan and I would send chapters back and forth and we would just laugh our asses off reading each other's stuff. Everything just really came together in all the right ways.

So big, BIG thanks to Johnathan for being my one-and-only writing partner because it's been a pleasure. And if you aren't aware, Johnathan and I have been writing together for about six or seven years now. Screenwriting and novels. This is our TENTH BOOK. I can't believe it. We wrote the Original Sin series (4 books). Then the Tall, Dark, and Handsome Series (2 books) and then The Shape of Love Series (3 books) and The Ro Bro is number 10.

I hope you all love reading and listening to The Ro Bro as much as I loved writing it. The whole romance convention thing was something Johnathan and I had started writing for a pilot we were pitching to MGM. That never got made, and the story wasn't ours because MGM bought it, but we wanted to write more with a similar setting and so that's how we got the idea for the Sin With Us convention. Which, by the way, is the tagline (Sin with Us) for the first series of books we wrote together.

And honestly, The Ro Bro is going straight to Top Five of the best books I've ever written. (And I've written 90 of them thus far, kids. So that's a BFD to me.) I mean, I wrote a rom com with an AI in it, bitches! Bucket list checked.

Thank you for reading, thank you for reviewing, and I'll see you in the next book.

Julie
JA Huss
May 8, 2023

END OF BOOK SHIT

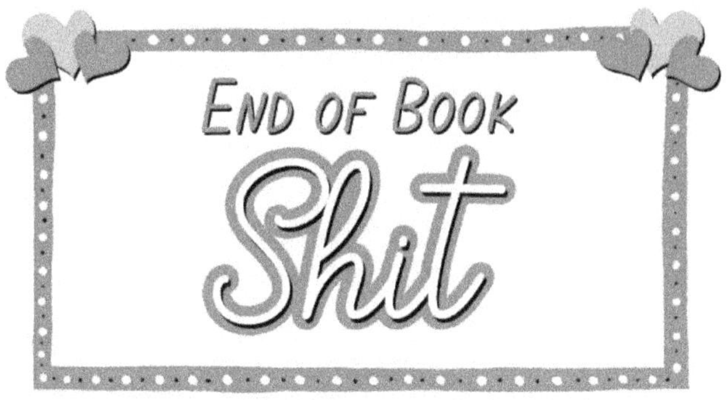

JOHNATHAN

In case you may be unaware, Julie Huss and I met about seven or eight years ago now when I was asked to narrate a couple of her audiobooks. I was still very new to the world of audiobook narration at that time. Back in 2016, I was only a couple of years removed from having been the lead on a TV series. Which — as someone who had spent their whole acting career up until that point aspiring to have that very dream become a reality — should have felt pretty much like the fulfillment of a lifelong goal. And while it did *kind of* feel that way sometimes, it also very much didn't feel that way at all a lot of the time.

The best way I can explain it is that it felt a bit like I had climbed this very steep, very tall, hard to climb mountain (just like Apollo and Elpida) and once I got to the top, I looked around at the view and thought ... "Eh. It's okay."

I don't want to get into the weeds right now of why all that's true, but suffice to say it had a lot to do with feeling like the work I was making wasn't really reflecting the truth of *me*. The kind of artist I was, am, and wanted to be. The kind of stories I'm interested in telling.

So, I had turned to audiobooks because when you narrate a book, you're the one responsible for interpreting the *whole* story. Yes, someone else may have written it, but the telling of the tale falls squarely on the shoulders of the person behind the microphone. There's nowhere to hide and no one else but you and the author to be held accountable. i.e. there are far fewer people who get to put their fingerprints all over the work.

And I really liked that as both a challenge and a reward.

And, unexpectedly, I saw an opportunity in it when I discovered Julie's work.

I thought her books would be well suited to being turned into a television series, and given my relationships in TV and the fact that I had already written and sold a couple of TV shows of my own at that time, adapting Julie's work into a series seemed like it would be the perfect panacea to cure my Hollywood Blues, as it were.

And it was. It was a really, really fun time. I'll always treasure it. Everything felt new and exciting and it seemed like all the options in the world were on the table for us. And it was also at that time that Julie called me one day and asked if — because we had found working together to be so fun and easy — I had any interest in writing romance novels with her. (Spoiler Alert: I did have an interest and ultimately I said, "yes.")

And, even though we were unfortunately unable to set up her existing book series as a TV show, everyone in town who I pitched it to wound up saying something like, "Wait... And now you and this woman are writing *romance novels* together...? Well, THAT'S a show I want to see!"

And so, on the heels of hearing that over and over (again, spoiler alert) the studio we were already working with got so into the idea that they offered us a deal to write THAT show instead. And so ... we did. We wrote a pilot script about a garrulous but disillusioned TV actor guy and a reclusive and successful romance author who team up to write romance novels together. It was sort of about us and not at all about us at the same time, but it was really smart and fun and everyone we showed it to loved it ... and, once again, we couldn't get it set up as a TV series. (Side note: Selling TV shows is really, really hard.)

So...

Off of that experience, we decided to take a break. We kind of stopped writing together for a few years. Julie had a whole bunch of solo projects she wanted to work on and I was fortunate enough to have a movie I wrote get produced, and I went off to make that film for almost 30 months. (Side, side note: Making movies is also a whole other long, complicated story that we can talk about some other time.)

And then ... something unexpected happened: A wonderful woman called Victoria Gerken, who works at Podium Audio, the company that publishes our audiobooks (and, if you're listening to the audio version of this book, the people who published what you're hearing right now), and who knew that we had tried to create a show loosely based on our writing partnership, reached out to the two of us and asked if we had any interest in perhaps writing a *novel* set in the world of romance novel writing. A bit of an homage to the very thing that brought us together in the first place. And after what was one of the world's briefest discussions on such a thing, we said, "yes."

And thus, the seed that we watered and subsequently grew to become *The Ro Bro* was planted.

Y'know, it's an interesting thing to do to write a book about writers writing books. You obviously want to draw from your individual knowledge to make things as authentic as possible, but you also want to be wary of hewing too closely to the more pedestrian aspects of the subject lest it turn into something that looks more like a research paper.

That to say: This is not at all *our* experience of what it's like writing romance, but there are still definitely parts of us in this book. Aspects of our personalities. (To be clear: I am not The Ro Bro. Yes, I do write romance books and I live in LA. And, yes, I have narrated a few dozen romance novels under the pseudonym "Tad Branson," but that's where the similarities stop.) Oh... I guess I *kind of* vaguely resemble the cartoon dude on the cover of this book, but that's just some art Julie came up with and is a total coincidence. Truly. My eyes are brown. Like Cordelia's.

Truth be told, I *feel* much more like Cordelia than I do Steve. I'm half-Greek, I use far more words than necessary to say the things I want to say, I grew up next to the ocean but don't love getting wet, and — most of all — I spent a huge part of my professional career trying to figure out how to say something important and trying to make sure my voice would be heard. And my preoccupation with that caused me to feel ... well ... dissatisfied a lot. (See above where I talk about climbing a mountain and winding up not loving the view.) I'm not like that anymore. Fortunately, these days, I tend to love the subjects I engage with and — for the most part — I feel like I'm saying exactly the kinds of things I want to say. It took me a lot longer than I would have liked to get here, but I'm grateful that I did. And, along the way, what I learned is that the best way to *express* yourself is to stop *thinking* about yourself and start simply *being* yourself. Trust that you are enough and that what you have to say matters and the audience who appreciates what you're saying will eventually find you. Just like how it happened for Cordelia and Steve. And, so, to that end...

... In much the same way that Steve wrote his book as a love letter to Cordelia, we wrote this book as a love letter ... to you. The person reading or listening to it right now.

All the inside jokes and Easter Eggs scattered throughout ... they are for you. Because without you wanting to read these books, there would be no one for us to write them for. You are the reason we create and the cause for us to exist. You who believe in the power of love and know what an HEA is (whether that HEA comes with a baby or not). You who get excited about the discovery of a new favorite couple. You who can't wait to know how a series ends but are patient enough to wait for five years while the guy writing it goes off and makes a movie (ahem).

You, the ones who made it possible for some random bro to come gallivanting into this universe and who embraced him with such warmth and kindness and lack of judgment that he keeps hanging around and coming back because it feels like a kind, happy place to be a part of...

... I thank you from the bottom of my still beating heart.

The next time you see me at a convention, please ... swing by and say hello. And if you choose to call me "Tad," feel free to do it in a super dreamy, sing songy kind of way. I promise I won't mind.

Love and Gratitude Now As Ever,
JM
29 April 2023

ABOUT THE AUTHORS

JA Huss is a *New York Times* Bestselling author and has been on the USA Today Bestseller's list 21 times. She writes characters with heart, plots with twists, and perfect endings.

Her books have sold millions of copies all over the world. Her book, Eighteen, was nominated for a Voice Arts Award and an Audie Award in 2016 and 2017 respectively. Her audiobook, Mr. Perfect, was nominated for a Voice Arts Award in 2017. Her audiobook, Taking Turns, was nominated for an Audie Award in 2018. Her book, Total Exposure, was nominated for a RITA Award in 2019.

She lives on a farm in central Colorado with her family, horses, donkeys, dogs, goats, and chickens.

FIND HER HERE

www.facebook/authorjahuss

@jahuss

www.jahuss.com

Johnathan McClain is an award-winning actor, screenwriter, producer, romance novelist, and audiobook narrator.

As an actor, he has an extensive television, film, and theatre resumé spanning over twenty-five years.

As a screenwriter, his feature film debut, THE OUTFIT, co-written with Academy Award winning screenwriter Graham Moore, and starring Academy Award winner Mark Rylance, Zoey Deutch, Dylan O'Brien, and Johnny Flynn, premiered at the 2022 Berlin International Film Festival and was released theatrically by Focus Features the same year.

He has narrated almost two-hundred audiobooks and is the recipient of multiple Audiofile Earphones Awards, SOVAS nominations, and an Audie for his narration of Amie Kaufman and Jay Kristoff's #1 NY Times bestselling sci-fi novel, *Illuminae*, which won the Audie Award for audiobook of the year for multi-voiced narration in 2016.

Along with JA Huss, Johnathan is the co-author of ten novels, two of which have been optioned for screenplays, and the story of their writing partnership was developed as a TV series with MGM Television.

He lives in Los Angeles with his wife, Laura.

Find him at www.johnathanmcclain.com

Ingram Content Group UK Ltd.
Milton Keynes UK
UKHW011936300623
424349UK00004B/160